Resounding praise for
FIONA M[...]
and her spell[...]
THE [...]

"Fiona McIntosh is [...] [...]ved
from my sofa f[...]ys, beguiled by
[*The Quickening*]."
Sydney Morning Herald (Australia)

"A rich, satisfying confection of vivid detail,
engrossing characters, and their dark doings,
all beautifully written. I was enthralled."
Lynn Flewelling

"Enjoyable. . . . McIntosh has taken the notion of
body snatching, given it a fresh twist and
come up with a winner."
Publishers Weekly

"[An] exquisitely detailed world. Strongly conceived,
believable characters and a swift plot."
Library Journal

"Fiona McIntosh's books move quickly
and unpredictably."
Robin Hobb

"Fiona McIntosh is an author who suddenly has found
herself not just rubbing shoulders with the important
writers of the world, but being one of them."
The Advertiser (Australia)

The Quickening Trilogy
by Fiona McIntosh

BRIDGE OF SOULS
BLOOD AND MEMORY
MYRREN'S GIFT

Forthcoming
The Percheron Saga

ODALISQUE

BRIDGE OF SOULS

THE QUICKENING Book Three

FIONA McINTOSH

An Imprint of HarperCollinsPublishers

This book was originally published in a mass market edition in 2004 by Voyager, an imprint of HarperCollins Publishers, Australia.

EOS
An Imprint of HarperCollins*Publishers*
10 East 53rd Street
New York, New York 10022-5299

Copyright © 2004 by Fiona McIntosh
Excerpt from *Odalisque* copyright © 2005 by Fiona McIntosh
ISBN: 978-0-06-074761-9
ISBN-10: 0-06-074761-7
www.eosbooks.com

First Eos paperback printing: January 2007
First Eos trade paperback printing: March 2006

HarperCollins® and Eos® are registered trademarks of HarperCollins Publishers.

Printed in the U.S.A.

10 9 8 7 6 5 4 3 2 1

GH . . . this one's for you

Acknowledgments

I'm aware that a great number of people have traveled this long and traumatic journey with Wyl Thirsk, so special thanks to the booksellers for recommending the series—especially Steve Hubbard in Minnesota and Jonathan Asay in Georgia, and my gratitude to all readers for giving The Quickening and this new writer a go.

The list to thank continues to extend: Gary Havelberg, Sonya Caddy, Pip Klimentou, and Judy Downs; the ever-increasing gang at the Heartwood Bulletin Board for their support and conversation; and Trent Hayes for a new Web site to make our international readers feel so welcome and appreciated.

Heartfelt thanks to Robin Hobb—quietly in the background, always full of encouragement, ever inspirational through her own work. And to Guy Gavriel Kay—not just for *Tigana*—but for his frequent and funny e-mails across the oceans. Also to Lynn Flewelling for such strong support and encouragement.

To my partner in crime, Kate Nintzel, a terrific editor whom I love working with, and to Jennifer Brehl, both at Eos. You're a wonderful team to be part of.

Sincere thanks to Chris Lotts at Ralph M. Vicinanza Literary Agency, for all the work on my behalf and for the regular laughs.

Finally, to Ian, Will, and Jack—who make it so easy for me to disappear into worlds beyond our own and yet are the trilogy of reasons I always return.

BRIDGE OF SOULS

PROLOGUE

It felt like an eternity to Fynch.

There was brightness, unbearably sharp, and combined with a hammering pain. He squeezed his lids tightly but the dazzling gold light hurt his eyes all the same as he helplessly relinquished control of his small body to the vast agony exploding through it. He believed he felt his body writhing uncontrollably, but in truth he was rigidly still, his teeth bared in a grimace as the force of magic gifted from Elysius radiated painfully into him.

At one point he thought he glimpsed the sorcerer passing through him to his death, like a distant memory he could not quite bring into focus. Elysius appeared whole again and he was smiling. Fynch vaguely sensed him offering thanks but was unable to lock on to it as the pain claimed all of his attention.

The sickening throb of power began to pulse through his body in time with his escalating heartbeat, each push harder, each more breathless in its intensity, until he lost all sense of himself. He no longer knew who he was or where he lay; he had to relinquish all to the excruciating pain until, finally, he glimpsed its end. The agony ebbed gradually but steadily until he realized he was bearing it. His pulse was fast but his heart no longer felt as though it might explode through his chest. The blinding light had dimmed to flashes of gold, as if he had been staring at the sun too long, and his breath was no longer panicked and shallow but came in deep, rhythmic drafts.

His wits returned. He had survived.

Trembling from the chill that now gripped him, Fynch

opened his eyes to slits. He registered a new layer of pain and closed them again; this time it was a headache that prompted instant nausea. He felt like crying. But where other youngsters might have had the comfort of a mother's voice and love, there was no such consolation for Fynch. He was alone. Wyl had gone.

Fynch hated the way they had parted. He knew Wyl had wanted him to leave the Wild immediately and he had watched his friend battle his inclination to say as much. Ylena's face was too expressive to mask what her brother was thinking. And yet Wyl had said nothing, had permitted Fynch to make his own decision and remain a little longer. Fynch felt a profound sadness for his friend who had suffered so much loss already and would suffer more yet, he sensed. He wished he knew of a way to spare Wyl more pain, or at least to share some of it with him.

He sighed. The nausea had passed. His eyes were still closed and he realized the pain had dimmed considerably. But the loneliness remained. There would not even be Elysius to offer solace. No. The boy suspected he was alone in the Wild, save for the four-legged beast who was his constant companion.

Full consciousness sifted through his shattered nerves and Fynch became aware of a pressing warmth at his side. Having sensed he was alert again, the source of warmth moved and growled.

"Knave," Fynch croaked through a parched throat.

Never far, a voice replied in his head. The unexpected sound made him flinch.

The boy turned toward the great black dog. "Did you speak to me?" he asked, tears welling. "Can I finally hear you?"

Depthless eyes regarded him and again he heard Knave's reply in his mind. *I did. You can.*

The friendly voice—one he had never thought to hear—was too overwhelming. Fynch managed to command his reluctant arms to obey him. Slowly, painfully, he wrapped them around the big animal's neck and wept deeply and without shame.

Elysius? Fynch asked after a long time, testing his newly acquired power.

The dog's response was instant. *Dead. It was quick. And he was glad to go.*

Where is his body?

Everywhere. He became dust. The massive transfer of power disintegrated his physical being and then dispersed him.

Did he say anything before . . . before he passed on?

That you are the bravest of souls. He agonized that he might be wrong to force this burden upon you, the dog admitted. *He regretted the pain you would experience and the journey ahead, but he believed there is no one else who can walk the path but you.* The dog leaned closer and spoke very gently. *In this I know he is right.*

Fynch pulled away from his friend, eyes still wet. There was so much yet to learn. *Knave, I don't know how to use this power. I have no—*

Hush, the dog soothed. *That is why I am here.*

The boy took the beast's huge head between his tiny hands. *Who are you?*

I am your guide. You must trust me.

I do.

The dog said no more, but Fynch sensed that he was glad, even relieved.

But there is something I must know, he went on, his tone almost begging.

Ask it. Knave's mental voice was so deep that Fynch suspected that if the dog could speak aloud, he, Fynch, would feel the sound rumble through his own tiny chest.

Who is your true master? Where do you belong?

Fynch sensed Knave's smile. *I have no master as such. But I do belong.*

Where? Please tell me.

I am of the Thicket.

Ah. Fynch's tensed muscles relaxed as understanding flooded through him. The neatness of the dog's answer pleased him. *Are there others like you?*

I am unique, although there are other enchantments within the Thicket.

So Elysius didn't send you to Myrren?

Elysius did not know me by flesh until we both came here, although he knew of me. And Myrren was not the person I sought.

This was a revelation. Fynch pressed his hands against his eyes in an attempt to ease their soreness and clear his swirling thoughts. *Then why didn't you just search out Wyl?*

Because Wyl was not the one I sought either.

Fynch looked up sharply. *Who, then? Who must we now search for?*

The search is over. It was always you, Fynch.

What? The dog's unerring gaze told Fynch Knave would never lie. *But why?*

You are the Progeny and I am the Guide.

I thought I was the Wielder, Fynch asked, confused.

That, and so much more, Knave said reverently. *You are many things.*

The Thicket sent you to find me?

The Thicket sent me to find the next Gate Wielder. It did not know that would be you.

But it must have known Elysius was dying in order to send you in search of his replacement?

Yes.

So your role has never been about Wyl or Myrren . . . or protecting Valentyna? Fynch sent wonderingly.

Knave's response was measured. *My task is to protect you. When the magic of the Quickening entered Wyl, the Thicket believed he was the next Wielder. Elysius wondered the same.*

Are you saying that it was pure coincidence you came into Myrren's life? Fynch asked, desperately trying to piece the puzzle together.

Not exactly. She was Elysius's daughter. Magic was part of her even though it was not strong in her. It was she whom the Thicket decided to keep a watch over. When Myrren made such connection with Wyl, we thought he might be the one. It was only when I met you that I realized it was you we searched for.

How can you tell?

There is an aura about you, Fynch. Unmistakable, and invisible to all but those of the Thicket.

Fynch sighed. *I was born with this aura?*

Yes. Your destiny was set.

Elysius never mentioned it.

Elysius didn't know. The Thicket told him who you are only as he died.

It talks!?

Communicates, the dog corrected.

Fynch held his head and groaned. These revelations were causing fresh gusts of pain to surge through his already aching mind. *It hurts, Knave. Will it always be so?*

You must control the pain. Don't allow yourself to become its slave. Master it, Fynch.

Is this how it will kill me?

The dog held a difficult silence between them.

I would know the truth, Fynch insisted. *If you are my friend—my Guide, as you say—then tell me honestly.*

He sensed the dog's discomfort as he began to explain. *This is the beginning. You must use your powers sparingly. Talk to me aloud whenever you can, although hearing my response in your mind will not sap your energies. The pain and other weakenings will only occur if you send the magic yourself.*

How long have I got, Knave?

The dog raised his head to look Fynch directly in the eye. *I don't know. It depends how strong you are, how sparingly you use this power.*

If Knave expected despair it did not come. Fynch wiped his eyes and, using his companion as support, raised himself wearily on unsteady legs. *I must rest,* the little boy said gravely.

And then we must go to the Thicket, Knave said, equally somber. *It awaits you.*

1

❧

THE VINEYARD SPRAWLED BEFORE THEM, THE LAND SUDDENLY sloping down in the distance to a small shingle beach and the channel of sea. The tang of salt in the air was invigorating and the bright day with its cloudless sky and sharp light reminded Aremys of how much he had missed the north all these years. He inhaled the air now and smiled. It felt good to be alive, despite the new and sudden complexities in his life.

With his memory now blessedly returned, Aremys felt much better equipped to accept the King's invitation to "walk the rows" of vines at Racklaryon. The mercenary learned that it was one of Cailech's great pleasures to see his vineyard bursting with new life each spring, showing the spectacular results of the savage pruning his vignerons insisted upon.

King and mercenary looked out now across the neat rows and Aremys could almost taste the wine this field would produce at summer's end. Bright green leaves, like the protective wings of a mother hen, shaded their yet-to-mature babies, bunches of fruit that hung like tiny green jewels, fattening and ripening daily as the plants sent out fresh tendrils to weave and curl their way along the special lines that supported the vines. The Mountain People had pioneered this method of support. In the south, the vines were left to themselves, to grow tall at first, stooping over when heavy with fruit. It made for a ragged, untidy vineyard but, in truth, did not affect the quality of the wine. In the north, however, vine support lines had been developed to air the fruit, as some months were humid and damp. It also looked more spectacular.

Cailech's people took pride in the ordered appearance of their vineyards. Not only were the rows straight but each vine was sung to as it was planted—a small prayer to Haldor that each new beginning might yield life of its own. At each row's end, the Mountain People planted a flower called a trineal. It was beautiful but fragile, very susceptible to lack of water or other natural attacks. Cailech's vignerons maintained that if the trineal foundered, they would have but a few weeks to find the solution to prevent the vines from following suit. It was an ancient tradition but one still faithfully adhered to. The bright rainbow colors of the trineal bushes were an attractive feature in this, Cailech's favorite vineyard, and they stood proud, colorful, and healthy at the heads of the rows. It would be a bountiful harvest, the men murmured.

The King was rarely alone; today he was flanked by Myrt and Byl. Aremys had come to know these particular fellows well since his curious arrival in the Razors. He felt comfortable in their presence and over the past few days had started to view them as companions as much as captors. Nevertheless, he had chosen not to reveal that his memory was fully restored. It suited him that these Mountain Dwellers knew only as much as he was prepared to share, until he could learn more about their intentions for him.

The small company had ridden to the vineyard beyond the lake and Aremys was sorry to see that the King had not chosen to bring the intriguing black horse that had caused him such fright on their previous ride. He mentioned his disappointment to Cailech.

"Ah yes, Galapek," the King replied softly, and Aremys felt the weight of the green gaze upon him. "I had the impression that he disturbed you somehow the last time we rode together."

It was said without accusation but Aremys felt the scrutiny couched within. Wyl Thirsk's warning burned in his mind: Only a fool took any comment by Cailech at face value. *Everything he says has a purpose,* Wyl had impressed upon Aremys during their journey together from Felrawthy. *He misses nothing.*

The mercenary thought back to the moment of disturbance the King spoke of. It had occurred only a few days ago. Aremys had initially admired the King's mount but, on casually touching the horse's strong neck, had felt a blast of dark, tainted magic surge through his hands. It had been an intense shock for Aremys—not only that the creature was alive with magic, but also that he could sense it—and he had jerked back in distress. Worse, he had been unable to regain his composure and had been forced to excuse himself from the party of riders. The entire scene had been embarrassing to Aremys, but, more important, no doubt had also appeared suspicious to his keepers at a time when he was striving to convince them that he was not a Morgravian spy or a threat to any of the Mountain Dwellers.

The only positive outcome was that the shock seemed to have caused his amnesia to dissipate and he had been able to piece together what he was doing in the Razors. He remembered following Wyl Thirsk, who now walked in the guise of his sister, Ylena, courtesy of the powerful gift, the Quickening. Together they had entered the mysterious region in the far northeast known as the Thicket. Aremys recalled Wyl asking him to whistle so they would not lose each other among the tangle of this dense landmark. He had obliged, could even remember the tune he had chosen, but then all had gone black and he had woken, disoriented and without his memory, on the frozen rocks of the northern mountain range. Cailech's men had discovered him there, and aided by his genuine confusion, he had managed to muddle his way through those early and dangerous stages. He felt convinced now that he had carefully won not only the trust of the Mountain warriors but that of their king as well. Wyl had warned Aremys that the Mountain King was changeable, capricious even, and had recounted the terrible night of the feast when Cailech had threatened to roast alive the Morgravian prisoners his men had captured and feed them to his people. This was definitely not a man to second-guess and so Aremys had been as honest as he could with the Mountain King, even disclosing his identity when it finally returned to him.

He had not, however, told Cailech anything about his connection to Wyl Thirsk, the former General of Morgravia, or that Wyl was possessed by a magic that had already taken the lives of three people—one of them Romen Koreldy, in whom Cailech had shown a keen interest. Aremys vowed that if the Mountain Kingdom held its own secrets, he would learn them and at least be useful in some small way to Wyl, who had promised to return to the Razors someday in search of his friends Gueryn and Lothryn, both of whom had offered their lives to save his.

Nor had he been honest with Cailech about his arrival in the Razors. It had taken Aremys hours of musing to accept that the Thicket must have somehow repelled him. It was a difficult notion for him to get his mind around. Until recently he had neither particularly believed nor disbelieved in magic, but growing up in the far north, on the Isles of Grenadyn, meant he held a loose acceptance that such a power might exist and was not necessarily something to fear.

Loose acceptance and indisputable proof were entirely different matters, however, and now—since he'd met Wyl and shared the sorrow of his plight—the legend of the Thicket had taken on a sinister character. Acknowledging that this enchanted place had purposefully separated him from the very person he had sworn to protect was disturbing enough, but accepting that the Thicket had also affected him in such a way that he now possessed the ability to sense magic was terrifying.

The horse itself couched a darker mystery. Just touching the animal had made him feel ill. It reeked of evil—and yet also of despair. Aremys needed to see the horse again, reach toward it once more. Perhaps his captors had no idea of the darkness in Galapek? But how else could Cailech know the horse was the reason for his disturbance?

Aremys realized Cailech was still watching him carefully. The mercenary, practiced at subterfuge, stretched a lazy smile across his generous mouth. "It had nothing to do with the beast, my lord. I felt very off-color that morning and I slept for many hours after that event."

"Probably out of your discomfort at almost spewing on

the King's boots!" Myrt added, safe in the knowledge that Cailech encouraged a more casual atmosphere when he was away from the fortress and the formalities of being their ruler.

Myrt's jest gave Aremys the opportunity he needed to navigate himself from the King's scrutiny. It suddenly occurred to him that Cailech knew more than he was giving away. His instincts had rarely let him down, so he listened to them now.

"It reminded me of the time," he said, seizing the opening, "when a very aged and strict aunt of mine came to visit the family." His companions, sensing a tale in the making, came closer. "She was a cantankerous woman who despised social gatherings, yet insisted on everyone celebrating her name-day each spring. Oh, how we hated that day and her arrival with all of its pomp and ceremony. But our family was obliged to her, for the rich crone had gifted much money to the town, and I would be lying if I said we had not benefited from her gold."

Aremys saw with relief the loose, expectant grin on the King's face as he bent to inspect a vine of juvenile grapes. He continued with his tale: a dare by his brothers that went horribly wrong and culminated in his tossing the contents of a chamber pot over the head of the town's special guest.

The men roared with laughter. Aremys noted that Cailech was less responsive but nonetheless amused; a wry smile crinkled the weathered face and sparkled in his eyes. "I would never repeat such a tale if that had been me," he said.

"Nor will I again," Aremys admitted, rather impressed himself by his telling of the story, which was wholly fabricated. "But I am trying to impress upon you, my lord, the level of my dismay. This sorry tale has now been relegated to the second most embarrassing moment of my life. I hope you can guess the first."

"You are forgiven, Farrow, and it's forgotten," the King said as the other two men began to wander away through the rows.

Aremys did not believe him. "Thank you, sire."

"Perhaps you would like to ride Galapek?"

Aremys had not expected this and he knew his hesitation was telling. The King was testing him and both of them knew it. The mercenary quickly gathered his wits. "It would be a privilege, my lord."

"Good," the King replied, his steady gaze unfathomable. "I will arrange it."

He looked beyond the mercenary. "Ah, here comes Baryn. He is head of the vineyard." The previous topic seemingly forgotten, he strode toward the man, calling back over his shoulder, "Don't you love the Thaw, Aremys? Spring unfurling her fronds, pushing through her shoots, warming the ground, and melting the ice?" Cailech pointed as Aremys caught up. "Just look at these vines, fairly bursting with joy as tiny green buds and tendrils begin their life journey."

"You should write poetry, sire."

The King smiled at the compliment. "I have a proposition to put to you, Farrow."

Cailech's sudden twist took Aremys by surprise. He would have to be careful; Wyl had warned him of this. "Sire?"

"I have been thinking about our conversation."

"Oh?" Aremys thought back over the past few days; he and Cailech had had many discussions.

"Regarding Celimus," Cailech clarified.

Aremys nodded. "I recall suggesting a parley."

"There is wisdom in what you advise and I have decided to act upon it."

Aremys raised his eyebrows but managed to keep the surprise from his voice. "Really?"

Cailech nodded. "Yes. I am going to Morgravia, and not under cover of disguise or stealth. Actually, let me correct that. *We* are going to Morgravia."

"You and your chosen men, sire?"

"Me and you, Farrow."

Aremys searched the King's face for any signs of guile, then realized that he would not be able to tell if Cailech was bluffing. The man was a master at hiding behind a granite expression—although on this occasion Aremys thought he detected the barest hint of amusement.

"Then I am honored, King Cailech," Aremys said diplomatically.

Cailech simply nodded. "You will set up the meeting, as you know Celimus. You will act as my emissary."

And with that the King strode away, leaving the newly appointed envoy for the Mountain Kingdom openmouthed.

"Close it, friend," Myrt said, returning to Aremys's side.

"He can't be serious," Aremys murmured, watching as the King's broad figure joined the vineyard manager among an ocean of green leaves.

"He never jests about such things. Take it as a compliment, Farrow. He must trust you."

"Do you know when we leave?"

"As soon as the streams run with the Thaw, he told me."

"But that's now!" Aremys turned to look at Myrt.

The man grinned. "True. Come on, we'd better head back—apparently you are to ride his prize stallion this afternoon."

A remys's stomach had clenched when he caught sight of the magnificent horse being led out of its stall by Maegryn, the stablemaster. The stallion flicked its tail constantly, as though angry. A weak sensation of nausea rippled through the mercenary. He forced himself to relax, for he had been holding his breath and was ashamed at himself for allowing this animal to have such a dramatic effect on him.

It's only a horse, damn it! he berated himself, but to no avail; the sinister feeling intensified.

"He's a beauty, this one," Myrt commented by his side.

Aremys fought the swirling dizziness. Did no one else feel it? "Is Cailech not joining us?" he asked through clenched teeth.

"No. Rashlyn will be riding out, though."

"Who is he?" Aremys asked innocently. He recalled Wyl's description of the man who seemed to have an unnatural influence over the Mountain King.

"The King's barshi—a detestable creature," Myrt said. "But if you ever claim I said that, I'll deny it first and kill you later."

Aremys grinned. "A man of magic, then?" he asked, watching as Maegryn saddled Galapek.

His companion nodded and Aremys felt his stomach twist again. "Can he sense other empowered people?" He hoped Myrt would not hear the anxiety in his voice.

"I have no idea. Why do you ask?"

Aremys forced a shrug. "Oh, no reason. I've always been rather intrigued by those with the power, that's all."

"To be honest I wish he'd leave the mountains. His influence upon our king is too strong. There are times . . ." Myrt's voice trailed off.

Aremys glanced toward his captor. "Go on."

The Mountain Man shook his head. "No, I speak out of turn."

Aremys could see it would not be wise to push Myrt further right now, although it pleased him to note that Myrt felt comfortable enough around him to be candid. Perhaps Myrt could become a source of information, or a key to escape.

It looked as though Maegryn was satisfied with Galapek. He was barking orders now for the other horses to be led out.

"Where did Cailech find this magnificent horse?" Aremys asked brightly, noticing that he seemed to be growing more accustomed to the nearby magic.

"It's the strangest thing," Myrt replied, clearly relieved to have moved away from the previous conversation. "I really don't know."

"What do you mean?"

"Well, the very best horses come from Grenadyn—as you would know—but this animal just turned up one day. He certainly isn't from our stock."

"You mean it just appeared out of nowhere?" Aremys asked, astounded. Perhaps the stallion had also been cast here by the Thicket.

Myrt laughed. "No, I didn't mean that. But Maegryn knows all the foals born here. And if we bring horses over from Grenadyn then it's quite a big event because they have to be shipped in. I don't recall this animal being brought across the channel—it would surely have caused a stir if he had."

Aremys was intrigued. It was not his imagination, then.

There was something mysterious about the King's horse. "What does his handler say?"

"Maegryn's very tight-lipped on the subject. I've tried to find out more but he's refused to discuss it. I get the impression that Rashlyn might have gifted the horse to Cailech, though I couldn't guess at where he would find such a beast. Perhaps the King has asked both to keep it quiet. Cailech can be quite unpredictable on occasion—in case you hadn't noticed." Myrt grinned.

"I have," Aremys said wryly.

"He is a great man, but he can be contrary at times," Myrt warned, before adding softly, "I know that worried Lothryn."

Aremys took a careful breath at the name of Wyl's friend. "Lothryn—that name sounds familiar. Who is he?" he commented absently.

"A friend. Formerly second in command to our king. A man I would have followed without question into any situation—but who betrayed us all."

Maegryn was leading the horse toward them now and Aremys again felt the sickening pull of magic. He forced himself to focus on Myrt's words. "Betrayed you? Where is he now?"

"Gone," Myrt said, ending the conversation. "Your mount is ready—and here comes Rashlyn. Be warned—he is a strange man."

The barshi was already mounted on a chestnut mare. He stopped just steps from the mercenary and gazed down upon the tall foreigner. "You must be Aremys," he said in his strangely hesitant manner. "Cailech suggested we meet. I hope you don't mind if I join you?"

"Not at all," Aremys lied, instantly taking a dislike to the wild-looking man with the dead eyes and unwilling smile. He raised his hand in salutation, deciding to avoid all physical contact with the barshi. If Aremys himself sensed the horse's magic through touch, perhaps Rashlyn could do the same with him. He wondered whether Cailech had specifically asked Rashlyn to watch how he reacted to the horse today.

Which would mean they are definitely suspicious of me, he thought. The stench of Galapek's magic buffeted his senses as the handler halted the stallion alongside the mare.

"Master Aremys, you'll be riding Galapek this afternoon," Maegryn said. "Be firm with him, sir. But also give him his head on the flat. He likes to gallop. Could use a good run today."

It was all Aremys could manage to nod agreeably and take the reins from Maegryn. How had he backed himself into this situation? Nausea threatened to overwhelm him, but he fought it and deliberately turned his back to Rashlyn as he mounted. He could not allow the barshi to read his fear.

Waves of revulsion pulsed through him as he took his seat in the saddle. It required all his courage not to leap from the horse immediately. "You lead," he said tightly to Rashlyn, hoping to get the magic man ahead of him.

Unfortunately, Rashlyn had his measure. "Myrt—you know the best paths," he said. "You lead. I'll bring up the rear."

The party of three set off, with Aremys now fully convinced he was under observation by the King's sorcerer.

2

MYRT SUGGESTED A PATH VIA THE LOWLANDS SURROUNDING the lake. Aremys grunted his agreement, still struggling to dampen his revulsion for the horse beneath him. Myrt did not linger for a comment from the barshi and set the direction. Once the horses were moving at a steady canter, Aremys felt better, and when they set them at a gallop, the exhilaration and the wind in his face alleviated some of the sickening taint permeating his body from below.

For the first half of the ride the men said nothing and Aremys was happy to be lost in his thoughts and the pure pleasure of being out in the breathtaking valley. The lake was mirror calm and he marveled at how it reflected the lower rises of Razors. The cacophony of the waterbirds drowned any potential for conversation, which suited him perfectly. Although the sun was high overhead, there was no real fire in it, and the riders were glad to feel its gentle spring warmth upon their shoulders, loosening winter's firm grip on the land.

Now that Aremys had been touching the stallion for some time, he was able to control his reaction to the horse. Whatever had initially caused him to gag wretchedly in front of the King had diminished to a constant queasiness, which he was mastering. His revulsion had given way to an intense pity for the animal. The beast moved beneath him with superb grace, all muscle and power, eager to respond to his rider's urgings, but Aremys sensed something beyond the physical, something he would almost equate with human emotion.

"We can stop over there and rest the horses." Myrt butted into his thoughts, pointing toward a cluster of rocky outcrops that formed a loose semicircle and a natural sun trap.

Aremys nodded. He would have preferred to keep going but was helpless, certain that this entire afternoon was all being carefully orchestrated.

They settled themselves against the boulders while the horses grazed contentedly on some tender grass, far enough away that Aremys could converse without the magical stench threatening to upset him. Still, he felt Galapek's pull. The more confident Aremys became in his resistance to the revulsion, the more strongly the horse pleaded to his senses. *What did it want him to do? What was this creature that it could generate such loathing as well as sympathy?*

A new thought struck Aremys: not *what* was this animal but *who*? The notion was so striking that it washed away his fear. *Who was this animal? Who was calling to him using the magic of the Thicket? Could the beast be under an enchantment, like Wyl—a man trapped in another guise?* The thought revolted him.

As he shook his head clear of such a shocking notion, the barshi embarked upon the expected interrogation.

"The King tells me you have lost your memory," Rashlyn said, without any preamble.

"I have," Aremys answered. "It is a terrible feeling not to know anything about oneself."

"I gather it is returning gradually?" the man replied, reaching to unwrap the hunk of cheese and hard biscuit Myrt had packed.

Aremys noted the man's grubby fingers and looked away. The Mountain Men were tough and capable of living rough, but he knew they bathed regularly. The King led by example: He was always scrupulously clean. As it had struck Elspyth not so long ago, Aremys had realized that the people of the Razors were a sophisticated race with great artistic and creative skills as well as a love of the land and a deep respect for one another. Since Cailech had stopped the tribal fighting and drawn the people together, that respect had extended beyond simple courtesies to living alongside one another in a manner that promoted cleanliness and protected them from disease. Aremys had noted with surprise the special ablution blocks that were built around the fortress, proof of how highly Cailech rated the importance of proper sanitation. The King was convinced of a link between human waste and disease, and so it was rare to see any Mountain Dweller squat in the fields or in a corner of the fortress to relieve himself. Instead, carts rolled away from the many ablution blocks daily to deliver the waste into pits dug deep in the ground, far from the main living areas, where it would harmlessly break down and return to the earth. It was part of the modern thinking—along with education and the maintenance of the old languages—that Cailech was beginning to impress upon his people. But this man, Rashlyn, with his dirty hands, his unkempt appearance and offensive manner, did not fit the Mountain folk's mold. How did they tolerate him?

Rashlyn was staring at him. "Yes, slowly," Aremys answered finally. "I know my name, at least, and where I hail from."

"Would you like me to check your skull for any damage?

I am a healer," Rashlyn offered, along with some of the cheese.

Aremys could not risk that the sorcerer might sense through his touch the Thicket's trace of magic. And Shar alone knew where those filthy fingers had last been. "Thank you, no," he replied. "I'm not hungry and my head is fine."

The man frowned. "It must have been a firm blow to knock your senses so. You really should let me examine you."

"No need," Aremys replied briskly, glancing toward his quiet companion, hoping to be rescued. "Myrt here has already looked me over. There is no sign of any damage."

Myrt did not deny Aremys's claim but did not support it either. Aremys suspected that he too was fighting a battle of loyalty. It was fairly obvious from his body language alone that the warrior despised Rashlyn.

"This business of your lost memory is odd, then," Rashlyn said. He spoke through his food and bits of the cheese crumbled and fell from his mouth into his tangle of a beard. Again Aremys looked away, disgusted. "How could a blow strong enough to cause you to lose your wits be entirely healed?"

"I have no idea," Aremys said, shrugging. He found the barshi's probing stare most unsettling; there was madness lurking there, he was sure of it. He stood and said politely, "Excuse me whilst I take a drink," glancing again at Myrt, this time for permission to sip from the stream.

Myrt nodded and Aremys walked as casually as he could to the stream's edge and bent down. He splashed freezing water over his face, enjoying the refreshing trickle of droplets that found a way into the front of his shirt and slid down his chest. As he straightened, flicking water in all directions, he sensed someone directly behind him. The thrill of fear that passed through him nearly unbalanced him into the stream. He turned abruptly, expecting to see Rashlyn reaching toward him, sinister and threatening.

Yes, Rashlyn was standing behind him, but instead of reaching out for the mercenary, he was digging in his pockets. Aremys felt stupid. He was definitely becoming paranoid, he berated himself silently and angrily.

"Apologies, I didn't mean to startle you," the man said, a little slyly, Aremys thought. He retrieved a tiny jar from a pocket. "Here—this will ease the headaches I believe you have been suffering."

"What is it?"

"A soothing blend of herbs for rest with a dash of laudanum. It won't harm you, or dull anything but the pain, I promise. Sip it every hour as you need."

Aremys was trapped. Rashlyn's filthy hand was extended toward him with the small bottle in its palm. He had to take it, or risk throwing yet more suspicion on himself. If the King was waiting to hear that Aremys had vomited again or had refused to ride his stallion, then he would be disappointed, but this moment might yet be his undoing. Aremys saw the healer's eyes narrow at his reluctance but still he hesitated.

"I can easily make up some more; you're not denying anyone by taking it," Rashlyn assured, the softness in his voice almost threatening. Aremys was sure the man was daring him to refuse.

He took a moment to shake his head free of the water droplets, then paused to wipe a sleeve across his face. "Thank you," he replied, reaching out slowly, hoping Rashlyn would simply drop the phial into his hand.

Before that could happen, Galapek alarmed all three men by rearing up behind them, screaming loudly as though in pain. Myrt reacted first, running toward the horse. Aremys took his chance, moving swiftly away from the healer. "Let me help!" he called.

The horse clearly wanted Myrt nowhere near him, rearing and screaming even more wildly as the warrior approached. To Myrt's surprise, however, the stallion calmed a little at the sound of the big mercenary's voice and allowed Aremys to sidle up to him.

Aremys reached for the reins and called again to the horse. "Galapek, there, boy. There, now. Settle, big fellow," he whispered. The horse stilled now, trembling and frightened.

"Poor Galapek, whatever has happened to you, I shall rescue you, I promise," Aremys said, stroking the animal's broad, magnificent face. "Be calm now, boy." He rubbed the stallion's neck, and for the first time, the stench of the magic did not turn his stomach. Whatever this curse upon the stallion was, it was somehow communicating with him, flowing through him and around him, begging him to keep his promise.

And then a word came into in his head. It was faint and desperately called but he sensed it clearly. *Elspyth*, he heard, just once, and then it was gone, like a sigh given to the wind and borne away.

Aremys was so shocked he stood rigid against the horse's neck, trying without success to recapture the word. Elspyth. Surely that was the name he had heard? Myrt's urgent voice broke through his haze of confusion.

"Farrow! For Haldor's sake, man!"

Aremys turned, surprised by the anger in the man's voice. Then he saw Myrt's expression—not angry, but distraught— and followed his friend's pointing finger. By the water's edge, where he had left him, Rashlyn writhed on the ground, shouting gibberish as spittle foamed and flew from his mouth. His arms and legs flailed wildly, then, suddenly, fell completely still.

"Check that the horses are secure," Aremys called over his shoulder as he ran to the prone figure. He hoped Rashlyn might be dead, but luck was not with him. He lifted the small man's chin to ensure a clear breathing passage, but stopped short of breathing any life-giving air into the barshi's mouth. "He has a pulse, I'm sorry to say," he risked to Myrt, who had come up behind them.

Myrt did not smile but something akin to a twitch of amusement flitted across his face. "What's happened?" the Mountain man queried.

"Is he prone to fits?"

"I don't know. I've not heard of any occurring before."

"Could it be the cheese?" Aremys asked.

"No, it's fresh. Nothing wrong with it."

"Something else, then. It seemed to occur at the same time as Galapek took fright."

"What are you saying?" Myrt squatted, saw the indecision in his companion's face. "Speak freely—I have protected you before."

Rashlyn lay rigidly still at their feet. Aremys lifted back the man's lids. The dark, madness-filled eyes had rolled back into his head. The man was unconscious; he could hear nothing.

"I'm not sure I should air my views. You're a loyal Mountain warrior, after all."

"Not to him!" Myrt spat disdainfully on the ground. "Like you, I wish he was dead. He's a danger to all of us."

"Because of his magic?"

Myrt nodded reluctantly. "He uses it for evil, I'm sure of it."

"I think it's his magic that has prompted this episode."

"I don't understand."

"I don't either, entirely." Aremys sighed and decided to take a chance on Myrt. He hoped his instincts would serve him truly. "Were you given any instructions about me and this afternoon's ride?"

Myrt frowned. "Nothing special. I was briefed to give you a chance to enjoy Galapek because you had expressed such interest in the horse."

"The King didn't tell you to keep a special eye on me?"

"My job is to keep an eye on you, Farrow. You're our . . ." —he hesitated—"our guest, after all."

Aremys grinned ruefully. "Myrt, you are more friend to me than most people I have met over the past decade. But let's be honest here: I'm a prisoner. I have to accept that. However," he went on, scratching his head, "your king is entrusting me with a very serious task, which means he has faith in me. Sadly, I can't be quite as honest with him as I can with you."

"Why not?"

"Because I suspect he is in the thrall of this man. You've told me as much yourself, and spending just an afternoon with Rashlyn has convinced me he's not someone to trust."

Myrt said nothing, merely frowned again.

Aremys pushed on. He glanced toward the horse. "I could be aiming completely off target here, but I think there's something very odd about Galapek. No, not odd. Enchanted."

Myrt rocked back on his heels as if slapped. "Magic?"

Aremys nodded. "Worked by Rashlyn, I'm guessing. And known of by your king." There, it was said.

Myrt stood and began pacing. He said nothing for a while and Aremys kept the silence, watching Rashlyn for any signs of consciousness.

"I don't believe this," the warrior hissed eventually, pointing at Aremys.

"You don't have to," the mercenary replied calmly, having anticipated the anger. "I'm just offering my own thoughts. I'm not suggesting that your king—whom I like and respect—is in complete agreement with Rashlyn."

"Then what *do* you mean, mercenary?" Myrt asked brusquely.

Aremys was sorry that he had pushed his friend so far. It was obvious from his anger that Myrt had suspected something not so far from what Aremys had suggested. But the blood of the Mountain People ran thick with loyalty. Wyl had warned him as much and he should not have presumed that friendship might override that loyalty—although, of course, it had in the case of the man Lothryn, who had chosen love and friendship over his monarch.

"I'm sorry if I've given insult, Myrt. It was not intended, especially not to you. I meant that I think Cailech—under the spell of Rashlyn, as you have pointed out—has permitted something unnatural to be wrought upon this horse."

"And how for the love of Haldor's arse would you know, Grenadyne? Are you a practitioner yourself, now, who knows when magic is being wielded?"

The harsh words bit at Aremys, as intended, but he could not ignore the truth. Could he risk divulging it to Myrt?

"Myrt, do you trust me?"

The man passed a weary hand over his eyes. "I'm not sure."

"What does your gut tell you?"

"That you are reliable."

"Good. That is enough for me. Now, we have to get Rashlyn back to the fortress. Help me lay him across his horse and I will tell you everything I know as we travel."

*   *   *

They took the same route home, although more slowly. Aremys had tethered Rashlyn's horse on a lead some distance behind them, so if the healer regained consciousness he would not be able to hear their conversation and would have to alert them by calling out. "An old mercenary trick," Aremys had said, winking.

On the return journey, Aremys began to share with his friend all the information he was prepared to risk bringing into the open. He cast a silent prayer to Shar that he had this man's measure, that he could trust him not to betray him. He said nothing of Wyl, of course, simply explaining that he had been in the employ of the Morgravian sovereign. Myrt accepted that the mercenary would not explain what specific task he was employed to do for Celimus, merely nodding when Aremys assured him that it was nothing connected with the people of the Razors.

"Let me simply say that I was tracking someone of interest to the Crown," Aremys offered.

"And that's what brought you so far north?"

"Yes. I've remembered that I came to a place called Timpkenny in the far north east of Briavel," the mercenary lied. "I believed the person I was following had passed through there."

"And these people who set upon you—just common bandits, you think?"

"Mmm." Aremys nodded. "Added a little something to my ale to make me feel sick so I would stagger outside the inn late at night. I'm guessing now—all of this is a little hazy, thanks to the drug—but they must have thrown me over a horse to remove me from prying eyes. They led me to the fringe of a region called the Thicket. Have you heard of it?" Aremys held his breath.

Myrt was staring at him intently. He nodded. "They say it has powerful magic."

"It does, my friend, or at least I think it does. The bandits left me there after robbing me. Something must have frightened them, because I expected to be beaten, at the very least." Aremys steered himself toward the truth. "The last thing I remember is a strange noise coming from the Thicket itself."

Myrt's eyes were huge. "A creature?"

"No creature I know makes that sound. No, I can still hear it—it was a sort of humming sound—and then the air became thick and oppressive," Aremys replied.

"Then what?"

Aremys made a gesture of apology. "Then nothing. I woke up to the sound of your men's voices and no memory of what had occurred or who I was. You know the rest. My memory came back gradually over the next couple of days, and it's still returning slowly." He shrugged, then added for effect, "I can even remember the faces of my family now."

Myrt, stunned, shook his head. Finally he spoke. "I believe you, Aremys. No one could make up such a tale, and we know of the Thicket's legend. It's just a shock to hear that its magical reputation is more than myth."

"For me too, Myrt. But I've been over it and over it and the only explanation I have is that the Thicket, or something inside it, had something to do with me appearing at a location in the Razors it would take days to reach by normal means. You checked the area; there were no signs of other people or animals, so I couldn't have been kept drugged and led in by horse."

"I believe you," the big warrior repeated, his hands raised in defense.

"Well, I don't want to put any strange ideas in your head, but my only explanation is that this place called the Thicket is enchanted—I too have heard the old tales—and it did not like my being there, let me tell you. I felt its animosity. I think it got rid of me."

"That's impossible, man!" Myrt said, desperate to cling to something rational.

"I agree, but there's no other explanation. You understand now why I had to keep this part of my story to myself? Obviously I couldn't tell that tale to the King. He would have laughed first and had my throat slit a moment later. As to how the Thicket rid itself of me—it repelled me. I can't think of any other way to describe it. It would be great to believe a nice family of tinkers found me, picked me up, and carried me with them on their journey through the Razors, but I think you'd agree we'd only be making up an explanation to help ourselves feel better about a notion we don't want to accept or understand. No, Myrt, I am convinced that magic has been wielded upon me. I have other reasons to suspect as much as well."

Here it was, the very core of his tale. Myrt would either give himself over entirely to Aremys now or brand him a madman and go running to Cailech. Aremys took a deep breath and waited for Myrt's inevitable question. He risked a glance behind. Rashlyn lay draped over his horse, still unconscious.

"What do you mean by that?"

The fortress was all but upon them now. Aremys could see the people working the orchards, driving carts and going about their chores. He shivered, noticing for the first time that a chill had descended into the valley and a slight breeze had picked up, sending ripples across the surface of the formerly mirrorlike lake. The disturbance matched his own mood.

"Aremys, what did you mean?" Myrt repeated.

Aremys reined Galapek to a halt and the other horses followed suit. He knew Myrt could tell this was difficult for him and was giving him time to find the right words. There were no right words, though—so he just told it as he saw it.

"I think I've been touched by the magic of the Thicket. It temporarily knocked out my memory with the force of its power, but it gave me something in return."

Myrt drew back warily and opened his mouth, then closed it again. Aremys hurried on. "It left me with the ability to sense magic." He held up his hand. "Before you jump in—no, I can't wield it. I just sense it. And magic is with us now."

"Where?" his companion whispered.

"Right here, beneath me."

Myrt looked toward the ground.

"Galapek," Aremys said. "This horse is not natural, Myrt. It is riddled with magic, bad magic. It's tainted—it smells evil and repulses me as effectively as the Thicket transported me all those leagues. This horse reeks of enchantment and I think Rashlyn is responsible for it."

"That's why you were so keen to avoid his touch," Myrt finished, tying together the threads of all he had noticed but had not been able to understand.

"That's right. That's why I disgraced myself on our first ride together when Cailech rode Galapek. The magic assaulted me and I had no control over my reaction to it. I didn't even know why I was behaving so strangely. It took me a while to work it out, but I know I'm right."

"And now?"

"The magic still revolts me, but I have it under control now."

The warrior whistled through his teeth. "So that's why you seemed nervous riding out this afternoon."

Aremys nodded. "I was terrified. I had no idea how I'd handle it, but I knew that Rashlyn had been sent to watch my reaction and so I had to be very careful."

"So you're saying the King sent him?"

"Of course. Cailech's too smart to allow my behavior on that first ride to go unnoticed. He's testing me."

"He speaks well of you, Aremys, you should know that," Myrt defended.

"Thank you. I've grasped as much, and yet I know he is suspicious of me—understandably so, because if he's got something to hide with this enchantment, anything that threatens it is a danger."

"You're risking much by telling me this."

Aremys nodded gravely. "My life is in your hands, Myrt. I trust you, and Shar knows, I had to tell someone. I was about to go mad."

"What do you want me to do?"

"Nothing. Just keep my secret for now."

"I cannot be party to anything disloyal to Cailech," the man said carefully.

"I wouldn't ask it of you. I just want to learn more about the horse—and Rashlyn, whom I wouldn't trust if he were the last man alive in this land."

"None of us would, except the King," Myrt replied, disgust lacing his tone. "And you think the horse's rearing and shrieking and Rashlyn's collapse are connected?"

"Yes. Something has tampered with their magic or disturbed the link between the two. I'll admit to something else . . ."

"Yes?"

"I felt it too, but only lightly. As Rashlyn was holding that medicine out to me, I became light-headed, slightly dizzy. I thought it was the fear of him touching me, but I think I know better now. The magic of the Thicket was resonating again . . . perhaps warning me. Or maybe something has happened, something connected with the Thicket that has also disturbed the horse. I don't understand what, or how. Maybe the Thicket can disrupt the actual enchantment on Galapek—why else would Rashlyn also react? They must be connected."

"But you don't know how?"

"No! It's frustrating!" Aremys frowned. "But I intend to learn more. Will you keep my secret?"

Myrt nodded unhappily. "I will keep it."

"Thank you. I won't betray you or your people—you have my word." Aremys banged his fist on his chest in an oath only another northerner would understand.

Myrt mirrored the movement and then the two men banged fists together in the traditional northern oath of loyalty.

After they had ridden on some time in silence, Aremys decided to push his luck with the Mountain Man. "Now that you know my secret, perhaps you would share with me whatever it was that you held back earlier about your great friend Lothryn?"

Myrt looked taken aback and uncomfortable. "It was nothing of importance."

Aremys shrugged. "It seemed to me that you were troubled by the mention of his name. I thought you might want to share your burden with someone who would not judge you for it—an outsider you can trust."

Myrt glanced back at the barshi's unconscious figure,

then looked around surreptitiously, his expression uncertain. *Come on, tell me,* Aremys urged silently. He knew if ever there was a moment to learn about Wyl's savior, it was now, while Myrt was in a fragile state of mind and the bond Aremys had built between them was new and strong.

"Lothryn . . ." Myrt spoke the name as if in veneration. "Brave Lothryn was brought back to the fortress after the Morgravians escaped—well, all but one."

Aremys bit back the question that leapt to his throat. He must not disturb the man's flow of speech. There would be time to learn about Gueryn le Gant later.

"Koreldy and the woman, Elspyth, managed to get away—because of Lothryn's aid and the fact that we were facing several zerkons. Lothryn and I fought back to back together on Haldor's Pass, a dangerous escarpment. We killed three zerkons that day and lost several men. When the battle was over my great friend turned to me and held his wrists out to be bound. He didn't ask for mercy or even a quick death—both of which I had expected, and might even have given him. I loved him enough to give my own life for him, and I knew Cailech would execute me if I showed such mercy. But Lothryn knew Cailech would have instructed me to bring him back to face his ruler. He allowed me to keep my faith with my king."

It was Aremys's turn to whisper. "What happened?"

Myrt's expression became distraught. His voice shaking with tightly held-back tears, he continued. "I delivered him to Cailech. It was a private meeting and I was not permitted to be present. I have no idea what passed between them. Later, all the King would tell me was that Lothryn was undergoing a special punishment and we would not see him again. I asked whether he was to be killed and I'll never forget the King's reply. He said, 'He probably wishes I would kill him.' I saw a mixture of pain and regret in his face, Aremys. The King loved Lothryn like a brother, and his betrayal cut deeper than any other wound ever could."

Aremys sighed. "And there's been no sign of Lothryn since?"

Myrt shook his head, deeply upset. "We've tried. I know

Rashlyn knows something, but he's as mad as a pit of burning snakes. He makes little sense at the best of times."

As if on cue, they heard a sound behind them, a weak cry from the man slung across the trailing horse.

"He's stirring. We've tarried long enough. We shall speak again when we next get a chance alone," Aremys said and, as Myrt dropped back to check on Rashlyn, he clicked Galapek on toward the mammoth arch that swallowed them into the great stone fortress.

YL'S PROGRESS ALONG THE DARKSTREAM WAS SLOW AS HE traveled against the current back toward the Thicket. His mind felt burdened rather than lightened by his meeting with Elysius and his heart was especially heavy at leaving Fynch. Further, his emotions were still in turmoil at the loss of his sister, Ylena, whose body he now inhabited, and by the disappearance of Aremys. He had precious few friends in his life now. To lose one so soon—especially one he trusted as he did Aremys—was devastating.

But it was leaving Fynch behind that troubled him the most. As he inched his way toward the Thicket, Wyl realized how important the youngster had become to him. Others, such as Elspyth and Aremys, had accepted the strangeness of his life, but Fynch had guessed his secret from the start and had protected him. Little Fynch, so humble and yet so wise, had saved not only Wyl's life but also that of a sovereign with his ingenuity. And then, following his own path, he had left the safety of Werryl, first to track down Romen's killer, and after obeying the pull of the Wild. The boy was deeply enmeshed in this whole business of Myrren's Gift, or at least in the curious life that Wyl was now leading, and Wyl was angry at himself for not insisting that Fynch leave Elysius and travel with him.

The truth of it was, he suddenly felt he needed Fynch. Their lives, strange though they both were, were entwined, and it suddenly occurred to Wyl that Fynch's involvement might be more than pure coincidence. Fynch had been at Myrren's burning; was it possible that he was magically tied to her gift, too?

Wyl sighed. Fynch aside, he was concerned about so many people that his only plan at this minute was to return to Timpkenny. He would stay overnight there before making a decision on his next move. The remainder of his journey up the Darkstream was curiously and happily uneventful—Ylena's fears mercifully remained at bay—and Samm was nowhere to be seen when he alighted, relieved, from the small craft. His intention had been to avoid the boatman and so it suited him that the cottage appeared deserted.

Wyl did not relish the notion of passing again through the mysterious Thicket, but he knew he could not wait too long to find the courage. Dark fell heavily and fast in this place, and he did not want to risk Samm coming across him. He walked briskly toward the dark line of yews that marked the border of the Thicket. Wyl was convinced that he could hear a dim buzz emanating from the enchanted forest; it frightened him, but as he had been allowed to pass through once before, he was counting on similar generosity again.

Wyl took a deep breath, closed his eyes reflexively, and pushed into the tangle. The Thicket's cool atmosphere chilled him instantly. The silence was disturbing. It was clear that the forest knew he was there, and the thought that this place could sense, think, and make decisions for itself was the most disconcerting notion of all.

Oddly, this time there were no snagging branches and no confusing pathways. Previously, when Knave had led him through, Wyl had felt sure that alone he would have lost himself among the yews for good. This time paths seemed to open themselves up to him. He shook his head with wonder. The Thicket was guiding him swiftly through its depths. It wanted him gone, was as glad to be rid of him as he was to have his back to it.

"Thank you," he whispered in genuine relief. Whether or not the Thicket heard he could not know, but he felt better for having offered his gratitude.

It was then that a terrible thought struck him: If the Thicket could guide him out, it was just as able to keep Aremys in. Was the mercenary still blundering around in the forest, trying hopelessly to escape?

Wyl overcame his intense fear, took the chance, and began to call to his friend. The somewhat desperate edge to his voice carried loudly through the dense overgrowth but did little more than scatter small animals he could not see. As if in response to the tension his concern for Aremys had created, Ylena's fear of enclosed spaces began to threaten again. He felt it first as a tightening in her chest, and recalled the identical tautness of emotion that had occurred just before he'd lost control of himself during his first journey on the Darkstream.

The familiar shallowness of breath hit him and he stopped moving. Was the Thicket's magic acute enough to sense this change in him? Instinctively, he began breathing into his cupped hands. He could not imagine how he remembered this trick, but it was something his father had taught Ylena when she was an infant. Panic, he recalled, had often overcome his young sister, prompted by any suggestion of being enclosed or hidden: the game hide-and-seek, looking into the dark depths of the well, or playing under Wyl's bed. To his knowledge, Ylena had not experienced this terror since she was a child, but obviously its ability to strike had traveled with her into adulthood. Wyl was grateful now for his memory of Fergys Thirsk's trick to calm his daughter; he quickly noticed a marked change in what had been steadily rising panic levels.

Whether or not the Thicket was aware of his discomfort, Wyl was fairly sure it deliberately steered him toward what might, at a stretch, be described as a clearing. His relief—or, more to the point, Ylena's—at the space was evident as her legs buckled, dropping him to the ground. It remained cool beneath the yews, but the oppressive atmosphere was not as marked, and Wyl knew that if he could get his breathing under control he would feel less anxious. He put Ylena's pretty head between her knees and forced her lungs to breathe slowly and deeply, as foot soldiers, suddenly overcome by fear of battle, were taught to do before the command to charge. He held this position for several minutes and was relieved that he could feel the anxiety lessening.

A soft sound above prompted him to raise his head and he was confronted by the largest owl he had ever seen. Strikingly marked, the majestic tawny blinked slowly and deliberately in the way owls do. Wyl watched it as intently as it was regarding him, wondering which of them would turn away first, if that indeed was what was expected.

He lost the staring contest. "And you are?" he said, feeling ridiculous but reminding himself that he had spoken to Knave without embarrassment. Why not this curious owl with such intelligence lurking in its large yellow eyes? He was rewarded for his faith.

I am Rasmus, the owl said into his mind, startling him.

"I hear you," Wyl replied, in awe of the splendid creature before him.

That was my intention, Rasmus said somewhat disdainfully, rotating its head in a disconcerting manner.

"How is it that we can communicate?" Wyl persisted. "Is it because of Myrren's Gift?"

The owl made a disgusted sound. *It is because I allow it, and because you are here.*

"In the Thicket, you mean?"

Where else could I mean?

Wyl felt an apology springing to his lips but resisted it. This creature was either baiting him or simply did not like him. "What do you want with me?" he asked, his tone direct.

Again the owl blinked. *We want you to leave,* it said firmly.

"Well, can't you just rid yourself of me?" Wyl replied, determined not to be cowed by this strange creature.

If we choose to.

Wyl sighed, irritated by the owl's superior manner. "Then choose it, owl, for leaving here is what I want too."

If you want to be gone from here, why do you linger? Rasmus asked, his tone suggesting he too was losing patience.

"I am not lingering," Wyl snapped. "I was guided to this spot, and if you're as magical as I suspect, you can probably sense the sorcery that has touched me."

I can.

"Then you know that this is not the body I was born with."

And so?

"And so this particular body does not care for the density or fearsome atmosphere of your Thicket."

It is not mine, the bird countered.

It was Wyl's turn to blink—with exasperation. He took a steadying breath; showing his fury would not help here. "The person whose body I walk in is scared of this place and was having breathing difficulties."

We gathered.

"Was this clearing deliberately created for my benefit?" Wyl was determined to find out the extent of the Thicket's abilities.

Yes. Are you ready to leave?

"Not until you answer a question."

I am not beholden to you.

Wyl took a gamble. "If you trust Knave, then you should trust me, for he and I are friends. I mean you and the creatures of the Thicket—or indeed the Thicket itself—no harm. The secret of your magic is safe with me."

There was a long pause. Wyl stood up, frustrated by the owl's stare and its silence. "You have let me pass through before. I know you have no intention of killing me."

Ask your question, the owl finally said, irritably.

Wyl curbed his enthusiasm and took a moment to consider how best to phrase his question. He sensed the owl would answer, at worst cryptically, and at best literally, so his question would have to be very clear.

"Where is Aremys living?" he asked carefully.

There was no hesitation from the owl. *He lives in the Razors.*

Wyl's relief spilled over. "Is he safe?"

I have answered your question, the owl replied, fractious now.

"Please," Wyl beseeched.

Rasmus made a peevish clicking noise. *Aremys is safe.*

Wyl wondered how much more the owl knew. The Thicket held many secrets; perhaps they could help him as he journeyed on. He had nothing more to lose other than the owl's patience, and that was already fast depleting. "Rasmus," Wyl began reasonably, "you have shared your name. Mine is Wyl. But then I'm sure you know that. Can we not be friends?"

Yet another tiresome question?

Wyl sat down deliberately. "Yes, I have questions. I know what you are concerned about, and I will not betray the Thicket. I owe it for keeping my friend Aremys safe and for helping me so far. I am your friend also."

The Thicket has no friends of your kind, save one. You are not he.

Wyl assumed the bird referred to Elysius. "Then let me ask what I need so I can help the others you do trust—Knave and . . . Fynch."

He had intended to say "Elysius," but "Fynch" came to his mind and slipped out first. He saw the bird react as he spoke his young friend's name, and the shrubs around him seemed to shudder. Was it the boy who interested the Thicket?

"I will protect Fynch always," he risked.

And was rewarded with a testy reply. *He does not require your protection. He has the protection of the Thicket.*

"I see," Wyl said, not really seeing anything but harking back to his earlier suspicion that Fynch had some special purpose in this dangerous game they were playing. Then a notion came to him as suddenly as a wasp sting and causing similar pain. "He's not coming to Werryl, is he?"

The bird said nothing at first, then sighed. At that soft sound in his head, Wyl felt hollow. He had lost Fynch. *Fynch has his own path to follow now,* Rasmus confirmed.

Although he had suspected as much, Wyl felt his heart sink at the owl's sorrowful words. Fynch's new path must be a dangerous one, he realized, or the owl would not have mentioned protection. Wyl also realized there was precious little he could do about it. The Thicket would not permit him to return to find Fynch, he knew. It obviously had its own reasons for helping the boy to follow this new road.

"Knave will be at his side, of course?" he ventured.

Always, Rasmus said.

"Thank you," said Wyl, and meant it. "I shall leave now. I am grateful to you, Rasmus, and the 'we' you speak of, for allowing me this time and for answering my questions."

He stood and bowed to the huge bird with marked respect, then walked away, presuming the Thicket would now guide him quickly to its fringe and toward Timpkenny. He was surprised to hear Rasmus call to him.

He turned. "Pardon?"

I said, where are you going? the owl repeated.

"I must make my way south to Werryl as quickly as I can."

We will send you there.

Wyl looked at the large bird quizzically. "Send me?"

Come back to the clearing.

"I don't understand." Wyl felt a thrill of fear run through him.

You will. Stand before me and close your eyes. Do not open them.

"I won't."

If you disobey us, we shall never allow you to leave, the owl warned.

Too much depended on his safe departure from this place. Wyl did as asked, wondering if this "sending" business was a small show of friendship after all.

Be still, the owl cautioned. *It will feel strange but you must trust us. Do not resist. Just let your body float. Remember, do not open your eyes.*

Wyl understood none of it but obeyed as a man used to taking orders.

Farewell, Rasmus said, and then Wyl felt a vast, chest-crushing pressure against his body. He wanted to open his eyes but fought the urge, having given his word. Breathing was all but impossible, but he refused to panic. He had to trust the owl.

Had he disobeyed the owl's strict instructions, he would

have seen Fynch before him. Wyl could not see the tears on Fynch's face or the goodbye the boy mouthed to his friend, but he felt the touch of the Gate Wielder as Ylena's trembling body was pushed through a thickened disk of air and disappeared.

It is done, Rasmus said. *Be at rest, Faith Fynch.*

W
hy do they refer to me as Faith?" Fynch whispered to Knave, who sat tall and imposing beside him in a special sunlit divide. Had he not seen it with his own eyes, Fynch would never have believed such a clearing existed in the Thicket. Curiously, the small light-drenched space added no particular cheer to the dense, dark, and brooding atmosphere, but Fynch was nonetheless glad for the brief respite from the chill.

It is how we think of you.

"What do you mean?"

We have faith in you.

Fynch wanted to ask more, but the words stilled in his mouth as creatures—many known to him only from folklore—began to gather at the fringe of the clearing.

"These are your friends?" he asked, his voice filled with wonder.

They are the creatures of the Thicket.

Fynch's attention was caught by a magnificent lion that watched him from the shadows. The animal shook itself and Fynch gasped to see wings extending from the proud cat's shoulders.

"Knave, that's the winged lion of legend."

No legend as you can see, son. He exists.

"I only know of him from the old tales and the carvings at Stoneheart. He . . . he is Wyl's mythical animal, who protects him."

And yours?

"Mine?" the boy said, awed as he caught sight of the equally legendary great bear. "My creature is . . ." He hesitated as a different animal invaded his mind, demanding to be named. He felt treacherous and pushed the thought away. "My animal is the unicorn."

He comes to you now, Knave said.

The other creatures fell silent as the beautiful animal emerged into the light. Its coat had a hue of the palest of blues, but the overall impression was of a pure, dazzling white; even its famed horn was a silvery white. It walked slowly and with such grace that Fynch held his breath, utterly captivated.

Tall and broad, the unicorn towered over the boy and his companion. *Child,* it said in a deep, musical voice. *It is my privilege to welcome you among us.*

Fynch was so overwhelmed that he began to weep. The unicorn bent its great head, careful not to touch the boy with its lethal horn, and nuzzled Fynch, who put his small arms around the creature's neck in worship. *My name is Roark,* it added, for his hearing alone.

"The privilege is mine, great Roark," Fynch whispered.

Be bright, Faith Fynch. You are our hope, the animal returned into his mind.

Fynch gathered his composure and dried his eyes. He looked about him uncertainly, registering the expectancy that hung in the air, and tried not to gawp at the amazing troupe of creatures gathered around him.

As one, they bowed, including Knave and the graceful Roark.

You must acknowledge them, Knave whispered into Fynch's startled mind. *Put your awe aside, son. You are to whom we give our loyalty. Assume your birthright.*

Fynch did not understand. He was a gong boy. A child of low birth and even lower rank. How could he acknowledge homage from these majestic creatures of legend? Who was he to assume such a role?

It was as if Roark could hear his thoughts. *Fynch, will you accept our obeisance and loyalty?*

Elysius's words echoed in Fynch's memory: *Perhaps the Thicket needs you for more than simply watching over a Gate.*

He could not escape his destiny, he knew this. His life was no longer his own to direct or to make decisions about. Choices had already been made and promises given.

Fynch steadied himself and found his voice. "Creatures of the Thicket," he called, "I will make myself worthy of your faith."

He bowed, low and long. When he stood upright again, he felt a new strength pulsing through him, from his toes through to the tips of his fingers. He realized that it must be the Thicket communicating with him, sending him nourishing power. He felt charged with it, and could not help the radiant smile that broke out onto his face.

"Tell me what it is I must do," he asked the creatures. "I am your servant."

It was Rasmus who spoke on behalf of the creatures and of the Thicket itself. *Be seated, Fynch,* he offered from his perch.

Fynch lowered himself to the ground. Knave and Roark remained standing, flanking Fynch on either side.

Child, you already know what it is we ask of you, the owl said.

"I do?"

Elysius shared the same desire.

"Rashlyn," Fynch murmured.

The creatures and trees all shuddered their shared hatred for the man.

Yes, Rasmus concurred. *You must destroy him.*

"What is it that frightens you so about this man?"

He is tainted, and he wants to use his power to corrupt all that is natural about the world. His evil is born of his jealously at being unable to manipulate Nature. More than anything, he passionately desires the power to control all creatures. With this at his disposal, he would rule all realms. Imagine him being able to call upon eagle or zerkon alike? Imagine him commanding them to do evil, the other animals powerless to refuse him? You must destroy him!

"I don't think I am capable," Fynch protested.

The Thicket and its creatures will help you.

Strengthened by the thrum of power that bristled through him from the ground of the Thicket, and emboldened by the love and loyalty that surrounded him, Fynch took a deep breath. "Then I ask for nothing more than your faith in me."

It was the right thing to say. Knave confirmed as much with a gently uttered *Bravo, child* into his mind while the creatures showed their trust and delight, some leaping into the air, others rearing to stand on two legs, still others squawking or braying.

Fynch laughed. He was filled with a joy he had never known before. He suddenly felt he belonged to all of them. He reached for Knave and touched the great dog's head.

I don't believe it, Knave said, his tone humble. *The King comes.*

"King?" Fynch repeated, puzzled. Since they had begun communicating via this special mindtalk, Fynch had found Knave's manner to be mostly serious, like himself. The dog was not one for jests or shallow thoughts. He spoke only when there was something to say, and during most of their conversations it had been his role to counsel Fynch. The boy knew of Knave's graveness, and the dignity that emanated from his solid, dependable presence, but never had he seen the dog show humility. And this was no small humility: Knave sounded filled with reverence for whatever it was that was arriving. "Knave—"

Hush, said the dog, and a powerful beating sound made Fynch raise his head and squint into the light above. Something plunged toward them—a suggestion of a shadow at first, that darkened until it cut out the light entirely and Fynch no longer squinted but was wide-eyed with both fear and awe.

"The warrior dragon," he breathed.

Our king, Roark said softly, veneration in his voice, as the mighty creature alighted in the clearing.

The creatures bent low to exalt the hallowed creature that stood before them, its famed, darkly shimmering colors gloriously filling the clearing.

Fynch needed no prompting. He fell to his knees immediately, then prostrated himself. Closing his eyes, he cast a prayer to Shar in thanks for the blessing of this day and what it had brought him.

Fynch, said a voice, as rich and mellow as treacle.

"Your majesty," Fynch replied, not daring to raise his head.

Come stand before me, the voice commanded. Fynch summoned his courage. With Knave and Roark's whispered encouragement, he opened his eyes and looked upon the King of all the beasts. There was no doubting that royalty stood before him, no wondering if this glorious creature was worthy of such exaltation. Fynch held his breath as every fiber of his being suddenly felt newly alive, restored somehow in the presence of such grandeur.

Like everyone else who looked upon the dragon pillar in the Pearlis Cathedral with awe, Fynch had believed the warrior dragon to be just legend. Associated with the Morgravian sovereign, it was the most impressive of all the mythical creatures but no more real than the winged lion. But now the King of Kings stood in all his glory before him, as real as Fynch himself.

Faith Fynch, the King said. *Be welcome.*

"Thank you, your majesty," Fynch stammered, bowing. "I am proud to serve you."

And we are indebted for that service, child, which is given so bravely by one so young.

Fynch said nothing. He had no response to such generous praise.

The warrior dragon continued: *And still we ask more of you.*

"I will give my life if it is so required."

The King regarded him through dark, wise eyes. *We shall do everything in our power to prevent you relinquishing something so precious.*

"Please tell me, my king"—*my true king,* Fynch thought to himself—"what it is that you ask of me."

The beast wasted no further time. *The King of Morgravia brings shame to his kind. He is of the warrior clan—of my blood, you could say—but he disgusts me.*

"Celimus is indeed shameful," Fynch agreed quietly.

That said, there have been Kings before who have disappointed and we have ignored them. The Thicket and its creatures do not meddle in the affairs of men, child. We have watched you kill one another for centuries and we have not involved ourselves. But on this occasion we have been

*drawn into the struggles of mankind because of the misuse
of magic.*

"You speak of Myrren's Gift, your majesty."

The King hesitated briefly. *That included, yes. It was
wrong of Elysius to channel his power through his daughter
to such a vengeful end. His power, once we granted him access to the Wild, was to be used only for the good of the natural world.*

Fynch felt compelled to defend Elysius. "I don't think he
fully realized what the repercussions would be, your
majesty."

*Magic is always dangerous, Fynch, even when used with
the best of intentions. There are always repercussions, although sometimes we are unable to see what they are until it
is too late. That is why the Thicket and its magic have been
deliberately shielded from men. Myrren's Gift has already
claimed four lives. Wyl Thirsk should have died; instead he
is abroad and carrying a deadly enchantment. None of us
knows where it could end.*

"Wyl didn't ask for Myrren's Gift, your majesty," Fynch
mumbled, trying not to sound petulant.

I know, my son, the King replied gently. *I feel great sorrow for Wyl, who is one of the best among men—as was his
father. It is the magic that troubles me, and how it will re-
verberate through the world of men. I mean to end it here.*

"You don't mean to destroy Wyl?" Fynch exclaimed.

In a way he is already dead, the creature answered.

Fynch did not like the resignation in the Dragon King's
voice. He grasped for placation, desperate to prevent this
powerful being from hurting Wyl. "The Thicket and its creatures have asked me to kill Rashlyn, your majesty, and with
their help I will endeavor to rid the land of the destroyer.
Both brothers will be no more. The magic will end."

*Not really, child, for now you possess it. Rashlyn wishes
to control the natural world. He is a corrupter of natural
things. He wants power over the beasts. But Celimus is just
as dangerous. He too wants power, although of a different
kind. I fear that if we do not destroy Rashlyn, these two ambitious men might join together. I know how the minds of*

greedy men work, and should they claim the Razors and Bri-avel, they will almost certainly turn their attention toward the Wild. With Celimus's help, Rashlyn will try to destroy the Thicket. The King sighed. *We do not wish to engage in such a confrontation.*

"What can I do to help, your majesty?" Fynch asked, desperation seeping into his voice.

I grant you permission to use the magic of the Thicket to aid Wyl Thirsk in his bid to rid Morgravia of its king, for without Celimus I do not believe Rashlyn's madness can be fully unleashed.

Fynch nodded thoughtfully, relief flooding his small body to learn that the Warrior King did not mean to attack Wyl directly. He recognized that the dragon warrior had not offered his own mighty strength or powers, only that of the Thicket. Fynch also knew that the creatures of the Thicket would insist on keeping their secrets. He already felt a part of this mysterious community and knew he would do everything in his power to protect them and their magic.

"Celimus has no heir," Fynch cautioned, even though he presumed the royal creature knew as much.

Morgravia will survive. Do what you must. Knave is your guide—use his wisdom well, child, and your own powers sparingly. I presume Elysius explained the price you may be required to pay?

Fynch nodded. "He did."

The King waited, wondering whether the child would expand on his brief answer. A plea for mercy perhaps, a query as to whether his life could somehow be spared. But no further words came. The King beat his wings in appreciation of the boy's humility; he was prepared to give everything of himself for those he loved and asked for nothing in return.

The warrior dragon's gaze penetrated deep into Fynch's heart and he was surprised to see there a startling and precious secret regarding this boy. He had not expected it, but the discovery warmed him. Should he share it? The child's life was already forfeit; what could be gained from adding more confusion? The King felt sorrow well up that they would use this boy so. But there was no other way. Fynch

was the sacrifice, though it cut him deeply to send his own
to die.

*Then we remain in your debt, Fynch. The Thicket and its
creatures will always hold you in their hearts. We bless you
and hold our faith in you with reverence.*

There was too much emotion swirling through Fynch for
him to risk another word to this mightiest of beasts. Instead
he bowed to show his complete acceptance. The royal creature acknowledged it with another powerful flapping of his
wings, driving Fynch to the ground as he lifted effortlessly
into the air and disappeared.

Roark and Knave were at his side again.

He has not appeared to us in an age, Knave said, the awe
still evident in his voice. *He came to pay homage only to
you, child.*

Fynch, overwhelmed by this fateful meeting with the
King of the Beasts, was unable to respond. Knave under-
stood and nuzzled his friend's small hand. *Come, Faith
Fynch, we have a journey to begin.*

4

Lost in bleak thoughts, Queen Valentyna leaned her el-
bows against the cool whitestone of the walkway that
linked two of the palace towers. It was her private place,
one she rarely shared. The last person she had permitted to
spend time with her here was Koreldy, and before him,
Fynch. She could not help but think of those two friends
now, both lost to her, both keenly missed. With her face
cupped in her hands she stared out across the Briavellian
moors she loved so much and marveled at a hawk hovering
far ahead in the distance, watching patiently as it waited for
its prey. Suddenly it plunged, arrowlike, toward the ground,

making the Queen breathless for the small creature about to lose its life.

That was how she felt. Vulnerable, and now suddenly exposed and helpless. Celimus of Morgravia was the hawk and she the creature giving up her life to him.

Rumblings of war were filtering back from Briavel's spies in Morgravia. By all reports, the Legion was preparing for battle and Valentyna did not have to ponder too hard to guess at their enemy. Was it a ruse? Just an empty threat? Her instincts told her it was, but she would still need to tread with the greatest of care. Her relationship with Celimus teetered on a knife edge and all that stood between peace for her subjects and almost certain slaughter was her written consent to marriage with the Morgravian King.

For that tenuous security, she owed thanks to Chancellor Krell, who had forced her hand and made her send the letter. And yet Valentyna could only hang her head in despair at the damage done by Krell's subsequent well-meaning but shortsighted interference in writing to his counterpart in Morgravia, Chancellor Jessom. Oh, she could scream just thinking about it. In fact, she was still so angry at the old man's actions it had taken all her willpower to maintain her composure at Krell's funeral. He had been quietly buried in the palace cemetery. No family had come for him; he went into the ground as lonely as he went to his god, believing he was despised.

Krell had diligently and tirelessly worked for the Briavellian royal family for nigh on twoscore years. He was like a piece of old furniture: comfortable, reliable, always there in the same place. Valentyna had grown up knowing that her father relied on him, and had come to appreciate his loyalty and advice herself. Despite her anguish that he had invited such ruin with an ill-considered move, Valentyna could not help but feel a keen sorrow that the good man would be remembered for that one poor decision among a host of wise ones during a solid and devoted career serving the Crown.

Now, in a quiet moment of reflection and private recrimination, she regretted her harsh words to him. She had no doubt that she had prompted his suicide and it was something she knew she would have to live with. Valentyna had shed her tears for him in private and she would be lying if she did not admit to herself that she missed his steadfast counsel. But she had also spoken the truth when she told him she could never forgive him for his terrible error. He had overstepped his authority and in doing so had risked the lives of all Briavellians.

Morgravia's king was vain, avaricious, and cruel, but he was not a dullard. Because of Krell's poor judgment, Celimus would now know about Alyd Donal's remains being smuggled into Briavel, and that the Queen he thought he had well and truly cornered was consorting with his enemies.

A man cleared his throat quietly at one end of the walkway to interrupt her musings. She looked toward him, knowing who it would be—one of the few she allowed to come to her here if duty called. All other servants were banned from tracking her down to the bridge.

"Liryk. Please join me," she said. He bowed in respect and walked to the center of the bridge.

"It's beautiful, isn't it?" Valentyna said, indicating the view before them.

"More than that, your highness," her army's commander admitted. "It feeds the soul."

"Liryk," she said, unable to help herself, "you're a poet."

Liryk smiled. It was good to hear her playful. That tone had all but disappeared these past weeks. "No, your majesty. I just never get tired of these moors. I'm always happy to see them when I return to Werryl after being away."

"And so how are you and I going to give this up?"

"My queen?"

"This," she said, moving her hand in a sweeping arc. "We will be giving this to Morgravia." There was a note of anger in her voice. "It will no longer be ours."

"Not giving, your highness," Liryk proposed gently. "I'd prefer to think of it as sharing."

"Celimus is forcing us to give Briavel to him," Valentyna said coldly. "He is blackmailing me, Commander, and there's not a thing I can do about it. If I want our young men to live, I have to give up the realm."

"Pardon me, your highness, but I—and I think I can speak for all your loyal subjects in this—do not view it that way. We applaud this move."

The Queen sighed. "And I am grateful for that," she said. "But will you thank me when King Celimus starts to stamp his own brutal form of authority across Briavel?"

Liryk had no answer, and in truth, the Queen did not expect one. "What news did you come here to tell me, Commander Liryk?"

"The Legion is preparing for movement east now, your highness. If we are going to placate our neighboring King, we need to do it soon."

Valentyna closed her eyes and took a deep breath. She cast one more fond glance toward the moors and then gave brisk orders.

"Have Crys Donal summoned, please. I will meet with you both in my study. Elspyth too."

"At once, your highness."

Valentyna watched him leave, hating what she was about to do.

The Queen dismissed the servant and poured the two men a glass of wine herself.

"Where is Elspyth?" she inquired of Liryk as he took the goblet from her.

"Your highness, she is nowhere to be found," he answered, silently happy for the woman's disappearance. He had agreed with Krell that Elspyth's influence on the Queen was dangerous. The Morgravian woman had fired their queen's spirit—made her feel strong and encouraged her to defy Celimus.

Valentyna glanced at Crys, who shrugged. "I haven't seen her for a couple of days, if truth be known. I thought she was with you, your majesty."

"Strange," Valentyna admitted. "Your search has been thorough?" she asked her commander.

"I've sent several runners to comb the palace, your highness. She's certainly not in any of the usual places."

"Has anyone checked her chambers?" Crys asked. "You

had lent her some garments, your highness," he added. "Are they still there?"

"You think she's fled?" the Queen exclaimed.

"Did she tell you about a man called Lothryn?" Crys replied, calmly sipping his wine. He suspected that they would not find Elspyth. She had mentioned several times to him that she was no longer needed here. He also suspected his own stay had worn thin, and who could blame the Briavellians with the Legion gathering in force across the border?

The Queen nodded slowly. "Only vaguely."

"There's a story attached to him," he explained. "It involves Koreldy." Once again it pained him to see the Queen react to that man's name. Wyl had given firm instructions that Valentyna was not to learn the truth about Koreldy, but it seemed to Crys unkind not to let her know that the person she obviously loved was not dead as she suspected but roaming the land in a new guise. Crys felt a lurch of despair as he remembered that terrible night at Felrawthy. The day after had been worse, but he knew he must not think on that now. *Bury your hurts,* his mother used to say. *Bring them out only when you're alone and strong enough to look at them.* And so he had somehow buried the despair of losing his family so cruelly and was trying not to dwell on their deaths.

"Crys?"

He was embarrassed to realize both the Queen and Liryk were watching him.

"I—I'm sorry. Lost myself there," he said, not wanting to say more.

"You were telling us about Elspyth and Lothryn," Valentyna prompted, deliberately avoiding mentioning Koreldy by name.

"That's right," Crys continued. "The Mountain Dweller Lothryn saved the lives of Elspyth and Koreldy in the Razors. No one knows if he survived Cailech's wrath at his betrayal. Elspyth is determined to learn his fate."

Neither of them referred to their knowledge that Elspyth was in love with Lothryn. "And you think she's gone back?" Valentyna suggested.

"I think she's capable of doing something that bullheaded, yes," he said, and smiled gently to reassure the Queen that he admired Elspyth for her courage.

"Into the Razors?" Liryk queried. "Alone?"

"I don't know, sir. She's a passionate girl. I don't think fear stops her from doing anything. If not for Elspyth, I would be dead with the rest of my family."

The new Duke of Felrawthy could refer to his loved ones now without threat of anger or tears. His brief time in Werryl, offering distance from all things familiar, and the new title by which everyone seemed determined to address him, had made the difference between his collapsing into inconsolable anguish or rising to the challenge of what he was born and bred to do. It was what his fine parents would have expected of him.

A knock came at the door. Liryk put his glass down. "Shall I see to it, your highness? It may be the messengers."

"Please," the Queen said, distracted as she pondered the business of Elspyth's disappearance. "I miss Krell," she muttered.

Crys held his tongue. No one had heard the exchange between the Queen and her chancellor that had preceded his death, but Valentyna had openly admitted that she had driven him to anguish with her harsh criticism. Crys had to admire the Queen for her forthright manner; she refused to shrink from blame but accepted and dealt with it as best she could. Krell's death had been a shock for everyone, most of all Liryk, but the doughty soldier had kept his feelings to himself and remained stoic throughout the funeral and the ensuing mourning that had gripped the palace.

Crys sipped his wine quietly, wondering why he had been summoned to what appeared to be a formal meeting. It would be better for Valentyna, he knew, if he were to leave Briavel. Perhaps he should offer and save her the trial of asking him to do just that.

Liryk returned to disturb his thoughts. "Your majesty, we found this note in Elspyth's chamber."

"Anything else?" Valentyna asked as she broke the wax seal. "Clothes?"

"Nothing, your highness," he replied, watching her frown as she quickly read the note's contents.

Valentyna looked up and sighed. "Your hunch is correct, Crys. She believes she has done what she came here to do and has taken her leave."

"Gone to the Razors?" Crys inquired.

"It doesn't say but I suspect you're right. I know how fond she was of this man Lothryn. If I were her, I too would want to know the truth of his fate."

There was another knock at the door. Valentyna could not disguise her frustration at being interrupted again. She stuffed the note into her pocket and stood. "Gentlemen, I'm going for a ride. We shall continue this meeting this evening, please, when we can talk without disturbance. There are many things to discuss and I need to think. Liryk, would you see to that?" She nodded toward the door. "I'll leave by the back way."

The two men stood and watched her go.

The highest point of the moors was the farthest Valentya could get from her subjects—or so she liked to believe—and the ideal place to vent her fears or frustrations. Her ever-present escort, however, was hovering nearby, so she swallowed the bloodcurdling shriek she longed to let rip. She gave a deep groan instead. Too many of those she loved or trusted had been taken from her or left her. She stared back toward the palace and counted them off softly to herself.

Her father: murdered. Wyl Thirsk: murdered. Romen Koreldy: murdered. Fynch, her little rock of strength: disappeared, and with him the strange yet somehow reassuring presence of Knave. Now Elspyth, her new friend and confidante, had disappeared as well, almost certainly advancing toward her own death as she ventured into the Mountain Kingdom to discover the fate of her beloved Lothryn.

Valentyna paused in her account of her personal sorrows to think on those of Crys Donal. An entire family slaughtered in one evening. So much death. And now, in order to protect Briavel, she would have to banish her latest friend too. That was what she needed to discuss with the new Duke of Felrawthy, but this afternoon, with all of its interruptions, conversation had proved impossible.

The Queen of Briavel shook her head with despair. Almost all of this destruction swirling about her was the work of one man. One cruel, scheming, greedy man. The man she would have to marry if she wanted to prevent further death.

She cast a disconsolate glance toward the soldiers shuffling in the shade of the copse a short distance away. Three were now being sent to shadow her every move. She hated it, but put up with it. Liryk's caution was well founded, but she missed her freedom. She inhaled the sweet air of the moors and felt even more despondent. Everyone seemed to be worrying about her at the moment. She sensed her advisers observing her, could feel their concern tightening around her like a bandage, constricting her free will. Valentyna knew what they feared—and they were right to fear it, for if she could find a way out of this marriage, she would renege in a blink. She knew such a dream was impossible, though. No one was going to save her. The nobles had told her to find Ylena Thirsk, but that was pointless. How could it make any difference? Ylena's word might convince them that Celimus was a cold-blooded murderer, but she knew it would not make them change their minds about the marriage.

She thought about Ylena Thirsk and the terrible things the young woman had experienced. Crys had explained to Valentyna what Ylena had been through just to get herself to Felrawthy. It had made the Queen shudder to imagine how Wyl's sister had coped with yet more terror after what she had already suffered at Stoneheart. Ylena was younger than she and had shown such courage. She would have to find similar courage now and face her destiny. Her father had fought to keep Briavel safe. She must do the same, just in a different manner. She would buy its peace with her body. Give it over to that hateful man, let him parade it before his minions and use her for his pleasures. But he would not have her love—ever. That belonged to one alone, and he was now dead. In giving her body to Celimus, however, she might still attain something untainted, something good. They might produce a child. And into that child she would pour all of her love, everything she denied Celimus and had hoped to give to Romen Koreldy. She would raise a proud sovereign to take the joint throne of Morgravia and Briavel one day.

Valentyna sighed as the soft breeze tousled her already messy hair. "Give me a sign, Shar," she said to the gentle wind, hoping it would carry her plea to the god. "Show me that marrying Celimus is the right decision."

She felt like weeping at her pathetic words. Instead she wiped away the single tear that had fallen, rubbed at her other eye just in case, and willed herself to be strong. She would live up to the woman her father believed she had become. She strode back toward the soldiers. They had already spotted her movement and busied themselves with preparing the horses to ride again.

Squinting into the sun, Valentyna did not see the bird at first. It was its gentle song that attracted her attention and she looked around for the music maker. It was perched on a low branch of the great elm she was about to walk beneath. She recognized its family immediately; King Valor had been a keen bird spotter and had gone to some pains to school his only child into recognizing various species. This bird was a beautiful little chaffinch and its pretty music made her smile. She whistled back at it as she passed by, and heard it continue to sing as she departed the copse.

It was only as Valentyna guided her horse onto Werryl Bridge some half hour later that she realized she had been humming a tune to herself on the journey back. The birdsong had reminded her of a traditional Briavellian ballad: "Wait for Me, My Love." Valentyna had always loved its melody and its lyrics were beautiful; in fact, her fondness for the song was well known throughout the kingdom and the court minstrel had serenaded her with it on her nineteenth nameday. She began to sing it now privately in her mind and the words stayed with her as she ascended into the palace proper.

Ranald, a stableboy, bowed and reached for the Queen's reins.

"Thank you, Ranald," Valentyna said, and found a smile for the eager boy.

"Your highness." He beamed, unable to mask his pleasure at serving the Queen so directly.

"It was a lovely ride," she said to him, enjoying his enthusiasm, wishing she could be a child again, without a care in the world.

"I'm glad, your highness. Bonny's a beautiful girl. My favorite," he chirped, ignoring the scowl from the stablemaster, who had come out to watch his young charge receive the horses correctly and no doubt thought him far too chatty.

"Mine too," Valentyna said, winking at Ranald. As she turned away from the boy the refrain of the ballad filled her mind again—and its resonance struck her.

> *Wait for me, my love;*
> *I shall return one day.*
> *Accept not another's words;*
> *With me only, I pray.*

Valentyna froze in the courtyard as the words played over in her mind. Men walked around her and horses neighed. Dogs growled over a bone and busy servants crisscrossed the yard on various errands, calling to one another. Among the activity, their queen stood still and silent, deep in her own thoughts. What had sounded so poignant and charming when sung on her nameday now sounded like a message from the dead. A warning.

"Romen!" she whispered fearfully, her breath catching in her throat.

"Your majesty, are you unwell?" she heard someone inquire.

"I'm fine," she stammered, coming back to the present and almost running from the courtyard. She flew into the palace and up the beautiful staircase, and up the next flight and the next. Servants watched, perplexed, as their sovereign ignored their salutations and curtsies, rushing past them toward her study on the topmost level, her boots clicking loudly on the flagstones. Finally she came to her father's former chamber and slammed the door behind her.

Leaning against its solid wood panels, she held her head as her breath came in great sad wrenchings. *Wait for me, my love.* Was this Shar's sign? Was this a message? What had prompted the song and its lyrics to come into her head? The bird! A chaffinch! Was this a warning from Fynch? Was he asking her to wait? For whom? Romen was dead! Cold, lifeless, bloodless . . . gone.

She realized she was sobbing and felt ashamed of herself for losing control. What was happening to her? Storming out of meetings, crying violently, listening to birds, believing in magic. She was going mad.

But she had asked for a sign. Perhaps this was it. She could be imagining it, of course, clutching at anything to save herself from Celimus, but it felt so right to believe it.

"But who am I waiting for?" she asked the quiet of her room.

She was startled by a knock at the door. "A moment, please," she called, instantly embarrassed at being found in such a discomposed state. She quickly splashed water over her face from a basin in a tiny closet and dried herself with a linen cloth, then smoothed back her hair as best she could.

She touched her fingers to her father's desk and drew strength from the solid wood, then took a steadying breath. Her mind was racing in all directions, but she had duties to perform. She needed to be steadfast. Briavel still looked to her for leadership, even as it collectively cast her to the wolves—or wolf, she thought bitterly.

Valentyna cleared her throat. "Come."

One of the older pages opened the door and bowed. "Your majesty, forgive my disturbance."

"That's all right, Justen. Who has sent you?"

"Commander Liryk, your majesty. He asked me to find you the moment you returned from your ride. He says it is urgent."

"Oh? A problem?"

"A visitor, your majesty."

Valentyna frowned. "Another one? Can't Liryk handle it?" she said irritably.

The page blinked, uncomfortable, and she felt immediately contrite. "Did Commander Liryk give you the name of this visitor, Justen?" she asked, more gently now.

"Yes, your majesty. It is a woman by the name of Ylena Thirsk."

5

AEGRYN MET THE RIDERS AND WAS ALARMED TO SEE THE state Rashlyn was in.

"He'll be all right," Aremys assured the anxious stable-master as he handed him the reins of Galapek and Rashlyn's horse.

"I couldn't care less about him," Maegryn said, and the vehemence in his voice surprised Aremys. "But the King will be alarmed and that makes us all uneasy. Did you have any problems with the horses?"

"Galapek got himself a little rattled over something, but he calmed quickly. Just skittish," Aremys answered, skirting the truth. The fewer lies he told the better. "He's more incredible to ride than I could have imagined. Thank you, Maegryn."

The man could not help himself; he smiled widely at the praise. "Yes, he's a beauty, this one. A real find."

"Where did he come from?" Aremys put the question casually.

"The barshi gave him as a present to the King. Had the horse sent in secretly from somewhere, apparently. He won't tell anyone from where."

"That's a little odd, isn't it? You'd think that if there were more like this one, the King would be keen to know."

Maegryn shrugged. "We're not allowed to ask too much about Galapek, sir." He looked embarrassed. "I'll be off, then, sir. I'm glad you enjoyed the ride."

Aremys knew there would be little further information to be won from Maegryn today. "Thank you. I hope you won't mind if I look in on him again?"

"I'm sure he'll be glad to see you, sir. You're one of the very few he permits near him. I think he's taken a shine to you." The stablemaster smiled.

Aremys stroked Galapek's twitching withers as the horse was led away. He was hoping for another sign from the animal but got nothing.

Myrt was barking orders for Rashlyn—who was lying on the ground still mumbling his strange nonsense—to be taken to his private quarters and attended by a physic. Then the Mountain Man turned to Aremys. "Come on," he said. "The worst is still before us."

Aremys sighed, needing no confirmation. Cailech.

They tracked the King down to his wine cellar, catacomblike chambers dug into the ground beneath a separate stone building. Descending the flagged stairs into the musty darkness, Aremys smelled earth and spice; mixed with the aroma of yeast and the oak of the barrels, it was a comforting blend. It was cool down here but not cold; the temperature would remain much the same year round, he guessed, and the vaulted ceilings combined with the peace and stillness to give the cellar a chapellike quality.

"We're sorry to interrupt you, your majesty," Myrt began.

The King turned from his discussion with the cellarmaster and grinned at the newcomers. *He's in a good mood,* Aremys thought. *What a pity we're about to ruin it.*

"Farrow, you have to try this!" Cailech called over the barrels. "It's to be our best vintage yet." The King slapped his cellarmaster on the back in praise, then lifted the long-handled tasting cup to his lips and drained it. "Ah, nectar," he said, delighted.

"Sire," Myrt bowed. When he straightened, his expres-

sion in the diffused light of the beeswax candles was sufficiently somber to win Cailech's attention. The King's smile
faded.

"You look like you've swallowed bad meat, Myrt. What's
wrong?"

"It's the barshi, sire," the warrior began. Cailech handed
the tasting cup back to the cellarmaster, who stepped aside.
"He's unwell," Myrt added.

"Oh?" Cailech looked toward Aremys. "Farrow, what's
this all about?"

Aremys was surprised to be brought into the conversation.
He wanted to clear his throat but knew this might make him
appear nervous, so he just began talking, sticking as closely
to the truth as he could. "We were resting, my lord, after a
ride around the lake."

"We were at the Ring, sire," Myrt interjected.

Cailech nodded. "Go on." Again he looked to Aremys.

"I was drinking at the stream and Myrt and Rashlyn were
leaning against the boulders. Rashlyn was eating, and was
seemingly in good health. We had been discussing my
headaches and he had just approached me at the water's
edge to hand me a small bottle of a concoction he said would
ease my discomfort—when the horses distracted us." Aremys had decided that the plain truth, rather than a version of
it, was the only course with Cailech.

"It was Galapek, sire," Myrt said. "Something startled him;
we don't know what. We couldn't see anything near him."

"And?" Cailech said, the hard green gaze impaling Aremys where he stood.

"Well, as I recall, I rushed over to help Myrt calm the stallion. It was over as quickly as it began—perhaps he was
stung by a bee or something irritated him. When we turned
back to Rashlyn, he was lying on the ground, seemingly
having some sort of attack."

"Attack?"

"Like a fit, sire," Myrt qualified.

"He lost control of his body for a few moments," Aremys
said, "and then he became rigid. I checked immediately for
a pulse—it was strong—but by then he was unconscious."

The King's face showed nothing of what he was thinking. "How long did this episode last?"

"It was over almost as soon as it began," Myrt said. "We laid him on his horse and got him back here as fast as we could." He dared not look at Aremys as he said this. Hurrying back to the fortress had been the last thing on their minds.

"And where is Rashlyn now?"

"He has regained his wits, sire, so I had him carried to his room and ordered that a physic attend him," Myrt reported.

"You have no idea what this is about?" The King looked between the two men.

Myrt shrugged and shook his head. Aremys figured the King needed more than sheepish shrugs. "I thought it might have been the cheese sticking in his throat, but his passage was clear," he fabricated. "And Myrt tells me the food was fresh, so we know he has not been poisoned. Does he suffer from fits, my lord?" he added innocently.

"It seems he does now," Cailech growled, the breezy mood blown through and replaced with what felt like a gathering storm. "I shall go and see him. How was Galapek, Farrow?"

The King switched subjects and moods so adroitly that Aremys was sure he would never learn to prepare himself for it.

"Even more magnificent than I'd hoped, thank you, sire. A truly beautiful creature. I hope you will let me ride him again sometime." He sensed, rather than saw, the glance Cailech and Myrt exchanged.

"I'm glad to hear it," the King replied. "Myrt, you can accompany me to the barshi's chambers. Farrow—"

"Sire?"

"I'll see you later. You will be leaving in the early hours of tomorrow for Morgravia."

Back in chamber with the familiar guard outside, Aremys sighed in frustration. He was not going to attempt an escape and felt sure Cailech knew this. But it seemed the King was keen to remind him that he was a prisoner and under the control of the monarch; hence the armed guard.

"Not for long," Aremys muttered under his breath as he flung his water flask into a corner. He would gladly leave for Morgravia in a few hours, and from there he would win his freedom. He liked the Mountain People. He did not even mind living here in the fortress among them, could almost see a pleasant life in the Razors stretching out before him, but he was beholden to no man, not even a king, and certainly not one who stopped just short of shackling him.

It irritated him that Cailech could be so friendly one moment and so domineering the next. Surely the King knew that Aremys would far rather give his help to him than Celimus? In truth, though, he could not blame Cailech entirely for remaining suspicious. One didn't become—or remain—a king if one trusted everyone, especially strangers who appeared out of the blue with no tangible explanation for how they had arrived. Especially strangers who reacted strongly to the King's own enchanted horse.

Aremys replayed the afternoon's events in his mind. Rashlyn's collapse had definitely coincided with the animal's shriek, he was sure of it, which meant something had disturbed them both. There had been nothing in the vicinity to alarm them or it would have created a similar reaction in himself and Myrt. No, this was something else. More like a disturbance in the strange magic that riddled the horse. Could it be that the wild-looking healer was bound to the stallion in some way? What if Rashlyn himself had cast some sort of spell upon the horse? Why, though? Why would he interfere with the animal?

Because Cailech had asked him to?

But why would the King ask something like that? Aremys thought it unlikely that Cailech possessed the cruelty that would prompt the idea of hurting an animal the way Galapek had so obviously been injured.

But what if the idea had come from Rashlyn? "Because Rashlyn could and Cailech allowed him to," Aremys said quietly into the silence of his chamber.

The notion took a firm place among his thoughts. He nodded. Yes, that made more sense. Aremys thought back to Wyl's account of Cailech's horrific actions during the feast, when he had presented the Morgravian prisoners as a dish to his people. Wyl had been sure Rashlyn had been behind that hideous episode, but that suggested the barshi was capable of persuading the King to do things not of his own volition. How could Cailech, usually so dominant, be so weak in the company of Rashlyn?

Aremys had no answer for that. He returned to his original puzzle. Something had disturbed the magic linking the barshi and the horse. It couldn't have been the Thicket or he too would have felt the effects, but perhaps it had resonated through the Thicket, thereby explaining his more subtle reaction. Had Wyl done something to disturb the balance? Unlikely, or the Thicket would probably have protested more strongly.

Aremys put his head in his hands, frustrated by his swirling thoughts that took him nowhere. *Think!* he commanded himself. Could it have something to do with Elysius? Had Wyl made it through and met the manwitch? Was that it? "Possibly," he muttered, but that did not help him get any closer to the riddle that was Galapek.

And then he remembered the most chilling moment of the whole sorry afternoon. How could he have forgotten it? The horse had somehow communicated a name to him: Elspyth. He began to pace now. It could be a coincidence, of course, but an unlikely one. The horse must have belonged to Lothryn, or somehow held the secret of what had happened to Lothryn.

Frustrated, Aremys punched the wall. If Cailech wanted to punish Lothryn, why hurt his horse? And how would a horse know about Elspyth, for Shar's sake!?

You're going mad, Farrow, he told himself. *Now you've contrived a magical talking horse.*

He decided to clean up and go in search of Myrt and more answers. Something else had begun to niggle at him and he wanted to find out if it had any basis in fact. Discovering he was right might not advance his cause, but it might provide some leverage if and when required.

Aremys opened his chamber door and explained to the guard, a nice young fellow with an unfortunate harelip, that he needed to find Myrt. The guard nodded, a shy smile emerging on his deformed mouth, when Aremys said, "After you." It was a joke they shared from the time when the guard, Jos, had first been assigned to Aremys; he had made the wry comment that if he proceeded first, the mercenary might bash him on the head and escape.

This, of course, had made Aremys laugh. "Look at you, lad," he had replied, grinning. "I'd need an ax just to dent you. You're built like an ox." He could see that Jos had taken the remark as a rare compliment coming from the bear-sized man. They had never spoken at length, but Aremys had been sure to keep the words they did share lighthearted and friendly and Jos always responded, albeit cautiously. The guard was only just into manhood and still establishing a reserve of confidence to draw upon, a process probably made more difficult by taunts about his affliction, Aremys figured. When they walked shoulder to shoulder, as now, the mercenary was careful always to defer to his guard in the hope that the young man might take some self-assurance from it.

They found Myrt at the main stables. The Mountain Man nodded when he saw them. "Go get your meal, Jos. Leave him with me. I'm getting our stuff ready anyway. We leave soon."

Aremys grinned at his young keeper. "Don't forget what I said about that young lady," he said, referring back to an earlier exchange. "You should tell her, for I sense from what you say that she doesn't trouble herself over your mouth—it only matters how you use it," and he winked.

Jos chuckled, a hand flying up to cover his crooked smile.

"What have you been filling that lad's head with?" Myrt asked.

"Nothing that didn't fill yours when you were his age, Myrt," Aremys replied, helping him to lift a heavy crate into a cart. "Why aren't you with a woman, Myrt?"

"Who says I'm not?" the man countered, somewhat sharply.

Aremys shrugged. "You haven't mentioned a wife . . ."

Myrt reached for another crate. "I have no wife."

"I see."

"Oh? And what do you see?"

"Nothing, my friend. What's wrong with you?"

The warrior flicked away what sounded like an apology. "Cailech's furious about what happened. Kept asking me what you were doing when Rashlyn passed out."

"Mmm, I thought he might. I told you he suspects me of knowing something."

"He's not so suspicious that he's not pressing ahead with the journey. In fact he's brought our departure forward—we leave at sundown. You, me, Byl, and two others."

"So what's all this stuff?"

"Gifts for the Morgravian King."

"Ah, goodwill."

Myrt grunted. "Help me load the rest of it."

They worked quietly and quickly for the next few minutes.

Maegryn appeared. "I've picked out the animals you'll be taking, Myrt. I've assigned Farrow Cherub."

"I'm a better horseman that that," Aremys protested. "I'll feel ridiculous calling out 'Whoa, Cherub.' "

"That's the joke, Farrow," Maegryn said, grinning. "He's anything but!"

The two Mountain Men laughed and Aremys joined in briefly, until Myrt gestured that they should leave.

"We're expected at the King's chamber," said the warrior. "He wants us to sup with him before we leave."

Aremys nodded. "Are we finished here?"

"Yes, I'd say so. Thanks, Maegryn. Be back later, then."

"As it suits you, Myrt. I'll be waiting." The stablemaster turned back to the stables.

"I need to talk to you first," Aremys said as they made their way toward the fortress.

"I reckoned you might. Follow me."

They walked in a companionable silence through several courtyards toward a part of the fortress he had not been to before.

"Where are we going?" he said.

"My home," came the brief reply.

Myrt stopped a few times to share swift words with various people. He asked one youngster to find Byl and have him call at Myrt's home after dusk. The big warrior generously introduced Aremys to all those he spoke with and the mercenary noted how they deferred to Myrt. He presumed the man had taken on a stronger leadership role since Lothryn's disappearance. He mentioned as much.

"I suppose so," Myrt replied. "I don't really want it, but Cailech finds it easier to rely on me to pass on his orders. I'd prefer everything to be back to how it was."

"With Lothryn as the King's second, you mean?"

"Yes, he was worthy of it and good at it."

"Why was he better than you?"

"Because he understood Cailech, and because he was not afraid of him. They grew up together, they were friends first and foremost. A bit like how it was between the old Morgravian King and his general, that Fergys Thirsk. They were great friends from childhood, I was told."

"So I've heard," Aremys said.

"Well, friendships made young like that have longevity and there's great affection there too. I'll never have that kind of relationship with the King. And when a relationship like that is broken, it hurts."

"You sound like you're speaking from experience, Myrt."

"In a way," the man muttered, hurrying Aremys down a short flight of steps.

"Did you know Lothryn from childhood as well?"

Myrt glowered at Aremys and his persistent questions. "Yes, as a matter of fact."

They emerged into the open again, into what appeared to be a walled community. The place took Aremys by surprise. "Shar! How amazing."

His obvious delight broke the tension. Myrt grinned. "More of Cailech's dreaming. This is his great social experiment."

"Explain it me," Aremys said, gazing around at the hive of activity.

"Well, not everyone chooses to live in and around the fortress, as I'm sure you've gathered. Originally the Mountain Dwellers were different tribes, spread throughout the

Razors. Cailech not only united us into one people but dreamed of forming a small city—he wants the fortress to become the true heart of the Razors and he is encouraging people to settle inside it. He dreams of his own Pearlis or Werryl, I suppose you could say. He has built homes for the settlers and has encouraged markets to be held regularly. He's even set up a school, which is very popular and getting bigger and bigger. Our king encourages education and at his urging more people are bringing their children to the classroom. Cailech has organized special rewards for families who set up home here permanently. It's really quite a new experience and a lot of our folk are watching to see how it goes. I think it will work. I believe Cailech will have his city in years to come."

"It looks like this community is thriving," Aremys said, unable to keep the awe from his voice. "I can see from the layout that it's been thought through very carefully."

"It has." Myrt smiled. "The King didn't want it emerging too haphazardly, so he put together a group of people who could plan a village, grow it into a town, and envision a city emerging one day. I was one of the first to live here and that encouraged others to come too. Lothryn lived not far from here, among a smaller group of senior people—formerly tribe leaders and family members distantly related to Cailech."

"Does Cailech have family?"

"Oddly, no. We Mountain folk tend to have large family groups, but Cailech was an only child. His mother died by accident, in a fire. Cailech was about thirteen when it happened. He was away with his father at the time, settling a dispute among the tribes."

"Does he blame himself?"

"No, I don't think so. He knew it was an accident. But Lothryn told me the King never really got over the loss. That's why he's keen on keeping families together, and he loves the youngsters. Part of his belief is that children thrive when they have elders around them and big family groups to teach them the right ways, and I agree with him."

"I would have thought he'd have a wife, then, his own family."

Myrt shook his head and Aremys thought he saw something painful flicker across his expression. The Mountain Man fought down whatever demon was rising. "He hasn't had time to take a wife, I suppose."

"And you, Myrt? What of your family?"

"I have a sister. I live with her. Her husband was one of those killed in the Grenadyn disaster. He was seventeen; they'd only been married a few weeks. I suppose you've heard of that incident?"

Aremys nodded. He knew only too well the story of Grenadyn's unwarranted attack on the Mountain People and the slaughter that ensued.

Myrt sighed. "Well, my sister never got over her loss. She all but raised me. Now, I suppose, I look after her."

"No love of your own, Myrt?"

The Mountain Man walked on. "One. That person did not want me," he answered in a thick tone, and prevented any further conversation by stopping to chat with a shopkeeper selling candles.

Aremys stared at Myrt for a few heartbeats. He was sure of it now, sure that the Mountain Man had a secret. Perhaps it could be exploited toward his own ends of helping Wyl. As Myrt finished his chat with the shopkeeper, Aremys took a moment to marvel again at Cailech's embryonic city. The laneways had been cobbled with stone from the mountains and more building was already under way, with more streets leading off the main one. It certainly was not Pearlis, but it was bigger than any village he had encountered, and there was a sense of sprawl about it; the place seemed well on its way to developing into a bustling town. He could not help but be impressed by Cailech: He was still a relatively young king but he had enormous vision. It was then that Aremys decided to give his all toward helping the Mountain People. If somehow he could influence the attainment of a working peace between the two prideful monarchs of Morgravia and the north, then he would. For Cailech and his ambition, yes, but also for Myrt and Byl, for Myrt's sister, for Maegryn and young Jos, and yes, even for Lothryn, wherever he was.

Like Wyl, Aremys wanted to believe that Lothryn was still

alive. And if he was, he intended to find him. He was convinced that the horse and its magic would lead him to the man it seems everyone had loved—even the King.

"Everyone except Rashlyn," Myrt cautioned, when they were sitting in his small house a short time later and Aremys brought the subject back to Lothryn.

"Rashlyn didn't like him?"

"More to the point," Myrt said, busying himself with a pot of tea at the hearth, "Lothryn despised Rashlyn and the barshi knew it."

"Why?"

"Cups are over there," Myrt replied, nodding toward a dresser. "Lothryn objected to the influence Rashlyn has with the King. He admitted to me not long before he disappeared that it had gotten to the point where he felt something had to be done about it."

Aremys almost made the terrible error of mentioning the cannibalistic feast. He stopped himself just in time and covered his near blunder by turning his back on the Mountain Man to reach for the cups.

He brought them back to the small wooden table. "What made him say that?"

Myrt poured boiling water over the leaves. "Let that brew, shall we," he said amiably. "Well, there were many reasons. Cailech had been making erratic decisions, out of character for him—there was one particularly disturbing incident involving some Morgravian prisoners. He wanted to make an example of them to send a message to the Morgravian Crown. They weren't even the culprits, for Haldor's sake, they were just a raggle-taggle group of farmers who were sent into the Razors with one old soldier as a leader."

Aremys held his breath. Myrt was almost certainly referring to Wyl's friend Gueryn le Gant. He kept his voice casual. "And?"

"The King's method of making an example of them was terrifying, to say the least. I don't want to go into the details, but it never sat right with me, or any of us, for that matter. Don't get me wrong, Cailech doesn't hesitate when harsh punishment is called for—as you know from the repercussions of the episode at Grenadyn—but he's not a cruel man by nature."

Aremys nodded; he remembered the events on his island home only too well. He had had a crush on Lily Koreldy for several years, but she was older than he and no doubt had never even noticed the lumbering boy who looked older than his years and who turned a beetroot color if ever he was in her presence. "That was a terrible business."

"Yes, but Cailech spared Romen Koreldy, even gave him a home and looked after him for a while. They actually became quite good friends by the end of it, despite the trauma that sat between them."

"I'm surprised Koreldy could forgive him."

"Don't be fooled. Koreldy never forgave Cailech and the King knew it, which is why he warned him when he left that if he ever set foot in the Razor Kingdom again, he would lose his life."

"So Koreldy was like me, eh? A very well-treated prisoner."

Myrt turned the pot three times and grinned at Aremys's perplexed expression. "Tradition," he explained. "Yes, Koreldy was dealt with in much the same way as we're treating you, except he was never entrusted with a mission for the good of our people."

"Did you ever see Koreldy again?" Aremys asked. Myrt poured the tea, not answering. "You know he was working for Celimus, don't you?" Aremys pressed. "In name only, though. Actually he was working against him."

That won the Mountain Man's attention. "What do you mean?"

"Koreldy hated Celimus, with good reason. The Morgravian King double-crossed him in an agreement they had. I know Koreldy stuck to the mercenaries' code of honor: He did his job and kept his counsel, but Celimus tried several times to have him killed for what he had learned in doing that job."

Myrt's eyes narrowed. "You're talking about the death of the King of Briavel now, aren't you?" he guessed, and was glad to see Aremys nod. "What do you know about that?"

"Plenty. What are you prepared to swap for it?"

"What?" Myrt said, astonished. "Swap information?"

"Yes," Aremys said, reaching for his cup. "Listen, Myrt, you know things and so do I. I would give you my knowledge happily, but getting information from you is like trying to get milk from a zerkon. Dangerous at best and fucking hard to boot!"

Myrt exploded into a rare laugh. "All right," he said. "All right, Grenadyne, you win. I haven't laughed like that in a while."

Aremys arched an eyebrow. "I can tell," he said. "Your turn, Myrt. The Morgravian soldier you mentioned—is he still alive?"

"Yes," Myrt said, serious now. He sipped from his steaming cup. "Your turn. Whose side are you on?"

"Cailech's. I will negotiate for him and will do all I can to help win this peace he pushes for. Understand this: I hate Celimus and will do everything in my power to undermine him. I am no enemy to the Mountain Kingdom."

Myrt said nothing, but Aremys saw something blaze in the man's eyes and sensed it was relief.

"All right, next question for you," the mercenary continued. "Is the Morgravian soldier called Gueryn le Gant?"

Myrt balked at this. "How do you know that? How do you know him?"

A little fib would help here, Aremys decided. "I know le Gant's niece. She's been distraught since he disappeared and I said I'd keep my ears and eyes open for any news on my travels north. Thank you for confirming it."

"He's in our dungeon."

It was Aremys's turn to flinch. "I have to see him, Myrt."

"Not until you answer my questions. Koreldy—where is he, do you know?"

"Probably scattered to the four winds by now."

"Dead?" Myrt could not hide his astonishment.

Aremys nodded. "Killed by one of the King's hired assassins. A woman," he said.

"Cailech must be told."

"Why? Did he want to kill him by his own hand?"

"He was certain that Koreldy, after his recent escape, would return to rescue le Gant."

"What will the King do when he learns of Koreldy's death?"

"Kill the Morgravian soldier."

"Then he cannot know of Koreldy's demise," Aremys said urgently.

Myrt scowled. "Says who? I've told you, I'll do nothing that smacks of betrayal of Cailech. Now answer me this if you want any more information or help: Why are you so interested in Lothryn? It makes me suspicious of you."

Aremys shook his head. "Don't be. Elspyth of Yentro is known to me—you could say we are friends, although we've not known each other long. I met her soon after she escaped from here and she was hoping to return to the mountains to discover Lothryn's fate. You know they were in love, she and Lothryn?"

Myrt grimaced. "I guessed as much. There would be no other reason for Loth to betray us as he did, and without sharing his decision with me."

Aremys was glad that the Mountain Man had not blinked at the coincidence that he claimed to know two separate women who just happened to know Gueryn and Lothryn. He could slap himself for such clumsy contrivance, but fortunately the big man had not been paying close attention. Aremys took his chance. "Myrt," he said gently, "I know that you loved Lothryn too, perhaps more than in just a brotherly fashion—"

The Mountain Man reacted as if burned. He stood up, pushing his chair away, eyes blazing with sudden hatred. "Fuck you, Aremys."

Aremys kept silent and did not so much as flinch when Myrt threw his cup and its contents into a corner and then kicked at his chair, smashing one of its legs. The big man turned to glare at the Grenadyne, daring him to make a move so he could punch him as well. But Aremys remained calm.

"I don't want to fight you," he said. "I want to find him for you."

Despite the warning, he was prepared for a fight: a black

eye perhaps, maybe broken fingers. So he was ill-prepared for tears, and when they came he hated himself for shattering the barriers that had kept Myrt strong. He sat there a moment bewildered, then did the only thing one person can do for another who is hurting: He put his arms around the Mountain Man's big shoulders and held him.

Eventually he spoke. "He's alive, Myrt, I know it. From all that you've told me, I don't believe Cailech would have killed him. That's why his reply to you was so cryptic. Lothryn lives and our only clue is Galapek. Help me and we'll find him together."

The tears were brief, dried away almost as soon as they had dared to arrive. They were replaced by wrath. "I can't!" the man roared.

"You can. We're all he's got. If you love Lothryn—as I know you do—then fight for him. Let's at least find out if he's alive and what state he's in."

Myrt stomped around his small cottage, a new battle raging within him now. Aremys had noticed that the dwelling showed a woman's touch—a jar of fresh hill flowers on the humble sideboard, dishes neatly stacked, floors swept, and surfaces dusted. It was as neat as a pin. He wondered where the sister was and asked Myrt.

"Due back shortly," the Mountain Man answered, distracted. "Listen to me, Aremys. I'll help you because of Lothryn, not because I'm threatened by what you've learned about me. If you ever repeat what has occurred here or been mentioned between us, I'll kill you. I might be in love with a man, but it doesn't stop me being capable of killing one. I want you to understand that."

"Your secret is safe with me. Whether you prefer men or women is of no consequence to me. I've trusted you with my life—I shall go on doing so. I'm only sorry that you have to be so unhappy."

"Don't trouble yourself. I've lived with it all my life," the Mountain Man said gruffly. "More to the point, what can we do? We leave in a few hours and I don't think Cailech plans for you to return here." Myrt's anger had dissipated, to be replaced with despondency.

"Well, that does change things. It might be that you must track Lothryn down without me." Aremys looked toward the ceiling, racking his brain for the best step. "Can you take me to see the horse again? I think it was trying to communicate something to me on our ride."

"You're jesting, aren't you?" When Aremys returned his gaze evenly, Myrt scoffed. "You expect me to believe the horse tried to tell you something?"

"Weren't you listening when I told you about the Thicket's magic? No, I'm not saying it talked, exactly," he lied, "but I felt something, and if there is more to learn, this is my last chance. I also want to see le Gant."

"No."

"Yes! He is not loyal to Celimus. He's like Koreldy and all the others that bastard has coerced and tricked, double-crossed and had killed. What do you think a soldier of that caliber was doing blundering about in the Razors anyway? Did you really think he wanted to be here with a gang of farmers who wouldn't know a sword from a threshing fork?" Myrt bit his lip. "Come on, man. This was set up by the Morgravian King. He wanted Cailech to kill Gueryn, but I have to see him to find out why."

"Because it might help in your mission?"

"Of course, why else would I want to see him?" Aremys lied again, and hated himself for deceiving this good man. "Keep the secret of Koreldy, I beg you—just a little longer. The King will learn of his death anyway once he enters Morgravia, or if you insist, I'll tell him myself."

"I do insist," Myrt said, staring hard at Aremys.

"All right. Just keep it quiet for now until I can learn some more."

Myrt nodded. "Where to now?"

"The dungeon," Aremys replied grimly. "Then Galapek."

6

GUERYN FELT FORGOTTEN. IT HAD BEEN DAYS SINCE MYRT AND his friend had walked with him and he had begun to think he would never smell sweet air again. Food and fresh water were being delivered daily, however, so he knew he had not dropped entirely from the Moutain People's consciousness. The jailer, Haz, offered no news or even conversation and Gueryn had given up trying to elicit any. In truth it was his own fault. Haz had made the effort to talk in the early days, but Gueryn's refusal to eat had brought the King's wrath down on his head. Now he ignored the prisoner, taking care of only the bare necessities.

Rashlyn had looked in on him twice since Gueryn had been returned to the dungeon, and was satisfied that his health was being maintained. The Morgravian had greeted the soft-spoken healer with only an icy silence on each occasion.

Having decided that he was fighting a losing battle in trying to kill himself, and realizing that he could do more good by regaining his health and learning as much as he could about the Razor King and his intentions, Gueryn had tried to keep himself fit. Once he felt strong enough, he had begun doing push-ups; now he was up to three hundred daily. As a result, his upper body was muscled again. And he walked. His cell was relatively narrow but quite long and he had used this length to pace relentlessly up and down. He lost count of the times he met each wall at either end because he had given up keeping track after a thousand. And with his physical health restored, he had begun to speculate on his situation.

The hated Rashlyn knew something about Lothryn, that much was clear. And he was smug about it. This suggested to Gueryn that perhaps the brave Mountain Man might not have perished as they had all assumed. Gueryn also knew the King was keeping him alive so that Koreldy would return to save him, but he had no idea why Cailech should believe there was any attachment between them. Gueryn had never met Koreldy until that time in the fortress. The odd thing was that until Gueryn's sewn-up eyes had been released of their stitching, he had believed Koreldy to be Wyl Thirsk! He had gone over it time and again in his mind, realizing that he had just wanted to believe it was Wyl. Nevertheless, something deep down told him there was more to the puzzle than what his eyes had confirmed. Even when he saw the unfamiliar face, he had still believed Wyl was somehow present. And how could Koreldy know the family battle cry? Or speak to him in the way Wyl would? Nothing added up, and the King's belief that Koreldy would return to rescue him further muddied the waters of his thoughts.

Gueryn was sitting in the corner of his cell, once again remembering Elspyth's death, for which he could never forgive himself, when he heard the key turning in the lock.

"You're early, Haz," he mumbled. He had no real knowledge of time, but his body and its regular functions gave him reasonable clues. And his body was not yet hungry.

A huge man stepped into the cell, a man he had never seen before. "Gueryn le Gant?"

Gueryn nodded, searching for a pithy rejoinder—any attack on his keepers felt good. "Who else did you expect?"

The man grinned, which confused him, and turned to nod to another person outside. Gueryn was sure he heard Myrt's voice saying that he would keep watch.

"What's going on?" he asked, alarm bells suddenly klaxoning in his mind.

"I have very little time, so you must listen as I explain something quickly. And you're going to have to trust me."

"Why would I trust you?"

"I'm a Grenadyne, not one of the Razor People. And

there's a single word I can say that I believe will make you trust me."

"Oh yes? What's that, Grenadyne?"

"Thirsk," Aremys replied abruptly. "Now hear me out. No interruptions. I am friend, not foe."

The name Thirsk was like a slap in the face. The big man had Gueryn's full attention.

"My name is Aremys Farrow. I am a mercenary and was employed by your king to hunt down and kill Ylena Thirsk."

"What?" roared Gueryn, pushing himself to his feet.

"I said, don't interrupt, soldier," Aremys warned. "I found Ylena, but instead of killing her, I took her to safety into the north of Briavel, where we parted company. I hope she has made it south to Queen Valentyna. I won't go into how I got to be here, but rest assured, although I might look like a free man, I'm as much a captive as you are. Cailech plans to use me to negotiate a parley with King Celimus. If I'm successful I might win my freedom, in which case I'll go looking for Ylena again and offer my protection. There is another woman—someone you know—who holds strong affection for a man called Lothryn. I understand that Lothryn betrayed the Mountain People in helping you, Koreldy, and this woman, Elspyth, to escape. Now that I've found you, as I promised Ylena I would," Aremys lied, "I'm determined to find Lothryn as well. My instincts tell me the King has kept him alive in order to make the punishment—whatever it is— of aiding your attempted escape the sweeter. You should know that Koreldy is dead." Gueryn closed his eyes as he heard this. "And that somehow I am going to get you out of here."

Aremys stopped. It was obvious he was sharing too much information; the prisoner looked too shocked to respond.

Then the Morgravian began to laugh. It was not the reaction Aremys had expected, and he gritted his teeth in annoyance. "A word of thanks might be more appropriate," he suggested.

"Thank you for coming, Grenadyne. Thank you for what you're trying to do, but I'm as good as dead, man. If Koreldy is no longer alive, that's my death warrant," Gueryn said, painful resignation in his tired voice.

"No one knows about Koreldy but myself and Myrt," Aremys assured.

"Myrt is a good man, but he is a loyal Mountain warrior. The King will already know."

"The King does not know. He doesn't even know we're here now. Myrt is outside keeping watch. He is protecting you."

"Why?" Gueryn demanded.

"It doesn't matter why."

"It matters to me. It doesn't make sense. Myrt has no reason to betray his king."

"Let's just say I have something on him that encourages him to help me."

Gueryn shrugged, suddenly tired. "Fine. Really, there's no reason for me to care. Everyone I have ever cared about is dead except Ylena, and it sounds to me like Celimus will kill her too."

"No chance."

"If you've met Ylena, as you claim you have, then you'll know she is a pretty, indulged, and fragile creature. She will not outwit Celimus—not without her brother's protection or mine."

"She has the protection of a queen . . . and mine."

"Oh, that's right, the protection of a new, inexperienced queen—by now under siege from King Celimus, I imagine—and a Grenadyne mercenary who is a captive of King Cailech. Forgive me if I don't hold my breath."

"I don't know why I bothered," Aremys muttered, stung by le Gant's ungracious manner.

"Neither do I. Save yourself if you can. I watched Cailech kill Elspyth with his own hands and enjoy it. He will do the same to me, and to you if he so chooses."

Aremys frowned. "Elspyth isn't dead."

"Yes, she is, mercenary. I'm sorry to upset you further. See this on my boots? That is her blood. Her life became forfeit when I refused to capitulate to Cailech's interrogation. I might as well have stuck the knife in her myself," he finished bitterly.

Aremys moved for the first time since entering the cell.

He crouched by Gueryn and dared even to place his hand on the soldier's shoulder. Hardly daring to breathe, he asked, "When did this happen?"

Gueryn shook his head. "I've lost track of time here. It was weeks ago, I'm sure."

"Gueryn, look at me. I saw Elspyth so few days ago I could count them on both hands and probably have a finger to spare. She, Ylena, and I were all together in Felrawthy."

"You lie! Why are you lying to me, you bastard?"

It was Aremys's turn to shake his head, but with compassion. "I'm not. We drank tea together, for Shar's sake! Elspyth is alive and determined to return here to discover Lothryn's fate. She was on her way to Briavel the last time I saw her. She'll be there right now, I'd wager."

A barrage of emotions raged openly across Gueryn's face as he considered what he was hearing. Aremys watched him take a deep breath. "Farrow, I watched Elspyth of Yentro die horribly. Now, one of us has been taken for a sap. I know your time is short, but I want you to tell me everything you know."

So Aremys did, as quickly as he could, while leaving out everything relating to Wyl's magical metamorphosis. The gruff old soldier would never trust him if he began to talk that sort of nonsense.

When Aremys had finished his story, Gueryn struggled to his feet and began to pace, deeply shocked by what he had heard. "The Duke of Felrawthy is dead?" he said, so disbelieving that he repeated it. "Dead? Jeryb?"

Aremys nodded. "I only discovered this piece of savagery myself a day ago from Myrt, when the news filtered into the Razors. It seems Celimus is making Cailech's people the scapegoats, but it was his men, his killing rampage—I presume punishment for the family's harboring Ylena. And no doubt it quashed any thoughts of an uprising from the northern duchy."

It did make horrible sense. "All of them?" Gueryn asked.

"So I'm told. Crys was seeing Elspyth to the border, so I'm not sure about him, but the Mountain People said the whole family perished."

"This is monstrous. That poor girl. Her husband, Alyd . . ." Gueryn closed his eyes in despair, then his courage rallied and he opened them again. This time they were flinty. "And you're now going to negotiate a parley between these two Kings?"

"To buy my freedom, yes. What about Elspyth? Do you believe me?"

"How can I disbelieve what I saw with my own eyes?"

"Because I'm guessing Rashlyn was involved, wasn't he?"

"He was, in fact."

"You do know he's a man of dark magic?"

"I've been on the receiving end of it," Gueryn replied bitterly, remembering the hideous sensation of being suspended in midair.

"Isn't that enough evidence?"

The Morgravian turned on the big Grenadyne, eyed him quizzically. "What do you mean?"

"Gueryn, he fooled you. Whether it was Cailech's idea— or, most likely, Rashlyn's—they duped you into thinking you were watching Elspyth die."

"Don't be stupid," Gueryn roared. "It was her, I tell you."

Aremys bit his lip in thought. He had not realized just how powerful Rashlyn was. "Yes, to all intents and purposes it was Elspyth. Have you ever heard of a glamour?"

"No. What is it—some kind of magic?"

"Yes, and I'm guessing that's what Rashlyn used against you. We northerners are more accepting of magic than you folks in the south and growing up we tend to hear about spells and sorcery of days gone by. My grandfather once told me about a powerful enchantment that can make one person look like someone else—a glamour. Only the most gifted can wield such power."

Gueryn wondered how many more shocks his heart could take in one day. He stared at Aremys in a stunned silence.

"Elspyth was alive and well when I left her," the mercenary went on. "I hugged her goodbye. I bet you didn't touch her."

Gueryn shook his head numbly. "I could only watch her die."

"It was another woman, le Gant. They took some poor

woman and placed a glamour on her. You said they were trying to get information from you. What was so important that they would murder a woman in front of you?"

"Cailech wanted to know about my connection to Koreldy. I have none, but it appears Koreldy had some connection to me." Gueryn barked a harsh laugh. "They stitched together my eyelids as part of my torture and I was blind when I met Koreldy. But do you know something, Farrow, I thought he was Wyl Thirsk." Gueryn began to weep, all his pent-up emotion spilling over. "I failed the boy. I failed the Thirsks."

"No, you didn't," Aremys countered helplessly, feeling the depth of Gueryn's emotion. "There's so much I'd like to tell you, but there's no time," he whispered. "Look, I have to go. You're safest here until I can work out how we're going to rescue you. You must hang on. Give nothing away of what we've shared."

He reached out and grabbed the man's hand, putting it against his own heart in the way of the Morgravian Legion. It was the highest form of commitment one soldier could make to another.

Gueryn was astounded by the action. There were only two men he had ever given such a signal to. Both were named Thirsk; father and son. Both were now dead.

"Wait!" he said, suddenly remembering. "Lothryn—you think he's alive?"

"I do."

"That horse has something to do with it, the horse called Galapek," Gueryn murmured, almost to himself, disgusted that he had not yet worked out an answer.

"What?" Aremys whispered, almost raising Gueryn's feet from the floor as he lifted him to standing.

Gueryn shook his head. "I don't know what I'm saying. I just have a feeling that the horse Galapek, Cailech's new stallion, has something to do with Lothryn."

"Why? What exactly do you know?" Aremys asked urgently.

Gueryn frowned. He had no idea why the Grenadyne was so excited. "Rashlyn knows the truth of what's happened to

Lothryn. I overheard him jesting smugly to Myrt and Byl that Lothryn was closer than they knew. And he went on to make some joke about the meaning of the word 'Galapek.' "

Aremys looked blank. "I don't know the word. Sounds like the old language," he mused.

"It is. And I do know it. 'Galapek' means 'traitor.' Cailech has named his new stallion Traitor, which, in my opinion, is just about the worst name you could give a horse."

Aremys looked stunned. Then he spun on his heels and called over his shoulder, "I'll be back, le Gant. Say nothing of this!"

The huge man all but ran from the cell, slamming the door behind him. Gueryn heard the lock turn. He had nothing but his sorrowful thoughts for company now.

Well?" Myrt asked, startled by Aremys's rapid exit from the cell.

"Let's get out of here first," Aremys said, his head swirling with fantastical thoughts, every nerve tingling with terror. It could not be true, could it?

Fortunately Haz was not in attendance at the jail. Myrt thanked the young, completely disinterested guard, who was obviously posted in the dungeon as some sort of punishment, judging by his scowl. He merely nodded when Myrt reminded the lad that Gueryn was to be walked daily.

Outside, Myrt grabbed Aremys's arm. "You got something, didn't you?"

"Do you know what the name Galapek means, Myrt?" Aremys asked, his voice hard and low. When Myrt shook his head, Aremys closed his eyes with a mix of anger and despair. What a cruel fate. "It's the ancient language of the north," he said. "Cailech's schoolchildren would probably be able to tell you. It means 'traitor.' "

Myrt looked perplexed. "All right, a curious name for a horse and even stranger connotations, but what's that got to do with Lothryn?"

"You fool. You poor sad fool," Aremys said, unable to help himself. "The horse is Lothryn," and his voice almost broke on those words. "Rashlyn has somehow worked his vile magic on Lothryn to turn him into an animal, and now your oh-so-proud King can keep his former friend as his servant until he's no good for anything but the knacker's yard."

Myrt opened his mouth to speak, but no words came. No sound at all, in fact. Aremys had once seen a man suffer a heart tremor; it had come quickly and gone as fast, leaving one side of the man's face paralyzed. That was how Myrt looked now: paralyzed. His facial muscles had gone slack and all color had drained from his cheeks, his eyes were like dull black buttons.

Finally he found some lucidity. "Cailech broke him. We all watched it. He did it in a special corral he'd had built. It took days. Days of painful, heart-wrenching breaking of this horse's spirit until it bowed its head before him."

Myrt began to weep. Aremys could feel tears stinging his eyes too; he could not remember the last time he had cried over anything or anyone. His sister perhaps, when he had seen her tiny corpse laid out, the vicious gores of the forest boar covered by a beautiful silken dress. He tore himself away from the memory.

"He said he would break him using trust," Myrt finished. "It was Lothryn all along. Lothryn who fought for days until he was too weak to resist his king anymore."

Aremys shook his head in wonder. "And that's why the horse made me feel so sick. The Thicket's magic sensed the sheer power and evil of the sorcery that had been wielded to turn a man into a horse."

Myrt's red-rimmed eyes stared at him. "Aremys, don't lie to me now. You said something earlier that I scoffed at—that the horse communicated something to you. Did it really say something?"

Aremys nodded miserably. "It whispered a name. Elspyth."

Without another word, the Mountain warrior turned and walked away to deal with his pain alone.

7

IT WAS THE FIRST TIME SINCE CHILDHOOD THAT CELIMUS HAD set foot in his father's beloved war chamber. Magnus had always loved the room, even in times of peace. Its windows faced east, toward the traditional enemy, and when Celimus had paid one of his few visits here, he had believed its views went on forever. He recalled now how his father had laughed a little indulgently when Celimus had voiced that notion. It had been a rare moment of shared enjoyment for father and son, and had passed all too quickly, Celimus forgotten the moment a messenger had arrived with a missive for General Thirsk, who always seemed to be at his king's side. Celimus was briskly told to find his tutor—although no one appeared to care where he went, as long as he left. He had understood with a sour realization that he had no place among these men. He had been nine years old, ready to watch and learn about kingship, but Magnus had not cared enough to teach him. That much had been obvious; Celimus had not returned to the chamber until this day.

It was here that men had smoked and argued with one another, plotted and schemed against Briavel. In this place many a war had been invented, but peace had also been designed. It was a room of ancient waxed timbers and leather smoothed from years of use, where, if you concentrated, you could still smell a hint of the sweet tobacco King Magnus had favored. A once magnificent, now faded tapestry depicting a famous battle scene from centuries previous hung across one wall, and a hand-twisted rug, threadbare in places, lay across the wooden floor, whose dusty boards had recently enjoyed a polish.

King Celimus held no sentiment for this chamber so loved
by his father. He hated it, in fact, equating it with the reason
he and his mother had never felt Magnus's love. But this war
room of his father's was where detailed maps of Morgravia,
Briavel, and other realms were stored. And Celimus needed
those maps now. He also needed to give the impression that
he was preparing to declare war on his neighbor, and this
was the place from which to do that.

In not appointing a general after Wyl Thirsk's death, Celimus had effectively claimed full leadership of the Morgravian Legion. This had shocked many of the noble families,
who had assumed that Jeryb Donal, with his brood of sons,
was the most likely successor. But Donal had refused when
such ideas had been suggested. His focus, he had assured all,
was firmly on the border between Morgravia and the Razors.
There was no better defense than Felrawthy and he had no
intention of moving to Pearlis. Celimus had made it equally
clear he did not require a general as such. He preferred to
work through the captains, leading the Legion himself.

To most Morgravians' despair, Celimus had recently
given the directive to mobilize the first few divisions of the
Legion. People had prayed that war between Morgravia and
Briavel was for the history books now. The coming marriage
had promised so much for the two realms' prosperous future
together. Still, no one could argue with this King. He was a
law unto himself.

It was Celimus's intention that his men start departing for
the Briavellian border today.

"That should give our queen something to think about,"
he said to Jessom, who was standing nearby, pouring his
sovereign a cup of wine.

The war room had been freshly cleaned, waxed, and aired
for Celimus. Someone had even placed a bowl of fruit and
vase of exquisite tannika buds in one corner. Celimus did not
particularly care for either, but he liked the splash of color in
this dull and dreary place. His mother, he recalled, had
adored the famed buds, which only flowered for a few short
weeks in spring. It afforded him an ironic amusement that
his mother's influence now held sway in Magnus's once

firmly private, men-only chamber. If he had any of her perfume, he would dab it over every surface so that Adana's scent permeated every corner and overwhelmed any lingering essence of Magnus. He smiled grimly at the thought.

"What are their orders, sire?" the Chancellor replied, handing the goblet to the King.

"Merely a show of strength at this stage. They await further orders," Celimus said distractedly, looking toward the flushed, dusty messenger being led into the war room by one of his aides. "Yes?"

The aide bowed, as did the messenger. "Sire," the aide said, "a courier from the north."

Celimus did not mask his irritation at being disturbed. "I take it this is urgent?"

"I'm assured it is, your highness, and to be given to you directly," the aide qualified. He would never dare interrupt the King and his chancellor unless it was important, although of course he did not mention this fact. "Say as little as possible" seemed to be the new creed among the palace servants when faced with their king.

The courier bowed again, overwhelmed to be in the presence of the King. It was clear that since arriving at the gates of Stoneheart, he had not even paused for a cup of water to quench his thirst.

Celimus leaned against the huge table where he remembered his father poring over maps and looked at the newcomer expectantly. With his arms folded and legs crossed at the ankle, the King suggested this was all most inconvenient and he offered no words to allay the messenger's obvious nervousness.

The man licked his dry lips. "Your highness, I was dispatched from the midlands checkpoint, having taken a message from another messenger, who had been sent by your captain at our northern base between Deakyn and Felrawthy." He paused to take a breath, not noticing the flicker of irritation across the King's face at the preamble.

The Chancellor did. "Get to the point, man, if it's urgent," Jessom warned, hoping to prevent Celimus from erupting. He had sensed his king's brittle mood that morning and experience suggested it would not do to test his flexibility right now.

"I apologize, sire," the man stammered. "The message I am asked to deliver direct to you is that King Cailech of the Razors seeks a parley."

A stunned silence filled the war room, then evaporated as exclamations ensued from both King and Chancellor.

"A parley with Cailech!" Celimus blustered. "Preposterous! Whatever for?"

The courier reddened. "My king, I am not privy to any background to this missive, other than to report that it was originally delivered to the Legion by a man called Aremys Farrow." He bowed, his task concluded. Celimus ignored him, glancing angrily toward the Chancellor. Before anything further could be said, Jessom dismissed both courier and aide. He stilled the King's coming explosion with a guarded look and both waited impatiently for the two men to leave.

As soon as the door shut, Celimus erupted. "Farrow!" he raged. "Working with Cailech?"

Jessom deliberately kept his expression clear of all emotion, although he too was startled by the news. "We don't have all the details yet, your highness. We cannot know what has occurred here."

"What secrets has he passed on?" Celimus demanded.

Jessom shook his head. "He knows nothing, sire. Besides, he will not share details of his paid missions with Cailech. Mercenaries of his caliber never let one hand know what the other is doing."

"Precisely my point, you fool," Celimus said. "How do we know that he hasn't been working for Cailech all along?"

Experience had taught Jessom to ignore such offense. "To what end, sire? What benefit has he gained? What secrets could he have learned during a few hours at Stoneheart? Both he and Leyen were watched on my instructions. Farrow did not leave his chamber, even washing up there. He did not emerge until supper with you, and during your meeting the only matter of note discussed was Ylena Thirsk—and presumably she means nothing to the Mountain King. Farrow returned to his room and was gone within two hours. With respect, my king, I think we are jumping to conclusions."

"Then what is Farrow up to?" Celimus roared, only mildly placated. "What is Cailech up to?"

"Well, let's think it through," Jessom said in a soft voice meant to calm his sovereign's rage. "An ambush, possibly?"

"Hardly," Celimus countered. "By all accounts, Cailech is not stupid. He's not going to risk himself on the vague chance he could hurt me. No, there is another reason."

"I have to wonder what he thinks the Razor Kingdom and Morgravia have in common, sire," Jessom said airily, about to expound further when the King cut him off.

"A mutual distrust of Briavel perhaps," Celimus replied, his mind now working its agile way around various scenarios. "Let's presume Aremys has no loyalty to either party—that he is working purely for personal gain. Perhaps he was captured by Cailech while he was on business for us, although that is unlikely; as you suggest, however, there could be other reasons he found himself in the company of Cailech. Let's give him the benefit of the doubt for now, shall we?"

"All right, your majesty," Jessom agreed, as if the more rational approach were all Celimus's idea. "So?"

"So, I agree to meet with Aremys Farrow on Morgravian soil. I am intrigued as to what Cailech has in mind with this parley."

"What do you propose, sire?"

"I shall see him somewhere that can be properly guarded. It will take too long for him to be brought to Stoneheart." The King began to think aloud. "Perhaps halfway—Rittylworth?"

"Felrawthy, my king," Jessom said in a tone of rich satisfaction. "What better spot?"

"Indeed," Celimus agreed, warming instantly to the notion of personally taking over the rich estate. "Who cares if Crys Donal is alive in Briavel? He is a traitor now, and Felrawthy belongs to the Crown. Make immediate arrangements. Send a message for Aremys Farrow to be brought to Tenterdyn. We shall meet him there."

"At once, your highness. And Briavel?"

"Can wait for now. Let Valentyna stew. Perhaps the sight of our men will soften her resolve. She would be a fool to go into battle."

"You would still marry her, sire?"

Celimus looked at his chancellor as though he were conversing with a dullard. "I don't want war, Jessom. I want her to capitulate. I don't want her as my equal—which is, tragically, how she sees herself—but I do want her as my queen. I want an heir from her. I want Briavel, man. And then I shall have the Mountain Kingdom too. I want it all!" he bellowed, storming from his war room, his energies charged.

A remys found the company of the Legionnaires easy and comfortable. With the Razors behind him, he was relieved to be back in Morgravia—and suddenly the chance of finding Wyl again felt possible. He still felt touched by Myrt's sorrow, Gueryn's imprisonment, and the shock of realizing what had become of Lothryn, but there was nothing he could do about any of that right now. He had a job to carry out for the Mountain King and his freedom to win.

He liked Cailech, in spite of it all. The man had a deep intelligence and quick mind, and Aremys was impressed that the King—who he sensed was capable of arrogance and too much pride—had not been too proud or arrogant to appreciate the benefit of a parley with the southern King. That Cailech despised Celimus was obvious, but he also had the capacity for pragmatism. He had admitted to Aremys that if he could stomach a meeting with Celimus and form some sort of loose bond, the long-term benefits were immense.

They had talked over a sumptuous supper before Aremys and his escort left. Myrt had been quiet, but then Myrt was always quiet. Only Aremys seemed overly sensitive to his silence; the King was focused on the coming meeting with his southern couterpart.

"Can he be trusted?" Cailech had asked bluntly.

"I doubt it. Can you?" Aremys had inquired, which had made the King bellow with amusement.

"You'll do well, Aremys. Go and set up this parley for me."

"And in return, Cailech," Aremys had risked, "what is my reward?"

"I allow you to live," the King had answered. The gregarious mood did not fool Aremys. He knew only too well that the King still held deep suspicions about him, but no mention had been made of Rashlyn other than to assure the two men that the barshi was well.

Aremys had not replied to the King's flippant comment. Instead he had held his ground, refusing to flinch under the King's scrutiny.

"All right, mercenary. I understand your need for an exchange of some kind," Cailech said, relenting. He smiled. "What would please you that I could provide?"

Aremys had decided to risk it. "I would have Galapek."

The King's reaction was dramatic despite his efforts to shield it. The eyes narrowed and Aremys saw the man's jaw tighten. His barb had hit home.

"What is your interest in my horse?" Cailech had asked, his tone bordering on anger.

"Only that I wish he were mine, sire," Aremys had lied. "He is the most beautiful stallion I have ever encountered— and that's saying something, coming from a Grenadyne."

"He is still new for me. I am fond of him."

"I see," Aremys had observed, keeping his voice light so no offense could be taken. It was time to pull back. "King Cailech, I will attempt to set up this parley for you in good faith. I need nothing from you in payment—not even your fine stallion. All I ask is that you grant my freedom once you have had the opportunity to work out a peace agreement with Celimus."

Cailech had instantly offered his hand, palm up. Aremys knew this was a rare show of friendship from a man who no doubt believed he had no equal, and once again he was struck by how quickly the King's mood could change.

"I will gladly seal hands on that, Aremys," the King had said. "I like your confidence that Celimus and I will find common ground."

Aremys had placed his own hand on top of the King's.

"You alone will make it happen, my lord. I have complete faith in you."

Cailech had smiled and this time there was no guile in his face, just open warmth. "I hope you will choose to stay among us, Grenadyne. But I will grant you your independence as soon as this deal is done."

Aremys had opted for a lighthearted response. "I must be free, your highness. My memory tells me I have a woman to find," and he had winked, much to the King's delighted amusement.

And so Aremys Farrow of Grenadyn had been provided with an escort, a fine horse, and a message to deliver to Celimus, which he had duly done, emerging out of the Razors with his hands held high, insisting that Myrt and his other two companions do the same.

Aremys had deliberately asked Myrt to lead him as close to Felrawthy as they could get, having learned from Wyl that these Legionnaires were the least likely to shoot arrows first and ask questions later. They had entered Morgravia via a pass known as Haldor's Tooth, which had led them into the duchy of Felrawthy, to a village mainly inhabited by soldiers about ten miles from Brynt proper. Captain Bukanan's men were well drilled to take prisoners for interview. Aremys believed he could thank Jeryb Donal for this mercy.

He had nodded gently at Myrt to allow the Mountain Men's hands to be bound. His too had been tied, and while the men of the Razors were led into a small dwelling, Aremys had been taken before Bukanan, who had listened to his story with an intense interest.

"A parley, you say?" the ruddy-faced Captain had repeated.

"Yes, sir. That's the message I bring," Aremys had confirmed.

"You understand how odd this is?"

"I do, sir. It's why I was chosen to deliver the message. I am known to the King and he will trust me."

Bukanan had studied him closely and finally replied: "You will remain in our care until we hear back from Pearlis."

"I understand," Aremys had said, smiling at the nicely couched words that really meant they were prisoners of Morgravia. "You must understand, however, that these men of the mountains are not to be harmed in any way and are to be released the moment you receive word from King Celimus."

"Who makes these conditions?" the captain had inquired politely, although Aremys had heard the edge in the tone.

"Cailech of the Mountain People. He insists his men are not to be compromised by King Celimus."

"And he's in a position to make such demands?" the Captain had asked, somewhat surprised at the audaciousness of the Mountain King.

"Captain Bukanan, I am merely the go-between for two powerful men. If my attempt to bring them together succeeds, you and I can continue our lives in peace. I think Morgravia wants peace, and what I want is to return to my life as a free man. Let us make this happen, you and I. If Cailech's men are harmed or kept longer than he considers fair, he will call off the parley and you may well be fighting a war on two fronts—with the King of the Mountains and the Queen of Briavel—which would be a shame, don't you agree?"

When it was put like that, Bukanan most certainly had agreed. His wife had just given birth to a son and the Captain had every intention of remaining alive to raise the child he loved with such ferocity. "We'll accept these terms, Farrow. Although you will have little to bargain with once Cailech is on Morgravian soil—for you may be sure Celimus will not agree to go into the Razors."

"Leave that to me," Aremys had said cryptically.

The Captain had shrugged. "As you wish. We will dispatch our rider this instant. Make yourself comfortable among us. It will take a few days."

8

LIRYK HAD PERSONALLY ESCORTED THE WOMAN WHO CALLED herself Ylena Thirsk to a small reception room. She was disheveled and spoke little, insisting that her business was with the Queen, who was expecting her. Liryk, despite the woman's high rank, had her thoroughly searched for even the smallest of weapons. The woman gave no protest and, in fact, carried nothing with her except the riding clothes she stood in. She certainly did not resemble the famed Thirsks. Apart from the golden hair—an obvious difference—she was beautiful, not a quality the Thirsk men had been known for. Liryk noticed that she carried herself erect and proud—clearly of noble status—and her defiant gaze when he tried to question her at the guardhouse had told him she was not intimidated by him or his men. Finally he had agreed to send a runner to the Queen.

"It is up to her majesty whether she will see you," he had cautioned.

"Rest assured, your queen will see me," the woman had replied, and had followed the soldier in silence to the chamber. The commander recognized that this sudden visit was fraught with danger for the now precarious marriage plans. The nobles had called for Ylena Thirsk and it seemed Shar had answered Valentyna's dearest prayers.

"Lady Ylena, my men tell me they found you in the woodland bordering the palace?"

"Yes, that is true," Wyl replied. "I was lost, Commander Liryk, and grateful for their guidance. I have already explained that my horse fell lame in Beeching," he lied, still a little shaky from his magical arrival into the Werryl woods.

"I left it there," he added, realizing too late that the Commander could easily check up on his story.

"And you walked from Beeching? Could you not buy another horse?"

"To tell the truth, sir, I did not have sufficient funds in my purse for that purchase. It wasn't so far."

"Most noblewomen would find five miles a difficult journey on foot."

"You forget I am a Thirsk," Wyl parried. "Even our women are tough," he added, working hard to keep vexation from his tone.

Before Liryk could reply, the doors of the chamber burst open and Valentyna strode in, her complexion slightly flushed from her hurried passage through the palace. Wyl had been anticipating her arrival with a hammering heart, and he felt it lurch now at the sight of her. He hurriedly dropped a low bow, glad that he had the excuse of riding breeches to avoid the more feminine curtsy. "Your highness," he murmured, his feminine voice catching in his throat. He could smell her soft scent of lavender. All he wanted to do was hold her, kiss her. He could do neither.

"Please, Ylena," Valentyna said, equally nervous but for different reasons, "be at ease."

Wyl looked at Valentyna's extended hand. He could not help himself; he took the Queen's hand in his own elegant fingers and kissed it—an unusual action for another woman. He saw her frown slightly as he looked up. Was it from consternation or had she recognized something in his eyes? He knew he was clutching at straws with such a notion. Surely all she saw before her was a ragged noblewoman.

"Thank you, your majesty, for permitting me an audience," he offered. It was all he could trust himself to say, and he was relieved to be rescued by the arrival of a servant with a tray of refreshments.

"Truly the pleasure is mine, Ylena," the Queen said, bafflement still evident in her expression. "Let us move to the balcony, shall we? It's a lovely morning." Valentyna led the way outside. "Liryk, you're most welcome to stay," she added, which of course was his cue to depart.

"I shall take my leave, your highness," he said, and saw the Queen's face relax at his decision. "I will leave a man outside the door should you need me again," he added, glancing toward Ylena Thirsk. His couched message was unmistakable. The Queen nodded at him, smiled her thanks at the servant, and offered to pour her guest a glass of sweet wine; Liryk was already forgotten. The Commander departed unhappily, his mood evident in his sour expression.

If Wyl's own sense of awkwardness was anything to judge by, Valentyna was equally unsure where to begin. He decided to take the lead.

"You have been expecting me, haven't you, your highness?" he asked, taking the cup of wine.

"Well, yes," Valentyna began, then shook her head slightly. "It's an odd thing, Ylena—may I call you that?"

I'd prefer you to call me Wyl, he thought. "Of course, your majesty. Please go on."

"Your letter said to wait for you and to trust you would come. My nobles insisted that without you they could not believe any of the recent claims against the Morgravian King, so I prayed for your arrival. And, curiously—please don't think me silly—"

"I would never do that," Wyl confessed, leaning forward and taking her hand. It felt so natural to do this and yet, he realized, it would strike the Queen as odd for her guest to be so instantly familiar.

Valentyna did not appear to be discomfited by his forwardness. "Even disheveled, you're really so beautiful—not at all like Wyl!" she exclaimed, and then burst into embarrassed laughter, covering her mouth. "My apologies, Ylena. I'm so surprised to see you my manners seem to have fled with my wits."

Wyl laughed. How could this woman say words that would normally offend and yet coming from her they seemed like playful affection? "Wyl was not handsome, your highness . . . and he knew it," he admitted.

"Ah," the Queen interrupted, "but Wyl, even though I knew him so briefly, was probably one of the most beautiful people on the inside that I will ever have the good fortune to meet."

Wyl felt himself glowing at the words. "I think if my brother could eavesdrop on this conversation, your highness, he would be more thrilled than you could ever know."

"He was so generous to my father and me," the Queen said somberly. "I can't quite shake the guilt of his death, knowing that he could have saved himself."

"It's probably not right of me to speak so openly, your highness, but Wyl was in love with you."

Valentyna felt a hot blush stealing up her throat. "How can you know this?"

"Romen told me," Wyl answered, and watched the Queen blink at the mention of her lover's name. It was wrong of him to do this, but he felt a little out of control in her presence. It was dangerous, though, feeling that anything was possible. He reined in his spiraling emotions.

"How well did you know Romen?" the Queen asked tentatively.

"We were together for several days, traveling to Rittylworth and its monastery. I got to know him well during that time, as people do when they eat together, ride together, and share thoughts that two strangers might not otherwise."

"Romen spent time here too. Did you know that he made a promise to your brother?"

"To protect us both. Yes, he told me."

"I—I would be honest with you," Valentyna struggled to say. "I was in love with Romen—I am still."

Ylena would have no way of knowing this and so Wyl framed an expression of gentle surprise on her face. He nodded, wanting to make it as easy as possible for Valentyna. "I can understand that, your highness. Romen was very tender toward me and I know he was a good man despite his occupation. I can see what a fine match the two of you would make."

Valentyna's eyes shone at the compliment. "Truly?"

Wyl nodded, hating himself and yet loving that he could lift her spirits so.

"No one else would agree with you, Ylena," the Queen admitted drily. "Romen might have been noble, but my realm has its collective heart set on a union between two royal households. But forgive me bleating on like this. I'm aware of your shocking losses, Ylena, and am ill at heart for you."

Wyl lowered his head but Valentyna reached over and clasped Ylena's hand. Her touch sent a tremor of joy through him.

"I have also heard about your courageous trip from Rittylworth to Felrawthy and know your brother would be so proud of you."

"How have you heard this, your highness?"

"Through Crys Donal."

Wyl moved free of her touch, surprised at such news. "Crys is here?"

The Queen nodded. "I'm sorry; perhaps I should have mentioned it earlier. There's so much to tell."

Wyl sat back, his pulse racing not with love now but with fear. What had occurred? "Please, tell me," he said.

"The Donal family was murdered."

Wyl stood abruptly, staggering slightly and gripping the balcony rail. He forced himself to breathe deeply. "You have proof?" His voice came out as a groan.

Valentyna's reply was soft. "Yes. Their deaths were confirmed by a witness." She paused to allow him to collect himself before she continued. "Crys was escorting Elspyth to the Briavellian border, which is how he escaped being killed too." Valentyna's voice was trembling. "It was Pil— the novice . . . You know of whom I speak?"

Wyl nodded without turning to look at her. He could not bring himself to explain that Ylena and Pil had traveled together.

"It was Pil who found Elspyth and Crys and alerted them to the tragedy, and Elspyth insisted the new Duke of Felrawthy accompany her to Werryl."

Wyl could not make his throat respond. It felt closed and as dry as tinderbush.

"My apologies, Ylena, I should have started from the beginning," Valentyna said. "It has been a shock for us all."

"Was it Celimus?" Wyl croaked.

"Apparently so. The men wore his colors, according to Pil and Lady Donal."

He swung around. "Lady Donal lives?"

Valentyna shook her head sadly. "I'm sorry, no. She died of her wounds, but the brave woman got herself as far as Brackstead, bringing the—" She stopped abruptly, realizing that what she had been about to say would only upset Ylena more.

"Bringing what?" Wyl insisted.

Valentyna stood, offered her hand, and ended up gently embracing her guest. She spoke softly. "Ylena . . . let me start again and tell you everything I know."

Wyl nodded glumly.

"Let's walk. I'll find it easier to revisit this painful story if I'm moving." She found a thin smile, but it was not returned by her guest. "Come, let us stroll in the gardens . . . if you're not too tired?"

"I'm not," Wyl said, numb from the shocking news but still glad for any time he could share with Valentyna. "Where is Crys now?"

"I'll send for him so you two can meet after our walk."

"And Elspyth—she's here too, I presume?"

At this the Queen paused and searched for the right words. She found nothing of comfort. Instead she spoke to Ylena in a straightforward fashion. "She disappeared during the night. You missed her by hours."

Wyl could no longer be shocked. He raised weary eyes to meet the searching blue gaze of the tall woman before him. "She's gone after Lothryn, then," he said, resigned.

"You know of him?"

He nodded. "What a mess," he murmured. "What a shocking mess my life is."

Valentyna did not understand the depth of his comment, but she nodded gently and took her guest's thin arm. "Come, the gardens will revive you even though what I have to tell you might not."

T he two women, strikingly different in appearance, strolled quietly through the peaceful herb gardens. The dark of Valentyna's hair contrasted with the gold of Ylena's. Both were in riding clothes and Valentyna was quietly delighted that the noblewoman walking alongside her had not so much as blinked at her appearance. It struck her as odd, because most women she met were surprised that she preferred this masculine garb, and Ylena seemed the kind of fragile beauty who would be horrified to appear in anything but a perfectly tailored outfit. Yet here she was, entirely unself-conscious in dusty trews, her hair tied back, her face smudged and fingernails hastily but not successfully cleaned. It did not match up with the woman she had imagined. Fynch had given her such a detailed description of Wyl's beautiful sister, how elegant and sophisticated she was, that it hardly seemed this could be the same person walking beside her. Of course, Valentyna reminded herself, Ylena had been through considerable trauma in recent weeks, and she was of Thirsk stock. The bloodline had to prevail, she reasoned. And it was true that Ylena reminded her more and more of the Wyl she had known so briefly.

She spared the young woman none of the details, telling her everything she knew of what had happened in Morgravia.

"Where is Alyd's head now?" Ylena asked. Valentyna was surprised by both the forthrightness of the question and the young woman's control. She had expected an outburst of grief, but Ylena had shed not a single tear.

"Ylena, I know this is very difficult for you," the Queen began, trying to step gently around the tender subject of Alyd Donal's remains. "I will do whatever you wish."

"Bury him here," Wyl said without hesitation. "Tenterdyn is soiled with enough blood of its own. Let him lie alongside his mother."

Valentyna nodded. "That's how Crys felt about Aleda. He wanted her to belong here for the time being." They had made several revolutions of the herb garden now. "Are you tired?"

"I must be but I couldn't sleep anyway," Wyl replied, shaking his head. "All of this news is shattering, but there are plans to make. Tell me about Celimus, your highness."

Bemused by her enthusiasm to share her anxieties with this woman, who could do little to help her, Valentyna told Ylena everything she knew.

"I can't believe Krell would do such a thing," Wyl said, alarmed at how rapidly the situation in Briavel had deteriorated.

"If you had known him, you would understand how very accurate your comment is," Valentyna agreed. "It was foolish beyond belief and so out of character for him to do something so rash. Celimus now knows everything."

"Not everything, my queen," Wyl cautioned, and Valentyna could hardly believe the thrill the fighting words sent through her. "He has no idea where I am. We must keep it that way."

"But it will soon get out. If I have spies in Morgravia, Briavel is surely riddled with his watchers."

"True. It was a mistake for me to announce my real name," Wyl admitted. "But it was the only name that was going to get me through the palace gates. I need some time to think, your highness. Perhaps I might take that rest now, if you will permit it?"

"Of course. I'm glad you're here, Ylena," Valentyna said, surprising herself with such naked truth. "You may not look like your brother, but your personalities are devastatingly similar. He made me feel safe, as you do, curiously enough."

Ylena's face shone with Wyl's pleasure. "I am your servant, your highness. As my brother once pledged his allegiance to Briavel, so I do too."

"I accept it with gratitude, Ylena, but what can we two women do against that treacherous King to the west? I marry him shortly, do you know that?"

"Perhaps you must, your highness, but not without a plan," he said reassuringly, even as his stomach clenched at the thought. "Gather up all the latest information you can—everything your people can report."

The Queen wondered at what point in their conversation Ylena had assumed such authority, but she nodded her agreement. "My intention was to ask Crys Donal to leave Briavel," she added.

"Yes, he cannot remain here. It will only inflame the situation now that Celimus knows he has survived. Besides, Crys may be far more help to our cause in Morgravia."

"What do you mean?"

"I'm not sure yet, your majesty. May we talk again in a few hours?"

"Surely," the Queen said, and then, unable to help herself, added: "It's uncanny . . ."

"What is, your majesty?"

"Either I'm going mad or Shar himself is conspiring to confuse me." She gave Wyl a long, searching gaze and he watched, discomfited, as her eyes misted. "It sounds so foolish, but not only do you echo your brother, you remind me keenly of Romen Koreldy in the way you talk to me. He and I plotted together not so long ago on how to keep Celimus and his marriage proposal at bay. I feel as if I am reliving that moment." A tear escaped and ran down her cheek. "Oh, forgive me, Ylena. I know I'm making no sense."

"Don't be sorry," Wyl said, reaching into a pocket and handing the Queen a handkerchief.

Valentyna gave a small, harsh laugh. "No, you don't understand. Our mutual friend Elspyth asked me just a couple of days ago to keep an open mind on people who might pass through my life."

"You're right; I don't understand," Wyl admitted, trying to lighten the moment with a grin.

Valentyna dabbed at her cheeks with the handkerchief. Something tweaked at her mind, but she paid it little attention. "I hate feeling this weak. A mention, a reminder of Romen, anything that resonates of him can undo me."

"Then use his memory to make you strong. If he was able to make you feel safe, call upon that feeling to give you courage rather than allowing it to undo you," Wyl urged.

The Queen sighed, handing back the beautiful square of linen. Once more she felt a tug at her thoughts, but again she dismissed it as Ylena spoke.

"What were you going to say about people passing through your life?"

"Oh, nothing really." Valentyna pulled at a stalk of lavender, crushing the flower between her hands. Wyl had to look away; it was a painful reminder of happier times, when Valentyna had crushed a head of lavender and held up her palms to Romen for him to inhale the scent.

"Elspyth is determined that I should lock Romen away and open up my heart to others who might love me," the Queen continued, shyly now.

Wyl heard alarms klaxoning in his head. "And what else did the wise woman Elspyth advise, your highness?"

Valentyna smiled at his gentle sarcasm, not knowing how terrifying this conversation was for her guest. "It was an odd moment—she was most intense about her words. We were in this very place actually, and she begged me that should someone ever remind me strongly of Romen to take notice of it."

Wyl felt his stomach twist with relief. Elspyth had obviously danced around the topic. She had learned the lesson of a loose mouth in the harshest way at Tenterdyn—and his sister had died because of it. Elspyth would not make the same mistake again, although it had not stopped her from alluding to his secret.

He needed to get away before the conversation became even more dangerous.

"I am proud indeed that I remind you of someone you loved so much, your majesty," he said, and bowed to kiss the Queen's hand and take his leave. As he did, he inhaled the scent of lavender as he had done not so long ago in the guise of Roman Koreldy, and felt a rush of adoration and desire through his body.

Wyl fled from the herb garden with its painfully sweet memories and was fortunate to bump into young Stewyt, the page who had looked after his needs when he was last in the palace, as Romen. He schooled his expression to show no recognition.

"Excuse me," he said, touching the youngster on the shoulder.

"My lady?" the lad said, bowing.

He had grown in the short time Wyl had been away. "What is your name?"

"Stewyt, my lady. May I help you?"

"I hope so. I'm a guest here and—"

"Yes, the household staff has been informed, Lady Ylena, and I have been appointed to wait on you, if that pleases?"

The boy had struck Wyl as sharp on their first meeting and it seemed this intuition had not been misguided. The page had been very sure of himself then and it had occurred to Wyl that Stewyt might be a spy for Chancellor Krell.

"It does please me," he replied now. "I was wondering where my chamber is."

"Let me take you there, my lady. Please follow me."

They engaged in small talk on the journey through the formal reception rooms of the palace, making their way up the beautiful marble staircase and then another flight—less ornate this time—toward the guest rooms. Stewyt was a competent guide, pointing out items of interest as they entered the western wing of the palace—a place Wyl had not been previously.

"We have arranged a suite for you, my lady. I hope you find the accommodation comfortable. Please let me know if there's anything I can fetch for you."

"Thank you," Wyl said, impressed by the lad's composure. He stepped past Stewyt into a freshly aired sitting room.

"The door over there leads into your sleeping chamber, my lady, and that other door is a dressing room where you might take your ablutions. Shall I send up a bath?"

"Please."

"Would you like a maid to help with your toilet?"

"Er, no, thank you, Stewyt. I would prefer to be alone right now." Wyl knew he should order some fresh clothes, but this new existence was hard enough. The riding clothes made him feel comfortable.

Stewyt nodded. "As you wish, my lady," and he bowed formally to take his leave.

It seemed to Wyl he would never escape the fragrance of lavender. A fresh bunch had been placed in a jar by the window and a light breeze carried the scent through the room. The stalks were mingled with mint, of all things. So typically Valentyna; he sighed. She'd probably ordered the arrangement herself.

He looked out from the window across Werryl Bridge. It was a magnificent sight from this high perspective. A procession of people crossed to and fro, in and out of Werryl city, and he noticed they all paid quiet homage to the newly erected statue of King Valor, who had taken his place among the other, more ancient royals who stood guard, made welcome and bade farewell to all who traveled the bridge. The people's love for Valor was evident in the way they paused to nod at his likeness or touch the statue's foot. It was poignant to watch and Wyl wished a similar tradition were followed in Morgravia to honor its revered dead. Then he stifled a nervous laugh at the mental picture that sprang to mind of the folk of Pearlis spitting on a statue of Celimus.

I must not falter now, he berated himself, knowing that being so close to Valentyna while trapped as Ylena was dangerous for him. He decided he should lie down, even if rest eluded him. Wyl was asleep in moments.

Fynch came to him in his dreams.

I cannot stay long. I am traveling with Knave into the Razors.

Fynch! Is it really you?

Wyl, sending to you is hard for me, so don't talk, just listen. I know what troubles you. Offer to go to Pearlis on Valentyna's behalf. Buy her more time.

Celimus will have me killed.

But you are already dead, Wyl. Farewell. I hope we shall speak again.

Fynch? Fynch!

Wyl woke trembling and disturbed.

9

FYNCH SAT DOWN HARD ON THE SMALL MOUND OUTSIDE THE cottage that had been built by Elysius. "My head throbs."

Knave prowled nearby. *It will. Each time you use the magic, the pain will become a little worse.*

"I had to."

Knave did not comment. Instead he offered some advice. *Take some sharvan leaves from the pot in the cottage. Elysius used them to alleviate the pain.*

Fynch nodded and forced himself to stand, despite the lingering ache. "Do we leave immediately?"

As soon as you feel strong enough.

"I wish we didn't have to leave this place. I feel safe here."

I understand, Fynch.

"Why did he come, do you think?"

Knave knew to whom the boy referred. *To thank you.*

"Something odd happened."

Knave remained quiet, although the silence was filled with unspoken questions.

Fynch touched the dog on his large head as he moved toward the cottage. "Maybe I imagined it, but I felt connected to the King somehow."

We all do.

"No, it was more than that. I felt like I belonged to him," Fynch said softly, slightly embarrassed. "Even though I know my creature is Roark, the unicorn."

The dog offered no explanation and Fynch sensed his friend was confused when he replied: *It cannot be a bad thing to feel connected to the King of the Beasts.*

Fynch understood he would get no more insight from Knave. He knew the Warrior King had also sensed something between them. He had seen recognition flare in the creature's dark eyes. But the King had gone now and there was no point in teasing at that problem.

Not when there was a journey to make, a man to kill, and another to save.

Despite his sleep, Wyl did not feel rested in the slightest, and Fynch's words had so disturbed him that he could not face putting his head back on the pillow. Soon enough, a gaggle of servants arrived to deliver the bath, hot water, fresh clothes, and a tray of welcome food and wine.

He took his time luxuriating in the steaming water and staring at the trio of gowns Valentyna had sent for him to choose from. He hated the sight of them, despised having to climb into a dress and curtsy before the woman he loved. And what was more, something terrifying was occurring in Ylena's body. At first he had been alarmed by the creeping hurt that had begun low and deep, almost at his groin. Sharp needles of pain had stabbed regularly at him since he had woken. The heat of the bath had soothed them but not taken them away, and then a fresh ache across his back had begun. When the dull throb of a headache gathered, he knew he was ill, but it was only as he was considering how to explain the discomfort to a physic that he understood what this was all about. He had Ylena's monthly bleed. A new wave of sickness passed over him. How much more humiliation could he take? Did he truly have to contend with this?

He took his mind back to easier times, when life was bright and happy for Ylena. He recalled how she would withdraw each month for a day at least and rest, but he had hardly been privy to much more information than, "Your sister is indisposed. She leaves a message that you should visit tomorrow when she will be feeling better." He smirked bitterly in the warm waters. *The first day is always the worst,* she had told him when he had dared to ask more than was polite. So he had to deal with this pain for one day—and then what? How long would the bleed last? He knew there was something about linens and regular changing, but that was a woman's world. *His* world now. He dipped deeper into the warmth of the bath.

Fynch's words haunted him. His friend was right: What did it matter if Ylena died at the hands of Celimus, or anyone else? Her death would buy Valentyna time. Wyl Thirsk would go on living anyway, he thought grimly. Perhaps he could persuade Celimus to do the ugly deed and end it once and for all. But just as he began to work out a plan, he remembered Elysius's warning that if he attempted to contrive his own death, the repercussions would be savage. He could not risk another person he loved suffering and he felt sure the penalty would be leveled on someone else rather than himself.

He dropped Ylena's head to her hands in deep frustration, but in truth his mind was made up. Fynch's advice was wise. Wyl could represent Valentyna to Celimus. The King of Morgravia would hardly turn down the opportunity to welcome Ylena back to Stoneheart—and no doubt directly into her former cell in the dungeon . . . or worse. He cared not. The sooner he was rid of Ylena's body, the better. He felt sick at heart that he would lose her again, but he would be glad to no longer walk in her skin.

Wyl pondered a plan as he washed Ylena's hair and readied her for dinner. A small glow of luck saw a maid arrive to clear his tray. He begged a favor and it was taken care of in minutes. She brought him strips of linen and a strange brown liquid that smelled awful and tasted worse.

The young maid smiled at him as he thanked her. "The pain will go quickly, my lady. I'll have some more linens delivered."

T he Duke of Felrawthy crossed the room and swept Ylena into his arms. "Wyl," he whispered into his prisoner's ear, "thank Shar you're safe."

Wyl felt self-conscious at the show of affection and yet knew it would appear perfectly normal to the Queen, who stood regally nearby, delighting in the reunion of her Morgravian guests. She looked dazzling in a dark brown gown of the simplest design. Figure hugging, with no frills or flounces, ruches or tucks, it flattered her tall, slim frame, the deep color accentuating the brightness of her eyes against her creamy complexion and the dark hair she had twisted up behind her head with a tortoiseshell comb.

When he was placed back on the floor, Wyl took the Duke's hand in his own and placed both their fists against his own heart. It was the gesture of a Legionnaire, and in Morgravian society would have looked not only odd but vulgar when performed by a woman. Fortunately, Valentyna had no understanding of the gesture, although Wyl knew Crys would instantly understand its intent. For Wyl, it was the only way he could show his true self and convey the depth of his feeling for what had occurred.

"I'm shattered by the news of your family," he said softly.

Crys momentarily lost his tight grip on the sorrow he kept locked away and Wyl saw it march slowly, painfully, across the handsome Duke's features.

"I can't—" Crys began haltingly.

"I know," Wyl said, fighting down the lump that was closing his own throat. "I understand. Stay strong, Crys. Their lives will not have passed in vain."

All Crys could do was gather up his hurts quickly and hide them again. It was either that or break down completely. He nodded as he turned away.

Valentyna rescued them both. "Ylena, Crys, come, I've had a table set up by the fire. Let us break some bread together."

Had the Queen deliberately chosen to entertain them in the same chamber in which Wyl had first met her father, with its secret doorway and huge tapestry covering the privy? He could not guess but it felt strangely comforting to be here again—as though he had come full circle. Nothing much had changed in the room, save a few Valentyna-esque flourishes. A jar of blooms, some fresh lavender and herbs scattered on the floor that would release their scent as they were crushed underfoot, a thick rug, and a charcoal-sketched likeness of Valor done by his daughter that hung unobtrusively in a corner. It was not a great work of art but had obviously been done with raw emotion and she had somehow captured the spirit of the man. The final brightening touch was a tiny puppy, gamboling about near the warmth of the hearth, teasing at a bone.

Valentyna saw Wyl's amusement at the little fellow as they seated themselves and shrugged. "I miss Knave." Then she whispered, "I hear you have the curse. Have you taken some raspberry-leaf tea?"

Wyl nodded, though he had no idea whether he had taken such tea or not. He was startled by her candidness. Did women discuss these maladies openly with one another?

Valentyna's smile was all sympathy. "The first day is always the worst."

Wyl wondered if his face was flushed red with the embarrassment he was feeling and was glad when Crys claimed his attention, drawing him away from the Queen's conspiratorial gaze.

"You've heard that Elspyth has gone?" Crys inquired of Wyl, the young Duke fully composed again.

Wyl felt proud of him. Morgravia could recover with young men like this to lead the future. If only he could rid the realm of its present monarch, there was hope. "Yes, into the clutches of Cailech, I suspect."

"What can we do?" Crys asked, not really expecting a response.

"I shall have to go after her."

"What?" Valentyna cried, and Wyl could understand how strange his comment must have sounded. "What can a tiny creature like you do against Cailech and his Mountain Men?"

"Oh," Wyl said, finding a lazy grin he was certain Romen would be proud of, "you'd be surprised, your majesty."

"But you've never been there. You have no idea about this man!" Valentyna spluttered, the noblewoman's arrogance reminding her of someone she had once loved.

"True," Wyl lied. "But Elspyth decided to risk it," he continued, "and we have time on our side. Presumably she is on foot?"

The Queen nodded. "She took nothing, not even the horse she rode in on."

"She'll be a while getting into the Razors, then. In the meantime, there's a realm at stake."

Valentyna found a sad smile for her new friend. "I was measured for my wedding gown this afternoon."

"As you should be," Wyl said, suppressing the nausea that rose in his throat at the thought. "You must be seen to be progressing with your plans for the wedding, your highness. Let the spies report that you are preparing as any imminent bride would be."

Valentyna put down her goblet, her expression one of disgust. "And in the interim allow him to intimidate my people by setting up his arrogant Legionnaires in camps along our border?" She briefed her guests on everything she had gleaned from recent reports.

Wyl considered this information, sipping quietly from his own wine, as a poultry course was laid before them. Valentyna's fare was simple but delicious, as was her choice in most things. He stared now at the roasted chicken before him, the heady scents of lemon and rosemary wafting up to tantalize him.

"The Legion's movements are purely that," he said, looking up from his plate and sounding nothing like a pampered young noblewoman.

"Pardon me?" the Queen inquired, a fork speared with meat balanced halfway to her mouth.

"You think it's a ruse?" Crys chimed in.

Wyl shook his head. "No ruse. Celimus would not hesitate to send in his men, if pushed, but he has a good soldier's brain. And he's a king now with designs on broadening his empire, not losing his subjects. No, I think this is what you might call stage one. I would do precisely the same in his shoes."

"Which is what, exactly?" Valentyna asked, stunned by Ylena's sudden likeness to Liryk or, indeed, her own father. The girl's brother, Wyl Thirsk, had sounded just as straightforward in the final few moments she had known him as he

had helped her escape the fate both he and her father had
met that afternoon.

"Parade the might of the Legion, remind Briavel of the
power that lies across the border. He knows you are aware
that war with Morgravia would be insanity and that you will
not permit it."

"Won't I?" she said, suddenly contrary. She sounded as if
she would rather fight. Ylena's presence, fragile though it
appeared, seemed to have given her a new rush of hope.

"No, your majesty," Wyl answered. Ylena's voice was
high-pitched and very feminine, but the tone he managed to
hit left no room for argument. "You will send him a declaration of your affections instead. A reinforcement, if you
will, of your commitment to the marriage and peace for the
region."

A hard blue gaze riveted Wyl to where he sat. He swallowed to loosen his throat, which felt suddenly tight. Oh,
how he would love to take her in his arms and kiss her, declare his love, and tell her everything, to hell with whether
she believed him or not. A roll of pain in his belly reminded him that the Queen saw a woman across the table
and certainly did not harbor the same sentiments. What
was more, her expression demanded an explanation of his
statement.

He was about to continue when they were interrupted by
a knock at the door. Valentyna called for one of her aides to
enter and Wyl saw the irritation flicker across her face. He
realized how much she would be missing Krell's competent
presence, knowing how much he had screened from her and
dealt with himself.

The man bowed. "Your highness, Commander Liryk said
you would want to have this information immediately." He
handed her a document.

"Thank you," the Queen said, standing as she took the paperwork and nodding to dismiss the messenger. She moved
to the fire to read it. "Excuse me," she murmured to her
guests.

Both watched her expression grow more serious as she
read, then darken. She let out a harsh sound, half laughter,

half despair. Wyl pushed his chair back and, despising the swish of his gown and girlish click of his heels, was at her side.

"Your highness, what is it?" He could see her pale before him.

Crys too was on his feet. "Your majesty?"

The Queen shook her head, eyes closed, jaws firmly clamped together as she gathered herself. She opened her eyes and they were filled with tears. "Our spies report that King Celimus of Morgravia is on his way north to Felrawthy, where he will meet for a parley with the Mountain King."

"Cailech and Celimus?" Wyl murmured in disbelief.

She nodded. "It's a reliable source too."

"What on earth would they have in common?" Crys said into the tense silence.

"Briavel!" Valentyna banged her fist against the mantelpiece and let out a sound of deep anguish. "They mean to destroy us."

"Wait, Valentyna!" Wyl cried, forgetting himself and all protocol. "Let me think." He began to pace.

Anyone who had known Fergys Thirsk, and perhaps his son, would be aware that this was a family trait. It had always amused Magnus to see his general pacing as he formulated battle or peace plans, and if Ylena or Alyd were alive, they would be able to confirm that Wyl was hewn from the same block. Neither of the two people watching Ylena pacing now had known Fergys or Wyl Thirsk that well, but Valentyna had known Romen and she had watched him perform this very action when thinking and plotting. It struck her so resoundingly she felt her breath catch in her throat. Even more disconcerting was the fact that Ylena was pulling at her ear as she paced, a habit Valentyna had teased Romen Koreldy about on several occasions during their short time together. There it was again, the tugging at the right ear, the relentless slow pacing, the face lost in thought. *Shar!* She was going mad. She looked away and reached for her wine, swallowed it in a single draft. The liquor helped steady her but did nothing to alleviate the shock of the news or the bewildering sense of Romen's presence.

Suddenly she was reminded of Fynch's strange suggestion that Wyl Thirsk and Romen Koreldy were of one mind. The boy had stopped just short of saying they were one person. How could it be that Wyl's sister now seemed to reflect similar traits? And then Elspyth's words blew through her mind:

I believe that some people are reincarnated. Perhaps you should listen more carefully to your friend Fynch. It is to this which he refers, I am sure. And you must promise me that should another person look at you and perhaps touch you emotionally as Romen did, reminding you uncannily of the man you loved, that you will permit it.

Permit them to love me, you mean? Valentyna remembered saying in amusement, almost teasing.

But Elspyth had nodded seriously and added, *Perhaps even a woman.*

Valentyna looked back at Ylena. *Perhaps even a woman.* She gasped, turning away to hide the sound and the frightened look on her face. What was happening here? What was Shar's plan? Something else nagged at the edges of her mind, something urging her to recall it. But it remained on the fringe, hovering and niggling, and her anxiety over this latest action of the Morgravian King won the battle and banished the thought. Valentyna had to focus on Celimus and his intentions, not her spiraling emotions and deranged thoughts that Ylena Thirsk was the embodiment of Romen Koreldy! *Fool!* she screamed at herself inwardly.

Crys urged Wyl to speak his thoughts.

Wyl swung around, the swish of his gown annoying him again. How he wished he could at least be Faryl, tall and strong in her masculine clothes. "I know Celimus," he said, just pulling himself back from blurting out, *I know Cailech too.* "And I have traveled with someone who knows Cailech," he lied.

"And?" Valentyna prompted, pushing away her own confusing thoughts.

Wyl raised Ylena's delicate hands. "Celimus despises Cailech. He is quietly obsessed with the Mountain King, your highness, and nothing would prompt him to organize a parley with a sovereign whose realm, I'm sure, he entertains visions of destroying."

"At least Celimus is consistent in his ambitions," Valentyna commented bitterly. "Go on."

"Everything I've heard suggests that Cailech hates Morgravia's new king just as energetically—has more reason to, in fact." Wyl's mind was racing. "So in truth, I can't see either of them making such a move of their own volition. Something has prompted it."

"As the Queen suggests, then—joining forces against Briavel," Crys argued.

Wyl shook his head, felt Ylena's hair bob from side to side, and grimaced to himself. "No. Celimus doesn't need the Mountain King to overwhelm Briavel. The Legion could crush the Briavellian Guard resoundingly. If he were of a mind to do so, he could take Briavel by force and then combine the armies to take on Cailech. That's the more logical scenario—no offense intended, your highness."

"None taken," she replied, frowning. There was no doubting it: She felt as if she were being briefed by a soldier. "Why the parley, then?"

"Does the letter say any more?"

Valentyna scanned it quickly again. "No, just the name of the man who brought the original message out of the Razors and delivered it to Celimus's people."

"Who was it?" Wyl said. No doubt someone reliable like Myrt, he reckoned.

Valentyna squinted at the page. "Dreadful writing," she murmured. "I think it says his name is Farrow. Yes, Aremys Farrow."

10

USING FRESH HORSES AT INTERVALS, KING CELIMUS HAD SWEPT through the gates of Tenterdyn earlier than he'd expected. He was impressed by the sprawling estate of Felrawthy's duke and delighted to see that the manor itself was exceptionally well appointed. For a provincial family, the Donals had not lived without creature comforts. Freshly bathed and changed now, and having taken ownership of Jeryb's magnificent study with its view over the heatherladen moors, Celimus nodded at his chancellor. "Bring him before me."

Jessom entered the small antechamber where Aremys Farrow had been asked to wait. "I trust there are no tricks up your sleeve, my friend," he cautioned the mercenary.

Aremys eyed the hook-nosed Chancellor. "Just earning my living, Jessom," he replied. "Lead on."

The man turned and showed Aremys into the main chamber.

"Farrow," Celimus said from the window where he had been admiring the vista.

"Your highness," Aremys returned, dropping a low bow.

"You are quite a surprise."

"That is not my intention, sire," the mercenary replied, straightening.

"Will you tell me how it comes about that you are working for my enemy?"

"Your highness, I am a man available for hire by anyone with coin to pay. I am always loyal to my employer, as your chancellor would know. You must not fear that I have shared any secrets with Cailech, just as he need not fear I will share any of his with you," Aremys said smoothly.

"So you admit he has secrets?" Celimus said, moving in his fluid, elegant manner to sit on the corner of Jeryb's old desk.

"We all have secrets, your majesty," Aremys said carefully. "It does not mean they necessarily impact on one another."

"Farrow, I would know how you came to be in the Razors when you were on paid business for the Crown of Morgravia," Celimus replied testily, tiring of the banter.

Aremys was prepared for this question. "Your majesty, I was following the trail of Ylena Thirsk, as instructed."

"Did you meet up with Leyen?" the King interrupted.

"No, sire. But I believe she may have discovered that our prey had visited this very house."

"Is that so?" Celimus said, olive eyes narrowing.

Aremys moved into the critical area of his fabricated story. He would have to be convincing. "I don't know what happened to Leyen. I presume she must have given up her pursuit because I haven't found any trace of her since Tenterdyn. Perhaps she had other tasks to perform?" he prompted carefully, and pretended not to see the glance between Chancellor and King.

"I gathered Ylena Thirsk had already left Tenterdyn before Leyen's arrival," Aremys continued, "and found myself giving chase to the eldest son of Felrawthy and the Thirsk woman, who seemed to be heading north to the very rim of the Razors before veering east."

Celimus nodded. "Into Briavel."

Aremys hesitated, a question in his expression. Perhaps the King knew something he did not.

"We have heard reports that Crys Donal is at Briavel's palace. Perhaps Ylena is with him."

Aremys wondered how in Shar's name the heir to Felrawthy had found himself in Werryl, although having heard with horror of the slaughter of Jeryb's clan, he wasn't terribly surprised that the young man had fled Morgravia. "Not necessarily, your highness," he said into the lengthening silence.

"What do you mean?" Celimus queried.

"Your spies have not reported a sighting of Ylena Thirsk, have they?"

"Not yet, no."

"Hmm," Aremys said, quietly theatrical, as though thinking through something complex.

"Farrow, you still haven't explained how you come to be with Cailech's people," Jessom prompted.

Aremys understood now why Wyl had disliked Jessom so deeply. He felt his own hackles rise at the interruption.

"I was getting to that, Chancellor. I overnighted in a border village, preparing to cross into Briavel the next morning to see if I could pick up the trail of Ylena Thirsk. There was no inn, just a shorrock house, and perhaps I had one too many, I don't know. I suspect my nip was spiked with something in order to make it easier for thieves to set upon me later. It seems I wandered away from the main village in a stupor, and I do remember stumbling onto a track which I presumed would lead me into the Razors proper. I was very cold, I recall, and desperate to lie down. I remember men following me from the village, which is what drove me toward the mountains. But I'm afraid I remember very little else, sire."

The King shook his head. "So what occurred next, Farrow?"

"I've pieced together that the thieves did attack me but were fended off by some men from the Razors, obviously using the track to enter Morgravia. They dealt with the villagers swiftly, by which time I was unconscious, and then decided to take me with them."

"Why?" Celimus demanded.

"I don't know, sire. Perhaps they knew I would die in the cold if they didn't. They could see I was drugged and had been set upon by bandits. They felt obliged." He shrugged.

"Obliged!" Celimus roared. "To help a Morgravian?"

Aremys was determined not to be intimidated. He kept his voice low. "They are not all murderers and thieves, your highness. The people of the Razors have scruples, families, a desire for peace—"

"Ah, you sympathize with the Mountain horde, Farrow?" the King interrupted, a definite barb in his tone.

"My king, I am a Grenadyne, so my soul is of the north. I like the notion that realms may prosper in peace rather than conquering one another through war."

"Is that what this is all about, then?"

"Yes, your highness."

"Cailech is holding out the olive branch to Morgravia?" Disbelief was thick in the King's voice.

Aremys nodded slowly. "You would like him, your majesty, if you'd agree to meet with him."

"This is rich beyond words, Farrow. When did the leap from drugged captive to King's counsel take place, might I ask?"

"King Cailech naturally wished to meet the stranger who had been picked up lurking on the fringe of the Razors. He learned that I was from the north, working as a mercenary in the south, and on business for the Crown of Morgravia. He does not know the details of my task for you, your highness. When the King interviewed me our conversation led us toward discussing the future of the Mountain People. When he said it was his greatest desire to create peace in the region, I asked him what was stopping him from discussing the same with the King of Morgravia. I mentioned that you were preparing for your wedding, sire, and that the two great realms of Morgravia and Briavel would soon be joined in peace. It fired his imagination, I think. He asked me to set up this meeting."

"That's it?" Jessom posed. "You are merely a go-between?"

Aremys did not look at the Chancellor but addressed Celimus. "Yes, sire, that is precisely what I am. Because I had been employed directly by you, Cailech thought it would be easier for me to seek an audience and set up this parley. He believed you were more likely to trust me than him."

"I don't trust anyone, Farrow, least of all mercenaries who have no loyalties."

Aremys said nothing but he did not shrink under the hard gaze of the King. He understood that Celimus was used to staring down others. *He must practice it in his mirror,* Wyl had once commented caustically. Aremys remembered that now and had to stop himself from smiling.

"King Celimus, I sell my services, not my soul," he finally replied, determined to stand his ground. "Cailech certainly does not own me—no one does. I am here to respectfully suggest that you, the reigning sovereign of a powerful kingdom, might consider it worthwhile to listen to what your northern neighbor has to say. Far more can be achieved around the dinner table, sire, than on the battlefield."

"So now you're a philosopher and peacemaker, Farrow? I could have you killed for your insolence."

"Yes, you could, sire," Aremys said in a tone that made it clear he knew that worse had happened to innocents around this man. "But I ask your forgiveness if I have given the impression of presumptuousness. What you need to understand is that my own life is at stake, sire."

That seemed to win the King's attention. He gestured for Jessom to pour some wine. "Carry on," he told Aremys.

Jessom offered Aremys a cup of wine and the mercenary was relieved by the gesture. Perhaps he would make it out of this meeting alive after all.

"Thank you," he said before continuing. "I give the impression of being a free man, sire, but I am in fact Cailech's prisoner. I have bought my freedom with the promise that I would attempt to set up this meeting. No money will exchange hands."

Celimus held his cup up toward Aremys in an ironic toast. "You play with your life freely, mercenary."

"It is mine to give, although I'm not sure I had any choice, your majesty."

"And did you think I'd just say yes?"

"I could only hope so, sire."

"In order to save your life?" Celimus mocked.

"No, my lord. To save Morgravia from war. I presume you'd like your marriage to be conducted in peace."

Celimus arched a perfectly shaped eyebrow. "So the Mountain upstart believes he can wage war on Morgravia—is that right?"

Aremys was tired of this but knew he was treading a fine line. Celimus walked his own knife edge of madness and would just as easily snuff out a person's life as swat at a fly. He needed to be careful. "No, your majesty. I think he believes he can achieve peace between his realm and yours."

Celimus smiled slyly and walked around Jeryb's desk to sit down. As he did so, Aremys had time to notice a child's engraving in the wood of the desk. The letters carved clumsily into the timber said ALYD and the mercenary was reminded of how that young man had been treated by this very King—his life taken on a whim, in front of his new wife and his closest childhood friend. That same friend who was now considered friend by Aremys. The mercenary felt a charge of anger as he considered that the two great families of Morgravia—the Donals of the north and the Thirsks to the south—had been all but wiped out on the command of the cruel man before him.

He watched Celimus lean back in Jeryb's handsome chair and sip from Jeryb's cup what was presumably a refreshment from Jeryb's cellar. Anger settled in his gut. He joined Wyl in hating Celimus more than any other man, alive or dead, and determined to bring about his demise.

"Farrow," the King began in a voice filled with tedium, as though explaining something obvious to someone stupid, "you know full well that I will not risk myself by going into the Razors to meet with your cowardly captor, a man who sends one of my own people—if I dare call you that—to do his dealings for him."

"I realize that, your highness."

"So I must presume that he is prepared to risk coming here alone, for I will not brook his men setting foot on Morgravian soil."

"They would set up camp at the border," Aremys replied, as though he and Cailech had already anticipated as much from Celimus. He felt relieved that the Captain had not reported that Aremys had been escorted into Morgravia by men of the mountains. Aremys inwardly saluted Bukanan's foresight at not risking anything that might turn this situation ugly. Presumably the man knew how vicious his king could be and that an opportunity to make an example of Cailech's men would prove irresistible.

"I see. So that means Cailech is perfectly comfortable about coming to meet me, in Morgravia, with no protection other than the sword of a Grenadyne mercenary who is in my employ and presently under my guard?" Celimus's tone was filled with ironic amusement.

"I am not his protector, sire. I am purely his emissary."

"Excellent. The situation is even more precarious, then, for Cailech is all alone and on Morgravian soil. What is to stop me from simply killing him?"

"Your desire for peace, sire," Aremys offered as reasonably as he could. "The men of the Razors can be damnably elusive and they do not forgive, my lord. I am guessing they would wage systematic attacks on your borders until their last man fell . . . the last woman, even."

"That does not scare me, Farrow," the King replied, lazily twirling his goblet. "Frankly, I'd prefer his head on a spike at Stoneheart to holding talks in my court."

"Of course he does have some insurance, sire."

Celimus laughed, genuine enjoyment spicing the mirth. "Of course he does! Now what could Cailech possibly offer me that I don't have and could possibly want?"

Aremys felt a tremor of fear pass through him. He was about to weave his most audacious lie yet, the only trump card he could produce from up his sleeve, and to a king who would have his throat slit from ear to ear this very second if he even suspected the ruse. "I believe there is one item you desire more than anything else, sire."

"I didn't know you possessed such magical insight into my desires, Farrow. Perhaps I should have you tortured and burned as a warlock?"

"No enchantments, sire," Aremys replied calmly. "Simple logic tells me what you covet at present."

"And that is?" Celimus said, a sarcastic sneer on his face.

"Ylena Thirsk, your highness."

The sneer vanished instantly, as did the casual posture. The King sat forward, suddenly alert. "You have her?"

"I will deliver her, your majesty, on the promise that both Cailech's life and my own are ensured your complete protection. We will come to Morgravia for the parley and you will allow him an escort of his men. Your two best captains, including Bukanan, who I gather is currently indispensable in the north, will stay at the border with the Mountain warriors. When the parley is complete, we will be escorted safely to the border of the Razors and permitted to depart into the mountains. When this promise is in writing and announced publicly to your people, I will arrange for Ylena Thirsk to be delivered to you."

Celimus ignored everything Aremys had just listed. "Do you have her, Grenadyne?" the King bellowed.

"I do, sire," Aremys lied, schooling his features to show an expression without guile. "Although I am not at liberty to tell you how that came to pass or where she is." He smiled. "I do not require payment for her capture, sire. I would not consider that fair," he added, and chanced a soft grin.

The idea to use Ylena as bargaining power had only occurred to Aremys when he had stood before Captain Bukanan and had arrogantly claimed that he had something in store that would keep Cailech's life safe. He had no idea where Wyl was or how he might reach him, but he reckoned Celimus would go along with the notion that Aremys was holding Ylena, not just because he was a mercenary paid to track her down, but because the King wanted her. Celimus's own greed and cruel desire to visit more torture on this last remaining member of the Thirsk dynasty far outweighed any doubt of Aremys's honesty—at least, that was what Aremys was counting on. How he would deliver on his promise or, more to the point, wriggle out of it, was a whole new problem, but for now he was bargaining for his life and Wyl was all he had. If he could win Celimus's nod with the lie, he would also win his freedom from Cailech. He reassured himself that he had no intention of betraying Wyl; he was simply using Ylena's name as the lure to buy some time and his own safety.

Celimus leapt to his feet. His eyes were dark and stormy with wrath, and Aremys wondered if he had misjudged the monarch. But he had not. The impending storm cleared as swiftly as it had gathered and the King began to laugh as he applauded Aremys.

"Bravo, Farrow. Bravo indeed. I shall guarantee your life
and that of King Cailech for the duration of his stay on Morgravian soil. Is that good enough?"

"With all the other provisos in place, sire."

"Yes, I agree. When?"

"When it suits you, your majesty. You are the host."

"Where, Jessom?" Celimus asked.

"Here, of course, sire. Tenterdyn offers easy access to and
from the border, plus the ambience of a provincial palace. I
would suggest a feast and entertainment, your highness.
Show Cailech that you are a magnanimous host and prepared to extend the hand of fellowship while you hear what
he has to say."

"Good. See to it all, Jessom." Celimus turned back to Aremys. "And Ylena?"

"I will start making preparations, sire," Aremys said, feeling very nervous now.

"Waste not a minute, Farrow. Return to your captor and
pass on your news. I expect the Thirsk woman to be delivered as soon as our talks are done."

Aremys bowed and departed, eager to be out of the
King's sight.

11

SO HOW DID THIS AREMYS FELLOW END UP IN THE RAZORS IF HE
was with you in Briavel?" the Queen asked, having
discovered why both her guests had reacted so dramatically
to the mention of the man's name.

"I have no idea," Wyl replied, feeling both relief and delight that Aremys was alive. "We lost each other in the north."

"How does one lose someone?" Valentyna said, sipping
her wine.

It was not a serious question and Wyl opted not to answer it. "Long story," he murmured. "I have an idea," he added hurriedly when it seemed the Queen might want to hear the long story. Fynch's suggestion would work now, with this latest news about Aremys.

"A plan?" Valentyna repeated, fractionally sarcastic. She folded her arms.

"Yes. But you won't care for it much."

"What's this about?" Crys queried.

"We have to buy some time with Celimus," Wyl explained, and Crys nodded. "So we buy it with me."

"He'll kill you!" Valentyna exclaimed.

"No, he won't," Wyl said, not believing it himself.

"He razed Rittylworth Monastery and its village, killing dozens, before turning on Tenterdyn and slaughtering my family," Crys said, his voice cold, "all to hunt you down. Don't tell me he won't kill you the moment he sees you." Then he added, quietly, "You know what will happen!" He was stilled from saying anything further by a dark glare from Ylena.

"What will happen?" Valentyna asked, sensing a new tension.

Wyl shook his head, ignoring the Queen's question. "He won't kill me because of Cailech," he said. "I'll make sure to time my arrival when the King of the Mountains is present. If they're planning some sort of treaty, Celimus won't be so stupid as to demand the death of a noble before his newly formed partnership, will he?"

"Won't he?" Valentyna said, an appalled expression accompanying her query. "You're gambling an awful lot on his sense of courtesy."

Wyl was relieved she had been diverted, and replied, "I know Celimus. I grew up around him. If he has one outstanding quality, it is his charm. No, I don't think he will harm me while he needs to maintain outwardly calm relations."

"And what about afterward, when Cailech's gone? Why will he care then?" she demanded.

"Because I shall be gone too. Aremys is there—he will help me escape."

"No," Valentyna said from the fireplace, her voice raised. "I can't let you do it. It's ridiculous and of no substance. I won't permit it."

Wyl took a silent breath. He would not enjoy this next statement. "I am not yours to command, your highness."

The words hit her as effectively as a punch. She struggled to control her expression as pain battled with her defenses. "My apologies, Ylena. I think I misunderstood our talk earlier," the Queen replied, her tone as tepid as the congealed gravy around the chicken they had all forgotten to eat.

"No, your highness. There is no misunderstanding. I am loyal to you and to Briavel. That will never change. But I will make my own decision on how to serve."

"You will be going to your death, Ylena!" the Queen snapped.

"I don't believe so, but I choose that path come what may."

"Not on my behalf! I will *not* have your blood as well as your brother's on my hands."

"I'm sure you tried to order Wyl around too, your highness, but it seems you lost that argument as well. I am just as stubborn when it comes to protecting those I love." The bit about love had slipped out. Wyl felt Ylena's face color afresh at the error.

Valentyna missed the slip. "Ylena, you are barely into your womanhood!" she exclaimed.

"And it is my womanhood which demands I leave your table, your highness. Please forgive me," Wyl said, suddenly feeling a most unpleasant release to the build-up of pain that had accompanied him all day. Still, it was a welcome excuse to get away from the Queen's commands.

Crys looked baffled but the Queen, still angry, could only nod. She understood precisely Ylena's predicament. "By all means."

Wyl fled toward his chamber, clean linens, and a fresh brew of raspberry-leaf tea. He hated being a woman. And he especially hated the disdain shown to women by others of the same sex. How dare Valentyna consider Ylena unworthy? *Well, that's not really fair,* he told himself as he ran up the last flight of stairs. Not unworthy, but certainly ineffective. He thought of Faryl and wished Valentyna had had the opportunity to meet her. Then the Queen would have seen a woman hold her own against a man.

He spent the next few minutes with an expression of disgust on his face as he sipped at the raspberry-leaf tea and replaced the linens. He felt quite worn out by the end of it all and, in a fit of pique, changed into his favored trews and shirt, although he had to admit the skirt was easier to wear in his current condition.

Shar, please deliver me from this, he prayed as he drank the bitter tea. *Let me be a man again.*

A knock at the door interrupted his plea. He was not surprised to see that it was Valentyna, but he was embarrassed.

"May I come in?" she asked.

"Of course, your highness," Wyl said, clearing his throat. "I'm sorry, I—"

"No, it's quite all right. It is I who should apologize. Forgive my interruption," Valentyna began. "Oh, good, I see you've brewed more leaf. How are you?"

"Oh, you know, first night," Wyl said, offering a half smile like an old hand.

"Had you hoped you were pregnant?" the Queen startled him by asking in her most gentle tone.

"No, your highness. I knew I wasn't," Wyl lied, unable to think of anything more enlightening.

"I'm sorry. I shouldn't have asked. I just thought that, newly married, you and Alyd had probably . . . well, you know . . ."

"Yes," Wyl interjected, disturbed by where the conversation was headed. He had never felt more of an impostor. "No baby, though."

Valentyna looked wistful. "You know, Ylena, there are moments when I wish more than anything that I had joined with Romen and that his seed had quickened my womb."

Wyl had to look away. This was too painful. He busied himself with tidying his discarded clothing.

Valentyna rallied a smile and changed the subject. "I see you've changed out of the gown. Not to your liking?"

"It's lovely, your highness. I just got so used to these comfortable clothes while traveling."

Valentyna nodded knowingly. "I often prefer my breeches myself. Men have it good. I often wish I was a man, don't you, Ylena?"

"I do, your highness. I'm wishing it right now in fact." Wyl had never spoken a truth with more passion.

She took his intensity in a different light. "Ah yes, I can understand why. You presumably get a lot of pain. I must admit that I escape the cramps. Shar is merciful with me."

"Do you look forward to children of your own?" Wyl asked, desperate to push away from the subject of women's ailments and yet not doing so very successfully.

"I do. I've decided it's the one good thing that might come out of this hateful marriage. Celimus won't have my love, but he can have my body. He will give me something far more precious than he takes."

Wyl grimaced as the fresh ache from his side joined with the pain of the image of Celimus siring a child upon Valentyna.

Valentyna filled the difficult pause. "I came here to apologize for my heavy-handed tactics earlier. Even as a little princess, I bossed everyone around," she said, trying to lighten the mood swirling about them. "I know I cannot permit or deny you anything, Ylena. I just don't want you to forfeit your life in order to save me from Celimus."

"I don't think I can save you from the marriage, but I can give you more time to get used to the idea," Wyl said, the resignation in his comment agonizing in its truthfulness.

"But you can't guarantee that you will escape."

"There are no guarantees in life, your highness. I have lost too much in too short a time to care anymore."

"But I don't want to lose you as well," the Queen said, her tone plaintive.

"You won't."

"What exactly is your plan?" Valentyna said. "No, wait, let's have some warmed milk sent up. We can lace it with some liquor to help you sleep and forget your pains."

Wyl nodded. Valentyna looked outside and called to

Stewyt, who had been positioned for the night outside the door, sending him to the kitchens.

"Now, tell me everything," she said, curling up next to Ylena on the deep sofa near the fire.

She was unbearably close but Wyl would have slashed his own throat sooner than ask her to sit apart from him. If this was all he could have, it would have to be enough.

"I shall go to Felrawthy, present myself before King Celimus—ensuring that King Cailech is in attendance—and beg Morgravia's indulgence."

"But what is your aim? I can't see the point if I have to marry him anyway."

"Well, among other things, to get the Legionnaires redeployed from Briavel's border. Their presence is making your people very nervous, and rightly so."

"But you said it was only a ploy."

"I am assuming that, your highness. I can't truly speak for Celimus's whims. Regardless, I would see the physical movement of the Legion away from the border."

"And you think he'll do it?" the Queen asked, amazed.

"Yes. I'll tell him that you are nervous, that you feel intimidated and threatened—which is, of course, his intention. I'll assure him that your personal preparations are well advanced and I'll give him a token of your loyalty to him and the truth of your claims."

"And what's that?"

"Me."

"So he can kill you!" Valentyna exclaimed, exasperated again.

"He won't do that in front of Cailech, your highness. But he will be appeased. He will realize that for you to relinquish me, you have been duly intimidated. The plan is perfect in its simplicity. My presence will confirm not only your commitment to peace and the marriage, but also your desire to appease him—you have gladly turned over his enemy who had run to you for protection."

"And how does that save you, Ylena?"

"It doesn't—but please, your majesty, let me worry about saving myself. I have a few tricks of my own."

"Oh, you're so frustrating!" Valentyna replied. "You sound like Wyl and Romen rolled into one." Then she stopped, shocked at what she had said without thinking.

"Do I? How odd," Wyl replied.

They stared at each other, the candlelight and flames from the fire combining in a soft glow across their beautiful faces. They were so close, Wyl realized. Too near. Close enough to kiss. A madness came over him and smothered his judgment. It was the move of a lunatic and he knew it, but still he leaned across the few inches separating his mouth from the Queen's and placed Ylena's lips to Valentyna's.

The Queen reacted as if burned by a spitting coal from the fireplace. She leapt to her feet, wiping frantically at her mouth. "Ylena!" she spluttered, shock and anger combined on her face.

Wyl felt frozen with horror at his actions. "I'm sorry," was all he could manage. "I beg your forgiveness, your highness."

The Queen appeared uncertain whether to flee or slap the woman before her. Then she gathered her wits. "No," she said, holding up a hand. "I must have been giving off all the wrong signals. Forgive me, Ylena, I should not have come to your chamber tonight. All this talk of babies and changing into men . . ." She laughed awkwardly and then that awful expression of disgust crossed her face again.

Wyl stood, feeling sorry for both of them. "The apology is all mine, Valentyna. I don't know what came over me. I've been through a lot these few weeks and the emotions have got me all confused," he offered. It was pathetic even to his own ears, but he pressed on, desperate to fill the vile and difficult silence that would surely prevail if he did not keep talking and backing her toward the door. "It's been a very long two days for me, without much sleep, and I shall put it down to the raspberry-leaf tea clouding my judgment, your highness."

"Yes," Valentyna stammered, none of her mortification dissipating. "I've heard it can make one hallucinate."

"You don't even look the tiniest bit like Alyd," Wyl said, hating himself for the weak jest at the expense of his beloved sister and friend.

There was a knock at the door and the Queen started, her hands wringing each other. "That will be the milk," she said, and Wyl heard the slightly hysterical note in her voice. He lowered his head, ashamed of himself as never before. "I'll leave you, Ylena," Valentyna managed with some grace.

"No, I'll leave you, your highness," Wyl said, bending to kiss her hand. He could feel her fingers pulling away with revulsion at the touch of Ylena's lips and could have wept at his own lack of control and stupidity of moments earlier. He would never forgive himself and she certainly would not.

The Queen, flushed and agitated, pulled open the door and pushed past the same serving maid who had helped Wyl earlier.

"Thank you," he said wearily to the girl as she placed the milk on a small side table. "Can you ask the page to bring me parchment, quills, and ink, please?"

There was not anything to pack, and nothing other than his memories to keep him here a minute longer. He lifted the letters from the desk and blew out the flickering candle, leaving behind the debris of his hurried toil—sealing wax, broken nibs, ink blotches, as well as various letters begun and crumpled on the floor, where he had tossed them in frustration. He bent now to pick them up and threw them into the embers of the fire he had not bothered to tend. The paper sputtered and curled before catching and burning quickly in a brief eruption of flames. He watched until his awkward words of explanation to the woman he loved were nothing but blackened flakes—just like the fragile relationship he had clung to and now ruined.

He cast a glance at the letter in his hand. After several attempts he had finally settled on being Wyl and the words were brief and to the point. There was nothing of Romen's charm, Faryl's cunning, or Ylena's courtesies, merely a simple apology for his unforgivable behavior and a reiteration that he was making for Felrawthy. No honeyed farewell, no promise of return, no attempt at reconciling their awkward parting. He would be gone from her life once and for all. Wyl had wished her well for her upcoming marriage and encouraged her to be brave and stoic in what she faced. To never forget who she was and to remember her promise to bring forth a babe who would rule both realms with honor and love. Wyl could not save her this trial or the destiny of an unhappy life with Celimus, but he could let her know that he had listened to her soft words and wished her the joy of loving a child. He suspected that this part of the letter might make her cry, but he knew she would read the rest with only relief that he had gone. "So be it," he muttered to himself as he strode across the room to the door.

Stewyt was sitting outside, straight-backed and wide-awake. No need to rub the sleep from those alert eyes, Wyl thought.

"Thank you, Stewyt, for waiting up," he said.

"A pleasure, my lady. I am here to serve," the page said, sounding mature far beyond his years. "May I take those for you?"

"Please," Wyl said.

"I will personally deliver them immediately, my lady."

"No, Stewyt, I would prefer if you would arrange their delivery in the early hours of the morning. I don't wish either recipient disturbed tonight and there is nothing of such import that it cannot wait until tomorrow."

Stewyt nodded, then hesitated, and Wyl saw him take in the change of clothes from gown to breeches. "Is there anything else I can do for you tonight, my lady? Perhaps I could send up some refreshment, have the fire stoked?"

Wyl cut him off with a gently raised hand. "Nothing, thank you," he said, forcing a smile. He had no intention of letting the curious page know of his movements. "I am very tired and sleep calls."

"I shall see you're not disturbed again then, my lady. Good night and sleep well." Stewyt gave a solemn bow and moved swiftly off into the shadows of the corridor.

Wyl waited for what felt an interminable time, making sure the inquisitive page did not see his departure. Eventually, he tiptoed from his chamber and made his way quietly down the various flights of stairs. At one landing he noticed a portrait of Valentyna he did not recall having seen before.

In the low light of the sconces, the tall figure seemed to be pulling away from the wall, advancing on him. Her expression struck him as accusatory, the faint smile mocking. If only she knew the truth, he thought, and regretted bitterly that he could not share it with her. He extended his hand toward the painting, hoping he could reach high enough to touch her on the lips, but Ylena's fingers only stretched to Valentyna's chest. It would do.

"Farewell, my love," he whispered, and then he was sprinting down the final flight of stairs and running toward a doorway he remembered from his time as Romen. It took him through the scullery, where he saw one sleeping attendant who should have been stirring the porridge that simmered continually through the night. The young girl looked exhausted; her lips were parted and a light snore punctuated the silence as she slumped on the table. Wyl smiled. Oh, for a simple life with only a dressing-down from cook in the morning to worry about.

He slipped out of the door into one of the many vegetable gardens, disturbing two cats fighting over a struggling rat. One took off, the dying creature still in its jaws. The other shrieked at its loss of the feast. Wyl looked around to get his bearings and made for the stables and his journey north.

12

ALENTYNA BROKE HER FAST EARLY AND PRIVATELY ON THE balcony of her bedchamber. She had changed rooms not so long ago. At first, after learning of Romen's murder, she had wanted to cling to his memory, to remember every word, every smile, every touch they had shared together, so briefly, in her bedroom. More recently, however, with her marriage looming, she had decided she must bury those memories and put aside anything that prompted their return. Hence the move into the new quarters. Her new room had been her mother's. It was from her mother that she had inherited a taste for simple, fine things, and this chamber and its suite of rooms used natural light and space to achieve a sense of calm. And calm was what Valentyna needed right now. She was still deeply upset from the previous night's events, and although not hungry after her fitful sleep and fretful awakening, she had adhered to her father's long-held advice that bad news and bad moods were best dealt with on a full belly. Nevertheless, she had ordered only the lightest of meals, consisting of a small sugared roll, a single lightly boiled egg, a sliced pear, and a pot of dark, strong tea.

She had left the letter from Ylena unopened by the side of her tray until she had picked over the fruit and egg, neither of which she tasted, and downed her first cup of tea. Valentyna suspected the letter would contain an outpouring of beautifully crafted yet cringing apologies and hated the thought of reading them, let alone facing the woman who had so misread her affections. She was sure her face still burned from the combined horror and embarrassment of Ylena's error, although Valentyna was uncertain whether this intense discomfort was for herself or on behalf of Wyl's sister. Both probably, she thought glumly.

She poured a second cup of tea, this time with a slice of lemon instead of sweetening honey, and waited until she had sipped from its steaming contents before breaking the seal on the letter. It was a sharp surprise to discover that it was not even close to what she had imagined. A brief and succinct apology for what Ylena called her unforgivable behavior was followed by an equally concise confirmation that she was already on her way to Felrawthy. She specifically asked not to be followed, and urged the Queen to write immediately to Celimus with news that she was sending Wyl Thirsk's sister as a token of her loyalty to the King of Morgravia.

The second half of the single sheet was softer in its intentions, if not in its words, and reminded Valentyna of things her father might say. Unlike her father, though, the words felt as though they had been written by someone not used to being openly affectionate, yet who cared deeply for her well-being. Frankly, Valentyna thought, drumming her fingers on her seat, Ylena simply did not know her well enough to write with such tender, albeit awkward, familiarity.

Tears stung her eyes and she hastily rubbed them away. She had not intended to cry, but weep she did, hating herself for these last days of such hysterical behavior. From Wyl's description of his sister all that time ago, she had expected Ylena Thirsk to be a gentle, fragile sort of character. Despite hearing how she had overcome such enormous trauma, Valentyna had still been stunned by the confident and direct woman who had presented herself at the court of Briavel.

She put down the letter, picked up her cup, and let the steam from the tea warm her face, which felt chill from being outside on this still brisk spring morning. It struck Valentyna that Ylena had behaved in a fairly masculine fashion throughout her short time at Werryl. This had occurred to her well before the kiss, even before the supper; it had begun to resonate as early as their stroll in the gardens. Ylena had showed all the poise and upbringing of a noblewoman, but she appeared to think like a man. Valentyna prided herself on being an adept judge of character, but Ylena's disposition was not easy to explain yet unusual enough to notice. At first she had thought she was imagining it, but during supper Ylena had taken over the conversation and led the discussion to Celimus and Cailech as though they were sitting in a war room. She had heard her father conversing with his soldiers for too many years not to recognize the similarity of the situation.

That aside, she wondered about Ylena's uncanny habit of pacing while she was thinking. That had rocked Valentyna only marginally less than the wretched kiss. The likeness to Romen was too painful to bear. Valentyna remembered how she had had to look away and how shallow her breathing had become as she watched Ylena. And then the worst part—that terrible incident in Ylena's chamber. Valentyna blamed herself for it. Ylena had lost so much—parents, brother, husband, the family friend Gueryn le Gant. And then she had learned of the tragedy at Felrawthy. The emotions had all boiled over, presumably, and she had sought affection from someone who seemed to be offering it. Valentyna made an involuntary sound of disgust. And yet the explanation sounded too neat and tidy, as though she were contriving every excuse to explain the curiosity that was Ylena Thirsk.

Far more likely, the practical voice in Valentyna's head suggested, the girl had a liking for women. But even that did not make sense. A woman who wanted to lie with other women surely did not have a male childhood sweetheart; nor did she marry that man as soon as they were both old enough. When Wyl Thirsk had told her and Valor about Alyd Donal's death, he had also described the great love between Alyd and his Ylena.

Valentyna closed her eyes in frustration. And then the nagging thought, which had called from the edges of her mind almost since Ylena's arrival, filtered to the top of her consciousness and set a new and chilling problem before her. Ylena's handkerchief—the one she had handed Valentyna when she had wept in the garden—was the same linen that she herself had given to Romen! How could Ylena possibly own it?

The Queen put down her cup, stood, and leaned against the balcony railing. Was she imagining things? No! It was her own handkerchief. She had even mentioned it to Elspyth at Aleda's funeral. Elspyth had been weeping for Aleda and Valentyna had put an arm around her petite companion and handed her a beautiful square of embroidered linen. She closed her eyes to remember the words she had shared with her friend: *I gave Romen an identical kerchief,* she had whispered. *You keep this. Now both my best friends own one.*

She repeated the words in her mind as she gazed down onto Werryl Bridge and its endless stream of activity. Romen had died in a brothel in Briavel, and Ylena's only contact with him had occurred between Pearlis and Rittyl-worth, she calculated. Then they had parted, and as she understood it, they had not seen each other again before he died. Valentyna had given Romen the handkerchief long after he had left Morgravia and the Razors, and he had lived the rest of his numbered days in Briavel.

A new thought struck the Queen. Perhaps that hateful woman, Hildyth, had stolen it from him. But why take a square of meaningless linen? And even if she had stolen it from Romen at the Forbidden Fruit, how could Ylena now have it in her possession?

Wyl, Romen, Ylena, and Hildyth—what did they have in common? Why was she even linking them in her mind? Wyl and Ylena were related; that one was obvious. Romen and Wyl had fought together in vain to save her father and had certainly saved her. Romen had rescued Ylena, keeping a promise to her dead brother, Wyl. And Hildyth? Hildyth was connected only to the man Valentyna had loved, through death—a blade in the heart.

But no. There was another link, was there not? She shook her head in a futile attempt at denial, but it whispered through her raging thoughts. A shining, clear notion that traveled brightly through the maelstrom of her mind and landed as sharply and painfully as an arrow. A notion that had been voiced by two separate people: Fynch subtly, and Elspyth more insistently.

Fynch had claimed that he believed Wyl and Romen were of one mind. Valentyna was immediately reminded of Knave and the talk of magic that swirled about the dog. She recalled Fynch's confusion when Wyl's cantankerous dog had taken so easily to Romen, and how Romen had called out the dog's name in Stoneheart, though he had never met Knave before. Even more baffling for Fynch was how playfully Knave had greeted the stranger. The Queen remembered Fynch describing how Wyl's eyes had changed color at the witch burning— more talk of magic she had ignored. And then along came Elspyth with similar murmurings. She had urged Valentyna to accept the notion of reincarnation, all but saying that she too believed Wyl somehow resonated within Romen, and that the Queen's beloved might well be spiritually present in a new person—a woman, even. Wyl . . . Romen . . . Ylena.

Valentyna startled herself by being sick, turning just in time to avoid soiling her clothes. She sank to the floor of the balcony, upending the crockery on the tray, and gave way to deep, dry sobs. Nothing made sense anymore.

She remained curled on the balcony until the cold and the smell of her vomit brought her back to the present and the one stark reality she could not escape: marriage to Celimus. Today was the all-important fitting for her gown. She must attend to her toilet, and tolerate the seamstresses' chatter and annoying pins and requests. The time between now and the night when the King of Morgravia would legally bed her could be counted on her fingers.

Valentyna collected her shattered wits, put all thoughts of reincarnation and magic to the back of her mind, and steeled herself for her regal duties in the coming days. Forging peace was all she would permit herself to focus upon. She had a war to prevent and a wedding to prepare for. She would do as Ylena Thirsk suggested and write a letter of appeasement to King Celimus using Ylena as barter. She might as well, now that Ylena had made her sacrifice.

Crys had risen later than Valentyna but read his letter before he dressed. Wyl suggested two options for him to consider. The first was that he try to catch up with Elspyth, who Wyl felt was on a foolhardy mission, although he did not believe she was in any immediate danger. Both he and Crys felt protective toward Elspyth and it was only right that, with so few allies, they all look out for one another. Failing this, he suggested Crys don a disguise and infiltrate Pearlis, particularly the Legion, spreading the word of Celimus's betrayal of Jeryb and his family. Wyl listed a few names of reliable men Crys should single out in particular. He was to tell them about the treatment of Ylena and Alyd as well. *Take the head of your brother,* he urged; *give them proof.* Crys was to be patient, though. He was to avoid doing anything rash and to encourage a similar self-control in any angry Legionnaires. Wyl asked him to lie low among the Legion until Wyl himself somehow got word to him. He reinforced the point that Crys was not to even hint at the truth should the Queen ask questions about Ylena. He signed off, wishing Crys luck and hoping that they would meet again soon. He added a note to Crys to remember the password, for he could not promise he would return as Ylena.

Crys smiled grimly at the postscript. Any stranger could walk up to him in the future and claim to be Wyl. *How frightening it must be for him,* he thought as he turned his mind to departure. Frankly, he would be glad to be on the move again, doing something constructive. He would leave today—this morning, in fact—and was sure the Queen would quietly sigh with relief when he did so.

Valentyna gritted her teeth and got through the gown fitting. As she had expected, the seamstress and her assistants tittered around her for almost an hour. Sadly, they did not poke her with a single pin, which might have at least given her an excuse to vent some of the frustration she was feeling. Somehow she found a smile when they stood beaming at their finished creation.

She had demanded simplicity, and simplicity she had been given. Madam Eltor was used to Valentyna's likes and dislikes, having designed gowns for the new Queen since she was old enough to attend formal engagements, but this time the dressmaker had surpassed herself. The gown had long, clean lines in a fabric that fell so beautifully into its natural folds that it took even the designer's breath away when she saw it hanging on Valentyna's elegant body.

"You're a woman now," she had whispered to Valentyna, whose eyebrows had raised slightly when she saw the plunging neckline. It revealed not only the shapely top of her arms but displayed the flawless creamy expanse of her chest, fabric meeting flesh just before any cleavage might show.

"You will have to be sewn in, of course, my dear," Madam Eltor warned through the pins in her mouth. Having known the Queen since childhood, the dressmaker had long ago been excused from the formality of using Valentyna's titles. "It's the only way we'll get this perfect fit across your bust."

Valentyna nodded distractedly. "Finished now?"

"No," came the reply. "Be still, child," and the Queen of Briavel could not hide the ghost of a grin at the reprimand Madam Eltor had been giving for so many years now they had both lost count.

The gown's only adornment was a tiny row of pearls sewn

along the neckline and around the cuffs, which ended three-quarters of the way down Valentyna's long arms.

"I'll wager all of Morgravia and Briavel will be wearing this new length and slim sleeve by summer's close, your highness," one of the assistants commented eagerly.

Valentyna and Madam Eltor shared a glance in the mirror. They had been setting new fashion trends in Briavel for years, despite Valentyna's lack of interest in her wardrobe.

"Would you like to see it with the veil?" Madam Eltor inquired, already knowing the answer.

"Not today, Margyt," Valentyna begged. "Next time, I promise. Right now I have some urgent things to attend to and a realm to run." She gave the older woman a beseeching grin.

The seamstress nodded, a look of long-suffering patience on her face. "Next time, then," she said kindly, adding firmly: "Which, your highness, will be in four days. Be warned."

Valentyna groaned. "Thank you, everyone," she said, wriggling hastily out of the dress.

"Flowers?" Madam Eltor asked.

The Queen sighed. "It is in hand. Your colleague Madam Pern is designing open creamy white roses and fairy's breath for the posy and a wreath of white buds for my head," she answered. "I'd prefer lavender."

"It wouldn't work," Madam Eltor commented, quite used to Valentyna's contrariness. "The white buds will echo the pearls and enhance the Stone of Briavel, which I presume you'll wear?"

Valentyna nodded. She had to admit the gown suited her, with its sleek look and sharp lines. She was not one for the rounded, softer look many of the court women preferred. The Queen liked the way her dressmaker had echoed her slightly masculine edge in the sharp plunge of the gown's neckline, and the lack of affectation and adornment made her feel she could almost get away with wearing her riding boots beneath it. She smiled inwardly. Her people graciously accepted her tomboyishness without reading all manner of sinister connotations into it—why could she not accept Ylena's masculine contradictions? "Because it doesn't add up," she argued.

"I beg your pardon, dear?" Madam Eltor said, the wedding gown held reverently across her outstretched arms, ready to be placed into clean muslin for the journey back to her chambers in Werryl.

"Nothing," Valentyna murmured, embarrassed to realize that she had spoken her last thought aloud. "Thank you, Margyt. I'll see you soon." She saw the seamstress and her chittering assistants to the door and called for a page.

"Find me Stewyt, please, Ross, and also summon the Duke of Felrawthy to a meeting in my solar. I will see him in an hour."

The boy bowed and ran off on his errands. Valentyna hurriedly tied back her hair. She wished she could wear it just like this at her wedding—combed off her face and plaited. She pulled at wisps she had not quite managed to incorporate into the main plait, then made a sound of disgust at their waywardness and left them alone. A soft knock heralded the page.

"Stewyt, thank you for coming so quickly."

"Your majesty," he said, bowing low. "How may I help?"

Stewyt often unnerved her with his mature manner. Talking with him often felt like speaking to Krell or someone of similar age and ilk. She saw that Stewyt would make a fine chancellor in years to come; he encompassed all the right qualities, from discretion to intense curiosity about everyone and everything. He was a superb listener and rarely needed to have anything repeated.

She cleared her throat and her thoughts. "I wanted to talk to you about Lady Ylena."

"Yes, your highness. You received her note, I presume?"

"I did, thank you. But you didn't deliver it. I was given it with my breakfast tray."

"That's right, your majesty. Lady Ylena did not want you disturbed last night. She told me the contents of the letter were of no immediate import and I was to ensure both were delivered this morning."

"Both letters?"

"The other was for the Duke of Felrawthy," Stewyt qualified. "Is there something wrong, your majesty?"

"No, not at all. I've been informed that Lady Ylena left
the palace during the night. Did she seem upset when you
saw her?"

Stewyt frowned. "No, your highness. She was very alert,
as I recall, and somewhat intense, if I might hazard that
thought."

Stewyt looked as though he had more to say. Valentyna
nodded, impressed as always by his composure. "Is there
more?"

"Forgive me, your majesty, but I took the liberty of watching Lady Ylena."

"Oh?"

"Yes, I felt her manner was a trifle odd. She went to some
trouble to impress upon me how tired she was and in need
of sleep, yet throughout our conversation she struck me as
being very much awake and caught up by a sense of urgency."

"And you were right, of course," Valentyna prompted.

"Yes," the lad said, not meaning to sound smug. "I set off
on my errand as requested but doubled back, just to see if
my instincts were right. Chancellor Krell taught me to follow my instincts, your highness," he added. "I watched Lady
Ylena hurry out of her chamber."

"She did mention in her letter to me that she intended to
depart last night," Valentyna replied, determined that this lad
should not think Ylena was up to any mischief. She could
not have gossip of that kind going the rounds and providing
any future ammunition. "You recall, Stewyt, I asked you to
keep her presence between ourselves, which is why I hand-
picked you as her page."

He nodded solemnly. "I have told no one of her presence,
your highness."

"Did anything else occur that you think is worth mentioning?"

"Well . . ." The page sounded uncomfortable.

"Yes?"

"She—" He stopped, and started again. "On her way past

your portrait on the first landing, your highness, she paused . . . rather deliberately."

"And?" Valentyna queried, not understanding the boy's hesitation.

"She touched it, your majesty. Touched your . . . er, your breast, your highness."

Valentyna felt a new thrill of alarm. "Did she say anything?"

"She murmured a farewell to you, your highness. In all truth, I would say that she was trying to reach your face but wasn't tall enough."

"I see. Thank you, Stewyt." The Queen quickly dismissed the page, following him out of her chamber and heading to her solar to meet with Crys Donal.

He was waiting for her. "Good morning, your majesty," he said, and bowed.

"Crys, you look readied for travel," she said, noting the cloak as she walked toward him, and surprised him with a brief kiss.

He blushed. "Yes, your highness, I've decided to leave. I think it's only right, what with your troubles with the Legion and so on. I know I'm a thorn in your side and I agree with Ylena that I can probably be of more use back in Morgravia, being a thorn in the King's side." He grinned but it looked hollow.

"You've spoken with Ylena about this?" the Queen asked, surprised.

"No. She sent me a letter which I received this morning. She suggested I infiltrate the Legion and start spreading news of the slaughter at Tenterdyn to help turn the army against their king, your majesty."

"Is that her plan?"

Crys shook his head. "I don't know what her plan is, your highness."

Valentyna sat down in her favorite window seat with her back to her guest so he did not have to look at her in the eye. "Crys, since when did the Duke of Felrawthy—or any Duke of Morgravia, for that matter—take orders from a young noblewoman?"

There was a difficult pause, as she had anticipated, and then an equally awkward laugh. "Your majesty, Ylena Thirsk is no ordinary noblewoman. The surname alone tells you the stock she comes from."

He was going to say more, but she cut him off. "The fact that she is the daughter of the famous Fergys Thirsk and sister to the revered Wyl Thirsk does not necessarily make her a military strategist, though, does it? I would have thought a woman like Ylena would have been taught to embroider beautifully and make polite conversation with strangers while making an elegant tour of a room, not the art of warfare."

"Just like you, your highness." Crys immediately regretted his gentle sarcasm as Valentyna turned to fix him with a stare. "Forgive me, your majesty, I meant no insult. I admire you tremendously for the dazzling way you balance being a beautiful woman and a strong ruler. It's not easy, your highness; anyone with half a brain can see that such skill requires both a feminine and a masculine side."

Valentyna dug deep and found a smile to show no offense had been taken—it was obvious that Crys was genuine in his praise, although just as obvious that he was protecting Ylena. "I don't know, Crys. I was under the impression that Ylena was a gentle, pampered young woman."

"Which she was, I'm sure, your highness. But plenty has happened to change that, and they do say blood will win out."

"They do indeed," Valentyna said cryptically. "If you'll forgive my digging into a painful subject—her relationship with Alyd, did you know much about it?"

"Only that they were madly in love. His letters were filled with his adoration of both Thirsks. They were his family during his time in the south. What's troubling you, your highness?"

She struggled. Could she tell him? She needed to share her secret with someone and Crys was as reliable as any of her own counsel. "You don't think she had leanings toward women, do you?"

The Duke looked shocked. "Ylena? No! Whatever gave you that idea?"

Valentyna made a face. "Oh, just something that happened last night between us. I don't really want to talk about it."

"Except we are," he said, grinning, understanding what must have occurred. That would now explain why Wyl had fled in the night. "No, Ylena used to write to us as well, your highness, and she was intensely in love with Alyd. It was all she could do to talk about anything other than him, their marriage, and children. They were planning a large brood."

"So they wanted babies immediately?"

"Oh yes, even Alyd said they would begin a family as soon as they could." He laughed. "They even married before we expected—couldn't wait for us."

Valentyna shook her head, baffled, recalling Ylena's confusion when she had mentioned pregnancy. "Well, she's not pregnant, I can vouch for that. It's why she left the table so suddenly—her monthly flux had arrived."

Crys tried unsuccessfully to stifle a laugh at the thought of Wyl dealing with women's ailments.

"I can't imagine what's so amusing, Crys," Valentyna said in a vaguely injured tone.

"There is nothing funny, your highness. My apologies."

Valentyna was sure he knew more than he was telling her, but she could not fathom what. "Is there anything else you know that could help me, Crys? Please, I feel like I'm navigating through a quagmire."

He gave her a look of tender sympathy. "Your highness, Ylena is true to you. After all that Celimus has perpetrated on her family and the family she married into, her loyalties have changed. We all love Morgravia, but we would rather fight on the side of Briavel as long as King Celimus sits Morgravia's throne." He surprised her by going down on one knee. "You can trust me and you can trust Ylena. She is fearlessly casting herself into the lion's den. Whether Celimus has her killed or not, it doesn't matter—we will never see Ylena again, that much I can assure you." The last was said bitterly.

Valentyna reached to touch his bowed head, moved by what he had said. "Oh, Crys, I don't want her death on my hands."

"She has nothing else to give. Your highness, Ylena doesn't want to live anymore—can't you see that? That is why she can give it up so recklessly for someone she loves."

He felt he had gone too far in mentioning the word "love," and Valentyna's anguished response confirmed it.

"I don't want her love, Crys!" The Queen was shocked by the pain that moved across the Duke's open face at her words.

"Then take her sacrifice graciously and use it for your own ends, as she asks."

"I don't even understand her intentions in going to Felrawthy," Valentyna replied bitterly.

Crys stood. "I imagine she means to disrupt those talks in the north," he said. "And somehow bargain for the deployment of the Legion back to Pearlis so your people can breathe easily again and get on with celebrating a royal wedding." He took her hand. "And about the wedding—I don't think you can escape that, your majesty, but you can demand equality. You can influence how this new era for Morgravia and Briavel will be felt by people. Believe me, if we can find a way to overthrow Celimus, we will, but you must proceed with this marriage."

She had heard it before from others and given herself the same sound advice. It was time she got on with living it now. "You're right. No doubt we shall see each other in Pearlis."

"I might not go straight to the Morgravian capital, your highness," Crys said, as if the decision had only just arrived in his mind.

"Not Felrawthy?" she asked, fear in her tone.

"No, that will have to wait, your highness. The time to seize back my family estate is not yet ripe. I've actually been thinking about Elspyth."

Relief softened Valentyna's expression. "You're going after her?"

"I think I should. She's a resilient woman and knows her mind, but she's still only a girl alone in a strange realm with no weapons or protection—"

"Heading off into the Razor Kingdom to rescue a prisoner of its king," the Queen finished, shaking her head. "I'm glad, Crys. Thank you."

The Duke shrugged. "Elspyth was good to me when I needed to be reminded who I was and what needed to be done. If not for her insistence, I would have gone tearing back to Tenterdyn."

"And lost your own life, and Felrawthy would have lost its duke."

"Yes," he admitted. "She saved me from my own stupidity and anger."

"Well, you still have every right to be angry, to want vengeance, Crys, and because of Elspyth's advice, you might yet get it."

He sensed the sorrow behind her encouraging words. "I'm sorry that you don't have the same opportunity, your highness."

She forced a small smile. "Oh, I'll find my own way."

Crys knew as well as she did that her comment was mere bravado, but he returned her smile with a squeeze of her hand.

"How will you follow her?" Valentyna asked, changing the subject.

"I'll start with Liryk, I suppose. I suspect your commander is rather gratified that Elspyth is out of your life, your highness"—he grinned as she nodded conspiratorially—"but he might help by asking his guards if they saw her leave."

"What good will that do?"

"Well, I imagine Elspyth was in a hurry to leave Werryl. That being the case, I believe she might have hitched a ride with someone." He shrugged. "It might help me follow her, that's all."

The Queen nodded. "Be safe, Crys. We shall meet again soon, I hope."

He kissed her hand with feeling, and then the last of her allies left the Briavellian monarch to her loneliness and bleak thoughts.

13

After leaving Werryl, Wyl made straight for a hide of Faryl's in Crowyll and dug up a pouch of money. He was pleased he could still remember some of the locations of her stashed coin, and although he did not care for using blood money, he was in dire need of it.

He galloped his horse as far and hard as the beast would permit, then traveled on through the night more slowly and spent most of his coin on a new horse the following morning. Although he had not slept, he was determined to press on and the replacement animal was fresh and happy to be given its head. His plan was to follow the border as closely as he could, entering Morgravia only when he believed he was far enough north to cross directly into Felrawthy. He could not risk stumbling upon any Legionnaires and being recognized.

At around midday the next day it was his good fortune to ride into the village of Derryn at a time when he not only had to rest his horse but needed food and sleep himself, and, most important, a chance to bathe. The pain had gone and he felt as well as could be expected, considering his fatigue, but it seemed that the bleeding would continue for a few days yet. How inconvenient and messy it all was.

Wyl hoped he would never be a woman again. The grooming, the curtsying, the requirement to be elegant and gracious at all times—these were merely a few of its annoying aspects. He pitied Valentyna, and yet he admired her too. Somehow she managed to balance the demands of being a woman with a strength of her own. Ylena, much as he had loved her, had delighted almost exclusively in her femininity—but then that was all that had been expected of her since the day of her birth. A daughter born into a wealthy noble family, particularly one as distinguished as the Thirsks, had one main task: to marry well. To achieve this she was educated in every possible pastime that could enhance her opportunities, from the effective running of a household to the art of embroidery. King Magnus had employed a small army of women to teach Ylena such niceties from her arrival at Pearlis at a tender age. And his sister had proved herself to be an adept student.

Fresh sorrow overcame Wyl as he pondered yet again how little Ylena deserved what had befallen her. She had always been ready with a kind word for everyone and her smile could banish even the gloomiest of moods. She had truly been a beauty in every sense of the word. That her mind had been empty of the thoughts and ambitions that drove Valentyna was not Ylena's fault. She was merely following form, whereas Valentyna was one of a kind. Yet Ylena's life had unraveled over a matter of weeks; what should have been the happiest time of her life had instead been the most cruel. Wyl felt a familiar nausea grip him and he knew he must stop grieving like this over his sister. Ylena was dead and no amount of soul-searching or tears would restore her.

Wyl knew his exhaustion and the monthly flux was contributing to his morbid feelings and was convinced that a decent meal and some rest would help to lift his spirits. As he walked the horse through the main street, he found there was no inn but discovered by asking a young woman passing by that a widow by the name of Mona Dey ran a guesthouse in the village. After stabling the horse, paying for its care, and making sure he could retrieve it with ease whenever he wanted, Wyl headed for the widow's place.

He paid Mona in advance, much to her delight, and was shown to a small, neat room at the back of her large dwelling. He learned from the chatty widow that her husband had been a wealthy though miserly trader with a wandering eye for other women, especially whores. According to Mona, her husband had died between the legs of a buxom twenty-year-old, a blade driven into his back up to the hilt.

She told the chilling tale with a sly relish and it brought back hideous memories for Wyl.

"A pocketful of silver—that's all the slut got for her trouble," Mona said smugly. "I got the rest." And she beamed. From then on she had lived her life to the full, deliberately spending her dead husband's money with abandon in revenge for his meanness, until there was virtually nothing left. "I held back just enough to keep me off the streets," she told Wyl, with no trace of bitterness, "and now I take paying guests and live a quiet life."

"I can't imagine it gets much quieter than Derryn," Wyl commented, surprised at the widow's candor.

"You're right there, my lady," Mona cried, and laughed as if he had cracked some great jest.

As open as Mona Dey was about her own background, Wyl appreciated that she showed not the slightest interest in his. Either she was entirely self-centered or she was very canny, knowing that most strangers preferred not to discuss their business. Wyl thanked the widow and paid her some extra coin for her discretion, for she had not even inquired why Ylena was traveling alone.

The evening meal, Mona told her guest, was served at sunset and no later. Wyl grimaced and politely asked whether there was any possible chance of a tray in his room now. He explained how tired he was and that his flux had fair drained him of all energy. A look of deep sympathy had come his way—definitely a special sorrow only women could share, he realized—and no doubt the generous coin rattling in her skirt pocket had encouraged Mona Dey to look kindly on the young noblewoman.

"I'll see what I can rustle up for you, dear," she said. "Oh my, I used to suffer it something awful at your age. And my Garth, he had no sympathy at all, still claiming his marital rights." Wyl quailed inwardly at the turn the discussion was taking but adopted the right expression and paid attention. "And pain! Shar save me, I thought I was fit to die," the widow continued. "My mother had no sympathy. She said I should get used to it, for it would curse me for most of my life—my mother was a bitter woman, you see. My father died on her young and left her with a brood of children and no money. Her bleed was bad too and left her in poor shape one week of each moon, and it meant she couldn't work during some of those days and we went hungry."

The widow looked set to carry on discussing her mother's moon cycles, but Wyl feigned a swoon, which effectively stopped the monologue and had Mona rushing for cold flannels and smelling salts. When he seemed recovered, the widow suggested the young lady take a soak. There was a room in the house already set up for bathing. "I have some herbs that will ease the pain, dear," she offered kindly.

Wyl was grateful to her and said as much, winning a wide smile from the widow. "And I'll fetch you some raspberry leaf," she added. "Chew straight on it, my lady. Tastes like hell but is far more effective for your condition than a weak brew."

Wyl stammered his thanks and allowed her to guide him to the bathing room, which had a huge old tub that more than swallowed up Ylena's exhausted body. He would have been happy to wash in cold water, but Mona wouldn't hear of it. "Heat is what you need, dear, for the ache."

Wyl did not want to start explaining that the ache was done; he just wanted peace and privacy now. So he let her fuss and organize for steaming jugs to be brought up by a small army of lads she paid to run to the smithy's where a huge cauldron of water was kept on the fire permanently. The joy of finally closing the door on Mona's chatter and climbing into the tub was second in Wyl's mind only to kissing Valentyna for the first time.

Afterward, he ate a meal of cold roast meat, potatoes simmered with cream, and some cheese, before slipping between the well-worn but fresh sheets on Mona's guest bed and drifting almost instantly into sleep.

When he awoke he was disoriented. It was black outside and as quiet as a tomb. Mona had kindly left a candle in his room, but it had burned down to a sputtering nub. He had been asleep for at least twelve hours, he estimated. Careful to make no sound to disturb the household, he relieved himself in the chamber pot and hurriedly dressed in his dusty but comfortable riding clothes. Wyl did not like to sneak away without thanking Mona but had no means to scrawl a note; the only way he could show his appreciation for her care was with money, which he left on the remade bed. He thought it unlikely she would think further on the young woman who had passed through her house, but if she did, she would remember Ylena kindly for her generosity.

He could not risk making his way through the house, so, thanking his lucky stars that he was on the first level, he climbed out of the window and dropped silently to the ground, rolling as he had been taught when he was a lad. He must have startled a badger or some night creature on the fringe of the small wood that skirted the town, for he heard the animal blundering disgruntledly back into the trees. He remained still, listening for any other sounds, but it seemed there was no one about. Nevertheless, he took the precaution of making his way to the stable via the back lanes. As he had anticipated, there was a sleeping stableboy in one corner who could barely rouse himself from his slumber at the young woman's oddly timed arrival. When he did, he recognized the noblewoman, pointed toward a stall, and mumbled something incoherent. Wyl was just glad to find his horse, saddle her, and be off as quickly and quietly as he could.

He ignored the fresh hunger pangs that gnawed at his belly and was out onto the open road again, Derryn behind him, moments later. One more day's riding, he guessed, and he would be able to cut into Morgravia and enter Felrawthy, back into the lair of Celimus, and perhaps have a chance to get into a new, more suitable body.

Cailech sat in a secret cave in Haldor's Tooth, pondering the situation that was about to unfold. The Grenadyne's suggestion to forge an alliance with Morgravia had touched the very core of everything the Mountain King believed. He was privately miffed that such an obvious idea had not occurred to him in the past, for treating with Magnus and his general, Thirsk, would surely have been easier than dealing with Morgravia's current monarch. But he had always derided any suggestion of forging links with Morgravia—wait, no, not always. In his early days as King, he had had notions of living as neighbors alongside the bordering realm, but had put them aside in more recent years. Rashlyn had always said the stones did not auger well for negotiating attempts, and eventually Cailech had stopped asking.

Nevertheless, when Aremys returned to the cave and reported on the meeting with Celimus, Cailech felt a surge of anxiety. "You're sure there is no trap?" he asked Aremys.

"No, sire. But I have made our way as safe as I can under the circumstances. Celimus is organizing for the hostages to be delivered as required, and I have taken out some additional insurance."

The mercenary explained that his bargaining tool was one Ylena Thirsk, daughter and sister of Morgravia's two previous Generals. The name carried weight with Cailech, and he had no qualms about using a Morgravian noblewoman to barter for their safety. He just had one question: "Well, where is she?"

Aremys startled the King by laughing and shrugging. "I have no idea, sire. But that is a worry for another day. You will be back on your own soil before I have to consider what to do."

Cailech smiled. He liked the way the large Grenadyne thought. Farrow had impressed him from their first meeting, and even though the mercenary clearly knew more than he was telling and had an uncanny interest in Galapek, Cailech privately considered the man a friend. He had never said as much, but they both knew it; there was mutual respect and admiration between them. Perhaps it was simply that, with his clear thinking and dry humor, Aremys reminded him of Lothryn. He missed Lothryn so deeply it actually pained him to dwell upon it.

It had been the most agonizing of discoveries to realize that his closest friend and confidant had betrayed him. How could Loth have chosen the Morgravians over his own people, over his own king? Cailech had ranted as much to Myrt, who had kept a dull silence throughout, but whose lack of words said much. Cailech quietly admired the man for his loyalty to his friend. Loth could have learned much from Myrt about brotherhood, honor, and trust. Cailech's pride would not permit him to show any mercy to his childhood friend, no matter how in love with the woman of Yentro he might have been. It made no difference why Lothryn had made his choice; it mattered only that he had made it, and made it incorrectly.

When news came that they were bringing Lothryn back alive, Cailech had wanted to slay him on the frosted stones of the fortress's threshold. He could not bear to see his lifelong companion—now a traitor—step even one foot across it. But then Rashlyn had persuaded him to exact a higher penance.

Somehow the King had been persuaded down the path of magic. Burning with a feverish anger, he had listened with fascinated horror to Rashlyn's suggestion that there was a far more subtle operation than an easy death by the sword. The barshi's repetition of the words "traitor" and "treachery" had fired the King's anguish into a white heat of vengeance. He had agreed to Rashlyn's plan, believing that by owning Loth, by breaking his spirit and forcing his subservience with Rashlyn's dark magic, he would somehow win his respect. His former friend and comrade would suffer the humiliation of knowing he would forever carry the King on his back, ever be subservient to Cailech, never forgetting who ruled whom.

Now, thinking about it, Cailech saw how distorted and poisonous such punishment had been. If he could reverse the magic he would do so, especially now that Aremys seemed to have such a dogged interest in the stallion. The truth was, his victory over Loth felt hollow. Painful, in fact. As with the threat to make cannibals of his own people, it had shown him to be base, led by anger rather than by his clever mind. How had he permitted Rashlyn to guide his hand toward inflicting such horrors? He shook his head.

"A silver for your thoughts, sire," Aremys said, approaching Cailech where he sat on a rock ledge with a clear view into Felrawthy. He brought with him a clay flask of wine and poured a cup for the King and one for himself. Myrt and the rest of the Mountain warriors were sharpening blades and checking the supplies of weapons, which everyone prayed would not be required.

"I was just thinking of Lothryn and how much you remind me of him."

"I shall take that as a compliment, sire. I have heard people speak highly of your second, despite his final actions."

"As they should," Cailech said, unable to hide the sorrow that had him in its grip.

"No one can tell me what happened to him, sire. I presume you executed him?"

Aremys heard the hesitation. "Yes, he is dead," the King replied flatly.

"Doesn't stop you missing him, though, I see."

Cailech nodded. "I miss him every day. We grew up together. We understood each other, we protected each other. That was what made his betrayal so shocking. We loved each other, Farrow. We were brothers in all but blood."

"With such love between you, could you not find a way to spare him?" Aremys prompted, hoping to lead the King into revealing more about Galapek.

"Only the barest thread separates the most passionate of opposites, Grenadyne."

"What do you mean, sire?"

"I mean that because I loved Loth so much, his betrayal stirred in me intense hatred."

"I understand." Aremys knew he would not get the admission he had hoped for. Instead, the silence stretched between them, before Cailech roused himself from his private thoughts and addressed the question that was no doubt troubling his men too.

"Is this a wise undertaking, Farrow?"

"Many would consider it foolhardy, given the Morgravian sovereign's reputation," Aremys replied. "However, I do believe that once he meets you, you, more than anyone, have the ability to convince him that an alliance is preferable to these regular skirmishes that could so easily escalate to war."

Cailech nodded, reassured by the Grenadyne's faith. "And his marriage?"

"Is still planned to go ahead shortly, which is why timing is of the essence. With Briavel's army at his beck and call, who knows what delusions might suddenly cross his mind?"

"I am told the Legion has been deployed to the Briavellian border. Hardly a loving wedding gift."

"Scare tactics," Aremys guessed. "There is no benefit to Celimus starting a fresh war with Briavel when he can conquer the realm through marriage."

"Intimidating the bride is a grand way to start a historic treaty between the two realms," Cailech replied.

"It seems Celimus knows no other way. From what I can gather, he has been a bully all his young life. Why should he change now that he is King?"

"Mmm—my thoughts exactly," Cailech mused.

Aremys could not work out what the King meant. Dismissing it, he reassured Cailech. "Nothing will go wrong, sire. Just don't tarry. Say what you have to say and plan to use emissaries to do the rest. The main thing is that you and Celimus meet and like what you see in each other."

Cailech nodded. "When are we expected?"

"Tomorrow. He is planning a feast in your honor. I suggest that only Myrt, Byl, and I accompany you, sire."

Cailech's green gaze narrowed. "A lean force."

"It shows trust."

"Even if I don't trust him."

"Exactly."

The Mountain King laughed again. "I hope, for your sake, Grenadyne, that you do not leave this meeting with my blood on your hands—or you will have hundreds of my warriors baying for yours."

Cailech raised his glass to Aremys, who followed suit. "To unions, sire."

"And friendship, Farrow. Thank you for your help."

"Does that mean I am a free man now?"

Cailech drained his cup. "It does, but I hope you will return to the fortress with us."

"If we are all still alive after this adventure, your highness, I would be honored to."

Celimus was riding on the moors that surrounded Tenterdyn and surveying what he now considered Crown land.

"It is beautiful, your majesty," Jessom said from his own horse, echoing the King's thoughts.

"I was thinking I would make Tenterdyn my summer palace and Argorn could become the royal winter retreat," Celimus replied with a smug smile, looking toward the majestic Razors, which reared up a hazy purple in the distance.

"Crys Donal and Ylena Thirsk might have something to say about that, your highness," the Chancellor cautioned, careful to hit a tone that did not suggest either reprimand or contradiction.

"Not from the grave they won't," his king snapped testily.

The notion had crept up on the Chancellor so quietly he had not realized it existed until this moment, but now it dawned on him that he had tired of the King's waspish manner and complete disregard for those who strove to accommodate his whims. Jessom's commitment to Celimus stretched to killing—and for no extra reward, certainly no thanks. Jessom was no fragile soul who shirked the meting out of death, but Celimus's settling-in period of brutality was, in Jessom's estimation, prolonged. The bloodshed seemed to be escalating, not diminishing, with the King's expanding power.

Celimus was young and brash, and his eagerness to stamp his own mark on his kingdom—and indeed beyond—was understandable. But since Jessom had first arrived in Celimus's life, he had hoped he might mold this brilliantly sharp young man into one who could be relied on to be subtle. Jessom had put all of his life experience and extensive range of talents at the King's disposal so that Celimus might learn from him.

Maris Jessom was the seventh son of a rich man, a moneylender who was involved in a number of ventures from bridge building to breweries. But even with such wealth, a son so far down the family's hierarchy was never going to be favored highly in the shareholding. His eldest three brothers were carving up the empire among them, and everyone else, including his three sisters, had to find their own way. In the case of his sisters, they had used their status to marry well. But Maris, thin and hook-nosed, had long ago accepted that he would never be a handsome man and so had decided from an early age to use his only real asset—his incredible intelligence—to get on in life. If the combined wits of his siblings were distilled into one, they still would not hold a candle to the speed, agility, and vision of their youngest brother. Although Maris kept this weapon a secret, it was obvious to him that his father should have chosen his seventh son to run his financial empire; it seemed that he alone had inherited the shrewdness, perceptiveness, and cunning that had helped his father to become one of the wealthiest men in all of Tallinor. But Jessom senior had never taken much notice of his gangly youngest son, and as soon as Maris was old enough, he had been encouraged to leave the family home to seek his own fortune. His mother, who loved him well, had given him a heavy pouch of gold. "Use it wisely, Maris," she had said, her eyes beginning to tear as she hugged her youngest farewell.

And he had, roaming the towns and villages of Tallinor from north to south and east to west as a traveling moneylender: an innovative and supremely lucrative scheme, and convenient for borrowers, who were surprised and pleased to have money coming to them. Perhaps people thought he would never collect on his lendings. But collect he did. Borrowers learned the hard way that Maris Jessom did not extend his loans. And because he never called in his loans early or was so greedy as to make the terms so cumbersome that they might be considered cruel, he always had the law on his side. The young Jessom was also ruthless, a characteristic that contributed to his rapid success.

It was not long before he had to travel with a bodyguard, and then two, for fear of being set upon by the new breed of bandits who seemed to think it was perfectly reasonable to steal from the rich, as they could afford to lose the money. This made Jessom's anger, normally slow to stoke, boil and he was soon traveling with a small company of his own paid mercenaries, who killed bandits for a hobby and kept all the spoils.

Jessom enjoyed two decades of this life, during which time he built a network of contacts and knowledge from all over the region, before deciding to settle down in Tal, not far from his original family home. Here he planned to establish his own permanent moneylending empire, using mercenaries to do the dirtier work of collection around the realm. By this time both of his parents had died and his less fortunate siblings were scattered across the realm.

It was around this time that King Sorryn of Tallinor declared moneylenders—whose number seemed to have tripled in Jessom's lifetime—to be "a pus-filled carbuncle on society that needed to be lanced" and systematically set about dismantling their terrible grip on the poor. Jessom saw the crackdown coming and fled Tallinor well in advance of the Purge, as it came to be known.

He fled to Morgravia, a wealthy man but homeless as well as landless and without the ties of family. Disillusioned, Maris Jessom decided on a change of career. He was too old to find the energy to establish a new empire and so he watched and waited. Garnering information, observing trends, and identifying needs were Jessom's talent. He saw an opportunity within the Morgravian royal family long before it occurred to anyone else that a king might need more than his general to be his closest counsel.

The position of Chancellor did not even exist during Magnus's reign, for he was a King who preferred the companionship and advice of his military strategist in all matters. But it was obvious to Jessom that the new King would not accept the guidance of Wyl Thirsk upon Magnus's death. Maris Jessom fancied himself a kingmaker; he had a network of messengers, mercenaries, informers, and spies who could help shape a kingdom, plus he had years of experience in finance as well as a shrewd understanding of human nature.

He watched Celimus for long enough before he became King to know the young man was problem-riddled and it would take years of smoothing and guidance to educate him on how to run an effective realm. Jessom saw the charm too, though; he sensed that Celimus could easily turn that talent toward his kingdom and use the energy he squandered in despising people into making them loyal to him. Jessom had to admit the proposal of marriage to Valentyna of Briavel was a masterstroke, but the killing of her father, Valor, had been plain stupidity. It was the act of an arrogant man, too inexperienced to realize that a suggestion of his power was more than enough. Jessom knew King Valor would have supported a union between Celimus and his daughter, which made his death pointless.

The murder of Thirsk had been another senseless move, although Jessom realized that there was a history there that affected the King's judgment and prevented him from being objective. Jessom had watched Thirsk too, long enough to realize the young General was loyal to Morgravia. Celimus could have molded that loyalty to his will—and the execution of the youngest Donal, the razing of Rittylworth, and the slaughter at Tenterdyn, not to mention various other deaths, including that of young helpless Jorn, need never have occurred.

Murder was dangerous. It had a nasty habit of coming back to haunt the perpetrator and Jessom could not help but think that there were too many corpses at the King's feet— with the Chancellor's involvement—for either of them to escape the outcry that was surely coming. All it would take was one voice of dissension. One voice that counted—be it that of Ylena Thirsk or Crys Donal or even Aleda Donal, wherever the hell she was. A few rumblings from Lord Bench could set off a catastrophic series of questions for the King to answer . . . and Jessom knew who would shoulder the blame. It would not be Celimus.

And yet, if only he would listen to Jessom, Celimus could still be a strong, powerful king who ruled prosperous realms. Not one or two, but three—the very empire the King dreamed of. All was not lost yet. Perhaps they could use Ylena Thirsk to their advantage—there was always a way— instead of simply murdering her.

He realized he was shaking his head and that Celimus, wearing a quizzical expression, had turned his horse to face his chancellor.

"Your majesty, may I speak candidly?"

"Of course."

"Well, sire, with the alliance you may well forge with the Mountain King, and what could only be described as the fairy-tale union with Briavel that is about to occur, you will have achieved what most sovereigns do not dare dream of, let alone attempt."

"And your point is?"

"My point, your majesty, is that you are now in the enviable position of essentially controlling three realms without resistance, without bloodshed, without the other two sovereigns realizing how powerful you actually are."

"Why is that a good thing, Jessom?"

"Your highness, there is a saying that holds good in almost every facet of life: Never allow one hand to know what the other is doing."

"Don't give me riddles, you fool. Speak plainly."

Jessom drew a deep breath to stop his disdain from showing. "Once married, Valentyna is beholden to you as wife, so she will be unable to rally any forces against you, which effectively leaves the Mountain King in the cold, should he suddenly decide the alliance is not working for him. I suspect he is much too canny for that, though—he will maintain the peace and enjoy the benefits of trade and free movement as well as increased prosperity. My lord, it is obvious to me that, handled with care, you will have the empire you have always dreamed of."

"Did you think, Jessom," Celimus replied, "that I could not work that out for myself? Is it your belief that I need you to spell out every scenario for me because I am too dimwitted to see beyond what is in front of my nose?" The tone was sarcastic and menacing.

"Not at all, sire," Jessom replied, with equal calmness but also with courtesy. "But with such an alliance so close to completion, I just think that killing Ylena Thirsk or Crys Donal might be . . . well, shall we say hasty, for want of a better word."

"So you would have me leave two dangerous mouths on the loose?"

"All I suggest, sire, is that you wait. You will have Ylena Thirsk in captivity shortly. Don't do anything too soon.

Think on the various situations that will inevitably present themselves. I imagine that Ylena Thirsk is feeling extraordinarily isolated these days. She has no parents, she has lost her guardian, and her beloved brother is dead. Her new husband and his family—her only allies—are fodder for the worms. Apart from Crys Donal, she has no one to turn to. She is a beautiful, vulnerable young woman who no doubt craves the security of being pampered again: her own private chambers, servants to wait on her, fancy gowns on her body, and money at her disposal. Think about it, sire. You could be her savior. You could put all this behind you and lavish your care and riches on the lonely girl—until she becomes your supporter."

Celimus listened this time without the smirk on his face. "She always was a spoiled little thing. I used to think she'd jump at shadows."

"That's exactly what I mean, sire. She may boast the name of Thirsk, but she is merely a girl. Her world has crumbled and been destroyed. What she needs now is resurrection from the rubble. If you provide that, it doesn't matter what excuses or tall stories you weave to excuse your behavior of the past; she will believe them all because what she will want is her life back again. Marry her off well—to your gain. I would go so far as to suggest you find her a high-ranking warrior from Cailech's brood. She will be no more trouble to you then."

The King's horse was restless. "Interesting idea, Jessom," Celimus replied. "I will think on what you have said. What time is the Mountain King due?"

"Midday, your highness. We had better make for the house."

"My summer palace," Celimus corrected, and smiled.

Jessom saw no warmth in the smile; if he was honest with himself, he would admit that he had never seen any genuine warmth in Celimus. Why it should bother him now was a surprise. This mood of dissatisfaction had taken him so unexpectedly that he recognized it as dangerous. He, like the King, had some thinking to do.

The King galloped on ahead, but Jessom rode back to Tenterdyn more sedately, silent and distracted.

14

VALENTYNA CRAFTED HER LETTER TO CELIMUS THE AFTERNOON of Crys Donal's departure. She wrote with great caution, outlining her decision to release Ylena Thirsk into his care. The words suggested her expectation that he would look after Ylena even though she was being given into the captivity of the Morgravian Crown. The Queen expressed her understanding that any known enemy of Morgravia could not be considered a friend of Briavel and that, as helpless as Ylena painted her situation, Valentyna did not wish to go against the express wishes of her husband-to-be. She felt sick writing the lies but pressed on, detailing her progress with her own arrangements for the wedding, not describing her gown but telling him a little of how well it looked. She discussed the party that would accompany her into Morgravia, which was not inconsequential, and then lightly touched on her desire to return to Briavel soon after the ceremony so that a second celebration could be held for her people. Much to her distaste, Valentyna felt she should ooze some special compliments here about how much the Briavellians were looking forward to seeing their queen with her new king.

By the end of it she felt revolted by the smooth way in which she lied to protect her own life as well as at how easily she was giving away Ylena's precious life. As terrible thoughts filled her mind about the ways Celimus might choose to kill Wyl Thirsk's sister—and kill her he would, she knew—the guilt of remembering how generously Wyl Thirsk had sacrificed himself for Briavel's heir nearly overwhelmed her. She was repaying his sacrifice with disdain for his family. Valentyna's fingers twitched with the desire to rip up the parchment with its treacherous contents.

But the memory of Ylena's hard words stayed her hand. It was Ylena's decision to give up her life and Valentyna realized she would probably aggrieve the young woman more if she did not carry out her wishes. Her life was forfeit anyway, Valentyna told herself. One way or another, Celimus would hunt Ylena down and complete his annihilation of the Thirsk line. Ylena seemed to feel that her sacrifice for Briavel matched that of Wyl's and would give some point to all the deaths that surrounded her tragic family.

"Too sad," Valentyna murmured at her desk. "Your life is given too cheaply, Ylena, for the gain is so little. I cannot escape marrying him."

She had the letter dispatched immediately, for fear of changing her mind, going so far as to take the parchment to the stables herself, placing it into the courier's hand.

"How long?" she asked. Briavel also used a relay network for messengers and she felt sure that once they were across the border, the Morgravian couriers would respect the urgency of this missive.

"Two days if we all ride hard, your majesty," the young man said.

"Then use as many couriers as you can. It is extremely important that King Celimus see this message as quickly as possible."

"I shall personally ride like the wind, your highness," he said, and with a bow from a saddle he was gone, clattering over Werryl Bridge and heading northeast as fast as his horse would go.

Valentyna turned away, feeling hollow and more lonely than she had ever felt in her life. Growing up as an only child had taught her to be self-sufficient and imaginative, but nothing could have prepared her for this complete loss of family, friends, and allies. And still, she realized, she could not begin to reach the depth of loss that Ylena must surely be experiencing. No wonder Wyl's sister was throwing her life away with such abandon. It might also explain why she was indulging in such curious affections. The Queen had not been able to shake the memory of Ylena's kiss; it seemed to haunt her every moment. There had been such tenderness in it . . . no, more than that. It had been filled with love. Valentyna had been kissed only once before in such a manner and that had been by Romen. Although this was a different mouth, different face, different *everything,* there was an aching familiarity to the passion behind that affection. But the memory of that physical love made Valentyna angry too. Angry enough to want to fight: not Ylena, but the person who had perpetrated all the pain. On her way back into the palace, in a state of resentment at the way her life was turning out, she sent a runner to find Commander Liryk.

He arrived slightly out of breath at her study door. "My queen, you wished to see me?"

Valentyna was struck by how old Liryk seemed to be all of a sudden. She had taken his and Krell's presence around her for granted, as if they would always be in her life, but this man was surely well into his seventh decade. The notion of him not being around one day bit deeply into her thoughts, reminding her that she might lose yet another of her supporters soon. It hardened her resolve.

"Yes, Commander, thank you for coming so quickly. In the absence of a chancellor, I would like you to summon the nobles for me."

"Of course, your highness," Liryk said, frowning despite his courteous manner. "All of them?"

"Yes. It is urgent. How swiftly are you able to gather them for a meeting?"

He paused and she wondered whether he was considering her question or her state of mind. He obviously anticipated that she was about to do something dramatic. "Three days, your majesty, if I get the couriers sent immediately."

"Do it please, Liryk. I'd appreciate it if you would give this the utmost priority."

"Of course, your highness." She waited, and of course the gentle objection came. "It is unusual, though. Perhaps I might give them some inkling of what you wish to discuss so urgently?"

She smiled. She had expected this. "State security, tell

them," she answered, and turned away, not unkindly but with sufficient firmness that Liryk knew he had been dismissed. "Thank you, Liryk," she added, just in case he thought to try to dissuade her.

Valentyna heard the soft sigh, the protest of his knee as he bowed, and then the sound of the door closing.

Wyl allowed himself to be picked up by Morgravian soldiers and was relieved to see that they were genuine Legionnaires and not mercenaries. It was a young company; although he recognized none of them, they certainly recognized his name. An awkward silence spread through the group of men as Wyl finished his introduction.

"You are General Wyl Thirsk's sister?" the startled leader qualified.

"I am," Wyl replied, his spirits soaring. He knew it was unlikely he could change the outcome of what was going to happen, but hearing his own name uttered with such reverence restored his confidence. And perhaps he might live to fight another day in another body.

He wondered whether Valentyna had taken his advice about writing to Celimus, claiming she was sending Ylena to him. Their parting had been so awkward and painful, he supposed the Queen was just glad to be rid of Ylena Thirsk.

The young officer could not help himself. "But what are you doing here? We heard you had disappeared."

Wyl was certainly not going to start explaining any more than he wanted to give away. "What is your name?" he asked.

"Harken," the young man replied. "Er, Captain Harken, I hope, by year's end."

"Well, Harken, firstly please remember whom you address. I am the daughter of General Fergys Thirsk, Duke of Argorn, and the sister of General Wyl Thirsk. Please treat me in the fashion you would any noble."

Harken flushed with embarrassment at the stinging rebuke. Blotches of red appeared on his cheeks and ears. "I . . . I apologize, Lady Ylena."

When he saw his reprimand had worked, Wyl deliberately

looked behind him as if suddenly fearful. He might as well continue with his planned charade and hope that the Queen of Briavel had complied with his suggestion. "Thank you, Harken. Have they gone?"

"Who, my lady?" the man asked, desperate to please. He looked over her shoulder and his companions followed suit, suddenly nervous.

"The Briavellian Guardsmen who brought me to this crossing point." Swords were drawn instantly, the ring of steel loud in the silence of the morning. "Fret not, gentlemen," Wyl assured. "They have no quarrel with you. They were concerned only with me." Wyl held his breath, hoping his detached manner and confident explanation would trick the Legionnaires into believing he had been brought to this point under armed escort.

"Why have they brought you here, my lady?" Harken asked sensibly.

"I am a gift," Wyl said, taking some grim amusement from the irony of his words. "For your king."

The aspiring Captain looked appropriately baffled as well as rattled. "I don't understand."

"You are not meant to. Your sovereign will and you will raise his ire if I am not taken to him immediately. I have no intention of trying to escape," Wyl added, glancing toward the rope that had appeared in one anxious pair of hands. "All you're required to do is escort me into Tenterdyn, gentlemen. Restraint will not be necessary."

"Put that away," Harken snapped at the lad, who was not much younger than he. "You do know who this is, don't you?" he added, more angry with himself, Wyl suspected, than with the youngster. "Lady Ylena! She is to be treated with respect."

"Thank you, Harken. I'm sure my brother would be proud of you."

"I never met him, my lady. He passed away the very week I entered the Legion. But your family's name means everything to me. All I ever wanted to do was join the Legion and be commanded by General Thirsk."

"Are you Laud Harken's son?" Wyl asked in surprise.

"Yes, my lady. I am surprised you know of him."

Wyl realized his error. "My brother spoke well of Laud Harken. How is he?"

"Dead, my lady. He fell in the north recently."

"How?"

Harken shrugged, embarrassed by the sorrowful tremor in his voice. "I was told it was a Mountain warrior's arrow, but, my lady, he was outraged by the Rittylworth scandal and no doubt said too much, too loudly."

Murmurings erupted within his group, reassuring Wyl that the name of Thirsk still resonated loudly within the Legion. He was counting on this very fact to help Crys to stir up trouble in Pearlis.

"I understand, Harken, and I am deeply sorry for your loss. Now you must take me to Tenterdyn."

The company remained on patrol while the young Captain-to-be provided the escort alone. This pleased Wyl, for it gave him a chance to learn as much as he could from the gullible youngster. They traveled in silence for a while before Wyl began to ease out some information.

"I imagine the missive from Briavel has arrived by now?"

Harken frowned. "I'm sorry, my lady, I'm not sure what you speak of."

Wyl felt disappointment slice him. "Apparently there was a courier coming from Queen Valentyna about my arrival."

Harken shook his head. "We can find out. I will make some inquiries as soon as we arrive."

"Who is your general now?" Wyl asked. He could see Tenterdyn sprawling in the distance. They would be there soon.

"The King is our general, my lady."

Celimus had finally gotten his wish and taken over the Legion.

"I see. And I hear he is expecting a parley with the Mountain King?"

"Yes—today. King Cailech arrives by midday."

"You sound excited, Harken."

"I am, my lady. If our king marries Queen Valentyna and this parley achieves a truce between Morgravia and the Razor Kingdom, there will be peace at long last."

Wyl made Ylena smile. "I thought most young men of your age dreamed of going to war?"

"I am engaged to be married, my lady. I dream of Alys more than I do killing for my realm." He returned her smile with a shy one of his own.

"Good for you. It is a worthy dream. So you trust your king to achieve these two coups?"

Harken smiled ruefully. "If anyone can, King Celimus can." Wyl suspected that Harken, young as he was, would not be drawn into saying anything openly traitorous, although his tone suggested he felt it.

"Peace for the region would be a rare achievement."

"Is the Queen as beautiful as everyone says she is?" Harken asked suddenly.

Wyl nodded. "More exquisite than you can possibly imagine."

"I was told you were a beauty, my lady," Harken began, then pulled himself back. He looked stricken. "Forgive me, my lady, I meant no offense."

"None taken. I imagine I look a real fright, dressed like a man and having ridden for days," Wyl admitted. "It is not easy to feel pretty in this situation."

"I'm sorry, Lady Ylena, that was tactless of me. Do you mind my asking why you are presenting yourself to the King? There was a rumor that . . ." He struggled to say more.

"That he tried to kill me?" Wyl finished. The young man nodded. "It is true, Harken. Your king is not a good man, I'm sorry to say, and I think you know it. You suspect your father's death was not as cut-and-dried as it was painted to be, and you are most likely right. If Laud stood up to the King's treachery at Rittylworth, then he would have paid in the most dramatic way. I am truly sorry for your family."

Harken's eyes were wide, the first hints of fear creeping across his innocent face. They were just a few yards from the compound of Tenterdyn now. Wyl spoke quickly. "Listen to me. I am here to frighten the King, but not to prevent peace. I hope the King's marriage to the Queen of Briavel will herald the beginning of the great union of our two realms, and that he will forge a peace with King Cailech, but

Celimus is not a man ever to be trusted. Remember that, Harken."

The young man heard the desperation in his companion's voice. "I don't want to take you in there, my lady," he said, further stricken. Both of them saw the gatekeeper stepping out.

"You must. But you must also do what your heart tells you."

"I don't understand," Harken urged.

"You will. You are Legion, used to taking orders, but one of the defining characteristics of an officer of the Legion is that he will never harm another Morgravian unless that person is a betrayer of the realm. Keep that in your heart. Do not allow Celimus to lead you and your men and the rest of the soldiers down the path of darkness. Be true to the Legion first."

"Ho, who comes?" The gatekeeper's voice ripped through the tension of their whispered conversation.

"Tell the truth," Wyl encouraged. "You cannot save me."

Harken spared an anguished glance toward the woman beside him. Wyl felt sorry for the youngster. He clearly sensed that he was involved in something deeply wrong by escorting Ylena Thirsk into Celimus's clutches.

"Come on, boy, we haven't got all day!" the soldier urged, irritated. "Who do you bring here?"

Wyl cleared his throat. "I am the Lady Ylena Thirsk, sir. I wish to speak to King Celimus."

The gatekeeper laughed. "Yes, and I'm the Lady Twinkle and plan to marry him. What is this?" he roared at Harken.

"Watch your manners!" Harken commanded, and the soldier glanced toward the badge on the youngster's uniform. This was an officer in the making and Wyl quietly smirked at the older man's error.

"This *is* the Lady Ylena Thirsk," Harken said, firm of voice now. "She has already been searched, but you may do so again if you are required."

The gatekeeper, far less chirpy now, signaled to another guard, who asked Wyl to alight from his horse. He was searched and Harken's papers were checked for authenticity.

They were permitted to enter the gate by the now slightly sheepish keeper. Another, more senior soldier arrived to ask questions and his eyebrows arched immediately at the name of the woman standing before him.

"Call the Chancellor," he said to his second. Then to Wyl, politely: "We wait, my lady."

He turned to the Legionnaire. "Thank you, Harken. We will take it from here. You may return to your men."

Wyl offered his hand to the young man. "Thank you for your escort," he said, although he hoped his gaze communicated far more. "Again, I am sorry to hear about your father," he added.

Harken looked distracted and anxious. "Sir, has a missive arrived from Briavel concerning the Lady Ylena?"

The man shook his head. "Nothing has arrived from Briavel. I am the first point of contact for all deliveries."

"Perhaps I should wait—" the young man began.

"No, Harken. A company of men without their leader stands at the Briavellian border. Return to your post," the senior man said, this time firmly enough that it brooked no further argument.

Harken bowed. When he straightened, Wyl alone saw the anger and concern in his eyes before the youngster saluted and departed the compound.

"Ah, here we are," the older soldier muttered, and Wyl turned to see Chancellor Jessom emerging from the the main house, a look of pleasure on his face. He swiftly adjusted it to a thin smile, but Wyl saw the satisfaction all the same. The Chancellor's reaction confused him. Surely astonishment, or at the very least irritation, would be more fitting, considering Jessom and Celimus must have hoped Ylena was dead by now?

Jessom's stride was confident and he covered the ground between the main dwelling and the gatehouse with surprising swiftness. "Ylena Thirsk. Almost perfect timing."

What? Wyl kept his expression deliberately blank as his mind raced to understand this new development. Jessom continued, "Our king was wondering when you would be delivered. This will be a special name-day present for him and no doubt he will reward Aremys royally for the gift of your life into his hands."

They were expecting Ylena's arrival? How could this be if no message from Valentyna had arrived—and what did he mean about Aremys? Wyl played for time. "I'm sorry. Do I know you?"

Jessom's smile thinned even further. "My apologies, we have never been introduced. I am Jessom, Chancellor and King's Counsel of Morgravia."

"Since when did King Celimus take advice from anyone?" Wyl replied as acidly as he could, watching the crease across Jessom's face, which passed for his smile, fade entirely.

"Thank you, Bern. I will take the Lady Ylena from here," Jessom said to the officer nearby. The man nodded and left their company, happy to pass on responsibility, but not before both Jessom and Wyl saw his raised eyebrows at Ylena's cutting comment. Wyl unhappily allowed Jessom to guide him away from the gates, but he noted that they were not heading toward the main house. The Morgravians must have other plans for Lady Ylena.

Jessom's voice was biting when it came. "You are in a perilous situation, Ylena Thirsk. I suggest you not make it worse on yourself," he advised.

Wyl made Ylena's beautiful face smirk. "How much worse could it possibly get, Jessom? The snake that sits upon the Morgravian throne is hardly going to show me mercy. I do not fear him."

"Nevertheless, I recommend you don't openly insult King Celimus. It could go very badly for you."

"You don't understand, Chancellor. I am not afraid of dying. I am not afraid of Celimus and his savage tortures. Any opportunity I get, sir, I will openly insult him and the bitch Queen who spawned him."

Jessom was normally in control of his emotions, but he drew back in surprise at the young woman's words. "When Aremys said he could deliver you, Ylena, I'm not sure our king understood how heroic you have become. It seems your struggles to survive have toughened you. That only means he will enjoy hurting you all the more. I am not a cruel man and I certainly do not condone the torture of women. Let me suggest again that you make this easier on yourself."

Wyl was happy he had managed to sting the man into losing his composure, even slightly. But more important to him was the second mention of his friend. *Aremys said he could deliver me? What is going on?*

"I am glad I have impressed you, Chancellor, but, frankly, that was not my intention. I will not plead for the King's mercy. He can do with me as he wishes."

"Then I wonder, what is your intention? What can you possibly gain through your defiance?"

"All will be explained, I am sure," Wyl answered cryptically. Valentyna's letter had definitely not arrived, then.

The Chancellor's face betrayed his bafflement. Wyl smirked internally. Jessom was used to knowing everything about everyone. Ylena's inexplicable behavior must be unsettling.

"The King will see you in good time," Jessom said, businesslike now. "But for the meantime, you will remain in here." They had arrived at an outbuilding: a storage hut built in the shade of a huge oak where Aleda had kept her cool pantry. "I'm afraid you have timed your arrival a little prematurely, Ylena. King Cailech is due any minute."

Wyl made a sound of disdain.

Jessom pointed to bucket of water. "May I suggest you clean yourself up. I can have a gown found for you, if it pleases."

"It does not please. I will see the King exactly as I stand before you, Chancellor. And by the way, your new status as servant to the King"—Wyl emphasized the word "servant" and was pleased to see that it struck home—"does not permit you to address a noble by anything but a correct title, sir. You will refer to me as Lady Ylena Thirsk or Lady Ylena Donal—take your pick—but you will accord me the small measure of respect I am due, prisoner or not."

The Chancellor was taken aback by the attack but composed himself smoothly and was quick to retaliate.

"Morgravia has forgotten you, young lady, and your family's name is being dragged through the mire at every opportunity. Climb off your pedestal, Ylena. I am not intimidated by your noble line. I'm wondering how long they will respect you when your head is rotting on a spike outside Pearlis. In fact, I'll do you a kindness—I'll hunt down Alyd Donal's head for you so you can both rot together. Romantic, eh?" he said, uncharacteristically cruel, as he finished tying her ankle to a huge timber post in the hut. "Now clean yourself up, woman, and make ready to meet your sovereign."

For the first time in his life Wyl spat at someone. It was the only comeback he could think of to show his hatred for this servile creature of the King's. He half hoped Jessom would kill him in a blood rush of anger. The Chancellor's body would accord him serious power.

But Jessom was not a man of violence; he was far more subtle in his methods. Instead he made a clicking sound of reproach, as a parent might do to a naughty child. "And you want to be treated like a lady?" He laughed; the sound was harsh and filled with hate. "I have been spat on all my life, Ylena," he said, wiping her spittle from his robe, "and I have always beaten my enemies."

He turned at the sound of the bell from the gatehouse, signaling that King Cailech's party had arrived.

"Farewell, Ylena. We shall summon you in due course."

15

FYNCH AND KNAVE STOOD AT THE FOOT OF THE RAZORS, about to step onto the tiny, unguarded track that would guide their ascent into the mountains. They had seen no soldiers and their journey from the Wild had been uneventful, and enjoyable for Fynch, who had needed time to think. Knave was not a companion who made conversation—he replied to questions, and prompted them if he considered them important, but otherwise he was silent.

"Why are we walking? Surely the Thicket could send us?" Fynch wondered.

You can send us, Knave said, a rare tone of amusement in his voice. *Too dangerous, though. We cannot take the chance of Rashlyn sensing a powerful spelling. Sending Aremys might have registered with him, but he would not have known what the magic was and we can only hope he dismissed it. However, since then we have had the transfer of Wyl to Briavel, the death of Elysius, the arrival of the Dragon King, and you coming into your power. So many surges of magic are not easily dismissed.*

Fynch nodded seriously. "Do you think he knows Elysius has died?"

I suspect he might have felt something. More important, I am wary that he would have felt the transference of power.

"How would he sense it? Would it be like a pain?"

The dog led them onto the narrow track. Neither of them looked behind, even though they were now officially leaving Briavel.

Possibly. More likely he would feel it as you might a seizure. Not pain so much, but loss of physical control and perhaps consciousness. It would bewilder more than hurt.

"But would he know what it was?" Fynch persisted as he pushed aside the branches of overhanging trees.

Who knows, Fynch? It would shock him to learn that his brother has been alive all this time, if indeed he did work out that the disturbance was Elysius dying, but I can't imagine he could begin to consider that his sibling's magic had been passed on.

"You are guessing, though."

Of course. But remember, your sensitivity to magic and your ability to embrace it and use it are known only to those of the Thicket. Rashlyn may be a sorcerer, but he is not sensitive to the natural world.

The track rose sharply ahead of them and they began to climb in silence, Fynch concentrating on the challenging, slightly slippery surface of decaying leaves. Many hours later they reached a plateau of rock, the trees below them now. It was cold in the open and a breeze had whipped up. Fynch shivered through his breathlessness. He did not like the cold; he felt it before most others because of his thinly fleshed body and he was glad of the thick fleece jacket Knave had found in Elysius's home and insisted he carry.

We must be wary, now that we have no cover for a while, Knave cautioned.

Fynch squatted on his haunches to take some deep breaths and rest for a few moments. He put on the jacket, relishing its instant warmth, then took a sip from his water skin.

"Are you hungry, Knave?" he asked, wondering if the dog should be allowed to hunt.

I don't need food, Fynch. I ate with Wyl to maintain a pretense of normality.

"No food at all?" Fynch was incredulous.

None. I am of the Thicket.

"You are real, though, aren't you, Knave?" There was a plaintiveness in the boy's voice.

Real enough; fret not.

Fynch sighed and confessed, "I rarely feel hungry either. I eat because I know I should, never because I want to."

That is because of who you are, what you belong to. The powers you have.

"How can that be? I didn't possess magic until the day Elysius died."

Fynch, you have always had the capacity to wield a certain magic. You just didn't know it until now.

Fynch shook his head, too distracted and surprised by Knave's assured claim to argue the matter. He took another draft of water to calm himself. "How long will it take us to get to the fortress?" he finally asked, wiping his mouth with his sleeve.

Yes, the fortress. I've been thinking about that, the dog replied. *It occurs to me that if we do our resting by afternoon, we might cover more ground at night.*

"Using magic, you mean?"

The dog did not answer immediately. Instead, he sniffed

the air and Fynch kept the silence, knowing Knave was pondering the most difficult of decisions.

Yes, the dog said at last. *I am hoping that if Rashlyn follows a normal pattern, he may not sense small bursts of power as he sleeps. In truth I don't believe he will know what it is even if he does feel it, but I have been reluctant to take any chances.*

"But you've changed your mind now?"

Knave's voice was gentle. *I think I overlooked how slight you are, Fynch. I don't believe we will be able to cover as much ground as I had hoped. It is a long way from Briavel's side of the Razors to Cailech's fortress on their western rim—I realize now it would take us too long. We shall have to take the risk.* He said the last few words with regret.

"But keep the distances small," Fynch added with trepidation.

The dog's dark eyes regarded him sorrowfully. *I am sorry to ask it of you. You will need to chew on the sharvan leaves regularly now.*

"Don't be sorry, it's my burden," Fynch replied, wishing he felt more brave than he sounded. He attempted a brighter tone. "This is how we traveled before, isn't it . . . from Baelup to the Thicket?"

Except then I had to rely on the Thicket and Elysius. This time we travel with all the power we need.

"Are you sure?" Fynch had no idea how he was supposed to effect such a magic. He had thought that after the transfer from Elysius he would feel a reservoir of power gurgling within, a well of magic at his beck and call. But he could detect no change within himself. He mentioned this to his friend.

Knave considered the question. Again Fynch waited patiently. The dog sighed. *It is different for me. I am of the Thicket, therefore I rely on it to feed me its magic when it needs to use me, and I feel an energy buzzing within. Anyone touched by the Thicket would feel it, I'm sure. I imagine Wyl might sense it echoing within him somehow and Aremys too. They have both been touched by the magic of the Thicket.*

"Then why not me?"

I think, Fynch, because you are more than us, the dog said gravely.

"More than you?" the boy repeated, not understanding.

Knave tried again. *I belong to the Thicket. Wyl, Aremys—and others, no doubt—have been touched by it, not empowered by it but affected somehow. But Elysius, and now you, are connected to it in ways I can't explain. We have no magic without the Thicket to feed it. You do.*

"Oh," Fynch replied, still feeling baffled.

But I think, my friend, there is far more to you.

"What do you mean?" Fynch frowned.

Knave gave a low growl of frustration, as if he could not put into words what he was trying to say. *It's as if you and the Thicket are one. While Elysius was merely passing through—for want of a better way of describing it—you belong to the Thicket and it to you. And the King of the Creatures never visited Elysius. I have never seen him before—most of us haven't.*

The gravity of Knave's explanation hit Fynch like a blow. The words and their intent terrified him. There was a finality to what Knave was suggesting; it was as if the Thicket had a hold on him that he would never escape. He did not want to think about it any further. Neither was he ready to consider the implication of the Dragon King's visit. That knowing in his eyes—it was all too bewildering and frightening.

"So what is your plan again?" he said, deliberately forcing the fear away by changing the topic.

Knave must have sensed Fynch's terror, for he switched smoothly from their previous discussion. *We travel on foot by day, then sleep from late afternoon for as long as you wish. We cannot travel by sending until the early hours of the morning, by which time I'm counting on Rashlyn being asleep.*

"But what if he's not?"

Knave shook his head in a doglike shrug. *If he can sense your magic, there's not much we can do about that. We will keep the sendings short so he never feels it quite long enough to tease at it. He cannot see you, Fynch. Not even with his own magic.*

"But he might feel me coming, is that what you mean?"

Perhaps; I don't know. But he won't know who or what it is, I believe.

"All right," Fynch said, giving up the train of conversation. To be honest, he had never been one for farseeing plans. He had taken each day as it presented itself and enjoyed all that life gave him during those days. He had been a sunny child and his mother had said often enough that he was destined for something special. He thought of his mother now. She had often disappeared for days, but she would always return, and when she did, she would be withdrawn, a little moody. One evening, returning late from his toil at Stoneheart, Fynch had overheard his parents arguing. His father had called his mother a slut. Fynch did not know what the word meant, but the vehemence behind it had shocked him. His mother had laughed in her tinkling manner and given some retort which had enraged his father further. A year or so later Fynch had learned the meaning of the insult and asked his sister about it. She had looked embarrassed and even pained by his query, but was a truthful person like her brother, so she had explained to him that their mother was a free spirit. "A sort of madness overcomes her," he remembered his sister saying.

"And what happens?" Fynch had asked, not really comprehending.

"Well, it takes her away from us," his sister had replied gently, ruffling his hair. "Sometimes she needs space and freedom."

Fynch was a child who needed clarity in all things and so he persisted. "What does she do when she goes away?"

He recalled now how his sister had sighed. "She allows men to take her, Fynch. It means nothing. Dad says it is a madness and best we leave it like that."

The little boy had finally understood. He knew his mother was fey—she saw things in her dreams and heard voices whispering to her. Most of the folk around their way thought she was bordering on insane, but in truth he could not imagine his mother any other way. He loved her just as she was, with all her curious ways, and although deeply troubled to hear of this new side of her life, he said no more about it. But he thought on it, wondering which men had taken their pleasures with his mother. She was pretty, there was no doubting it, with her petite frame and elfin looks. And when she let her golden hair down, and bathed and put on a fresh dress, she still took his father's breath away. He loved her so, which made her inclinations all the more hurtful. His father would drink himself into a stupor each time she disappeared, no doubt hoping the liquor would take away the grief.

Soon after learning his mother's secret, Fynch had become troubled by thoughts that perhaps he had not been sired by his father. Fynch did not resemble any of his siblings closely—they were all dark and solid like his father, while he was fair, golden in fact, with the same elfin qualities as his mother. Though he had worked hard at convincing himself that he simply took after his mother, the thought still troubled him. He had never shared this anxiety with anyone. Well, not with any person. The Dragon King had seen it in him, though—Fynch was sure of it. The dragon's eyes had flared as they penetrated the boy's soul—had seen the truth of Fynch's secret fear.

As he climbed farther into the Razors, Fynch thought about what the King of the Creatures had asked of him. Perhaps, in his heart, he had always known that his life would be brief and so had given his energy to enjoying the moment he lived in. So be it. He was not scared of dying anymore, but he would make his death count. As much as the Dragon King saw destroying Rashlyn as his priority, Fynch knew that his own loyalty lay with Wyl. Somehow he had to help Wyl defeat Celimus. It was why he had risked more headaches in sending Wyl to Werryl. And, against Knave's counsel, he had sent Valentyna the chaffinch to whistle a tune he hoped would prompt her to wait for Ylena. He had even risked more pain to send dream thoughts to Wyl, urging him to face Celimus and to die again, if necessary.

Fynch was utterly committed to the cause of ridding Morgravia of its present king while also protecting Valentyna and

Wyl. Deep down he believed Valentyna would have to marry Celimus—she could not both prevent such a union and secure peace for her realm. He wondered whether she could survive such a marriage, for he knew the cruelty of Celimus. But far worse was his deeply held belief that Wyl would fail in his bid to become Celimus. When he tried to interpret this chilling thought, the only explanation he could come up with for his fear was that Wyl hated Celimus so much he would never be able to live with himself in that guise. If Wyl could not achieve the end of the Quickening by becoming Celimus, however, it could mean an infinite lifetime of changing bodies. Or perhaps the opposite, he reasoned. Perhaps Wyl would die in the body of some lonely guard, an arrow through his back. Fynch grasped—perhaps more than Wyl did—that in any of his guises Wyl could be killed through an accident or natural causes. The Quickening, as Fynch intuitively understood it, only worked if the killer was still connected to Wyl via a weapon or touch, which was why Myrren could not have used the magic to save herself. She had died at the stake; the flames had taken her life.

Knave interrupted his thoughts. *We had best keep moving. We are too exposed here.*

Fynch stood, adjusted the sack across his shoulder, and buttoning his fleece, followed the dog.

What were you thinking about? Knave asked.

Fynch was surprised. The dog rarely asked questions on such a conversational level. "Myrren," he replied.

Oh?

"She must have known that the Quickening could not save her, that she would be consumed by the flames. So she took revenge instead. If only she hadn't," he finished, more bitterly than he had intended.

It wouldn't have changed Wyl's fate, Knave said softly. *Celimus would still have sent him on the journey of treachery into Briavel. Wyl would have died by Romen's sword; Ylena would have wasted away in the dungeon; and Gueryn would have died in the Razors.*

Fynch nodded wearily. "Yes, you're right."

I don't approve of what Myrren and Elysius did, Fynch,

but Wyl's life was forfeit from the moment Celimus took the throne. It might be worth your looking upon the Quickening as a gift rather than a curse.

Fynch rubbed Knave's great head to acknowledge the kindness in the dog's voice. No one could approve of the Quickening, but perhaps some good might yet come of it. He thought about the zerkon that could so easily have killed Wyl in the Razors. If the beast had succeeded, that would have been the end for Wyl, for Elysius had told him the magic worked only between humans. They had a lot to thank Lothryn for, if he still lived. The fate of a kingdom had shifted on that one man's bravery.

Fynch was not aware that he had voiced this thought aloud in his mind. It was only when the dog responded that he realized he needed to learn how to control his new abilities more thoroughly.

Fynch, do you not realize yet that the destiny of all three realms rests with you? the dog said. *It is your actions—not Lothryn's or Cailech's, not those of Celimus or Valentyna, not even what Wyl might achieve—that will save the land. You will decide the destiny.*

Tears rolled helplessly down the small boy's face. *I am the sacrifice,* he thought privately, hauling himself up another small ledge. *So be it.*

16

ASHLYN AWOKE FROM HIS STUPOR, ANGRY AT FEELING HANDS at his brow, wiping away the sweat of his ragings. He swung at the person tending him, hitting her in the face and drawing blood at her mouth. "Begone, woman!" he roared, searching his wits to identify his location. He was in a strange chamber; it was dark outside.

"Wait!" he called to the woman, who had turned her back on him.

She looked at him then, a line of red trailing from the corner of her lip to beneath her chin. Rashlyn could see the hate in her eyes and dismissed it, used to such a reaction.

"Where am I?" he demanded. "Why am I not in my own chambers?"

"The King said we were to watch over you here until you fully recovered," the woman replied sullenly, touching her mouth and bringing away bloodstained fingers. "He said you would not like anyone in your rooms."

He ignored her injury. "How long have I been here?"

"Two days."

That shocked him. "Where is the King?"

"Gone." She spoke the word as a threat. "He left with the Grenadyne the night of your seizure."

She called to someone and a man entered the chamber. He took one look at the woman and glanced darkly toward Rashlyn.

"I suspect I am no longer welcome," Rashlyn said to the man, hoping to unnerve him.

"You have never been welcome, barshi," the Mountain Man replied, not at all intimidated. "We permitted you in our house only because our king asked it. My wife has taken good care of you."

"And I regret my odd form of thanks, Rollo," Rashlyn answered, recognizing the pair now. She was a midwife, a capable nurse, and the husband, Rollo, was a senior and trusted warrior of Cailech's. It would not be wise to insult them further.

"My apology, Kaylan," he said, getting slowly to his feet. The dizziness was still there. "I must have been dreaming. I am sorry for your wound."

"Leave, scum," Rollo growled.

Rashlyn was not surprised. Without Cailech around, the people of the mountains did not maintain the deference they attempted to show him in the King's presence.

"Be careful, Rollo. I understand your daughter is with child. We wouldn't want anything untoward to occur to the infant, now, would we?" Rashlyn said conversationally as he pushed by the couple.

The man roared, lunging toward the barshi, but his wife held him back. "Don't, Rollo. Who knows what he is capable of," she said, terrified now, her bleeding lip forgotten, her pride tattered as her pleading eyes beseeched Rashlyn to leave the family be.

That's better, Rashlyn thought, smirking at the cowed Rollo, pleased by the fear in Kaylan's tone. One day he would make them all pay for their disdain. He left the stuffy dwelling and gulped deeply the fresh air of the mountain night. Limping across to the nearby well, he drank two long refreshing cups of the clear water. It revived him sufficiently that he could make his way, without staggering, to his lonely chambers.

Once inside, he bolted the doors, double-checking the locks. Only then did he begin to relax; only then, in the safety of his isolation, did he permit himself to release his fright at losing two full days of his life. What had happened? He was aware that his periods of darkness, when he spiraled into his other self, were extending, but had no idea they could stretch so long. Until now, the longest he had lost himself to such madness was half a day, and that had frightened him enough. But two days! Usually during these black periods he functioned reasonably well, but it was as though he was someone else. Rashlyn did not dislike that other self; at such times he was confident, flamboyant, certainly creative. His mind was at its most sharp and great innovations often came to him. He felt invincible in this state. No drug he knew of could induce such a constant euphoric sense of power. But when he was able to think clearly, Rashlyn understood that the euphoric moods were dangerous too. During these times he was unpredictable, capable of anything. The surge of power forced him to relinquish control over his actions. It was a madness, he knew. It had been creeping up on him for years. His brother had seen it in him first and his father not long after. Curse their souls!

And yet this time it did not feel quite the same. His body was still trembling from the seizure. Normally he would emerge out of the darkness, realize he had lost himself, and discover what had occurred in his "absence"—there was no better way to describe it. But this occasion was different. It sounded as though he had simply collapsed. Cailech must have seen him in a considerably weakened state to have ordered his care. Who else had seen him, apart from the King and the two who cared for him? Where had he been when the seizure overcame him?

Rashlyn was famished but ignored the growling plea of his belly. Using a spell to summon a flame, he lit a fire and brought some water to boil. He added verrun bark and a handful of arkad petals and tried not to think about anything but the brewing and cooling of the infusion. As soon as he tasted the first bitter sip of the brew, he felt his mind begin to clear.

He sat at the window, inhaled deeply of the numbing air, which also helped to freshen his thoughts, and continued sipping. The tea began to work; the blurriness cleared and he was able to move backward through the past days.

It came to him. He had been riding with the Grenadyne and Myrt. His suspicions about the stranger had not lessened for knowing him; Rashlyn was convinced there was a mystery attached to the foreign mercenary. If he could make physical contact with the man, he was sure he could find out more. It had unnerved Rashlyn to hear from the King that Farrow had reacted strongly when he had stroked Galapek. Clearly he had felt the magic in the stallion, which could only mean the mercenary owned power himself or had been touched by it somehow. Cailech had wanted to dismiss the incident, but Rashlyn was not convinced such a reaction could be passed off as coincidence. And so the King had agreed to force Farrow into riding Galapek with the proviso that Rashlyn accompany him to observe him.

The barshi recalled now how the mercenary had not reacted in the manner described by the King on his first meeting with the enchanted horse. Either the Grenadyne had wrestled his emotions back under his control, or the King had been mistaken and the man's claim of being fatigued from his adventure in the mountains was true. And yet Rashlyn was sure Farrow was hiding something. The stranger seemed too confident, too aware that he was being tested. He had parried Rashlyn's questions smoothly and then, just when Rashlyn had gotten close enough to touch him . . . something had touched Rashlyn instead.

The barshi closed his eyes and took himself back to the moment. The shrieking of the horse had echoed his own instinctive reaction to the immense pressure he had felt throughout his body. There had been no pain, but the experience had been followed by intense nausea . . . then darkness. The woman, Kaylan, had called it a seizure, so presumably he had thrashed about in his unconscious state.

"It was not my madness that caused this," he murmured. "So what did?"

"Magic," he answered himself, and laughed briefly. "Powerful magic," he whispered, remembering it more clearly now.

Galapek had felt it and had screamed. The barshi wondered if the horse had experienced a similar weakness. But there was more to the strange event than his physical reaction . . . there was also a sense of dread. The ominous notion that something was coming toward him was strong indeed. For the first time in a long time Rashlyn felt very fearful.

Elspyth had decided to slip away from Werryl Palace when everyone's attention was diverted toward Brackstead and Lady Donal. She felt bad about leaving without a farewell to both Crys and the Queen. Valentyna had welcomed them warmly when they were in need, had sheltered and protected them without hesitation. Elspyth's secret departure would surely be considered a slight and this bothered the woman of Yentro. But she wanted to leave with no fuss, no teary farewells, and definitely no one trying to talk her out of it—which the Queen most certainly would attempt. It seemed right to go quietly, taking nothing, not even the horse she had ridden into Briavel.

What she regretted most was the seemingly sly departure, which might be construed the wrong way, and not leaving a note for Wyl. She owed him that much. Why could she not have taken a few extra minutes and scribbled a second note for the Lady Ylena Thirsk? Elspyth was sure Wyl would find his way to Werryl, and she could have given him an assurance she would not do anything rash, along with a promise of her return. But her head had been filled with Lothryn and seizing her chance to leave without creating a commotion. She knew Liryk would be glad to see the back of her; his and Krell's surreptitious glances and grimaces had left her in no doubt of their displeasure at her presence. She knew they did not appreciate her speaking her mind about Celimus. There were moments Elspyth had been sure either one of them would have gladly silenced her with something more painful than stares.

So, as soon as she saw the royal party depart across Werryl Bridge, she grabbed her small sack of goods and fled via a small, barely known courtyard gate which Valentyna had admitted making good use of as a child. She stepped out of the palace grounds and walked through the town of Werryl rather than across its beautiful bridge. The main township was walled and Elspyth intended to make her escape by blending in easily with the traffic that drifted into and out of Werryl daily through its most northern gate. She felt confident she would find someone to hitch a ride with into Crowyll, and perhaps from there she could buy a nag and use four legs instead of two to get to Banktown in the far north, before turning west and crossing the border into Felrawthy.

It was the brewery driver's child who spotted her first. The cart rolled level with Elspyth as the big horse's ponderous tread caught up with the slow-moving crowd passing through the gate. The guards did not seem to be paying close attention to those leaving town and Elspyth was confident she was unlikely to be stopped or questioned. It wasn't as if anyone would be looking out for her at this early stage of her journey. Nevertheless, her previous adventures had taught her to take precautions. She needed an innocent cover—just like this family here, she thought, eyeing the little girl, who smiled tentatively.

"Where are you going?" the child asked.

Elspyth smiled brightly. "I'm going north," she replied.

"And what will you do when you get there?" the child said.

"Well, I'm going home actually," Elspyth lied, and cast a gentle rescue-me expression toward the driver, who shrugged his apology for the youngster's inquisition.

"Do you have a family?"

"No," Elspyth said, surprised at the question. "I have no one in my life who worries about me, but north is where I come from and where I feel comfortable."

"The north of Briavel?"

"The north of Morgravia," she said theatrically.

"And where's that?"

Elspyth laughed. "A long way away. I come from a town called Yentro."

"And you have to walk all that long way?" the little girl exclaimed.

"Hush, Jen. Let the lady be," the man said, embarrassed. "I'm sorry, miss," he added, looking at Elspyth shyly. "She gets bored easily on these trips and we've hardly begun."

"It's all right, really," she replied, making a swift decision. This was her ride. She looked toward the girl again. "I once knew a pretty lady called Jen and she had beautiful red hair like yours." It was a lie, but Elspyth needed any leverage she could create and quickly.

Jen's eyes grew wide with pleasure. "Am I pretty?"

"I think you are. I'm sure your father does too."

"Would you like to ride next to me?" Jen asked.

Elspyth swallowed her delight. It was the invitation she had hoped for. She looked deliberately toward the man. "Oh, I don't think your father would . . ."

He reacted precisely as she had intended. "You're most welcome to ride with us, miss," he offered kindly. "We're going as far as Coneham, if that helps?"

"Oh, I'm sure it will." She smiled. "Where is that, exactly?"

"North of Brackstead. Hop up."

Elspyth climbed into the back of the cart, near the little girl. "Thank you," she said, with relief. "Will we be stopping in Brackstead?" she added as innocently as she could, not liking the idea of running into Valentyna and Crys.

"No. We don't stay in inns or the like, miss," the driver said. "We just curl up in the back. We carry everything with us."

Elspyth smiled. It was perfect. "That sounds wonderful. I'm sure I can help to keep your Jen amused on our journey."

"My name is Ericson," the man said, an expression of gratitude sweeping across his tired face. Elspyth felt a tiny pang of guilt at how adroitly she had manipulated the kind fellow.

The cart rumbled through the northern gate, Jen chattering incessantly about anything that came into her head and Elspyth doing her best to agree where necessary and answer when required. She pulled her blue cloak more tightly around herself, for the morning was chill. As they passed the soldiers at the gate, she tried not to catch anyone's eye, but she had never quite grasped how attractive she was and her dark hair and pert features could not help but win attention.

"Shar guide you," the guard said to her. It was a common blessing used by Morgravians and Briavellians alike to bid others a good journey, but it was the wink that came with it that made her grin. "Don't stay away too long, now," the guard added, encouraged by her smile. "I won't sleep until I see your pretty face again."

Elspyth made a gesture of admonishment, as if to say it was improper of him to talk like that in front of her family, but the cart had already rolled on and the young man missed her mock annoyance.

It had been a long time since Elspyth had felt as lighthearted as she did at that moment. *I'm coming, Lothryn,* she silently cast. She hoped Shar would take pity on her and she might soon be reunited with her beloved.

As Elspyth was privately celebrating her escape, Gueryn was arguing with Rashlyn, who, now recovered, had decided to visit the prisoner.

"Who would it hurt?" Gueryn demanded.

"No one, but I don't understand your request," the barshi said.

"Because I am rotting here."

"Why is that my problem?"

"Because you're meant to take care of me," Gueryn said, his tone as acid as he could make it. "Either you make it possible or, I promise you, Rashlyn, I'll find a way to kill myself, even if it means banging my head against this wall until I knock my senses clean out!"

Gueryn knew he sounded desperate; he could hear as much in his tone, and he also knew it was highly unlikely he could fashion any genuinely expedient method to cause his own death. Still, he had made the threat and the barshi looked thoughtful. Gueryn decided to press his luck. "The King insisted that I be looked after. I refuse to sit here day after day in your stinking dungeon."

"Isn't that what prisoners do?"

The man's light voice irritated Gueryn further. "Let me work, damn it! I'll provide an honest day's toil for the chance to breathe fresh air and work my muscles. You can keep me chained if you must."

"Oh, I will," Rashlyn murmured.

Gueryn felt himself losing his temper; the only thing that stopped him reaching for the barshi's throat was the memory of the magic Rashlyn had once used on him.

He tried again, a little more humility in his tone. "The King agreed to allow me daily walks so I can remain as healthy as possible considering my situation. I am prepared to work for them, for Shar's sake."

"Where?"

That took Gueryn by surprise. He stopped his pacing and turned on the healer. "Where what?"

"Where would you work?"

Gueryn knew he had to negotiate carefully now. He forced himself to keep the exasperation in his voice, as if the chance to escape the loneliness and despair of the dungeon were all that mattered. No one, especially Rashlyn, must guess his true intent. "Where? Anywhere! The kitchens, the vineyards, the stables . . ." He ran an unsteady hand through his tangled graying hair to give himself an air of distraction.

"Your preference?"

"Does it matter?" he retaliated, wondering whether Rashlyn was testing him. "I'm good with horses; I'm not afraid to work in an open field; and if you want me scrubbing pans, I'll happily do that. Why don't you choose?"

"The kitchens would not want you, Morgravian," Rashlyn mused. "And I don't want you around knives or any potential weapons." He scratched at his wild beard and something fell out of it. Disheveled as Gueryn himself looked and as dirty as he felt, Rashlyn's grubbiness revolted him.

"Then let me work in the stables," he said. "I'll muck out, rub down, water, exercise the animals—whatever the stablemaster wants."

Rashlyn stared at him. The eyes were tiny and dark; no evidence of warmth flickered in that cold gaze. "I shall speak to Maegryn," he said, after a long pause. "Remember my lesson, soldier. With the King gone, you have no protection to count on, other than what my rule deems fit."

"I had no idea you hailed from royal blood," Gueryn risked.

"Be very careful, le Gant," the dark man warned, his lips twisted in a cruel sneer beneath the filthy beard.

Gueryn emerged into a sharply bright spring morning, his eyes stinging from the sunlight but his body rejoicing in its warm caress and the chance to breathe the opposite of the stale mustiness of his cell. He stood between two guards, neither of whom he knew, and watched a man approach. Rashlyn was nowhere to be seen.

"I'm Maegryn, the stablemaster," the man said, coming to a halt.

Gueryn nodded. "Thank you for allowing me to work in the stables. I'll not let you down."

Maegryn made a low sound of disdain. "You wouldn't want to, soldier. Come with me."

Gueryn followed as fast as the rope binding his ankles would allow.

"You're not going to make him wear that all day, are you?" Maegryn complained to the guards.

"Rashlyn's orders," one said, shrugging.

"And who is he to be giving orders?" Maegryn said, adding under his breath, "Haldor spare me."

Gueryn took a chance. "He told me he is the King's voice when his highness is not here," he said to Maegryn, who was now slicing through the rope with a blade.

The stablemaster stood, his deep-set eyes giving away little of the man inside. "And I'm the fucking King of the Stables, so Rashlyn had better look out when he gives orders in my domain."

The guards laughed.

Gueryn bowed. "Your highness," he said, and knew he had made a fragile conquest when Maegryn grinned in response. "Thank you," Gueryn added, looking toward his unshackled feet.

"Don't get too excited, soldier. Jos here will be hanging around to keep an eye on you."

Gueryn eyed the huge, lumbering lad beside him. "Nice to meet you, Jos."

The big guard nodded, a sloping grin pulling at his deformed mouth. "Don't give me trouble now," he warned, the words slightly mangled.

"You have my promise," Gueryn assured, looking toward Maegryn too.

"But is it worth anything?" the stablemaster teased.

"As an officer of the Legion, most certainly."

"I wish your king showed similar manners."

"My king is a ruthless, lying, cowardly murderer."

Maegryn gave a low whistle. "Well, I hope our king watches his back, then."

"What do you mean?"

"I gather our people are about to make a peace alliance with your people, soldier."

"What?" Gueryn's eyes narrowed; surely this was a jest.

"If our Cailech has his way, then the Razor Kingdom and Morgravia are soon to be allies," Maegryn clarified.

Gueryn was shocked. "Celimus cannot be trusted."

Maegryn shrugged. "So long as you can, le Gant. I'm only King of the Stables, remember? What happens for the greater good of our realm is not something I have any control over. Now, I think you need exercise as much as my horses do—follow me."

Jos stayed with Gueryn all afternoon and the Morgravian noted that Jos followed his orders dutifully, taking his responsibility of watching over his prisoner seriously. The deformity was a pity—it gave the impression that Jos was a dullard when he was anything but. It also gave the other guards reason to tease him, as Gueryn learned from the lad's shy admission. He found the youngster pleasant, courteous, and charming. Jos laughed at Gueryn's small jests and even made a few of his own. Gueryn made a promise to himself to make a special effort with Jos. Confidence was all the lad needed. The harelip would fade to invisible if Jos's personality were allowed to shine through.

Gueryn had to admit he was enjoying himself after so many weeks of despair. He had walked, rubbed down, and watered six horses now and was pleased with himself, despite the twinge from aching muscles and tired limbs. He had not counted on being as weak as he felt.

"A good afternoon's work, soldier," Maegryn said, offering him a linen rag. "That's good honest sweat there."

"Call me Gueryn," the soldier offered. When the man nodded, he added, "Can I come again?"

"Tomorrow's fine. I'll be glad to see you. Perhaps Jos can bring you this time."

"What about Rashlyn? Will you speak with him?"

"The man's insane. No one follows his rules. We won't say anything—he probably won't even come looking."

Gueryn's relief showed. "Until tomorrow, then."

He nodded at Jos to let the guard know he was ready to be returned to the dungeon and gave him a grin. He was building tenuous friendships here, and was a big step closer to Galapek. That made the aches all the more satisfying. Tomorrow he might see the horse the stranger, Aremys, had claimed was Lothryn. It still seemed too incredible to contemplate, but Gueryn could not forget the touch of Rashlyn's evil magic on his own body or the murder of a woman made to look like Elspyth. There was no knowing the limits of Rashlyn's power.

Until tomorrow, then, he said privately as he fell into step with Jos.

17

RYS ADMIRED THE WAY THE BRIAVELLIAN COMMANDER, DEspite his busy duties, offered his help. If Liryk minded, he did not show it.

"Forgive me for dragging you away from important affairs, Commander Liryk," Crys said. "I'm just a little worried about Elspyth, as is your queen."

"And rightly so, your grace," Liryk said sharply. "She is a young woman abroad alone. No matter how I tighten the net around bandits and cutthroats, they still exist, and she makes the softest of targets."

"Too true. Where should we start?"

"Let's find out who was on duty first during our absence in Brackstead."

"How many gates are there?"

"Five main ones, but as you rightly point out, she was leaving as anonymously as possible, so I imagine she would have used the busiest outlets—Werryl Bridge or the northern gate."

It took them an hour to find and question the relevant men, drawing a blank until one young man was hurried back from a meal. He wiped his mouth in haste, concern on his face. His superior introduced him. "This is Peet. He was one of three guards on the northern gate for the morning watch."

Liryk and Crys had already questioned the other two from the morning and all from the afternoon rotation. Crys was sure this man would offer no further insight and had resigned himself to a fruitless search following a trail that was already stone cold.

"Sir," Peet said to his commander, nervously nodding at Crys. "My lord."

Liryk cleared his throat. "Relax, man, you're not in any trouble here. We're seeking your help."

"Oh?" the guard replied, none of the anxiety leaving his tone or expression.

"We're hoping you might remember a young woman who left Werryl yesterday. We think she might have departed via the northern gate and we're pretty certain it would have been on your watch, the early-morning guard."

Peet nodded, relieved, looking between both men. "I'll try, sir. Can you describe her?"

Liryk looked at Crys, who obliged. "Well, she's petite. She has dark hair and is comely. Very pretty, in fact." He grinned at the young man. "She stands about yea high to me"—he measured a point halfway between his elbow and shoulder—"and I'm guessing now but I think she might have been wearing a soft brown skirt, pinkish sort of blouse, black boots. I really can't be sure, but that was what she was wearing when she arrived in Werryl." He knew Elspyth had not taken any of the items Valentyna had given her to wear.

Peet's expression became forlorn and he sounded embarrassed. "Hundreds of people pass through that gate each day, my lord. That description could be any of a dozen women from yesterday." He held his hands out in a gesture of helplessness. "So many people, you don't really scrutinize anyone unless you've been ordered to."

Crys nodded, understanding. "I know, it was a long shot."

Liryk sighed. "I'm sorry, my lord." He was genuine in his commiseration; he did not like the antagonism the woman of Yentro had stirred up, but he certainly was not happy at her going off alone into the mountains. He thought Crys had been far too flippant about her disappearance when it had been first discovered; obviously the Duke had had a change of heart, but a little too late, he thought privately. "Thank you, Peet, you can return to your meal," he told the guard.

"Oh," Crys said suddenly, "she did have a cloak with her. The morning was cold, so presumably she had that on. It's blue, if that helps."

Peet, who had been turning away, swung around. "Blue cloak?"

Crys nodded. "Does it jog anything?" he asked, noticing the man's keen attention.

"Why yes, my lord, it does. I do remember a woman in a blue cloak. Her hair was dark, I think, though she had it covered though with the hood, so I can't be sure."

Liryk stepped forward. "Well, tell us, man. Hurry now."

The soldier bit his lip in thought. "I wished her Shar's speed, my lord," he said, looking toward Crys. "I added something along the lines that she should hurry back to Werryl because I wouldn't be able to sleep until I saw her pretty face again." He shrugged. "It was harmless really—I was just passing the time of day with a lovely girl."

Crys smiled. "That's all right, Peet. Was she alone?"

"No, as I recall she was with a family. I thought it was hers."

"Come on now, son. What do you remember?" prompted Liryk. "Bring the scene back. Remember all those exercises we've been doing about how to recall a moment in detail?"

"Yes, sir, I do," Peet said. "I can remember it well now. She was traveling with a little girl and a man who was driving the cart they were in. They—the woman and the girl— were laughing. It was a cart with one horse."

"Did she say anything?" Crys asked.

"No. Seemed happy, though."

"The man—what do you remember about him?" Liryk added.

"Not much, sir. He said he was going to Coneham. His cart had brewery barrels on it, which, come to think of it, strikes me as a little odd."

"Why is that odd?" Crys asked.

Liryk turned to him. "Because our brewery is situated northeast of the city. There would be no need to pass through Werryl itself, let alone the northern gate, for deliveries to Coneham. It does sound suspicious." Liryk addressed the officer. "Find out whatever you can on this fellow—if there's any information among the men. Get Peet here to give as detailed a description of him as possible. Anything at all he remembers, record."

"Is the lady in trouble, sir?"

"No, lad. But we need to find her and your information can help us track her down."

Peet nodded and took his leave, following his superior officer.

"Not much to go on, I'm afraid," Liryk admitted to Crys.

"It's something, though. I'll wait around a little longer—Peet's information might jog someone else's memory."

"Let's give it another hour."

"And then I'm heading for Coneham, come what may," Crys promised.

The cart slowed to a stop and Elspyth was roused from the snooze she had fallen into. She presumed they were breaking for something to eat and felt embarrassed that she had no food to share with her hosts. She did, however, have some coin Crys had insisted she keep during their journey to Werryl. "You may need it if we get separated," he had cautioned, and she was grateful now for his generosity. At least she could offer to pay for her keep while traveling with Ericson and his little girl.

Elspyth noted a hut not far away. She knew they had taken a route off the main road, which Ericson had said was a shorter route with less traffic. "How long have I been dozing?" she said, stretching. She didn't recall feeling tired, or falling asleep, but apparently she had needed rest more than she thought.

"Oh, hours," Jen said in a singsong voice. "The tea always makes the women drowsy."

Elspyth smiled at the youngster without understanding. They had shared some tea at the roadside not far out of Werryl. She had thought it odd, because they had only just left the city, but Jen had insisted she was thirsty and hungry and Ericson had said tea and a hunk of cheese would satisfy his daughter, who rarely ate breakfast. Elspyth had been happy to go along with them and had enjoyed the curious-tasting brew. "Where are we?" she asked, imagining they might be a couple of hours north of the city.

"Just outside Sharptyn," Ericson replied, jumping down. Jen followed.

Elspyth was taken aback. "Sharptyn! No, wait," she said, frowning. "That can't be right." Her mind raced across her imaginary map of Briavel. Sharptyn was to the west, almost into Morgravia, and many hours from Werryl. She shook her head free of the befuddlement of sleep. Perhaps she was mistaken in her mapping. "Are you sure?"

He grinned and there was something unpleasant in it. "Oh yes, very."

"But Sharptyn is far west. You said you were heading north," she said, a pang of fear tingling through her body.

His nasty smile remained. "Did I? Well, we're here now, Elspyth."

Ericson no longer looked tired or kind. He looked predatory and smug. "Jen?" Elspyth looked toward the child, bewildered and frightened.

Again the singsong voice. "Sorry, Elspyth. So, so, sorry," Jen chanted, not even looking at the woman. "Ericson chose you. I didn't want to. I liked you."

"Ericson!" Elspyth shrieked as men appeared out of the hut. "What's this all about?"

"It's not personal," he said, acknowledging the new arrivals with a nod. "Just business. Get her, lads," he added.

Elspyth had no time to think; she lifted her skirt and ran. She forced her legs to move faster than they ever had before, and she screamed, unleashing every ounce of her strength and spirit. Even escaping from Cailech's fortress had not been as terrifying as this. She could hear the shouts and taunts of the men chasing her. They were laughing at her.

She thought of Lothryn. Her pathetic attempt to rescue him had achieved nothing more than getting herself trapped, and probably killed. He would never know that she had tried to reach him. She screamed one last time as she sensed a man about to launch himself at her. He crashed from out of the bushes, knocking her sideways and crushing the breath out of her. The others arrived panting, some laughing still. And then Ericson forced her to swallow more of the tea she had drunk earlier. It all made sense now: She had been drugged. Elspyth tried to spit out the liquid, shaking her head from side to side, deliberately gagging. Ericson hit her, which shocked her into opening her mouth, giving her attacker the chance to pour the drug down her throat.

The men let her go. She just had time to count six of them, including Ericson, before the sky began to reel. She sensed something reaching toward her, something powerful trying to connect with her—or so she imagined—but it was too late. Elspyth lost consciousness again. There would be no more screaming now.

Fynch had felt Elspyth's fear as she fled from the men, sensed it when she fell. He had never met this woman of Yentro, and yet somehow her terror and helplessness assaulted him. He reached toward her and could see her now: prone, presumably unconscious, with men standing around her.

Knave looked back to where Fynch stood rigid on the small ledge. The wind was whipping around them and Knave wondered whether he and the boy should be harnessed together somehow. Fynch was so slight, Knave feared that a stiff, rogue gust of wind would blow him off the ledge.

Bewildered by the boy's closed eyes and fixed stance, the dog returned to him. *Fynch! What happens now?* he asked. When Fynch did not respond, he nudged the boy, suddenly disturbed that he could not lock on to whatever was troubling his companion.

Fynch staggered and finally opened his eyes. "It's Wyl's friend Elspyth. She's in trouble," he said, holding his head.

Knave knew it hurt to use the magic. Elysius had been very careful about the power. His channeling to Myrren had near enough killed him, for she had needed his company and strength for a sustained period. But Fynch was so small and inexperienced and seemed to be opening himself fully to the magic. He did not know yet how to shield himself from it. He must have accidentally latched on to this woman's plea for help. Well, she was not Fynch's problem. He had a task to fulfill.

We must press on, Fynch, Knave began.

"No. She's hurt, in trouble. Elspyth is the woman who escaped with Wyl from the Razors. She helped him. I cannot forsake her," Fynch murmured through his pain.

Chew some sharvan, Knave suggested, determined not to show his annoyance at this new setback.

Fynch poked into his sack and retrieved a handful of the dried leaves he had taken from Elysius's stock. He sat down and quietly chewed as suggested.

How do you know this? Knave asked.

"I have seen her," the boy answered.

I'm not sure I understand. Is Elspyth empowered? How can she reach you otherwise?

Fynch shook his aching head. "I don't think she's empowered. Wyl did not mention her having any sentient ability. I'm not sure, to tell the truth, whether she even knew I was there."

What do you mean?

"She did not call to me, exactly. I felt her fear and then I heard her scream. I followed her trace." Fynch looked at Knave with large, serious eyes that were full of pain and the dog felt grief for the small boy. "I think it's the Thicket."

Sending you her message, you mean?

Fynch nodded once, carefully. With the pain slowly clearing, he did not want to reawaken it. "You said something earlier about Wyl being touched by the Thicket and therefore sensitive to magic, even though he cannot wield it?"

I remember.

"Well, Elspyth is the niece of the Widow Ilyk—the seer Elysius knew and used once. Do you recall that?"

Yes.

"So perhaps Elspyth, though not empowered herself, has a vague awareness of magic's touch. Wyl mentioned that she once dreamed of Lothryn calling to her."

And?

Fynch shrugged. His head felt better, the dizziness gone, with just a reminder of the pain lurking. He spat out the pulp of the sharvan. "I'm guessing that she cast out her fears without realizing she could, and it just so happened that the Thicket was listening. The Thicket has connected us all, you might say."

It was plausible, Knave thought. *So what are you thinking now, Faith Fynch?*

"I have to find out more about what's happening to her."

We cannot be diverted from our journey, Knave warned gravely, hoping to impress on Fynch once again that nothing mattered but what the Dragon King had asked of them: to destroy Rashlyn and rid the world of his evil.

"I know. I'm going to send a spy," Fynch said, and chanced a grin at his black friend.

Then use a fast one. We must get on.

Fynch looked out across the hazy landscape. He knew what he was searching for and sure enough he found the kestrel, high on the wing and hovering, staring down toward the ground. He closed his eyes and drew on his magic to summon the bird of prey.

Knave saw the bird tilt its wing and knew that was the moment Fynch had connected with it. The kestrel swooped and banked high again, turning in their direction, and then dived toward them fast, no doubt curious. When it arrived it perched itself on Fynch's outstretched arm and even permitted the boy to stroke it, in thanks for answering the summoning. Knave was impressed. He had been told that Elysius had achieved something similar once before, but not as easily; according to the creatures of the Thicket, he had cajoled and beseeched them when he needed help. But the answer to Fynch's call had been immediate.

Knave would not normally be privy to what passed between boy and bird, but Fynch generously opened his mind so the dog could listen in as well.

I need you to find someone for me, Fynch asked.

Who? the bird replied casually. Knave wondered if the kestrel knew who Fynch was.

It is a woman—this is what she looks like, and Knave saw the mental image Fynch gave to the kestrel.

Where?

Two miles east of Sharptyn. Another picture was given: an aerial map of Briavel. Knave was spellbound; was the Thicket supplying Fynch with this practical information?

And when I find her?

Let me know what you see. I will send help.

With your powers, can you not look for yourself? the bird asked cheekily.

I could, my friend, but I lose strength and a portion of my life each time I draw on my powers. You can save me some of this loss if you will make that journey and be my eyes.

I shall do what you ask if you will give me your name and tell me who you are.

Gladly. My name is Fynch. I am from Morgravia and was a cleaner at the castle of Stoneheart.

Oh, but you are much more than that, surely, the kestrel said, scorn lacing its voice at the boy's humility. *I must know the truth before I make this journey.*

All that I have said is true, Fynch replied evenly.

But there is a secret, the bird encouraged. Its inquisitiveness was infectious and Knave realized he too was holding his breath. Fynch said nothing. The silence hung between the three of them, heavy with the knowledge that one of them was reluctant to share.

You must tell me, the kestrel urged. *I am like you, Fynch. I need facts . . . and I need the truth.*

The boy hesitated, and then, *I am Fynch,* he replied, his voice filled with a power Knave had never heard before. *And I am the King of the Creatures.*

At the last word, he passed out, crumpling to the ground. The kestrel lifted from the boy's arm just in time to avoid falling with him and launched itself into the air and away from the mountains. Knave was too stunned by Fynch's words to move. He gazed after the bird until it was no more than a tiny speck on the horizon. Then, as it disappeared from his far-reaching sight, he roused himself from his disquiet and lay down, curling around Fynch to keep his friend warm until he regained consciousness.

18

AILECH WAS FLANKED BY ONLY TWO OF HIS OWN MEN AS HE
slowed his horse at the gates of the Tenterdyn Estate
of Felrawthy. On one side of his rode his loyal warrior
Myrt, and on the other a man he now called friend: Aremys
Farrow.

Despite certain misgivings, the King had decided to trust
Farrow. Cailech considered himself an able judge of character and his instincts about people had rarely let him down.
Lothryn had been his only error—but it had taken almost
forty years of friendship to discover his mistake. His mouth
twisted at the thought of Lothryn's betrayal.

"Sire?" Aremys said, noting the expression on Cailech's
face.

"I'm all right," the King replied. "Just wishing Lothryn
were here." He expected Myrt to agree and was surprised by
the grim silence at his right. He did not miss the sly glance
his warrior gave the Grenadyne. What did that look mean?

"You don't need him for this, my lord," Aremys assured
him. "Only you can achieve what we're setting out to do
today."

"He had a way of making me feel calm."

His companions remained silent. What was there to say?
Aremys believed Cailech had no right to feel sorry for himself after what had been perpetrated on Lothryn, but he was
hardly in a position to comment.

Myrt saw the Morgravian guard approaching. "Are you
ready, sire?" he asked.

"As I'll ever be," Cailech replied, glancing toward his new
friend, who nodded encouragement.

"Lothryn would be proud of you for this," Aremys said.

"He would, wouldn't he, Farrow. This is something he would applaud."

"Then you honor him by it."

Cailech smiled. There was gratitude in his expression and something unreadable in his eyes—sorrow perhaps? Aremys hoped so.

The guard arrived and the mercenary addressed him. "I am Aremys Farrow. You're expecting our party, I gather?"

The guard nodded. "We are. Wait here, please." He whistled to the gatehouse and gave a hand signal.

"You might care to bow in the presence of a king," Aremys suggested while they waited for the gates to open.

He was relieved to see the man looked abashed, had worried for a moment that due respect was not going to be accorded to Cailech.

"Forgive me, sire," the man stammered, and bowed low. Cailech and his companions exchanged satisfied glances.

An officer met them. "Welcome, your highness," he said with appropriate respect. Then he looked toward Aremys and nodded. "Farrow," he acknowledged.

Aremys gave his reins to the men who had arrived to take care of the horses. "Captain Bukanan, sir. Good to see you again. This is Myrt, Second Warrior of the Mountain People."

Celimus was watching as the King of the Mountains arrived at the gate, exchanged a look with Farrow, and then jumped gracefully from his magnificent stallion. The Morgravian sovereign was surprised. For some reason he had imagined that the Razor King would be dark, stocky, and bearded, with hooded eyes and a secretive countenance. He had not expected this golden-haired warrior, tall, clean-shaven, and artless of dress. The man wore no jewelry to proclaim his royal status, and his clothes were simple and yet frustratingly elegant. Celimus would have liked to own the cloak that hung so magnificently across the broad shoulders and seemed to shimmer in the daylight. And yet for all the understatement in his presentation, the Mountain King oozed confidence. Celimus suddenly felt like a strutting peacock in his bright courtly clothes. He pulled angrily at the circlet around his head.

"I don't think I need this," he muttered to Jessom, who, as ever, was nearby.

"I'll take it, sire," the man replied, nothing in his tone to suggest that he was inwardly smirking at the insecurity one glimpse of the Mountain King had provoked in his king. "It is time," he added.

Celimus remained silent, distracted by his thoughts. He turned from the window and strode past the Chancellor toward the main steps of Tenterdyn, where he had intended to arrange himself so the Mountain King might come cringing toward him. But there was absolutely nothing in Cailech's demeanor to suggest he would comply with that idea. In fact, if anything, he seemed utterly assured. It was the opposite of what the Morgravian had expected, and baffling.

Celimus forced away his puzzlement, replacing it with a beautifully contrived bright expression, as he emerged to meet his fellow sovereign.

*S*o far so good, Aremys thought as he looked toward the movement at the front of the large house, which not so long ago had been filled with the Donal family. He felt a sudden flurry of fear as he saw the King, flanked by his chancellor and various other military people, emerge from the huge main doors.

"Your majesty, King Celimus is here to greet you. May I accompany you?" Captain Bukanan offered.

Aremys thanked Shar that Celimus was playing this out according to strict protocol. It was a heartening sign that the King of Morgravia was treating his sworn enemy with courtesy and equality, although Jessom no doubt had been a guiding hand.

"Thank you, Captain," Cailech said. He threw a final glance toward Aremys, who noted the glint in the King's eye and read it as a combination of pleasure and mischief. He truly admired this man who walked so boldly into his enemy's camp, unarmed and with nothing to offer but promises.

Aremys closed the gap between himself and Myrt to fall into step behind the King. He admired the superb cloak that the King had donned for this most formal of occasions. It was a pewter color, made from the softest of wool, spun repeatedly until it shone, from the coats of the shaggy polders—a rare cross between goat and sheep, found only in the mountains. Cailech's people took good care of the two large flocks they had gathered. The animals' long hair was impervious to moisture and felt like silk to the touch. The women of the Razors had done their king proud with this beautiful garment, which kept the natural silvery gray of the polder as its background while yarn dyed crimson and black had been woven into an eye-catching, intricate pattern along its entire length. Aremys marveled at how the clever design made the already tall man look even larger. Cailech was certainly a match for Celimus in height and looks, although the Razor King was older and more rugged than the vain southern monarch.

Myrt nudged Aremys out of his thoughts and they stepped forward for the party from the mountains to be introduced to King Celimus.

The dance of Kings had begun.

"King Cailech, welcome to Tenterdyn, our summer retreat," Celimus said, his tone full of largesse. He noted a twisted expression flicker across Farrow's face and wondered what it meant.

"King Celimus, it is a true honor to meet you." To the Morgravian's astonishment—and indeed to all who were privy to this historic meeting—Cailech bowed his head and shoulders toward his southern foe. "Thank you for this parley."

For once in his life Celimus was at a loss for words. He had not anticipated such graciousness from his northern foe. He was irritated further by the man's surprisingly deep voice, which made him feel like a boy greeting his father. His stomach clenched.

Everyone waited for Celimus's response. Finally it came. "I am intrigued, King Cailech," he said, reaching for the right words, "by this opportunity for Morgravia. Come, we are here to talk." He gestured for Cailech to enter the Donal estate.

Captain Bukanan, already briefed on the format for the day, returned to where Myrt stood. "I believe I must accompany you; is that correct?"

Myrt nodded. "We will return on horseback to a spot of my king's choosing and await word of his safe return. There are others coming with us, of course." He stopped himself from using the word "hostages."

It made little difference. Bukanan knew he was a hostage. The Captain nodded his understanding and took his leave from his king, as did Myrt from Cailech.

Inside, the party was led by their regal host to a huge chamber Aremys had not seen on his previous visit to Tenterdyn. At each end of the large space was a glorious stone fireplace and a long table stood in its center. Tapestries softened the walls, as did huge windows with bench seats and elegant shutters, each one crafted with the Donal sigil. Aremys realized that the room's simplicity deliberately allowed the dazzling scenery of the distant Razors to do all the work of impressing visitors with the beauty of the chamber.

"I thought you would be most comfortable seeing your home from here," Celimus said, his charm more evident now that he had taken a minute to gather his thoughts.

Cailech smiled in return. "Having never witnessed its beauty from this vantage point, I thank you for such a treat."

The response pleased Celimus. He indicated the thin man at his side. "I took the liberty, King Cailech, of retaining only my chancellor, Maris Jessom . . ."

"Your majesty," Jessom said on cue, bowing his head to the Mountain King.

" . . . to match your Aremys Farrow. I believed we would be most comfortable with the fewest ears."

"I am grateful for the consideration, your highness."

"Please, be seated," Celimus continued. "Let us offer you some southern refreshment."

Jessom nodded toward a waiting servant, who brought drinks and wafers to the large table. Celimus gestured for Cailech to be seated at his right so the Mountain King could see the Razors through the magnificent picture windows. Aremys was offered a seat at his left.

"I will bear witness alongside the Chancellor," Aremys said, as deferentially as he could manage, and moved to stand beside Jessom.

"As you wish, Grenadyne," Celimus said, unfazed.

"Smart move, Farrow," the Chancellor murmured under his breath. "You would fare well in court."

"I don't belong here, Jessom, and you know it," Aremys shot back, relieved to be out of Celimus's gaze.

"Shall we dispense with our regal titles, Cailech?" Celimus said brightly, raising his goblet.

"I thought you'd never suggest it," the Mountain King replied, grinning and raising his own cup.

"To us, then," Celimus said with a flourish, tapping his goblet against his guest's and noticing the glint of humor in Cailech's light green eyes.

"To Morgravia and the land of the Razors!" Cailech responded, and both men drained their goblets.

"Again!" Celimus called to the servant. His cheeks were suddenly flushed with the gravity of this historic moment.

"Would your father be proud of this parley?" Cailech asked as their goblets were refilled.

The Morgravian was unprepared for such a disconcerting question. "My father?" he repeated, angry at himself for doing so.

Cailech nodded and again Celimus saw amusement sparkling in the man's eyes, although his facial expression gave nothing away.

"Er . . . I'm sure he would."

"I think he would be shocked," Cailech said.

"Why do you say that?"

"I believe he did not see such a vision of peace as you have, Celimus."

Aremys silently congratulated the King of the Mountains. With a neat twist of words, he had given Celimus credit for bringing together two enemy nations.

Celimus searched for a hint of guile behind the words but saw nothing except openness on Cailech's rugged face.

Again he was not ready for the man; such praise from the enemy was something to be savored. "I would like to think that I can bring together our realms, Cailech," he began, warming to the vision of himself as peacemaker, "as well as Briavel."

"Indeed. In the space of a just few days, you could achieve such an amazing feat that your jongleurs will recite great tales about it, bards will sing stirring songs of homage, and I have no doubt your artists will record the events so that future generations will understand this momentous time in Morgravia's history."

Aremys felt Jessom shoot a warning glance his way. Cailech's praise was honeyed, but it was in danger of sounding insincere. So far, however, Celimus was lapping it up, Aremys noticed, certain that the Morgravian King would personally commission the songs, plays, and artworks should they not arise unprompted. Wyl had told him that the man was vain, but Aremys also recalled Wyl's warning that Celimus was clever, that behind his charm and looks was a stunningly sharp mind. Yes, Aremys thought, Cailech would have to be a bit wary.

The servant had been dismissed now. It was just the four of them.

"And tell me how you fit into all of this, Cailech," Celimus said, leaning back in his chair.

"Quite simply, I wish us to stop being enemies. I see no reason for it other than our own stubbornness and I am offering you the hand of friendship and alliance from hereon if you wish to take it. My people will respect your boundaries utterly. There will be no further threat of raids, no incursion into your lands without your permission."

Celimus nodded. "And what will your people gain from that?"

"Freedom of movement without harassment or threat of injury. We wish to have permission to trade freely with the people of Morgravia and Briavel. I would also suggest you sanction a delegation of your people to visit the Razor Kingdom in order to gain a greater understanding of our people, our culture, and our living standards. Perhaps you will allow a similar delegation from the Razors into Morgravia? I firmly believe that the more we can appreciate each other's culture, the more peacefully we all will live."

"Interesting. I am not averse to anything you have suggested, Cailech. There would have to be a governing body made up of delegates from both realms to supervise the . . ." —Celimus searched for the right word—"the melding of our kingdoms."

"Of course. My thoughts entirely. But I don't believe we could ever live as one, King Celimus," Cailech cautioned, addressing his counterpart with highest courtesy. "Our ways are too different from yours. By the same token, there are many areas in which we are similar. I want the same things for my people as you want for yours. I want our young to be educated and literate; I want free trade so commerce can flourish between our realms; I want my people to eat and sleep well, secure in the knowledge that their own are safe no matter which borders they are moving across."

Aremys could have applauded Cailech for building his case so eloquently. He doubted Celimus could find fault with anything Cailech was presenting and it seemed the Morgravian King was paying genuine attention and not just lip service. Aremys listened as Cailech continued.

"Nevertheless, my people don't want to be Morgravian and I know you have no intention of taking your people into the Razors. Let us agree that we are different—but will tolerate each other's differences. We will learn to admire these subtleties that make us the people of the Razors and your people the sophisticated Morgravians."

"Bravo," Jessom whispered to Aremys under the guise of softly clearing his throat.

Before Celimus could respond there was a knock at the door. The King looked toward his chancellor, irritated. "See to it, Jessom," he said unnecessarily, for Jessom was already making for the door.

The other three remained silent as the Chancellor listened to the hurriedly spoken message. He turned. "My king, apologies for the interruption. There is an urgent missive from Queen Valentyna. Apparently you have insisted that anything arriving from Briavel be delivered to you immediately."

Celimus nodded. "Forgive me," he said to Cailech.

"Never keep a woman waiting, Celimus—least of all a bride, and a queen at that," Cailech responded with mischief.

Celimus laughed. "Bring the messenger in," he ordered.

The man was permitted to enter. He bowed and moved toward Celimus. "Your highness, this was sent in haste."

Celimus waved his hand at him, saying nothing, having already broken the wax seal. He scanned the letter. Jessom shooed the messenger out of the door. He, along with everyone else in the room, was holding his breath. Aremys had not realized how much tension had been created by Cailech's proposition; it was only now that he saw that he had been hanging on Cailech's every word, waiting for Celimus to agree once and for all to a formal union. This messenger could not have come at a worse time.

"Nothing wrong?" Cailech queried, his voice casual, although he glanced toward Aremys for guidance. Aremys shook his head, glad that no one noticed the exchange.

"Farrow," Celimus said, taking Aremys by such surprise he almost jumped.

"Yes, sire?"

"The delivery of Ylena Thirsk . . ."

Suddenly the King's tone sounded cunning and his body language was sly. Aremys felt the first stirrings of alarm.

"Yes?"

"It is in hand, as agreed?"

"It is, sire," Aremys lied, resisting the urge to tug at his collar, which suddenly felt a tad tight.

"Interesting," Celimus said, standing. "Listen to this," and he read Valentyna's letter aloud.

When he finished, Aremys was convinced he could hear his heart pounding, the silence in the room was so profound. He made himself look directly at the King. "That's right, sire," he confirmed. "I sent a message to the Queen to release Ylena."

Celimus frowned. "*You* did!"

Aremys nodded.

"You know Queen Valentyna personally?"

"Not personally, sire."

"Well, how exactly do you know her, then?"

"I'm sorry, sire, I can't divulge my sources. You understand that, I'm sure."

Jessom could see that his king's ire was stoking frighteningly fast, but there could be no scene right now with Cailech quietly watching this event unfold. Jessom felt abashed that he too had been caught out by this missive. He had presumed Ylena had been brought to Tenterdyn via whatever means the mercenary had at his disposal. The fact that Queen Valentyna had become involved was something of a shock.

"Your majesty," Jessom interrupted as gently as he could, "Ylena Thirsk is already here."

"Here?" Celimus repeated, a storm gathering in the olive eyes.

"Yes, your majesty, she arrived just minutes before your guests. Circumstances prevented me from bringing her before you."

The King gave his chancellor such a murderous look that even Aremys, who could not have cared less about the conniving servant, felt his blood run cold. But Aremys also realized that the King had been diverted: His wrath was directed at Jessom now, rather than himself, and he pressed that advantage.

"As we know, sire, Ylena went to Briavel. I have contacts there, and before I was attacked in Timpkenny, I sent word to follow her and keep her under observation."

"Why, by the hairs of Shar's arse, would you do that, Farrow, when I wanted her in Morgravia? Why not have her captured, man?"

Cailech laughed openly at the curse. "I shall have to remember that one, Celimus."

The King of Morgravia caught his famous temper, the laughter reminding him that he was being watched carefully by another sovereign.

Aremys, smoothing an innocent expression across his face, began to embellish the lie, his mind already racing toward how he might get to Wyl before anyone else to ensure that their stories coincided. If Wyl told a different tale, they were both as good as dead. "I figured that the noblewoman would be dangerous wherever I held her in Morgravia, your highness. And as I didn't have her in my own hands, I thought it best just to have her watched. I knew I could get to her whenever I needed to so long as I knew where she was based. I also felt she was a captive of her own fears, sire. If she felt safe in Briavel, she would not leave the realm and I would not have to give further chase."

"But when did you plan to carry out your mission for me?" Celimus asked, following the Grenadyne's line of thought.

Good question, Aremys acknowledged silently. Again Wyl's warning about Celimus's sharp mind nudged him. "Immediately, sire. I was in the north, and Ylena Thirsk was presumably well south by then, which meant I didn't have to hurry and run unnecessary risks of being discovered. I knew my people would pick up her trail and keep watch until I was ready to make my move. I didn't expect to be carried into the Razors, sire. That was a surprise." He glanced at Cailech, whose mouth was, as he had expected, twisted into a wry grin. "And a good thing too that I had people on task in Briavel."

"So then what?" Celimus persisted. The mercenary began to wonder if the King was simply toying with him before calling for the death squad.

"My people are tactically placed, sire. It was simply a matter of getting word to them from the Razors."

Celimus switched his attention to his royal guest. "You were aware of this word being sent, presumably, Cailech? If Aremys is your prisoner, as he tells me, surely you didn't give him such freedom as to pass messages out of your realm to enemy states?" It was phrased as a question, but no one could miss the challenge in the Morgravian's words.

To his credit, Cailech did not so much as hesitate. Aremys had told him about his plan to use Ylena Thirsk as bait; he would have to trust his new friend. "I permitted him a message, yes. It was to Briavel, to a dignitary in the Queen's court. You must remember, Celimus, that you and I were enemies until just moments ago. I would have done anything to undermine you. Allowing this man to send a message into Briavel did not disturb me. Had I known at the time that he was working on your behalf, I might not have been so generous."

Satisfied, Celimus returned a steely gaze to Aremys.

"Anyway, Celimus, has this not achieved the outcome you wished for?" Cailech's question surprised everyone.

"Pardon me?" the King of Morgravia managed.

The Mountain King waved a hand in mock disgust. "It's just that we seem to be wasting time over petty details. You wanted this woman, you have her. Aremys has delivered as he said he would. Why is there a case to argue?"

There was no accounting for the moods of Celimus or the shifts in his thinking. His whole body seemed to relax as he considered Cailech's question, and Aremys could not help but compare the two kings' capriciousness. They made a good match.

"Why indeed, my friend?" Celimus echoed. "You are right," he added, nodding slightly at his guest and then returning his attention to the mercenary. "Thank you, Aremys, for delivering Ylena into my hands. To be honest, I hadn't thought you would trust me sufficiently to hand over the bait you dangled in front of my nose *before* you and your new employer left my realm for the safety of the Razors. After all, it was to be your insurance." His last few words were not lost on anyone in that chamber.

Aremys took the moment to bow, covering his relief. Straightening, he said, "Your majesty, as I have explained before, I am a mercenary and always for hire. You have shown me nothing but generosity and I would have been foolhardy not to trust such a powerful monarch." He nodded at the King. "I would like to be able to work for you often, sire. Ylena Thirsk is nothing to me. My communication to your queen simply suggested that the person to whom she offered sanctuary was your open enemy, and that she would be wise not to risk her new king's wrath by sheltering her."

"And it worked, by Shar!" Celimus said. "You are a cunning man, Aremys Farrow."

As are you, you snake, Aremys thought; instead he said: "I am simply a man for hire, my lord. I take opportunities where and when they present themselves. Do you still wish me to kill her, sire?"

"I think I can manage that myself if and when needed," Celimus said, a cruel smile flitting over his mouth. Cailech frowned but held his tongue. "So where is she?" the King continued, looking at Jessom.

"In one of the outhouses, sire. I said you would summon her at your pleasure."

"And how is she?"

"Surprisingly feisty," Jessom commented.

"The Thirsk girl has found some spine, has she? I shall enjoy seeing this. So will you, Cailech. Do you know of the Thirsks?"

"Only by reputation," the Mountain King said. "This is the daughter of General Fergys Thirsk, I presume?"

"Mmm, yes, the sister of Wyl Thirsk—finally back in my care." Celimus laughed. "Have her presented to me during this afternoon's feast, Jessom. I should like Cailech to see how we deal with treachery in Morgravia."

Aremys felt his blood run cold. He needed to warn Wyl. The thought that his friend would probably die again in a few hours disturbed the Grenadyne so much that he could not breathe. He loosened his collar.

"May I see her?" he said, shocked that he had spoken without thinking it through.

"Why?" Celimus looked at him sideways.

Aremys thought quickly. "She knew I was following her, sire. I just want to remind her that I always catch my prey."

Celimus clapped. "You have a nasty streak, Grenadyne. By all means. Jessom will go with you. Get her ready for us," he said to his chancellor.

He turned to Cailech. "Let us get some air. How about a ride—just us? That horse of yours looks splendid. I should like to try him out for myself."

The Mountain King smiled. "Delighted. Am I to assume that we are done here? Formalities concluded?"

"Well, my friend," Celimus replied, Cailech noting this

was the second time the southern King had addressed him in this way, "I am about to be married to the most beautiful woman of our age. Aremys here has just kept his word and delivered to me the last of the Thirsks, whom I shall see die before my eyes shortly. I can't think of anything I feel like dealing with less right now than the threat of war between our realms—which is what I presume is the alternative to an alliance?"

Cailech watched his counterpart carefully as he spoke. This man had no intention of honoring a union. What he wanted was sovereignty over Briavel and the Razor Kingdom. The marriage achieved the first, and the pretense of friendship would achieve the second. The green gazes of two powerful men met and each understood the other very clearly.

"It would mean war, yes," Cailech finally answered, realizing what a sham this whole event had been. His thought that he could charm this man or appeal to his good sense amused him suddenly. He had been carried away by the vision of the Grenadyne, but both of them had misunderstood the main point: Celimus did not want friendship or even harmony. All the King of Morgravia wanted was absolute authority over his neighbors. Neither Cailech nor Aremys had factored in the southerner's avarice or his self-delusion of might. They had entered into the parley like excited boys, stupidly believing that Celimus would also be seeking peace, trade, community. How innocent and how ignorant they had been. And now he was trapped. Would Celimus allow them to leave here alive? He might not care for the lives of those he held prisoner, and Aremys had delivered Ylena Thirsk early. Why? What had he to gain from that?

"That must be avoided, then," Celimus commented. Cailech had to remember what he was referring to. *Ah yes, war.* It was time to unleash his final trick then, all that stood between him and certain death at the end of this man's sword—or more likely, that of one of the King's henchmen. It was unlikely Celimus would dirty his hands with Mountain blood.

"King Celimus," Cailech said, standing now to look at his

enemy eye to eye. "My emissary here, Aremys Farrow, may be far too trusting, but I am not. Until now I could not be sure you would see things in a similar way to me. I had to take the precaution that your desires might differ from mine."

Aremys felt the temperature in the hall drop. The gently crackling fires at either end of the room had no effect on the cold that descended. He had to admire Celimus when the southern King barely twitched at the couched threat that now lay between the two monarchs. What had Cailech kept up his sleeve?

Celimus asked the question that burned at Aremys's and Jessom's lips. "Ah, further insurance, I gather. Tell me, King Cailech, so that I understand clearly, why is it that, although you don't trust me, neither do you fear me, even though you are on my land, in my house, under my guards' watchful eyes?"

"Please don't take it personally, Celimus. It's simply the caution of a king who knows how easy it is to give trust too quickly."

Celimus nodded indulgently as if to say he truly understood.

"There are two thousand Razor warriors currently gathered in the foothills," Cailech said.

"Two thousand!" The number clearly took the Morgravian's breath away.

Cailech grinned good-naturedly. "And another two thousand camped a little bit higher."

Aremys closed his eyes. He had definitely underestimated Cailech—as had Celimus.

"And what are their instructions?"

"To hit Tenterdyn with full might if my second, Myrt, does not give the all clear by nightfall."

"Nightfall? You hadn't factored in much time for the feast, my friend."

"I wasn't sure I'd make it to dinnertime."

"Bravo, Cailech. You are a man after my own heart. You will make your rendezvous with your men."

"Alive?"

"Alive," and Celimus laughed, genuinely now.

Aremys felt his stomach unclench. He took what felt like his first breath in minutes.

"I hope you and Farrow will at least agree to dine with me," the King went on.

Cailech nodded, green eyes ablaze with triumph. "And our union?"

"Begins today," Celimus lied. "My men will be instructed that people of the Razors are no longer targets. I will put together a delegation, to be led by Jessom here, and I suggest you do the same. They can hammer out the details of how we shall run this union. Let us clasp hands, before our two witnesses, to signify the formal alliance of our two realms."

The King of Morgravia held out his hand and King Cailech of the Razors gripped it firmly. "To peace," he said, although he did not believe it could happen as long as this King sat upon the southern throne.

"To peace," Celimus echoed, privately laughing.

19

YL HEARD THE APPROACHING FOOTSTEPS BUT HAD ANTICI-pated soldiers arriving, not the two men who entered the hut.

"Look, Ylena," Jessom said, a note of triumph in his voice, "I've brought you a visitor."

Aremys spoke before Wyl could answer; it was his only chance for a warning. "I thought it would be polite of me to introduce myself, Lady Ylena, as I was the one pursuing you on behalf of King Celimus. It was I who encouraged your protector to hand you back to Morgravia."

He watched the surprise leave Ylena's face. There was a

momentary hesitation before she replied, but so slight he was sure he alone had been sensitive to it.

"Congratulations, sir," Wyl said. "Do come closer and allow me to spit on you and the trade you ply."

Bravo, Wyl, Aremys thought. *Thank you for saving my life. Now how am I going to save yours?*

"You high-and-mighty Legion wives and daughters are all the same—don't think your men are any different. I've heard what happened at Rittylworth—"

Aremys was interrupted by the arrival of a Legionnaire at the doorway.

"Chancellor Jessom, the King wishes to speak to you before he leaves on his ride."

"I'll be just a minute, Farrow," Jessom said. "Try not to make the wildcat too angry—her claws are sharp." He smiled thinly as he left the hut.

"What are you doing here?" Wyl whispered.

"Listen to me, Wyl!" Aremys urged in an equally terrified whisper. "They are going to kill you."

"And that's supposed to frighten me?"

The big man frowned. It had not occurred to him that Wyl might welcome the next stage of the Quickening. "I . . . I suppose not."

"That's why I'm here—I want him to kill me."

Aremys shook his head. "This is all too much for me," he groaned. He stole a look over his shoulder to the courtyard, where Jessom was conversing with his sovereign. "Look, I used you as a bargaining tool. I told Celimus I could deliver you to him—it was my insurance to get Cailech and myself out of here alive."

"I gathered as much," Wyl said, just a touch of sarcasm in his tone.

"I had no idea you would deliver yourself. It was just a ruse—to buy us time."

"Well, I'm here now. What intrigues me is how you and Cailech come to be here together."

"It was the Thicket. It separated us."

Understanding dawned on Ylena's face. "Ah. I suspected as much. Any plan in mind for yourself?"

"None," Aremys said, and looked at Ylena's lovely face with despair.

She nodded. "When do you leave?"

"Tonight," Aremys replied, then heard Jessom's footsteps approaching. He gestured to Wyl, who quickly switched Ylena's expression to one of rage.

"Get out!" he screamed.

Jessom entered to hear her shriek. "Oh dear, I did warn you, Farrow."

"Don't worry, I'm going. What are you going to do to her?"

The Chancellor looked thoughtful for a moment. "Well, the King wants her dead, as you know." It was a callous comment designed to frighten Ylena.

"Good, I can't wait," Wyl said.

Jessom was unable to hide his astonishment at Ylena's reckless statement. "I was going to say that I was hoping to persuade him otherwise, but the young lady seems determined to die." He shook his head. "I imagine King Celimus will make an example of her."

"That's risky, isn't it?" Aremys queried.

The Chancellor sighed. "He will want to impress his regal companion."

"He won't—not in that manner," Aremys said, desperate to prevent Wyl's death, no matter how much his friend wanted it.

"We shall see. Come, Farrow, I trust you have gloated sufficiently. Farewell, Ylena. Prepare yourself to meet your king."

"He is no King of mine, Jessom!" Wyl called out after the two men. A memory of kneeling before King Magnus filled his mind, and he recalled how he had pledged his life for Celimus. "And gladly will I give it," he muttered now. He hoped Shar would hear and let Magnus know.

Cailech allowed Celimus to ride the exquisite white stallion that had been bred in the Razors. The Morgravian King's silence as they guided their horses toward the back of Tenterdyn where the lush plains stretched toward the mountains, attested to his enjoyment of the beautiful beast.

"He's extraordinary," Celimus finally said when they halted beneath a small stand of trees.

"He is yours."

"I could not—"

"No, really. Let me gift him to you to seal our historic union. It is appropriate. I reared this one from a newborn foal. He has a twin brother, identical. His mother is one of my most treasured broodmares and his sire is a tough old rogue with perfect bloodlines. He suits you as much as he does me. Now we shall both have white stallions of the same family. Fitting, don't you think?"

Celimus gave Cailech one of his dazzling smiles. This gift pleased him more than anything the Mountain King had brought with him; it meant more than the alliance itself. "Thank you. I will think of you whenever I ride him."

"His name is Wildfire, like the falling-star trails we see on a clear night in the Razors."

"And what can I give you in return?"

Cailech shrugged. "Oh, I'll think of something," he said. Both men laughed.

"Whatever you want, it is yours."

"Be careful. That promise sounds wide reaching. I might choose your bride-to-be."

Celimus gave a wolfish grin. "Whatever you want that is here in Felrawthy, then."

"I know I mentioned this before, but I feel compelled to repeat it: Our fathers would be proud of this alliance," Cailech said, his voice suddenly wistful.

"Not mine. I never made him proud."

"What you have done today, and what you have achieved between Morgravia and Briavel, should make him sit up in his tomb and applaud."

Celimus liked the notion. He laughed, respecting his companion despite himself, despite his plans to betray him. He and Cailech were similar. Not in looks of course but in . . . what was it? He reached for that intangible something he had recognized in Cailech. Texture, that was it. They had a similar texture. Both Kings, both ambitious. Celimus believed the Mountain King was as ruthless as he

himself was. The likeness pleased him. Cailech's personality, though less flamboyant, was just as large and domineering as Celimus's own. His father had seen these facets
of his son's nature as flaws, and yet here they were reflected in a man his father had considered powerful, talented, intrepid. Celimus shook his head.

"My father hated me, Cailech. We hated each other, in
truth. He killed my mother—I'm sure of it—and were I not
his only heir, no doubt he would have seen me dead too."

"You will carve your own way for your own realm, my
friend. Forget him. He is dust. Not forgotten, I grant you—
you will always feel his shadow falling over you—but remember, that is all it is. A shade, no substance. He cannot
hurt you now, or command you. You rule Morgravia and you
have vision. Your people are fortunate."

Celimus's chest swelled with pride to hear his fellow sovereign speak of him with such respect, but it deflated as he
pondered the last few words. "No, they don't see it that way.
They fear me."

Cailech reached down to stroke the neck of the borrowed
horse he was riding. "Is that such a bad thing?"

"Your people are in awe of you. My people are just frightened of me."

"You have the power to change that, Celimus. And within
weeks, not just your people, but the citizens of Briavel, and
even my people, will see what you have achieved: peace
throughout the whole region. What an extraordinary time
this is—and you are the one who has brought it about. I am
proud to be a part of it."

Celimus searched the Mountain King's face for guile,
suspecting this man was simply oiling him up, but he saw
nothing but the hard green gaze of a man determined to
forge peace. In that moment he made a decision that went
against everything that made Celimus who he was. Charged
by this man's encouragement and pride, he decided to maintain the alliance. He would not betray Cailech as planned; he
would keep his promise and spare lives. He would ensure
that the union worked, even though it meant compromising
his grand plans of imperial domination. In one of the rarest

moments of his life, Celimus smiled and meant it. "Let it be so, then," he said, his voice almost catching with the emotion he felt.

Cailech saw the change and realized that he had just saved hundreds of lives and ensured a new peace for his kingdom. He felt invigorated by what had been achieved by a simple conversation on horseback. "Remind me to gift you a horse more often," he said, his eyebrow arching.

Celimus threw back his head and laughed boyishly. "I'll race you across the fields and show you how fine this stallion is."

Wildfire sprang forward and Cailech followed. But inside he felt a tinge of regret, for the Morgravian's words had reminded him of Galapek and his growing sorrow at what had been worked upon the poor beast.

Gueryn was permitted to walk without being shackled this time. Even his hands were free to swing at his side as he luxuriated in the warmth on his back from another beautiful morning.

"How are you today, Jos?"

"Just fine," came the mangled reply, but Gueryn understood.

"Only one of you today?"

The big man nodded. "We trust you," he said, offering his crooked grin.

"I won't run away if you have more important duties to attend to," Gueryn assured.

"You're my most important duty. I can't let the King down by losing you."

"All right, I do understand. But you have my word," Gueryn offered. It was crucial now to build a friendship and some trust. His chances at escape were increased if he could lull his captors into believing he would never make such an attempt. Descending the Razors was no easy prospect, and vivid memories of the arrow thumping into his body discouraged him from such an idea, but it was spring and there would never be an easier time, with the King and Myrt away.

"Morning," Maegryn called, stepping back from a horse whose hooves he was inspecting.

"And what a fine one it is," Gueryn replied.

"Did you ache from your work?"

"Yes, but it felt good."

"A treat for you today. A ride, with Jos here and another guard."

"Oh? How come?"

"Three of our stallions need some proper exercise."

Gueryn could see his own pleasure reflected in the grin from the stablemaster. "A ride." He said it as though the words were brand-new on his tongue.

"I'd come myself but one of the King's broodmares is in labor and I have to be around for the delivery. She's struggling a bit, so I can't risk not being close."

"Can we help?" Gueryn asked reflexively. He had been around horses since he was a child and had been involved in enough births to be useful.

"I appreciate it but I'm hoping the little one will be born before you lot return. And the mother's best with fewer fussing around her." Gueryn showed his understanding with a slight nod. "Jos, you'll be on Charger—he's out sunning himself over there in the paddock. He's a fiery character but let him loose. He needs a good run. Rollo will be accompanying you. He's on Dray, the older stallion."

"And me, Maegryn?" Gueryn asked.

"Well now, Morgravian, I thought I'd allow you to ride something very special. You might have to prove your worth as a horseman today because you'll be calling on all your skills."

Gueryn grinned. "Do your worst, Maegryn. I'd ride a donkey right now just for the chance to be back in a saddle again."

"This is no donkey, le Gant. This is the King's most prized horse and he's a flighty one. That's him you hear right now making all that noise."

Gueryn frowned. "He does sound agitated. What do you call him?"

"Galapek."

The joy of learning he would be on horseback, however briefly, had temporarily sapped Gueryn of his wits. It had not occurred to him that one of the mounts could be the very horse he was trying to track down.

"Galapek," he repeated, taking a moment to gather himself and ensure no recognition showed in his expression. "That's a sorrowful name indeed for a fine stallion."

"Oh? I've been told it's from the old language. How could you know old Northernish?" Maegryn asked, intrigued.

"My ancestors on my maternal side were from a place even more north than here. The old language stayed alive in our family. I learned some of it as a child."

"So what does it mean? We've all been dying to know," Jos chimed in.

Maegryn grimaced. "I think Rashlyn said that none of us know what Galapek means."

"It means traitor,' " Gueryn answered, surprised. So none of these men had an inkling about the stallion, not even the irony of the King's choice of name.

"Traitor?" Maegryn repeated. "What sort of a name is that for a horse?"

Gueryn shrugged. "Perhaps your king has a sense of humor."

"Stupid name, if you ask me. This is an extraordinary beast, le Gant. You Morgravians have never clapped eyes on anything so remarkable. He's the most beautiful stallion I've ever seen."

"Grenadyne?"

Maegryn's eyes seemed to sink into his skull even further, if that were possible. "He was a present. I have no idea who sired him."

Gueryn sensed the withdrawal. He had worked too hard to forge this precious friendship, however fragile it was, and didn't wish to lose it. "Well, let's see this splendid beast. You've made me feel envious already."

"Here he comes now," Maegryn replied, forthcoming again. "Admit it, le Gant. He's the finest horse you've ever seen."

Gueryn felt his breath catch in his throat. The horse was massive through the chest. He came toward them, proud and majestic in gait. He shook his head and his long mane flicked in a shiny wave of fluid movement while his black coat sparkled in the bright morning. He was beautiful, there was no denying it, but Gueryn saw the ugliness in the horse's eyes. They were wide, as if in permanent fear, and his flesh appeared to twitch incessantly.

"Ah, here's your other companion," Maegryn said. "Rollo is one of the King's most trusted men, le Gant. No tricks, eh? He's also one of our best archers and won't hesitate to sink another arrow into that shoulder of yours."

Gueryn smiled at Rollo. Rollo did not smile back, and Gueryn recalled with vivid intensity his aborted escape, the arrow ripping through skin and nerves, muscle and bone. He was in no hurry to feel that sensation again, yet knew he would risk it if the opportunity for escape presented itself. "Have no fear," he assured, lying easily.

Maegryn gave some final instructions regarding the horses and Gueryn submitted to having his hands loosely strung together.

"You can still handle the horse with ease. Just a precaution, you understand?" Rollo said.

Gueryn pulled a face to suggest it was of no consequence to him and then made use of Maegryn's offered leg up to hoist himself into the saddle. The other men followed suit, and after a nod from Rollo, the party eased itself away from the stable compound.

20

THEY HAD TRAVELED A SHORT DISTANCE THROUGH THE NIGHT using magic. The boy had performed the magical transportation and then slept restlessly, sometimes crying out, presumably in pain. Now awake, he squatted, pale and quiet, chewing sharvan leaves.

Knave wanted to ask Fynch what he had meant the previous day when he answered the kestrel's question so audaciously, but he did not dare. When Fynch had finally roused himself from the curious stupor he had fallen into after the bird's departure, he had been withdrawn and Knave had sensed it was no time for talk. Movement was best and so he had suggested they walk for a time and then sleep until the early hours, which they had done. When the time came, Knave had marveled at the speed with which Fynch had conjured the spell to create what could only be described as a bridge to the Thicket. When the Thicket responded, Knave felt a pulse like a thick plume of air punched into his side. The next moment he landed, breathless, alongside Fynch on a safe ledge deeper into the Razors and closer to their prey.

"All right, Knave?" Fynch had whispered.

Yes, he had replied, and that had been the end of the conversation. Fynch had settled immediately and slept. Once again, the dog had lain down beside his companion and kept the youngster's body warm with his own.

Now it was time to move again. *Are we waiting for something?* Knave risked.

"For Kestrel. I feel him."

How is the pain?

"Not unbearable," Fynch answered. "Thank you," he added, and Knave knew he meant it. Then: "Kestrel speaks," and Fynch opened his mind to share the communication with Knave. *Where are you?* he asked the bird across the leagues that divided them.

Just outside Sharptyn. I have found her.

Good, he replied calmly. *What can you see?*

She seems to be a prisoner—she walks with shackled hands and feet. There are others, all women. Men guard them. And there's a child—a small girl belonging to one of the men, I think. The girl talks to your friend.

Is Elspyth injured?

Pretty name. There was a pause. *Not injured, but she looks frightened.*

What are they doing now? Fynch pressed his temples and Knave knew the pain was back.

I can't really tell. I would guess that they are stretching their limbs because they came out of a shed a short while ago.

Fynch. You must stop, Knave urged.

Fynch nodded. *Kestrel, I am so grateful to you. Can I trouble you to remain there awhile longer?*

No trouble.

Thank you. I'll talk again shortly. Fynch closed the link.

You cannot keep doing this, the dog cautioned.

"We must save her." Fynch's tone was stubborn.

How?

"You must go to Valentyna and get her help." The dog's silence made his exasperation clear. "Please, Knave."

We have a task to complete.

"And I will finish it as promised. But I also promised that I would help Wyl's cause. I will not forgive myself if Elspyth perishes."

We are helpless.

"Not helpless. Just distant. I can fix that."

No, Fynch.

"Yes. If you won't go, I will."

A difficult silence lengthened between them as the huge dog regarded the trembling yet implacable boy. Knave knew the suffocating pain Elysius had suffered, even though the sorcerer had used his magic infrequently and with utmost care. Knave could not imagine the burden Fynch was bearing right now.

You'll send me?

"And bring you back when you've delivered her a note."

That will still take days.

"Not if I send you the entire distance."

Fynch! It will kill you.

"Trust me. I am stronger than you think."

The dog felt helpless. He had no doubt his companion would send himself back to Werryl if he did not comply. *And you will promise to continue on alone?* he asked.

Fynch covered his face, pushing his fingers against his eyes. His answer was mumbled and weak. "Yes, of course."

Rashlyn will sense the magic, Knave warned.

"I don't care. Elspyth could die."

So could you.

"I am already sacrificed."

Oh, Fynch.

"I'm sorry. I don't mean to sound cruel, but you must do this for me. I will prepare a note. Valentyna can send help."

Can you write? the dog asked, looking for a reason to prevent this madness.

"I know some letters . . . enough to convey the urgency."

Knave looked at him gravely. *There is a cave over there. You must rest for a while before you travel on.*

"I think you're right," Fynch admitted. He dug into his sack for a scrap of parchment he had had the foresight to throw in, but although he had brought a quill, he had forgotten ink in his rush. "I'll use blood," he said matter-of-factly, and, without hesitating, dragged a small knife across his palm.

He scrawled five words only, spelled incorrectly but clearly enough: Elspyth, Sharptyn south, huts, danger. He had to dip the quill frequently into the pool of blood in his palm. Knave could not watch, disgusted with this turn of events but also feeling helpless.

"For Valentyna only, you understand?"

I understand. Knave allowed Fynch to tie the parchment around his neck with some trailing grass vines. It was fragile but would make the journey.

"Ready?"

Do it! the dog instructed, unable to conceal his dissatisfaction any longer.

"I'll wait to hear," Fynch said, hugging the dog briefly. Without wasting another word, he sent Knave tumbling through a magical tunnel arcing from the Razors to Werryl.

Knave landed softly on all fours, checked that the parchment was still in place, and then took his bearings. He was in the woodlands just beyond Werryl city, where the Queen liked to ride. Sighing to himself, he set off at a lope toward the palace.

Back in the Razors, Fynch retched pitifully, but there was nothing to be expelled. He curled up, exhausted, in his cold but dry cave and, chewing on his decreasing supply of sharvan leaves, drifted toward sleep—the only place where respite from his aching head was to be found.

It was late afternoon of Elspyth's second day as prisoner. The first had passed in a blur caused by the drug and the shock of her situation. She was still too stunned to take in all that had happened to her, but she had been able to realize that she was among women only; there were no male prisoners. Released from the huts, she found the courage to speak to one of her fellow prisoners.

"What are we doing here?"

"Finally found your voice, then. Don't worry, we're all the same when we first arrive."

"What is this place?"

"We're prisoners. They trick us, trap us, and keep us here."

"What for?"

"Who are you? You're not Briavellian, are you?"

"My name is Elspyth. I'm from Yentro, northern Morgravia."

The woman raised her eyebrows. "You're a long way from home, Elspyth, and you'll certainly wish you'd never been duped by Ericson. I'm Alda, from southeastern Briavel."

"He's trapped us, you say?"

Alda nodded. "For his sport."

Elspyth gaped at her companion. "Sport?" she repeated.

"Well, it's for all of them, really. He just gets paid a lot for finding us."

"Alda," Elspyth said, her voice shaking now. "What do you mean?"

A bird screeched in the tall trees. Both women glanced up but neither could see the kestrel perched there.

"We fight and they bet on us. After three wins, we're sold on. I've got one more win to go to get out of here."

Elspyth opened her mouth to speak but had no words. Finally she croaked, "Sold?"

"There's a good slave trade out of Morgravia's south. Didn't you know?" the woman asked, clearly surprised.

"I had no idea."

"Oh yes. A very good trade. Ships from the Exotic Isles slip in and out of a tiny bay called Cheem, east of Ramon, west of Argorn. They pick up slaves regularly." She shrugged at the disbelief on the newcomer's face. "At least it's an escape from this—but you have to survive three bouts, of course."

It was too much for Elspyth to take in. "What sort of fighting is it? Bare hands?"

Now the woman laughed harshly and Elspyth heard a hint of despair in her voice. "Blades, you fool. To the death. You will be fighting for your life tonight, my girl, and for the right to be shipped off as a slave. Forget your former self—it doesn't exist anymore." Then she became wistful, the bravado shattering. "Perhaps one day I'll see my family again, track down my son, but right now I have to make it through one more fight."

Elspyth grabbed her companion's arm. "Alda, I don't know how to fight."

"None of us know, girl! It's pure animal instinct that has kept me alive. I suggest you find some of your own or your blood will be splashed across the main hut's dust tonight."

Elspyth, shocked and upset, could not help the tears that began to trickle down her cheeks.

Alda pushed Elspyth's hands from her sleeve. "Expect nothing from me, or anyone else, for that matter. No one has friends here. We don't know who we'll have to kill next to survive. Two days ago I killed someone I liked. I don't want to know you or feel sorry for you, because you might be the woman I have to kill tonight." She paused, and her tone softened slightly. "Ericson dreamed it all up apparently. Did he use the young girl to lure you?"

Elspyth nodded blindly through her tears.

"No good blaming yourself. I fell the same way, accepting a seemingly kind offer of a lift, trying to get back from Werryl to my family more quickly than I could on foot. They're experts at picking the perfect mark."

"What were you doing in Werryl?" Elspyth asked, desperate to prolong any conversation that might take her mind off what was hurtling toward her. She heard the shriek of the bird again but ignored it, finding herself on her knees in the dust, clinging to Alda's skirts.

"It doesn't matter. I don't want to share anything more with you. Don't think we're friends. I can't help you—won't help you. You'd best prepare yourself. It's either kill or be killed. Get that straight now."

Alda ripped herself away and hurried to the other side of the compound. No one saw the tears she shed there over her own cruelty. What sort of monster had these men turned her into?

Wyl too was preparing for death, except he welcomed it. Dying again would be his salvation and he wondered who he would become. In truth he did not care; all he knew was that he could not bear to be Ylena for much longer. He knew that ultimately he would have to become Celimus, but he clung to Fynch's quiet belief that random acts could change the course of Myrren's Gift. He desperately wanted to believe in anything that might spare him living as Celimus. As much as he loved the idea of marrying Valentyna, the notion of walking in the body of the present King of Morgravia was repulsive. Every time he saw the vision of Celimus's face before him, he had to draw on all his strength to force it away.

In the end, to distract himself from his downward-spiraling thoughts, he washed Ylena's face and combed her hair. Wyl tied it back once again, not prepared to allow the soft waves of golden tresses to pool around her narrow shoulders. He also refused to change out of his riding trews. There would be no curtsying today. He did, however, dust his garments as best he could, having decided that Ylena should not die looking ragged and filthy. Wyl knew appearance and presentation had been high on his sister's list of priorities and looking pretty was the least he could do for her considering that he was contriving to bring about her death—a second time.

He glanced at the small tarnished mirror that Jessom had provided. Not even its rusted surface could hide the ethereal radiance that shone from Ylena's visage. She was gaunt now, but somehow that only added to her ghostly beauty; it reminded Wyl of how their mother had looked when she was laid out following her death.

The wasting fever had shrunk his mother's willowy figure to a skeletal state, and she had died gasping for one more lungful of air, but in her death repose Helyna of Ramon remained breathtakingly lovely. Ylena would be the same, Wyl promised himself as he stared out through eyes that were so full of sorrow that they looked even larger than usual.

Wyl threw the mirror down, shattering it across the flagstones, glad that it would never reflect that sad, haunting face again.

He turned at the sound of footsteps. It was Harken, together with the older officer from earlier in the day.

"I thought you had gone," Wyl said, gathering his unraveling emotions.

"Our company was called back this afternoon to guard the arrival of the Mountain King."

"You have been summoned," the older soldier cut across them both. "The lad here seemed determined to see you again."

"And how kind of you to let him," Wyl said, bitterness lacing his tone. "It is a pity you don't feel the same loyalties to General Thirsk that I would expect from a soldier of the Legion."

"He's dead, or hadn't you noticed?" the man answered with a cruel grin. "Thirsk is no good to us now. We're stuck with the nasty royal brat and the only way any of us will survive is to follow his orders."

Wyl mustered as much contempt as he could on Ylena's face. "You sniveling coward! The Legion could overthrow him in a blink if it would only find its spine. What has happened to all of you?"

The man did not bother to reply, simply held out the manacles to be put around Ylena's wrists. Wyl obliged; there was no point in wasting energy on a man like this. He turned his attention to the dumbstruck Harken.

"I'm so sorry," the young man finally stammered. "I just had to see you again."

"And I'm happy you did. There is nothing you can do for me, but I urge you to rally your men against the Crown."

He expected the old soldier to strike him for saying something so treacherous, but the man simply laughed. "Don't be daft, lad. These are the ravings of a condemned woman. Follow orders—that's the Legion's way, isn't it? And you have yours."

"Harken, look at me!" Wyl commanded. "Do this, if nothing else. Throw your support behind Celimus's bride. When he marries Valentyna of Briavel, she will be your queen. Help her. Don't let him crush her as he has all of you. Make your men pledge their allegiance. She is your only hope against his brutality."

Harken, stunned, could only nod. His companion gave Ylena a shove. "Come on, lass. Let me follow my orders. I've got just another winter to get through and then I'll be out of the Legion and off mending fishing nets in the northwest. After that I don't care what the young bloods do. Right now we have instructions to bring you to his majesty and that's what we're going to do."

Wyl rubbed at Ylena's burdened wrists. "Let us go then," he said.

Elspyth stood with about sixteen other women in what was akin to a cattle pen, which Ericson and his cohorts had built inside the main stone building. She had been forced to strip herself of clothes and given a grubby length of linen to cover whatever she could. One end of the cloth was stained with blood and it was all Elspyth could do not to scream at the testimony of another's injury, perhaps her death.

The men had been drinking for most of the afternoon. They were well and truly intoxicated now, eager for the naked women, for fighting, for killing. The volume of noise in the building rose noticeably when the women were herded into their pen, clutching at the useless fabric that barely concealed their modesty.

The smell of liquor, combined with sweat, vomit, and the unmistakable scent of congealed blood, made some of the jumpier women gag. Others began to wail. They knew what was coming and that, in the next hour or so, they could be taking their last breath. Elspyth could cope with the stench, but her rising fear would surely undo her. She had learned that the men had not found "fresh meat" for a week or more, and one kind soul had told her she would be a definite item on tonight's menu. There were no more tears to cry and there was no one coming to save her. If she was to survive this, Shar help her, it would be because she managed to kill three of her fellow captives.

Elspyth looked around the pen and wondered who she might be partnered with tonight. She noticed all of the women were in relatively good health, no one older than around thirty-five summers. She smiled grimly. Of course they wouldn't choose anyone much older—the naked bodies would not offer the same spectacle.

"I've heard they sometimes rape the winner," a woman nearby murmured, no doubt awaiting her first bout, her eyes panic-stricken.

"They're not here just to look, you fool," her neighbor warned.

Elspyth gritted her teeth and turned away, her glance catching that of Alda on the opposite side of the pen. The other woman looked calm yet menacing, as if violence lay just behind that expressionless exterior. Madness and the threat of death whirled around them all, but Alda's attention was riveted on Elspyth alone. It was unnerving. When Elspyth saw torches being lit around the central area, and a man approaching to get the first fight under way, her emotions frayed. She would not let the men see her fear, but inwardly she screamed her pain toward Lothryn, knowing he too was helpless, but needing to say farewell.

She reached Fynch instead.

T he boy woke, consumed by Elspyth's anguish. *Lothryn, I love you, I'm so sorry! Shar, help me!* Her scream came through a gossamer-thin link that threatened to tear away at any second. But this time Fynch was quick enough. *We're coming. You must hold on,* he reassured her, and then the link was ripped away, her terrified voice a memory. But her fear was contagious and it remained like a bad smell, festering around him. Fynch shivered. The pain was back in his head; he was not sure it had ever left or that he would ever be free of it again. He wanted to chew on more sharvan but resisted, knowing he was turning to the leaves too quickly. Knave had counseled him to fight the pain, not let it control him.

He focused on Knave now. *Where are you?*

At the palace gates. I believe I've just enraged a number of Briavellians with some ferocious barking.

Fynch smiled despite himself. *Thank you for going, Knave.*

How are you?

I'm all right. I've just woken. Elspyth reached me again. She sounds in desperate trouble.

The note is intact. Here they come now. I hope they re-member me.

No one could forget you.

We'll speak again soon. Chew some leaves—you'll need them after this.

Fynch did not reply. He broke the bond and cast a silent prayer to Shar to guide the message into Valentyna's hands. She alone had the power to save Elspyth.

Knave barked again, for good measure, as the guard limped toward the gate. "Shar's mercy, look at the size of that thing," he muttered to his younger companion. "I'll send an arrow into its heart if it doesn't quiet down."

"Wait! That's that black dog of the boy's, isn't it?"

"Which boy?"

"You know—that Fynch lad. One of the Queen's favorites."

"Shar spare us, so it is. I must be going mad not to have recognized it."

"Do we let it in?"

"Search me. You take a message to the Captain."

"Looks like it's got a note tied around its neck," the young soldier said, nodding toward the dog as he left.

"You'd better hurry," his companion called after him.

Several minutes passed, during which Knave stalked the breadth of the gate impatiently and the older guard watched, mesmerized. Knave was convinced the man was half-asleep. He barked, just to make sure he had the fellow's attention, and the soldier nearly leapt out of his skin.

"Bastard animal," he murmured, then turned to see his superior approaching. "Captain Orlyd, sir," he said, nodding stiffly.

"Barnes," the Captain acknowledged. "Ah, the dog. Yes, I believe that's the same one. Commander Liryk says it's to be given entry."

"Right-o, sir. You're sure it's not dangerous?"

"It's a dog, Barnes. Haven't you seen it playing around these very grounds with the young lad Fynch?"

"Er, once or twice, sir."

"Then you'll know it's harmless. Move, man. Let's see what the note is about."

When the gate was raised, Knave padded in and obediently sat so that Fynch's note could be taken from his neck. Fynch had taken the precaution of scrawling a "V" on the outside, as he had seen on some of Valentyna's personal items.

"This is for the Queen," Orlyd said as he patted Knave's large head. "Good fellow. You'd better come with me." He shook his head as Knave stood to follow him. "Smart too, eh?"

Man and dog took the quickest route toward the royal apartments, where the Captain knew Liryk had been having a meeting with the Queen and the Duke from Morgravia.

Orlyd gave a message to the man acting as the Queen's secretary and wondered again at how sorely missed old Chancellor Krell was. If Krell had been at his desk, Orlyd would probably have been taken directly into the Queen's chamber. The former Chancellor had had an uncanny knack of knowing when something was important enough to warrant such attention. Orlyd was sure this was one of those occasions.

Liryk emerged with a quizzical expression. "I trust this is urgent, Captain?"

"I believe it is, sir." He held out the note.

"Shar strike me. It's Knave," Liryk said as he took the note, and at that moment Valentyna appeared at the doorway, looking for one of her servants. She squealed with delight at seeing Fynch's dog and their reunion was filled with licks and joyful sounds.

"Is that a note?" the Queen asked, still grinning from Knave's particular form of salutation.

"It appears so, your highness," Liryk replied, handing it to her.

"It will be from Fynch, of course. I've been dying to hear news of him. I presume he is nearby if Knave is with us," she said, unraveling the parchment from its leafy twine. It took only seconds for her to read it. "Shar save us!"

Liryk, who was in the process of dismissing his Captain, turned back in alarm. "Your highness?"

"It's Elspyth. She's in trouble."

"How does the boy know?"

"I have no idea. But I'm glad Crys was lingering over his farewells. He won't have gone yet, will he?"

"At the stables still, I imagine. Captain Orlyd, please prevent the Duke of Felrawthy from leaving until the Queen has spoken with him."

"Right, sir."

"I'll be straight behind you," Valentyna called after him. She looked toward Liryk. "She's in Sharptyn. You know what this is, don't you?"

He nodded, his expression grim. "It ties up with a few other disappearances we can't explain."

"I'm sure of it," she said, eyes blazing. "And now we have the location of where these scoundrels are holding the women. Come, Liryk, Knave. We'll send the guard with Crys."

The old man broke his usual sense of protocol by grabbing the Queen's arm. "I trust the Duke is not to be put in charge of my men, your highness? We have been chasing clues regarding these men for many months now."

Valentyna realized that in her excitement she had overlooked something important. She reminded herself to learn from it. Her impulsiveness could make her careless—her father had told her this many times, even though he was usually referring to her horse riding. "No, Liryk," she said, covering his hand with her own. "You are in charge." Her voice was gentle. "I will send Crys because Elspyth is his friend and she trusts him. It will give him a reason to leave us too." Liryk nodded. "It also means I send one less man of our own."

"Thank you, your highness."

Valentyna continued speaking, her voice serious. "Commander Liryk, I cannot do all that is ahead without you. I hope you understand how much I rely on your counsel and support. I don't see myself as an island."

It was an odd comment and yet a timely one for the old soldier, long in need of assurance from his sovereign. He found a smile. It felt like his first in a long time.

"I am obliged, your highness," he answered in a thick voice. "I sometimes feel we old fellows are no longer much use to you."

She frowned. "You've been part of my growing up, which makes you all the more important to me now. I hope you understand I will never do anything that is not in the interest of Briavel." Valentyna knew the statement referred to virtually everything that had happened since she had taken on the monarchy—from her relationship with Koreldy to trusting the Morgravians and dismissing Krell.

"I don't doubt you, your highness. But you are under more pressure than most royals face in their first year of rule. Let us get this girl rescued before it's too late."

"I know you don't like her, Liryk," Valentyna added, determined—while they were talking so candidly—to take this opportunity to discuss Elspyth. She wanted to exert her authority as the ultimate decision maker for the realm. She often felt as if she were serving some sort of apprenticeship, with Krell and Liryk guiding her, smiling benignly at choices they considered wise and grimacing when she went against what they thought was right. Elspyth came under the latter category.

"It's not personal, your majesty," Liryk began. He

searched her face, as if the words he looked for were written across her forehead. She gazed back at him intently, giving nothing away. "It's just that Chancellor Krell and I felt she was a dangerous influence here."

"A dangerous influence on me, you mean?"

He sighed. "We felt she was driving you to say and do things that might put the realm at risk."

"Never, sir. Never!"

"I'm sorry, your majesty."

"You're entitled to an opinion; indeed, I'd be troubled if you didn't have one." She raised an eyebrow. "But I am also entitled to like whomever I choose without sanction from the people around me." Valentyna saw her words bite; she had meant them to. "Elspyth knows things we don't. This marriage with Celimus is not as cut-and-dried as you think. My instincts are screaming at me that it is wrong, that it is a bad decision for Briavel, and yet I can't convince anyone of it. The nobles refuse to hear any dissent, from any party, and the rest of Briavel can speak of nothing but the years of peace to come. I seem to be the only one concerned by the fact that the Legion is breathing down our necks on the border, seemingly preparing to invade. I know I have no choice in this, Commander Liryk," she said, deliberately lowering her voice to just above a whisper. "I have to marry Celimus. And yet people like Crys Donal, Elspyth, and Ylena Thirsk truly believe it is the worst decision I could make."

Liryk felt it was his turn to be forthright. "Your majesty, with all due respect, if you don't continue with your preparations for the wedding, we will go beyond the point where a marriage can save any of us. The King of Morgravia is threatening war. It is a war we cannot win, your highness, not even if we recruited every man of able body. The sheer weight of the Legion will crush us, your majesty." His voice wavered as emotion swelled through his words. "This is not King Magnus, your majesty. Celimus is not a man of compassion. He will brutally slay every Briavellian man and his son, and his son's son, if necessary, if we choose to go to war against him. What we are seeing now is only the threat. He is making sure we understand the consequences of your backing out of this marriage, your highness. If you love Briavel and you love its people—"

Valentyna stepped back, aghast that he could think otherwise. Liryk continued, ignoring her shock. "If you love Briavel and its people," he repeated, more gently this time, "you will hurry up and marry the King of Morgravia."

He bowed, refusing to react to the telltale glisten in the Queen's eyes. "I shall prepare to leave for Sharptyn, your highness, and I shall bring back the woman of Yentro for you. I give you my word that I will achieve this for you or die trying."

Valentyna was unable to speak. She watched Liryk's broad back go down the corridor and she felt hollow.

21

ELSPYTH WATCHED THROUGH HER TEARS AS THE BODY OF THE woman who had been wailing earlier gushed its lifeblood steadily into the sawdust. The killer, an older woman, stood bowed above, bleeding from several wounds and no doubt in shock. The victor had struck a lucky blow at the top of the wailing woman's thigh, which had hit a major artery in her groin. Death had followed not long afterward. The men did not even give the woman the grace of a peaceful death; instead they cheered hysterically while the winners gleefully collected on their bets.

The women in the pen watched in silent horror as another soul was collected by Shar's Gatherers. Most did not know the dead woman's name. As Alda had cautioned Elspyth, there was no point in getting to know one another; it only made the killing harder. The corpse was dragged away by the hair, to be burned later with the rest of the dead, their bodies piled up from the evening's entertainment. The victor, still frozen, her eyes glazed over, was led roughly out of the arena.

"It's her first kill," a voice said close by.

Elspyth started, unaware that Alda had sidled up beside her during the fight. "And the dead woman?"

"She was on her third fight. If she'd won tonight, she'd be on her way to the boat. Stupid fool—she could have won easily. Still, one less for me to kill."

Elspyth looked up at the taller woman. She felt sorrow that a mother had become so hardened. And yet it was because of her child that this woman plotted to win at all costs. Elspyth shuddered in disgust. "Get away from me."

The Briavellian made a sound of disgust. "I hope you're next!" she said, nodding her head toward the man approaching. "Time you found out what it's like out there."

Elspyth ignored her, her gaze fixed on the obese fellow waddling toward them with his hated parchment of names.

"Next up, ladies, is Olivya," he said in a jovial voice.

No one moved. Terrified gazes met the more resolute ones of those succumbing to a sense of fate.

"Come on, now. Small, pretty, dark. Ah, there you are, my dear. Cast off that sheet now," he said to Elspyth. "It's your turn."

Elspyth had forgotten she had given a false name. Her legs felt too weak to hold her body up, let alone carry her across the pen and into the arena. She began to weep.

"Come on, lass. Haven't got all night," the man urged, scowling now.

Alda pushed Elspyth forward viciously. "Who's she fighting?"

"Ginny. Where are you, Ginny?"

"Let me fight her instead."

"You're not down to fight tonight, Alda," the fat man replied. "We're going to make you lose some sleep over your third." He smiled without kindness, sweat running down his oily face.

"I'll make it a real spectacle," Alda said desperately.

Elspyth felt her chest constrict, trapping her breath. What was Alda thinking? She could see the bloodlust in her face, and knew the Briavellian was looking forward to an easy kill.

The idea that she was considered a pushover dragged Elspyth from her stupor. She sucked in air with a huge angry gasp and suddenly the noise, the smell, the woman's blood still wet and gleaming on the floor, and now, the fat man and Alda bargaining over her death, galvanized her. Elspyth felt the fear leave her in a tingling, angry rush. It pushed upward through her throat and exploded in a cry of fury, and something she had never felt before oozed from every fiber of her being. It was rage, bubbling through her as a white-cold flame, torching her thoughts, sparking her emotions, scorching her with its devouring wrath. The fear that had left a puddle of urine around her feet only minutes earlier fled.

Elspyth stepped away from her own mess, cast aside the flimsy linen, and addressed the man in a voice that was animalistic and predatory. "Let me fight Alda!"

The fat man looked at her. This was new. Normally the women fought one another under protest, all but helping their opponents into the ring, apologizing for having to hurt one another, then weeping over each death. But these two women were eager for the fight; with those sorts of emotions, the spectacle was sure to be especially entertaining for the men.

His thick tongue flicked out to wet his rubbery lips as he considered this option. "My, my," he said, unpleasant smells wafting toward Elspyth as he moved closer to her. "You must be confident."

"Just announce it," she answered, eager to get the fight done. If she was going to die, she'd rather do so now than spend further hours agonizing.

Alda clapped her hands with pleasure. The Morgravian had admitted she did not know how to fight. It was going to be easy.

"All right, then," the man replied. "Don't say I never give you girls what you want," he added with a lecherous chuckle. "Off with your linen, then, Alda. Both of you oil up. I'll make the announcement."

Wyl walked between the two men, his arms in front of his body and tied at the wrist. He did not feel scared. This was the death he wanted; he just wished he could somehow spare Ylena's body from being mistreated in the process. He spent the time during the frigidly silent walk toward the main hall contemplating what would be the kindest death for Ylena and decided a blade into her heart was ideal—just as Faryl had killed Koreldy. That way, when her body was cleaned, covered, and laid out in Argorn, as he fully intended it to be, no one would have to see the ugly wound that had felled her. She could remain beautiful for eternity in their minds.

But it nagged at Wyl that Celimus was unlikely to have in mind something as straightforward as a knife. He would draw this out as if it were a game; in the same way that he had taunted Wyl—forcing him to witness Alyd's death and Ylena's suffering—he would now mock Wyl's sister in front of his honored guests. Except he was in for a surprise. This Ylena walked to her death with a light heart.

"Are you all right, my lady?" Harken whispered.

"I am fine. Remember all I have told you. If you think well of the Thirsk family, be assured they would have sworn their allegiance to Valentyna the moment she became Queen of Morgravia as well as Briavel. Do the same, for all of us."

Wyl sensed Harken's fear but also his pride at being singled out. "I will do it for you, my lady."

"Then I am glad to have met you."

"Be quiet," the older soldier warned. "We're here now."

Dusk had fallen so quietly Wyl had not noticed. The north draped itself with evening's calm without the south's cacophony of noisy birds telling the world it was time to roost. There was still sufficient light, however, that Wyl had no doubt as to the identity of the man waiting at the grand doorway of Tenterdyn.

"Good evening, Ylena," Jessom said, all politeness. Wyl did not reply. "As you will," the Chancellor replied, not at all offended.

"Thank you, gentlemen," Wyl forced out of Ylena's lips. It was meant only for the young soldier and he qualified his words with a brief glance toward him. He was careful not to name Harken. Jessom was far too sharp to let the soldier leave if he thought any sort of alliance—no matter how tenuous— had been formed.

"We'll take her from here," Jessom said to Ylena's escort. Two burly guards stepped out from behind the Chancellor and took position on either side of Ylena. "Follow me."

Wyl was led past familiar rooms toward a part of Tenterdyn he had not seen on his former visit. He heard the murmur of voices and small explosions of laughter, which grew louder as they approached a wing that he recalled had been shut off by doors. They were wide open now, the corridor lit by torches and guarded by yet more soldiers. Two kings were present; it was little wonder that the level of security was so high.

"Wait here," Jessom commanded, touching Ylena's arm. Wyl shook off his hand and the man's thin smile returned. "I must let the King know his lamb has arrived."

There was no mistaking his meaning. If Ylena's mouth had not been so dry with tension, Wyl might have tried spitting again at the Chancellor, for the amusement of soiling his robes, if nothing else.

Jessom disappeared around a corner. The sounds of men eating and entertaining themselves filled the frigid silence between Wyl and his guards. The aroma of food wafted toward them and one man's belly acknowledged it with a growl. Wyl turned toward the sound and met the culprit's abashed expression.

"Do you know that I'm being brought here to be killed for sport in front of your king?"

The guard shrugged, although Wyl sensed there was embarrassment hidden behind it.

"We just follow orders, my lady." It was the man on his other side who answered.

Wyl looked at him. "And as a Legionnaire, you are comfortable with the notion of slaughtering an innocent woman—a noble no less—from a fine family that has given its life to the Legion? You are old enough to have known my father."

The man did not respond, but the pity in his eyes betrayed him.

Jessom rescued him. "Come, Ylena Thirsk. Your king awaits you."

*   *   *

Elspyth stood at the fringe of the rough circle mapped out with string tied around small stakes in the earth. She was naked but no longer cared, ignoring the sounds of appreciation from men enjoying the sight of a lovely body. All that mattered right now was the person on the opposite side of the ring, also naked, also breathing hard, and no doubt hoping that her cold stare would be enough to intimidate her opponent into submission without a blow.

The fat man was stirring up the excited crowd, but Elspyth ignored him too. She knew where Ericson was sitting and briefly entertained the idea of flinging her knife, Koreldy-style, at his bulk. She had a vision of him flailing in shock as the blade hit him squarely in the throat. She sighed, knowing she could never throw true. The blade would probably make it only half the distance and then clatter pathetically on the ground, undoubtedly to wild applause, leaving her defenseless, to be slaughtered by Alda. A bell sounded and dragged her back to the insanity before her. She knew her knuckles were white as she clutched the single small blade that was her weapon.

She heard the fat man remind her that this fight was to the death, then his explanation that Alda was fighting for her third win and her right to be given over to slavery. The men cheered, no doubt imagining profit from her sale as well as her win. Elspyth forced herself to withdraw completely into her mind. She recalled the long night journey to Deakyn with Wyl—he walked as Koreldy then—and how he had told her that a warrior preparing for battle must draw every ounce of his conscious self into a closed section of his mind that no one could penetrate. She had smiled a little indulgently at his description at the time; now she understood completely what he had meant.

The bell sounded again and Alda began moving, circling. *This is it,* Elspyth thought. *Kill or be killed.*

"To you, Lothryn, my love," she murmured, remembering how he had given his own life in order to save others. She suddenly felt sure that Lothryn's feelings at that moment of decision—the knowledge of certain death, the grief of losing his

new son, the sorrow that their love had remained unspoken—
were identical to her own. It was a tearing free of all ties, a casting loose of all fears in the pursuit of one thing: kill or be killed.

Alda lunged and Elspyth's mind went blank.

Wyl stepped into a large chamber that was warmed by
fires at either end. A few men milled around, holding
goblets of wine. He recognized none of them, which meant
there was no one who might object to Ylena's mistreatment.
His boots crunched on the floor and he realized he was
walking over the remains of Aleda's fine cranberry-colored
glassware. Like the loyal family of the north, it was now
shattered, forgotten.

And then he laid eyes on the man responsible for it all.
Celimus, brimming with self-importance, sat at the head of
Jeryb's oak table, goblet in hand, making some toast, his
cheeks slightly flushed from the wine and the general jovi-
ality. To his right sat Cailech; the Mountain King looked less
comfortable and there was less debris about him, as though
he had been more cautious in his enjoyment of the repast.
Wyl knew the man well enough to recognize that the smile
fixed on his face was fake. Cailech raised his glass in answer
to whatever Celimus had said but did not drink; meanwhile
his penetrating gaze soaked up all around him as effectively
as a sponge. He was bare-armed; the muscles sculpted and
tensed, as if he was ready to leap to his feet and charge, like
an animal disturbed. No, Cailech was not happy here, but he
was pretending well enough. Next to him sat Aremys, un-
smiling and rigid, no sign of wine or food about him.

The three men noticed Ylena's arrival at the same time.
Celimus looked savagely delighted, his eyes darkening with
pleasure at what he knew was coming. Cailech, however,
looked taken aback. His roving gaze settled intently on
Ylena and the contrived smile faded. Her beauty had taken
him by surprise, Wyl realized. Poor Aremys looked like a
chained dog; one that knew it was about to take a hiding. He
paled, his already unhappy expression settling into a blank
mask, as if he was steeling himself. He could hardly make
eye contact with Wyl, such was his despair.

The room quieted as people noticed their presence, but Jessom allowed the hush to settle fully before he spoke. "Gentlemen, may I present Lady Ylena Thirsk, daughter of the late General Fergys Thirsk and sister to the much loved General Wyl Thirsk, may Shar bless their souls."

Some repeated the last few words and Wyl took bitter delight in seeing the Morgravian King's mouth tighten. The smile turned acid and Wyl knew he would pay for that loyalty to his family with blood.

"Ylena Thirsk, how enchanting to have you back among your fellow Morgravians," Celimus said, flashing a bright smile toward his honored guest. "Come, Cailech, you must meet the woman who escaped my punishment through the aid of a mercenary who goes by the name of Koreldy."

Cailech turned a cold green gaze onto his fellow king. "Koreldy?"

"You know him?"

"I will flay the skin from his bones when I find him again."

Celimus, fired by the excellent wine from Jeryb's cellars and feeling very pleased at being about to do away with the final member of the hated Thirsk dynasty, threw back his head and laughed with delight. "Then I have done you a service, my friend. Koreldy is dead."

The Mountain King did not react. His face was set in stone, his eyes unreadable.

"Well, actually," Celimus continued, noticing the lack of reaction and pleased by it, "I think we have my bride-to-be to thank for his death."

"How so?" Cailech asked tightly.

Celimus drained his goblet of wine and slammed it down. Droplets of red launched from his mouth like blood as he shook his head. It was fitting, Wyl thought, for blood would flow tonight. "Koreldy fled to the safety of Briavel, pretending to be a champion to my queen." He made a gesture of nonchalance. "She was unaware of his identity, of course, until I revealed it to her."

"Why don't you admit it was the only way you could escape

death from Koreldy's sword, you sniveling coward," Wyl shouted.

Exclamations rang out in the hall and Celimus's eyes shone with hatred. He walked toward Ylena until he towered above her. "The Thirsk bitch lies. She wasn't there; how could she know? Where were you, Ylena? At Rittylworth, wasn't it? Cringing in the cellar of a monastery before your flight to Felrawthy. It is fitting that your journey ends here. No one can save you now."

"Nor do I want them to, you son of a whore. Thank goodness your father killed your mother. The only pity is that he did not do it before she birthed you—"

He got no further with his insult. The punch to Ylena's face was expertly leveled and the room went dark for Wyl. Everyone else was frozen in shocked silence. Jessom was the first to gather his wits; he nodded toward one of the guards to pick up the woman sprawled across the flagstones, her head bleeding from where she had gashed it on the table.

Cailech glanced toward Aremys and saw his stricken expression. He didn't know what was going on here, but he didn't like it one bit. There was clearly a connection between Aremys and the woman. More than that, and perhaps more disturbingly, it seemed that Celimus was putting on this whole charade for his benefit. If Celimus thought his northern neighbor would get pleasure from watching a noblewoman humiliated and injured in this fashion, however, he had entirely misjudged. Cailech was the first to admit that he was no softhearted monarch; he had not flinched at having the Morgravian woman staked out for roasting, or killing her later to trick Gueryn. But she had been a prisoner of battle. This Thirsk woman struck him as a pawn in whatever game was being played out between Celimus and the Thirsk family, and Cailech wanted no part of it. He raised an eyebrow in silent question to Aremys, who glared back at him, as if demanding that he do something.

Celimus turned to his guests and rubbed his knuckles. "Don't worry, she has a head as hard as stone—like all the Thirsk trolls." Nervous laughter sounded in the room. "Get her ready!" he ordered Jessom, who escorted the guard holding the prone woman out a side door.

Cailech wanted to bring the evening to a rapid close. It was time to get away from here. But the sight of the golden-haired beauty and her magnificent defiance of the man everyone in Morgravia feared compelled him to learn more. He knew Celimus was watching him and so he said smoothly, "You were telling me about Koreldy," as if the interruption had been of little consequence.

Celimus continued with similar aplomb, seating himself and bidding everyone do the same. "Yes, forgive the disturbance. I revealed Koreldy's true identity to Queen Valentyna, who was mortified—as you might imagine—for the mercenary had killed her father, King Valor."

"I see. And?"

"Well, she banished him, which made it possible for one of my assassins to deal with him. I had no intention of allowing Koreldy to roam the land after he had betrayed me."

Cailech sucked in a breath. "You have proof of Koreldy's death?"

"A finger, still wearing a signet ring with a deep bloodred stone and marked with the family insignia."

"I know the ring," Cailech replied, feeling suddenly empty. He had been looking forward to dealing with Romen Koreldy himself, it was true, but he had not expected the acute sense of sorrow that pervaded him. In spite of their differences, not to mention the bad blood, he had respected the man, and felt sure Koreldy would have preferred to be felled by a Mountain warrior's sword than a Morgravian assassin's blade. "I always thought the man had lives to spare," he commented, trying to hide the bitterness in his tone.

"Well, he used them all up once he crossed me, my friend," Celimus boasted, and urged more wine to be poured.

Cailech had tired of being referred to as friend by the Morgravian King. He gave a subtle nod toward Aremys, who understood its meaning but made no move; instead he glanced again toward the door beyond which the woman had been taken. Cailech frowned. What was it between those two?

"That woman—what is to happen to her?" he asked, twirling his half-empty goblet.

"She will be executed in your honor, sir," Celimus answered.

Cailech spilled some of the wine in his surprise. "Certainly not in my honor!"

The King of Morgravia shrugged. "Well, she is to die anyway—I'd like her to be my gift to you. You're not squeamish, are you?" It was a challenge.

Cailech had had enough. He liked neither the sound of the gift nor the suggestion of his gutlessness. "Celimus, we have enjoyed your hospitality long enough. You will forgive me if I take my leave now."

"I could not forgive you if you did, my friend."

"Why is that?" Cailech asked, gritting his teeth.

"We still have time before the appointed rendezvous and I would like you to partake of the evening's entertainment."

"Which is?"

Celimus's voice was sly. "Tell Jessom we are ready," he said to a waiting servant.

It was terrifying. Elspyth had never fought in any sort of hand-to-hand combat in her life, not even as a child, enacting pretend sword fights and mock battles with other children in the pursuit of laughter and competition. Now she found herself facing a woman who seemed utterly determined to kill her. Elspyth had no tricks to draw upon, no skills that might help her protect herself.

Alda's lips was drawn back in a tight snarl. There was no doubt in Elspyth's mind that Alda saw herself as the predator and her opponent as the cornered, helpless prey. The older woman laughed, springing forward and feinting toward her right. Elspyth fell for the bluff and tried to dart in the opposite direction, but found that path cut off, a blade slashing toward her. She shrieked and twisted away, feeling the knife cut cruelly down her back.

The men roared; more bets were exchanged in Alda's favor. The cheering and jeering continued without respite as the audience insulted Elspyth, shouting that Shar's Gatherers were running toward her so fast, she might as well give up now.

Again Alda pounced, this time trying to slash her opponent's face—which was all the prettier, many men in the audience conceded, for its pleading expression. Elspyth reacted instinctively and put both her arms up, which won her a nasty gash on the arm, where bright blood bloomed instantly. The arm she held her blade in began to go numb almost immediately. She cried out in despair.

Alda was enjoying herself. Elspyth realized the woman was simply playing with her. She had promised the fat man a spectacle in exchange for being allowed to kill the opponent of her choice, and she was delivering on that promise. How many more slashes would she make before the killing blow came? Elspyth wondered through her tears as Alda leapt again, missing so slightly that Elspyth heard the whistle of the blade through the air. Alda laughed again. Elspyth's exertions were making her blood flow more freely. She could feel it was running down her back, and her front was splashed with blood from her arm wound.

The numbness made it hard to feel her hand gripping the blade. That was probably Alda's intention, she realized, impressed. Not all for show, then. Her would-be killer was making strategic wounds, designed for disabling as much as for exhibition. No wonder Alda had made it to her third fight. No doubt she would make it to the slave boat.

Elspyth felt the sadistic bite of the blade again, this time expertly delivered across one breast, and rapidly followed by the wet sensation of blood spouting forth in concert with the vicious pain. Elspyth staggered, hardly daring to look down at the ruin of her body. When she did she saw only red, running freely and draining her of strength and the will to remain standing. Opposite her swaggered Alda, free of cuts or injuries but covered in blood nonetheless . . . Elspyth's blood.

And then Alda did something she had no idea would awaken the primeval instinct in her opponent. Responding to the chanting of the male audience, now calling for an end to the ragged young woman, Alda slowly licked at the blood that spattered her mouth. The men, driven into a frenzy of lust and greed, shouted all the more fiercely for the killing blow.

But Elspyth, watching that theatrical gesture, as if Alda thought Elspyth was hers to consume, felt the searing white flame of anger once more. She straightened, threw back her greasy hair, and screamed. And her fury traveled and hit its mark, cutting through the shields of sorcery, streaming loudly into the consciousness of a man trapped in the body of a horse.

It was as if, for just a moment, he saw it all.

Kill her, Elspyth, he cried. *Survive!* And then he was gone, slipping away from her mind like sand through fingers.

"Lothryn!" she shrieked, but silence was all she heard. Thick, dark silence and Alda's sinister presence.

"It's time, Olivya," the woman called sweetly, like a mother to her child. Except the sweetness was tainted and false.

"Do it, then, bitch! End it!" Elspyth screamed back over the excited clamor of the audience, who knew the blade would fall only once more.

Alda was not prepared for this. She had anticipated begging and weeping, but not aggression. Then she frowned; Elspyth was crouching as if in disabling pain, placing her blade in the sawdust.

"I have no more to give," Elspyth whispered, "no more."

Her opponent became angry. "You gave nothing! You didn't even try to defend yourself, you weak fool. At least now I have my escape from here. Thank you, Olivya—your life has bought something precious." She sneered as she quickly covered the ground between them.

"Make it swift," Elspyth pleaded.

"I will," the woman said, wiping blood from her mouth, hardly able to see flesh through the red liquid covering her opponent's body. "Bare your throat!"

Elspyth turned her head slightly sideways, knowing she looked like a lamb with its neck exposed for a quick killing slash.

In her excitement, all Alda saw was the girl giving herself

willingly to death. She did not notice Elspyth's hand reaching slowly for the blade by her side. Some of the men did, and began screaming for Alda to beware, but she could not hear them in the cacophony. She had eyes now only for Olivya's creamy throat and raised her blade high into the air.

Elspyth watched the weapon reach the zenith of its arc . . . Now! She moved faster than she ever had before. It was a once-only effort and it had to be accurate. Wyl had told her that in battle, when you sense the opening in someone's defenses, you have to strike as fast as your body allows and put your full strength behind it, as a cat does when it pounces. Elspyth was that cat now. She felt her legs push up hard as she poured every ounce of her courage and love for Lothryn into one savage leap. Propelling herself upward, she thrust the blade before her and, unbelievably, saw it embed itself in the center of Alda's throat.

Elspyth felt pain as Alda's knife, intended for her neck, missed its mark and sank deep into her shoulder. It hurt, more than she cared to think about, but it would not take her life . . . unlike her blow. Alda's spluttering surprise was cut short by a horrible gurgle, and she fell to the sand.

Elspyth, trembling with shock, knelt beside Alda's slumped figure and took her hand. She did not want her to go to her god amid hate. The woman tried to speak, but her eyes were already glazing over. Did she feel regret that she had lost her chance for the slave boat or sorrow for the cold-blooded actions that had brought her this far? Elspyth would never know, but she felt the slightest squeeze of her hand as the dying woman struggled not to release her soul to the Gatherers.

A hush blanketed the audience in eerie silence. Much money had been lost this evening; the underdog had won against the odds.

Alda's blood mixed with Elspyth's, forming a pool between them. "I'm sorry," Elspyth whispered, unable to control her tears. "May Shar guide you to his peace." Alda died with a crooked smile, as if in thanks for Elspyth's blessing.

The strangled silence of disbelief was broken by the angry shouts of soldiers bursting into the building. One of them was Commander Liryk, roaring orders, but it was Crys who saw Elspyth first.

The sight of the two bloodied figures in the middle of the makeshift arena horrified him, stopping him in his tracks. One woman was obviously dying, perhaps already dead, and the other was sobbing.

"Elspyth," he called into the rabble. She did not hear him. "Elspyth!" he yelled, fury overtaking him as images of his own dead family scorched a path to the front of his mind.

She looked up, her body trembling. "Crys?" He saw her mouth move hesitantly, as if she was unsure she could believe what she was seeing.

He was at her side in a few angry strides and scooped her into his arms, the blood that covered her body wet against him. Unable to force out another word, all Crys could do was bury his face in her lank, bloodied hair and weep with her.

Kind arms finally loosened his grip on Elspyth and a blanket was thrown around her shivering body. Liryk squeezed Crys's arms. "Steady now," he said, and Crys was grateful for the reminder that he must hold his strength in front of the men. He nodded, communicating his thanks silently to the senior soldier. "She's hurt," he said, at which point Elspyth sank to her knees.

"Get her out of here," Liryk barked to one of his men.

"No, wait!" she begged. "Have you got the leaders?"

Liryk shook his head. "Are you up to helping us with that?"

"Can't you see her wounds—"

Elspyth interrupted Crys. "It's all right. Please. Ensuring their heads roll at the swipe of an ax means everything to me."

"Good girl," Liryk said, impressed, for he had seen the woman of Yentro's injuries and knew they must be extremely painful. "Point them out."

Crys helped Elspyth to her feet and wiped her face with a damp towel a nearby guard handed him. The cool water and the cleaning away of the blood revived her slightly.

"Come," Liryk encouraged. "They're rounded up outside."

"What about the women?" she asked.

"They're being taken care of," Liryk assured her, then gave a low whistle. "I'm shocked by this. We had no idea of its extent."

"You knew about it?" Elspyth could not help the accusation in her tone.

"Suspected it," Liryk corrected. "But we've been waiting for something or someone to give us a lead to follow."

Elspyth made a sound of disgust but said no more, feeling Crys's slight pressure at her shoulder, suggesting she hold her tongue. She turned to follow Liryk, but when she tried to walk unaided she fell down.

Crys picked her up gently and Elspyth felt warmed by the sad smile on his face. "Let me support you, Elspyth, if you won't permit me to carry you," he said, and circled her waist loosely with his arm so she could lean against him as she needed to.

"Thank you," she whispered. "How did you find me?"

"Later," Crys replied. "Let's get this ugly business done."

Outside, Elspyth pointed out the men who had led the betting and then took much pleasure in asking Crys to take her to where Ericson was trying to stand unnoticed in the mob.

"That's him," she said. "He calls himself Ericson. He is the leader of this rabble, the one who acquires the women for his sport." She said the last word as if it was poison in her mouth.

Ericson was dragged from the crowd and bound and shackled alongside seven other men who had been involved.

"Is this it?" the Commander asked.

"Yes. The rest are just cruel onlookers."

Liryk nodded wearily. "Right, men, hear me." He addressed his soldiers. "I want proof of the name of each man here. If he has no proof, he will be executed. Those who provide proof are to receive forty lashes each. If they survive the whipping, they can drag their sorry arses home and explain it how they will. Remember," he said, turning back to the prisoners, "we will have a record of your names and the towns you hail from. If you err again, at any time, your family will be stripped of its assets—homes, land, money, belongings. Is that clear?"

Elspyth saw the men blanch with fear on hearing about the physical ordeal ahead. Perhaps now they might understand a tiny measure of what they had put the captured women through. She had no sympathy in her heart for them, and wondered what Liryk had in store for Ericson and his band of followers. She did not have to wait long.

"The leaders will have their heads removed from their bodies," Liryk said, glaring at the cowardly Ericson, who visibly staggered at the sentence.

Silence gripped the crowd, soldiers and prisoners alike too stunned to make a sound.

"What are you waiting for?" Liryk said calmly to one of his captains.

"I'm sorry, sir. Do you mean now?"

"I do. All of these men are to watch, as a reminder that Briavel's queen does not show mercy to those who break the most sacred laws of life."

Despite her flagging strength, Elspyth had the energy to feel sorry for the Captain, who, to his credit, gave a crisp salute despite his sudden pallor. She stayed conscious long enough to bear witness to Ericson's sobs as he was forced to kneel and lay his neck across a log. She looked around for his daughter, but the girl with the singsong voice was nowhere to be seen as the ax fell and her father's head rolled from his body.

"They say the head knows it has been removed from the body for several seconds afterward," Crys commented blandly, still supporting her with his arm.

"Good," Elspyth mumbled, and, her strength gone, slumped against his shoulder.

22

YL WAS BROUGHT BACK INTO THE HALL OF THE ÐONALS, where an air of expectancy greeted him. He glanced at Aremys's stricken face and wished he could reassure his friend that death did not frighten him anymore. Any escape from the sheath of Ylena's body was welcome.

At Jessom's bidding, and with an awkward silence prevailing, he was taken by the two guards to a spot at one end of the chamber where his hands were tied to a timber framework, no doubt hastily erected for his benefit. His ankles, still manacled, were unnecessarily tied to the timbers as well. *This is novel,* he thought. Celimus was obviously getting more creative. He stared defiantly at the Morgravian King.

Celimus took a swig from his goblet. "The last of the great Thirsks, strung up for our pleasure, gentlemen. Call in the archers," he said, then glanced toward the stony-faced Mountain King. "Come on, Cailech, I thought you people were . . ." He paused.

"Barbaric?" Cailech offered.

Celimus smiled, sly and cunning. "Fun loving, I was going to say."

Cailech did not reply. He turned to look at the intriguing woman and was met by a hard blue gaze, fiery with hatred and anger. He felt his breath catch, as it did each time he looked at her. He admired the defiance, her complete disregard and indeed disrespect for the company she was in, and the lack of fear for what she surely knew was coming. She had the courage of the Mountain People in her soul, he thought fancifully, caught by the golden hair that had fallen loose. Ylena Thirsk looked dirty and disheveled, but she was nonetheless desirable, he admitted to himself.

He had to look away from her fierce stare. "No trial?" he asked as two archers were brought in.

"None required," Celimus said. "She pays the price for the treachery of the men of her family."

"Shar won't grant you forgiveness for this, you evil scum, Celimus. This is like the witch Myrren all over again, isn't it?" Wyl forced out a laugh as the similarity of the situation struck him. He saw that it struck home with Celimus too and took pleasure in seeing the King flinch. "She got the better of you and so will I. I won't scream, I won't give you any satisfaction, you cowardly—"

"Shut her up!" Celimus ordered a soldier.

But Wyl was going to have his say, even as the embarrassed guard moved toward him. "Your father wished many times that my brother could be King, so you got rid of both of them—and the King of Briavel, Romen Koreldy, and the Donal family. Watch out, Cailech, he'll be planning to kill you next. And no doubt his bride. He'll slaughter everyone until—"

Ylena's mouth was bound. Although he could not make himself understood, Wyl continued to rage at the man who had destroyed the lives of so many good, loyal people of Morgravia. He saw Cailech shake his head, noticed that the Razor King wore an expression of wonder.

"Where are you going, Aremys Farrow?" Celimus asked loudly over Ylena's accusations. "Be quiet, Ylena, or I'll slash your mouth so it can't move properly."

Wyl quieted. He had promised himself he would keep Ylena as unmarked as he could. There was nothing more to be achieved anyway by his unintelligible ravings. He joined everyone else in the chamber in looking toward the mercenary.

Aremys had hoped no one would notice him slipping away from the hall. He could not witness this. "Apologies, sire. I thought I should go and check on the horses so that we would be ready to move out after the . . . entertainment."

"Everything will be readied for your departure, Farrow.

I'd prefer you to stay. In fact I rather thought you'd like to see your prey be felled."

"Not in this manner, sire," Aremys risked.

Celimus did not react as Aremys thought he would. In truth, the King was enjoying everyone's discomfort. "Your king has remained, and as this is in his honor, I expect you to share in this gift," he ordered.

"Of course, sire. As you wish," Aremys said, glancing toward Ylena and privately agreeing that it was probably for the best. He would need to know which of these men Wyl would become. And then a chilling thought occurred to him. Did Myrren's Gift work only if Wyl was slain by hand—that is, if someone was physically connected to the weapon? His mind raced. Wyl had never mentioned it, but then perhaps Wyl did not know! Koreldy had been killed by Faryl, who had plunged a knife into his heart with her own hand. Faryl had been killed by Ylena, who had held the blade that slashed the assassin's throat. If Celimus was planning to loose arrows into Ylena, no one would be connected to the weapon when it landed in her body. Ylena would surely die . . . but perhaps so would Wyl.

The sense that he had stumbled across something important so terrified Aremys that he shouted into the thick, expectant silence: "Sire!"

"Yes, Farrow?" the King said, his temper rising.

Aremys looked at Ylena and then at Cailech—saw the Mountain King frown and knew he suspected something between him and the woman. "King Celimus," he began, clearing his throat nervously, "this is a messy end, sire, particularly for a celebration. Why don't I just take her out the back and kill her for you?"

"You had your chance, Farrow. Now I will show you how to finish a job."

"But, your majesty . . ." His words died away and he felt a twinge of fear as Celimus turned to stare at him, no longer indulgent toward the emissary of the Mountain King, no longer prepared to be generous.

"Don't push me Grenadyne, or you'll find yourself staked out like the Lady Ylena there."

"I would have to object to such treatment of a protected guest," Cailech warned icily, nodding at Aremys to continue.

"Let me finish what you asked me to do, King Celimus. I will cut her throat here and now before you." It was his last desperate try. At least he could be sure Wyl would live on.

Celimus found himself cornered. He wanted to have some fun with Ylena's death, but he could tell he had overstepped the mark where Cailech was concerned in threatening Farrow. He knew from the expression on Jessom's face that the Chancellor was urging him to take the easy way out: have the mercenary finish off the woman. He was angry but this was not the time or place to make a scene.

"Well, at least her blood will not be on my hands." He smiled. "Go ahead, Farrow. Finish the job I paid you to do."

Aremys risked a glance of thanks toward Cailech, convinced that without the Mountain King's timely comment and brittle tone, Celimus might not have relented. Cailech returned the gaze with an expression of utter bafflement.

"I will need a blade, sire," Aremys said.

Celimus gave an order and one of the soldiers at Ylena's side pulled a mean-looking knife from his belt. "It's sharp," he murmured. "Make it quick."

Aremys nodded. Everyone wanted this ugliness done with. He took a deep breath. This was it. He was about to die, to sacrifice his body to Wyl. He stood close to Ylena. "As One," he said, and grinned sadly at the irony of the words. He saw the tears well in her eyes as she heard the Thirsk family motto.

Aremys raised the blade, knowing precisely where to strike to slash the jugular for a swift death. As he did, however, Ylena began to scream and struggle desperately.

"Arrow! Arrow!" Wyl shrieked in Ylena's high voice, determined to stop his good friend from giving up his own life.

"What's she saying?" the Morgravian King inquired, determined to drag out the agony.

"She's simply yelling my name," Aremys answered.

"Er, I think she's saying 'arrow,' sire," one of the guards objected.

"Oh, perhaps she'd prefer to be killed by the archers?"

"No, sire," Aremys said as firmly as he dared. "This is best."

"Wait!" the King replied. "Let's ask her. It's the least we can do, isn't it?" He cast an appealing glance around the hall, playing the magnanimous sovereign.

Aremys glared at Wyl. "You fool," he said angrily, under his breath.

The guard ripped away the bindings around Ylena's mouth.

"Step aside, Farrow," Celimus said, enjoying himself hugely. The big man did so reluctantly, but not before glaring at Cailech, who frowned again, taking in all the strange nuances of behavior on display here.

"Ylena," Celimus said; it sounded almost tender. "As a final act of generosity toward your family, I'm going to allow you to choose how you die: by Farrow's blade across your throat or by an arrow fired by one of my expert archers?"

"By the arrow," Wyl said fiercely, not daring to look at Aremys.

"As we suspected. Good choice, Ylena," Celimus replied, stopping just short of rubbing his hands in glee. "Thank you, Farrow. It seems your job is complete. Move away."

This time Aremys looked at no one as he returned to his spot near the door. He stared at the ground. He would not watch Wyl die.

"Ylena, my dear, I did have some sport planned with the archers, but as everyone here seems to want you to have a speedy end, I'll send them away and instead I will do the necessary."

"As you wish," Wyl replied without blinking, knowing he was spoiling Celimus's fun by being so accepting. It worked. The King's face darkened with a scowl.

"Give me a bow!" Celimus said, his tone furious. "Let's finish this."

"Why don't we?" Wyl said, in the most bored tone he could achieve. He could hardly believe his luck that Celimus had chosen to do the deed. He would become the Morgravian King within the next few moments, and much as he hated the thought of living as Celimus, what pleasure it would be to finally kill him. "Hurry up, sire! I am eager to be gone from here." He saw Cailech give a grin of astonishment at Ylena's bravado. Celimus took aim. Wyl switched his attention briefly to Aremys, but his friend refused to look at him. Wyl could not understand why: Aremys knew he would live again, this time as King.

"Farewell, Ylena Thirsk. May Shar send you to wherever your predecessors have ended their days." Celimus stretched the bowstring taut. "Heart or eye? Or shall I let it be a surprise?" he asked with a cruel smile. Everyone could hear the slight strain in his voice caused by holding back the string so tightly.

Wyl refused to answer and instead closed his eyes. Celimus was an excellent shot.

Cailech's astonishment erupted. This woman was extraordinary; she should not be wasted in this manner. Ylena Thirsk stirred more emotion in him than any woman had in his entire life. Cailech had been accused of being cold toward women, but that was not true. He liked women well enough; he just had never met anyone who truly excited him. But Ylena Thirsk provoked in him a swirl of inexplicable feelings. He wanted this woman! And he was not about to let her die trussed like an animal at the end of one of Celimus's arrows.

He moved fast as a pouncing cat and pushed the Morgravian King's wrist up just as the arrow was loosed. It shot high into the air of the hall, burying itself with a resounding thump in a solid beam overhead. Everyone followed the quivering motion of the shaft, not sure whether to be horrified by Cailech's action or relieved. Wyl opened Ylena's eyes with angry disbelief. Aremys had to ball his hands into fists to stop himself from clapping.

Celimus turned the darkest of stares onto his fellow king.

"I've just decided about that gift you offered me, Celimus."

The Morgravian's expression did not change, nor did he utter a word in response.

"I want her," Cailech said, pointing toward Ylena.

"What?" Celimus roared.

"You heard me," Cailech replied calmly. "I shall take

Ylena Thirsk from you. She will travel with us high into the Razors and will never trouble you again."

"What possible interest could you have in her?"

"I'm sure if you think about it long enough, you'll work it out," Cailech said, winking.

Impossibly, Celimus began to laugh. Jessom slowly let out his tightly held breath. Cailech had certainly taken a risk, but the Chancellor could not think of a better way to handle this situation. Had he not suggested to Celimus that he marry Ylena off to a Mountain warrior? There would be little chance of her escaping the Razors, and once the royal marriage was complete, no one would care about the Thirsk name, so deliriously happy would they all be that Morgravia and Briavel were unified. "My lord, this is an opportunity," he risked.

Cailech grinned. "You see, Celimus, even your own counsel likes the idea."

Wyl began to rage, Ylena's voice becoming hysterical. "You bastard! You killed my brother and I'll see you in hell for that. Let me die. I want to die!"

"Oh, someone get her out of here," Celimus said, more exasperated now than angry. He could not help but like Cailech's idea as he watched Ylena being dragged away.

"You did promise me a gift. Anything, you said," Cailech reminded him.

"That's true, I did," Celimus agreed, looking at Cailech. "There would have to be conditions, though. Koreldy tried something similar."

"I am not Koreldy." Cailech bristled.

"Why do you want her?"

"Why would any red-blooded man want her? Does she not affect you so?"

"No. Her mere name sickens me."

"All the better for me, Celimus. I think she's a beauty. Let us truly bind ourselves in our treaty—I will take a Morgravian as my wife."

"Your wife?" Celimus exclaimed, unable to hide his incredulity.

"Yes, why not?" Cailech was grinning widely now. He

glanced at Aremys, who could hardly keep his own smile in check.

"You jest, surely?"

"I never jest about anything so grave as the sacrament of marriage. If you can marry a Briavellian, Celimus, why shouldn't I complete the triangle of our realms and marry a Morgravian?"

"Why not indeed, sire?" Jessom said, daring to join the conversation. "It is indeed a perfect union." His eyes pleaded with his king. This was better than any of them could have dreamed. Surely Celimus could see that?

"There would be conditions," Celimus said again, frowning as his agile mind ran through this new turn of events.

"As you said," Cailech replied. "Although I can put your mind at rest. Ylena Thirsk would not be permitted to leave the Razors. I make that pledge to you now."

"Ever?"

"Ever."

"And as your queen, she would not be permitted to make any decisions that might affect Morgravia—or our treaty will be nullified and I will wage war on your people. Not just the Legion, Cailech, but the full might of the combined Morgravian and Briavellian armies."

"She will be Queen in title only. I am the power in the Razors."

"Done. Now how do we effect this?" Celimus asked, looking toward his chancellor.

Cailech took the lead. "I will take her with me now. Your men can escort us to the border and see that she is safely transported into the Razors, from where she will never emerge. Your chancellor here can draw up the paperwork and your delegates can talk with mine. I will sign whatever you need to effect our treaty and this new understanding regarding the Thirsk woman."

Celimus shook his head. He could find no ruse; Cailech seemed earnest in his desire for Ylena. "All right, I agree. Ylena Thirsk is yours to take. She is my gift to you."

"Thank you," Cailech said, surprising himself by how delighted he felt. He turned to his companion. "Come, Aremys. Ready the Thirsk woman for travel. She rides with me."

23

IN THE END, WYL WAS GIVEN HIS OWN HORSE FOR THE FIRST part of the journey. He sat sullenly astride the bay next to Aremys, a thick and uncomfortable silence between them as the two Kings made their official farewells.

"You have no idea how angry I am by what's happened tonight," he finally said in a low voice to his companion.

Aremys bristled. "This was Cailech's idea, not mine, but I'd be lying if I didn't say I'm not ready to kiss the ground he walks on because of it!"

Wyl glared at his friend. "What's that supposed to mean?"

The Grenadyne cast a glance around to check that they were not being eavesdropped upon, particularly by the Chancellor. "It occurs to me," he muttered, a bite in his tone, "that perhaps Myrren's Gift only works when the killer is still in touch with you somehow."

Wyl frowned. "I don't get you," he replied.

"Did Elysius explain how the gift works?"

Wyl shrugged. "What's to know," he said, bitterness underpinning his reply as he watched the sovereigns clasp hands and shoulders in the tradition of parley and peace.

Aremys sighed. He understood Wyl's angry mood; it would be ludicrous even to pretend he could imagine what it felt like to be trapped as Wyl was, or how much courage it must have taken to welcome the agony of whatever form of death Celimus had wished upon Ylena Thirsk. "I began to wonder, back in that hall, whether whoever killed you had to be connected with you through the weapon."

That won Wyl's attention. He paused in thought. "I've never considered that. You mean if the arrow had been shot

I might be fully dead, but if you'd slit my throat I would be you?"

"Exactly," Aremys muttered beneath his breath. "You might truly have died and then all would be lost. That's why I acted as I did."

Ylena's face looked newly distressed. "So I do owe Cailech my life."

"Possibly, is all I'm saying. I don't care to test my own theory," Aremys admitted. "And I'd prefer it if you didn't either."

Wyl glanced at Aremys again and this time Ylena's expression was chastened. "Thank you," was all he had time to say before Cailech was striding back to their party.

"My lady," the King of the Razors said. Wyl did not understand the soft tone or the gentle expression on Cailech's face. All he could do was nod.

Aremys felt a new fear thrill through him. He had not had time to explain that although Cailech might have saved Wyl's life, the new situation was just as dire. Although he knew Wyl had to be told, he was relieved that he had not had to give that explanation just yet or deal with its consequences.

When Cailech was seated on his horse Celimus strolled up. "Safe travels, my friend." Cailech simply nodded. The Morgravian turned to his prisoner. "Another lucky escape, Ylena Thirsk, but this time I fear it is your last. I won't be seeing you again."

"Oh, you'll see me, Celimus," Wyl promised, a determined, somewhat sly smile touching Ylena's lips. "In a place I call hell."

Celimus laughed. "Good luck with her, Cailech—as I understand it, her husband plowed the furrow only once. She'll be nice and tight for you. Remember your promise to me."

Celimus's words shocked Wyl, but he put them aside in order to take his final opportunity to have the last word. He had never heard Ylena's voice sound as cold and threatening as he made it now. "And you remember my promise to you, Celimus. When we meet again, you will die and I will bear witness to it. Just you and I, Celimus—as it should be."

The words sounded strangely prophetic to Chancellor Jessom. The threat felt so very real on this cold night in the north, and yet how could it be, coming from a helpless captive, a young woman at that? Nevertheless, a chill passed through him as he watched Ylena Thirsk stare at the Morgravian King. She was too confident, too unfazed by Celimus—she had demanded her own death, for pity's sake. It did not make sense. He glanced at Aremys and was surprised to see the mercenary watching him. The clue sat between Aremys and Ylena; Jessom was convinced of it. He narrowed his gaze in thought and saw the Grenadyne nod toward him as the party, escorted by Legionnaires, moved out of Tenterdyn.

Jessom watched them depart in silence, seized by an unshakable notion that, despite what both Kings promised, they had not seen the last of the Thirsks.

The journey back to the border was uneventful and mostly silent. That suited Wyl; he was content to let his horse follow the party while he contemplated this new turn of events. It was frustrating being pulled farther from Celimus, but then Fynch had warned him of the randomness of Myrren's Gift. Perhaps this was one of those occasions. He expected to meet Celimus again—and next time, as he had promised, he would not fail. His mind turned to what the King of the Razors might have in mind for him. Why had Cailech stayed the hand of Ylena's would-be murderer? He felt a sudden gratitude to the Mountain King, for perhaps Aremys was right; so far all his deaths had involved someone killing him with a weapon they held. He noticed Cailech beckon to Aremys, who nudged his horse to draw alongside the King, but he could not hear their conversation and lost himself in his thoughts again.

"What lies between you and the Thirsk woman?" Cailech asked Aremys, direct as usual.

"Sire?"

"Don't play the innocent with me. I'm sure I deserve better."

Aremys sighed. "It's true, my lord. I did not want to see Ylena Thirsk murdered."

"That much is obvious. But why?"

"She is innocent of all that Celimus lays at her feet."

Cailech made a soft sound of exasperation. "I worked that out for myself, Grenadyne. Tell me something I don't know, something that accounts for that look in your eyes that fairly begged me to step in and halt the proceedings."

Aremys knew he would have to skirt the truth as carefully as possible. "When I was picked up unconscious in the eastern part of the Razors by Myrt and his companions," Aremys began, "I had lost my memory, as you know." The King nodded but said nothing. The horses slowed to a walk. They could see flaming torches being waved in welcome from a distance. It would not be long now before they were reunited with their men. "As my memory returned I remembered the task I was involved with at the time of being set upon by the thieves in northern Briavel."

"I'd like to hear the end of this before we actually reach the others, Aremys," Cailech admonished gently.

Aremys nodded and got to the point. "I was hired by King Celimus to track down and murder Ylena Thirsk."

"Right. So I gathered."

"Celimus has, as I understand it, my lord, designed the deaths of Wyl Thirsk, Romen Koreldy, King Valor of Briavel, perhaps even his own father, and no doubt countless others."

"You knew about Romen?" Cailech interrupted.

"It only came back to me recently. I didn't know him, my lord, only of him."

"Why do you think you mentioned him when you awoke from your stupor?"

Aremys was reminded again that Cailech missed very little. "I suppose because Ylena Thirsk mentioned to me that he carried a blue sword."

"So you did actually meet up with her?" Cailech said, his mind moving swiftly now.

"Yes, sire. I met with her at Felrawthy, but had no intention of killing her as instructed. We talked of Koreldy because she was so grateful for his help in saving her life the first time. Having learned all that had befallen the Thirsks, and realizing that the girl was obviously an innocent, I followed Koreldy's lead and decided to help her. Mercenary I may be, sire; cold-blooded murderer I am not. It was I who took her into Briavel, where I felt she would be safe. We lost each other at Timpkenny when I wandered out for some air and got set upon." His story sounded horribly thin. He continued quickly. "We'd already discussed her going to Werryl and throwing herself on the mercy of the Queen, so she must have followed the plan in my absence."

"But the note to Valentyna of Briavel that you claimed to have sent was a ruse, correct? Despite what I told Celimus, I would never have permitted you to send a missive to Briavel, certainly not without knowing what you were sending."

Aremys nodded. "Right. I had to lie—I was trapped. But who would have thought the Queen would give her up in the fashion she did? I had both your life and my own at stake, as well as Ylena's. You'll recall when I told you about my insurance that I said I had no idea how to deliver the Thirsk woman."

Cailech nodded. "It does seem that Ylena Thirsk wishes to die. Do you think she forced the Queen's hand?"

"Perhaps, and frankly, who could blame her?" Aremys offered, not wanting to say much more, cautiously grateful that he had gotten this far on lies.

"And your need to rub salt in the prisoner's wounds was actually your way of warning Ylena—am I right?"

"Again, yes, sire. I needed Ylena's story to match mine, or I feared none of us would leave that hall alive."

"The Chancellor knows nothing?"

"Nothing, my lord. He watched Ylena and me argue, nothing more. I was fortunate that a message came for him during that time in the outbuilding. I had but a few moments to brief Ylena."

"I see," Cailech replied. He fell silent. They were almost at the rendezvous point, could see Captain Bukanan and the other dignitaries being brought down to be exchanged. "One more thing, Aremys."

"Yes, my lord?"

"Why do you care about Ylena Thirsk? What hold does she have on you?"

And here we come to it, Aremys thought, struck suddenly that he had no answer to this question. Cailech waited as the mercenary's mind raced to find something to offer the King. The carefully constructed web of lies could all fall apart now if he said the wrong thing.

"What is it, Aremys? Why do you hesitate?" Cailech pressed, more pointedly. "Are you hiding something I should be concerned about?"

"No, my lord. It's not that—"

"Then what!" Cailech demanded. Aremys saw Wyl glance behind at the disturbance of Cailech's raised voice. "You will tell me, Grenadyne, before we meet our men . . . before I permit you to enter the Razors again, before I—"

It was Aremys's turn to interrupt. "Because I love her!" he blurted, shocked by the vehemence in his voice. But the last thing he wanted was to be separated from Wyl again and this was the best reason he could manufacture. It was not so far from the truth: He had come to love Wyl Thirsk like a brother, regardless of the guise in which he walked.

Cailech looked at him, astonished. For a moment neither man spoke and Aremys knew he must hold the Mountain King's hard gaze no matter what. To look away now would be interpreted as weakness or deception.

"You jest," Cailech said eventually.

"I do not, sire," Aremys said sadly.

"But—"

"Let us not speak of it anymore, my lord," Aremys said, glad for the cover of darkness. "I have not yet expressed my deepest thanks for what you did today for Ylena. Let me do so now."

"By Haldor's arse, man, I didn't do it for you," Cailech said, still rocked by the Grenadyne's admission. "I did it for purely selfish reasons. I would be lying if I did not admit here and now that I desire her more than I have desired any woman. I meant what I said."

Myrt arrived. He took one look at his king and knew

something was awry. He nodded to his sovereign. "Welcome back, sire."

"Get rid of the Morgravian escort, Myrt, and make the official exchange," Cailech said abruptly, turning back to Aremys.

Myrt accepted the salute of the Legion's senior officer and the departure of the men. When he returned, he glanced uncertainly between Aremys and the King, sensing the new tension.

"We'll be right with you, Myrt," Cailech said. "Take good care of the noblewoman we've brought with us."

Myrt took the reins of Ylena's horse and led creature and woman into camp without another word.

"I mean to make her my wife, Aremys."

"Without even knowing her," the mercenary replied softly, careful not to sound judgmental.

Cailech looked toward the stars and gave Aremys the truth. "I've never been so affected by a woman and I've barely shared a word with her. She is disheveled, dirty, angry. She is magnificent. I want her."

"She is certainly different from any woman I've ever known," Aremys admitted, unable to help himself. "Be careful, sire."

"Of what?"

"Of getting your heart broken."

Aremys meant it sincerely. He knew Wyl would shout loud and long when he heard of the King's intentions and Aremys only wondered how long Ylena would keep her life once Wyl set his mind to losing it again.

Cailech, however, took the mercenary's meaning a completely different way. A dawning realization spread across his expression. "Oh, poor Aremys. The Lady Ylena has rejected your advances."

"No, my lord," Aremys corrected. "I have never made them."

"She doesn't know?" the King asked, aghast.

The Grenadyne shook his head. "I prefer it that way, sire."

"Then what do you mean about getting my heart broken?"

"Only that she loved her husband, Alyd Donal of Felrawthy, passionately and completely. She will never love another."

"We shall see," Cailech said confidently, then: "We have cleared this between us, then?"

"My lord?"

"I can't have you mooning around the woman while I'm wooing her, man! I don't want us to fight over her."

Aremys smiled for the first time in a long time. "Good luck to you if she will have you, Cailech."

The King of the Razors grinned and held out his hand palm up in absolute sincerity. Aremys laid his own palm over it. Cailech grinned. "You constantly surprise me, Grenadyne. Now, if you'd be so kind, I'll ask you to introduce me to my bride-to-be."

E lspyth was laid out on a makeshift pallet on the ground, blankets piled over her small frame to keep out the bite of the cool spring night. A nearby torch lit her face a ghostly color.

"Am I dying?" she asked Crys.

He mustered the crooked grin she loved. "No, but we've got to get those wounds closed up. Drink this," he said, helping her to sit up slightly. "It's warm, sweetened tea. Good for shock, my mother always says." He sighed. "Said."

"Crys, take me home." It was a plea. She squeezed his hand. "I know you've probably got better things to do than travel to Yentro, but I just want to get back to the north."

"To Lothryn?" he asked, his voice gentle.

"Both. I can get well more quickly at home and I feel closer to him with the Razors in sight. I've had enough of roaming the land. The last time I slept in my own bed, ate in my own cottage, did something simple like go to the market, seems like a lifetime ago. I need to see if by chance my aunt is still alive, and I need to return to my life. Wyl doesn't need me now."

"Will you promise me that you won't go off into Cailech's lands if I do take you home?" Her pause was telling. "I won't let you waste yourself, Elspyth. You know how I feel about you—"

"Don't, Crys," she begged softly.

"I don't mean it like that," he urged. "I know where your heart lies. But I care too much about you to let you risk yourself, and Wyl would kill me anyway if I did."

She found a smile for him. "He'd be wrathful, for sure. You saw him in Werryl?"

He nodded and then laughed. "Supremely cranky too. He'd got the flux and he made an inappropriate move on the Queen."

Elspyth spluttered into painful laughter and then groaned at the way it tore at her wounds. "Oh, I mustn't laugh at him," she said, "but I can't help it. I wish I'd known Wyl before Myrren's Gift."

"It's true what they say—he was no painting," Crys commented, determined to see her smile again. His timing, as always, was perfect and she found herself giggling once more.

They were interrupted by Liryk. "Well, this is heartening."

Crys cleared his throat. "Anything to keep her conscious and her mind off her woes," he said to the soldier, winking at Elspyth.

Liryk nodded. "Elspyth, I am so sorry for all you have been through."

"Please, Commander Liryk, the fault is all mine. It was stupid of me to leave as I did and even more naive to fall for that man's cruel trap. Did you find his daughter, by the way?"

"We did. We'll take her back to Werryl and see if we can find the rest of her family."

"Good. She was part of the scheme, I know, but she's so young. Her father used her as much as he used the women."

"Well, he's gone to Shar to answer for his sins now. Now, on another note, we need to get you stitched up, my girl. Those wounds risk infection and that could be life threatening even if the injuries aren't."

"Do you have a physic in the company?" Crys asked.

Liryk gave a nervous smile. "No, but as it happens a Master Rilk passed through an hour ago. One of my men recognized him and hailed him."

Elspyth nodded. "Physic Rilk?"

The Commander looked sheepish. "Well, not exactly. He's a tailor." At Crys's exclamation of protest, he held up a hand. "Hear me out. Next to Madam Eltor, there isn't a more adept person with a needle and thread in the whole of Briavel. Rilk crafts for the top nobility in Morgravia too."

"A master tailor to sew me up?" Elspyth queried.

"He has the finest silken thread and a light touch, Elspyth. It's the best we can do. Those wounds need to be sutured, and rather than let one of my men do a hack job, I'd far prefer a talented craftsman to work on your skin."

Crys was frowning. "I suppose, under the circumstances, this is the best option."

Liryk nodded; he had already motioned to the soldier behind him to bring the tailor forward. "This is Master Rilk," he said, and looked at the craftsman. "This is Crys Donal, Duke of Felrawthy, and our patient, Elspyth."

Crys shook the tailor's hand. "She's got four major cuts." The little man was already perspiring, even though it was a cool night, and Crys had to wonder if he was up to such a grisly task. "Can you stomach it, sir?" he added.

"Oh yes. I've done something similar for my son's beloved pet. I'm sure Miss Elspyth will have far finer skin." He chanced a grin but no one returned it. Rilk's tone became brisk and businesslike. "Can we have her gently moved to a table, please? I'll need lots of light and clean linens and hot water. I presume you have some antiseptic?" Liryk nodded. "Good, I'll need plenty of it. Do you have any shorrock or liquor with you?"

"We'll find some," Liryk said.

"Do it quickly, please, and get some down Miss Elspyth's throat to dull the pain. Not too much, mind, just enough to help her drift off a bit."

Elspyth had already drifted, frightened yet too exhausted to keep her attention on what was about to happen.

Knave was back at Fynch's side. The boy was pale and trembling from his efforts to return the dog to the Razors. *This is exactly what I was afraid of,* Knave growled.

"I'll be all right soon. I just need to sleep."

Have you taken some sharvan?

"No. Just let me be."

Knave looked around, quietly exasperated. Fynch had made no progress since they had parted. He was obviously too weak to send himself anywhere.

"How was Valentyna?" the boy mumbled.

Worried about you. Liryk and company left immediately.

"Good . . . ah, wait, here is Kestrel." It took Fynch some pain to open up his mind, but he wanted Knave to share this.

Kestrel's thin voice entered their heads. *Elspyth is safe. Quite badly injured from what I can tell, but alive and talking to some of the men who arrived.*

What are they doing? Fynch asked.

Perhaps I can show you? Kestrel replied.

Yes, let's try, the boy said, a new excitement cutting through his pain.

Knave sighed. If Fynch did not stop exerting himself unnecessarily, he would die before they even left this plateau.

Fynch concentrated. His eyes were squeezed tightly shut. *That's right, Kestrel. Open your mind completely to me. I won't hurt you, I promise. I just want to see through your eyes, if I may.* There was a pause and suddenly a picture appeared in Knave's mind.

I see it, he admitted grudgingly to Fynch.

An awning of sorts had been set up. Torches burned brightly around it and some men held candles as others bent over a prone figure. Kestrel must have perched himself on a low branch nearby; his sight was keen and they could clearly see all that they needed to.

"They seem to be sewing her," the boy said. "There's Commander Liryk. And . . . oh, wait, is that Master Rilk?"

You're right, Knave said. *It's the tailor.*

"He's mending her," Fynch said in wonderment. They watched Rilk snip a thread and then step away and arch his back. *She's pretty, isn't she?* Fynch said absently. *I'm glad we were able to help. She's going to be all right.*

Is that enough, Fynch? Kestrel asked.

Enough, Knave answered, determined now that his charge would rest.

Perhaps I'll follow the pretty lady, the bird added. *I've got nothing better to do.*

Thank you, Kestrel, Fynch replied weakly, his head pounding.

We'll speak again soon, the bird said, taking to the air.

Knave bristled. *I can feel the echoes of your pain, Fynch. You've got to stop using magic for a while.*

"I can't," the boy moaned, retching helplessly into the bushes.

We have no choice. You must recover your strength before we proceed. We'll make camp here. I'm going to find you some food. You may not feel like eating, but your body is mortal, Fynch. It needs nourishment.

The boy did not reply. He had fallen asleep, collapsed into a small, curled shape like a tiny animal.

24

ALENTYNA LOOKED AT HERSELF IN THE MIRROR AND GLUMLY permitted a brief, silent admission that the dress was exquisite.

"Oh, my queen, you make the most glorious bride," Madam Eltor said. "The fit is perfect." She looked at the breathtaking woman before her and sighed. "A smile would help."

"I'm sorry, Margyt."

"I have to ask you to try on the veil now, my dear," the woman continued, affixing the confection of cream gauze and seed pearls to Valentyna's dark hair. She stood back and looked at her finished creation with satisfaction and pride.

"Thank you, it's lovely," was all the Queen could force out.

"You know, Valentyna, perhaps it's not my place to speak, but we would all like to think that you enter this union with some joy."

The Queen and her seamstress had known each other too long for lies. "I'm sorry that I cannot," Valentyna said. "I bring it about for Briavel, Margyt, because I know it brings us peace and, I hope, new prosperity, but I cannot love him."

"Because of another?" the woman risked.

Valentyna shook her head gently. "No. Simply because I don't love him. We can't help our feelings, can we?"

"No, child. In that you're right. My husband and I could never claim to have loved each other as I know other couples do."

"But you have a good partnership," Valentyna said.

"More than that, to be honest. We are the closest of friends. But yes, we also have a great partnership—as you will with King Celimus. You will make it so. You will give us heirs and make us proud."

A smile ghosted across Valentyna's mouth. "That is my fervent wish."

Margyt Eltor patted her queen's hand. "Let me snip those threads now and release you."

"Are all the preparations in hand?"

"Yes, your majesty," Madam Eltor said, back to her formal role. "I shall be taking two dressers and a couple of other girls for errands and any other needs we might have. The various gowns we spoke of are also ready."

"And the new riding clothes?"

"Completed. You didn't want new boots too, did you?" the seamstress asked, frowning, her mind already racing toward how quickly the cobbler might work.

"No, I like my comfortable old ones," Valentyna replied.

"As I understand it from our earlier discussion, your highness, we depart for Morgravia in ten days?"

"Yes. The wedding was supposed to be at the close of spring, but I see no point in holding off and will send a message today to King Celimus. It should please him. I'll have

one of my assistants confirm everything with you shortly.
We'll take it slowly with a view to four days' journeying. I
can visit some of the towns and villages along the way to
pay my respects to our people."

"I imagine the party will be quite large," Margyt commented as she sliced through the threads that had ensured
the gown's perfect fit.

"I suppose so," Valentyna said, not really caring. "Perhaps
Commander Liryk will split it into smaller groups and send
them by different routes."

"Yes, that would be sensible," the seamstress agreed.
Then: "Are you giving the King a ring, your highness?"

The Queen nodded. "Studded with jewels in the colors of
Briavel."

"Lovely," Margyt said, helping her sovereign to lift the
gown over her head.

"Why are you alone this time?" Valentyna's voice was
muffled from beneath the garment.

"Because I don't want my girls twittering that our queen
goes to her marriage as if to a funeral," Madam Eltor admonished. "I sensed from our last fitting that you were not
getting any pleasure from the preparations. I thought privacy
was best, your highness."

"Thank you again, Margyt. Your sensitivity always makes
you my favorite," Valentyna said, finding a playful tone.

The seamstress responded, glad of it. "Oh? I hear Master
Rilk gets plenty of your business, your highness," she said
archly.

"He wanted the wedding gown," Valentyna replied, tugging her more casual day gown over her head.

"The cheek of the man!"

The Queen laughed. Madam Eltor and Master Rilk had
been married for as long as she could remember. And between them they crafted everything Valentyna wore.

"I will take my leave, your highness. There's still plenty
for me and my girls to do."

"You're a treasure. I promise to be smiling next time we
see each other."

"Make sure of it, child. You will be preparing to take holy vows in the grand Pearlis Cathedral the next time I stitch you into this gown."

Madam Eltor's words remained with Valentyna long after she had departed, reminding the Queen that there was no way off the path she was now on.

Nothing and no one was going to save her from Celimus. She wasted no further time in sitting down at her desk and crafting, with her own hand, a message to her groom to set a final date for their wedding ceremony.

Wyl recognized Myrt and several of the Mountain warriors, all of whom treated Ylena courteously. He was not sure what to think of this new situation. It felt dangerous—all his senses told him so—but at the same time it was reassuring to be back with Aremys.

Someone handed him a bowl of broth. "My lady." It was Myrt, Wyl realized, when he lifted Ylena's chin to glance at the owner of the soft voice. "The King tells us you have been treated inhospitably in Morgravia."

"He speaks true," Wyl admitted.

"I'm sorry there is still a long journey ahead, but he hopes you will eat something before we leave."

"We leave tonight?"

"Yes, my lady. We wish to be deep into the Razors by midnight."

"So you travel comfortably in the dark?" Wyl wondered.

"We need no light but the moon," Myrt said, with a polite nod, then left.

The broth was surprisingly good, hearty and rich with the flavor of meat. As Wyl finished the bowl, glad for the warming nourishment, Aremys arrived in the cave, holding a candle. He looked distracted and hesitant; Wyl figured it could not be easy for the mercenary to find time alone with the Mountain King's new captive.

"We're breaking camp now, leaving immediately. How are you?"

"Fed," Wyl said. "Myrt brought me food."

"Does he know you recognize him?" Aremys asked, alarmed.

"No, I've been careful about it."

"Good. He's sharp."

"How much aren't you telling me about this turn of events?"

Aremys hesitated. "Cailech insists on knowing why I have aided you."

Wyl nodded and Aremys paused, embarrassed. "I was cornered and had to come up with something."

"So you told him . . .?"

"That I loved you." He watched uncomfortably as Ylena's face transformed into a look of incredulity. Fortunately, whatever Wyl was going to say was cut off by the arrival of a messenger announcing the party's imminent departure. Aremys asked the man if scouts had checked that Celimus had sent no tracking party. The man confirmed that they had done so and there were no spies trailing them.

During this exchange, Wyl had composed himself. "So, are you going to tell me the rest?" he asked. "We don't seem to have much time."

Aremys scratched his head. It was best to give it to Wyl straight, he decided. "Cailech's taken a fancy to you."

"Oh, Shar save me!" Wyl groaned. "You're serious, aren't you," he said, and it was no question.

"It gets worse," the big man continued.

"How can it?" Wyl asked, letting Ylena's head drop between her knees.

"During your absence from the hall, Cailech declared to Celimus that he would make you his wife." Wyl looked up sharply. His horror was reflected in the Grenadyne's despondent expression. "It took everyone by surprise. There was nothing I could do."

"I understand, Aremys," Wyl admitted, bile rising in his throat. "You were helpless back there. But we're not helpless now," he declared, standing to Ylena's full height, which barely reached halfway up the mercenary's chest.

"Please, Wyl," Aremys said, cautiously glancing around. "Go along with this for the time being."

"Go deeper into the Razors, back to that fortress?" Wyl hissed. "Are you mad? I've escaped it once. I don't think I'll be able to do it again."

There was nothing for it but to tell Wyl all that he knew. "I've found Gueryn," Aremys said firmly, knowing it would stop Wyl's tirade.

It did. Wyl grabbed his shirtfront angrily. "You're sure it's him?"

Aremys nodded. "We spoke briefly. I said I'd come back for him. He's in the dungeon and, considering his situation, looks quite good for it, but now that Cailech knows Romen Koreldy is dead, I fear for his life. And then there's Rashlyn, the most unpredictable factor in all of this. Apparently he's used magic on Gueryn a few times now."

"What do you mean?"

"Too long in the telling now. Suffice to say it's been used for good in healing the arrow wound, but bad too, and it's rattled your old mentor."

Wyl paced, pulling at his ear, thoughts racing as to what would be the best course of action. He did not want to go with Cailech—the Mountain King's intentions for him were just too revolting to contemplate. But Gueryn's needs called strongly. He could not desert his dearest, oldest friend, not after the sad way they had parted.

Aremys sensed that Wyl needed a final push and gave it. "I've also found Lothryn."

Ylena's eyes blazed in the soft light. "He's alive? I knew it!"

"But not how you remember him, Wyl," Aremys cautioned.

"How so?" Wyl asked. His frightening dream at Felrawthy, of the man's voice screaming from behind a barn door, returned to haunt him.

Before Aremys could reply, Cailech appeared at the mouth of the cave. "I hope I'm not interrupting anything."

"I can't imagine it would matter if you were," Wyl replied, flustered by his friend's various revelations and the discomfort of seeing his captor—his husband-to-be— smiling so disarmingly at him.

"No, I suppose it wouldn't," Cailech agreed, his smile broadening. "I hope my men have treated you deferentially, my lady?"

"Thank you, sire," Wyl replied, remembering Ylena's manners, but aiming a glare toward Aremys.

Cailech did not miss the glance between them. "Ah, I suppose Aremys has explained why you're here."

"He has, King Cailech." Wyl was at a loss for words. He understood his friend's reasons for wanting him to return to the fortress, but this was a perilous situation for him now.

"Don't be frightened, my lady. In the south you know us as barbarians, but we may surprise you."

"Romen Koreldy spoke highly of you, my lord. He told me much about the ways of the Mountain People and I have an appreciation for your sophistication," Wyl said, believing it best to reveal now that he knew something of the culture. Any misjudgments he made in seeming too familiar with the Razor Kingdom he might now be able to hide behind Romen's teachings.

"Did he now?"

"He liked you," Wyl offered.

"I hope you will too, Ylena. Come now, we must journey."

There was nothing for Wyl to do but follow the King's guiding hand. "You will ride with me, my lady," Cailech added, and it was fortunate indeed that the King did not see the look of despair that swept across Ylena's face.

Wyl gritted his teeth and allowed Cailech's strong hands to help him into the saddle, tensing uncomfortably as the King climbed up behind him. Cailech's arms passed around Ylena's tiny waist and took the reins from her.

"Allow me," he said graciously.

Wyl grimaced toward Aremys, who looked away in embarrassment.

"Comfortable, Ylena?" the King inquired.

"May I not ride a horse of my own, sire?" Wyl risked.

He sensed the King's wry grin. "It is good for my men to see me take ownership of you, my lady. It is critical they understand how highly I regard you. Life in Morgravia is no longer possible, Ylena, you surely agree?"

"I do, my lord," came the grudging reply.

"And it seems your life is now worthless in Briavel too, where a queen must bow to the whims of her powerful neighbor and soon-to-be husband. So the only realm where your life can be protected—and, might I add, revered, my lady, is the Razor Kingdom. My men are surprised by your presence, I'll not lie." Cailech's mouth was so close to Ylena's ear that Wyl felt sickened. "But in seeing us together like this, they will now offer you the highest respect, my lady, as befitting a noblewoman and my future wife."

Gueryn was still smiling from the thrill of riding Galapek. Not even the sound of his cell door hammering closed or the key turning in the lock could tarnish the day's experience.

He, Jos, and Rollo had taken the horses around the lake and beyond for several hours, returning late in the afternoon. Gueryn had felt exhilarated. He had not had a chance to confirm his suspicions about Galapek, unfortunately, but the joy of being in the open and on a horse again was exquisite. He had wept as they neared the stables at the close of the ride, embarrassing himself.

Jos had given him a consoling pat on the shoulder. "I'm sorry you are our prisoner, Gueryn," the young man had offered.

"I too am sorry," Gueryn had replied, "but thank you for this wonderful escape, however brief it has been."

"What do you think of our fine stallion?" Maegryn had asked on their return.

"That I wish he were mine," Gueryn had answered truthfully.

The stablemaster had laughed. "Everyone does."

"Can I rub him down?"

"Most certainly," Maegryn had said, but sadly for Gueryn, who had hoped to be left alone with the horse, the head of the stable had remained.

Despite Maegryn's presence, Gueryn had managed to whisper once to the horse, begging the animal to give him a sign that he was Lothryn, but nothing had occurred. And yet he could not doubt the sincerity of the stranger, Aremys. As the incredible words had tumbled from the big man's mouth, horror lacing each one, Gueryn had believed them. His brief but terrible experiences with Rashlyn were all he needed to draw upon to believe that the mercenary had hit on the truth.

Being Morgravian, Gueryn had always been scornful of magic—frightened of it too. Along with most Morgravians, he had accepted the persecution that had not so long ago been visited on anyone perceived as a witch or warlock. But now, after hearing Aremys's story and feeling the effects of Rashlyn's power for himself, Gueryn was forced to accept that magic must be at the heart of the mystery surrounding the horse Galapek, and indeed Wyl himself.

Myrren of Baelup came to mind and, inevitably, Wyl's attempts to protect her from further suffering. The memory surfaced fresh and clear now. At the moment of the witch's death Wyl's eyes had changed color, reflecting the exact strange hues of Myrren's eyes. The very reason for her persecution was mirrored in Gueryn's own beloved Wyl Thirsk. And he was not the only person who had seen it. The tiny gong boy, Fynch, had shared the experience. They had not both imagined the presence of some magic.

Gueryn's good mood evaporated as the sour thoughts overtook his mind. If he could accept that Wyl had been somehow touched by the magic of the witch, then surely it was possible that Lothryn could be so remarkably changed by sorcery, especially when wielded by one so deeply wicked and heartless as Rashlyn. But what about Wyl? How had Myrren's magic affected him?

He was still wrestling with the question, haunted by the memory of how Romen had tricked him into believing he was Wyl, when the key turned again in the lock. Gueryn was startled. He moved back into the shadows, away from the nub of candle and its light which was now permitted him as a small kindness.

He instantly recognized the figure that appeared in the doorway and his stomach clenched in fear.

"Le Gant," Rashlyn said, in his light, irritating voice. "You can't hide from me in this dungeon."

"Have you come to share my ration of water, Rashlyn?" Gueryn asked, forcing himself to fight back his fear.

The small man laughed. "After tonight's proceedings, I imagine conversation will be the furthest thing from your mind. Take him," he commanded to the two men who now pushed through the doorway. Gueryn recognized neither. His heart lurched with new terror.

"There will be a reckoning with your king over this, Rashlyn," he warned in desperation, all bravado gone now. If he were to die at this man's hand, who would back up Aremys's claim?

"But it was the King who gave me permission, le Gant. He agreed that I could use you for my own . . . interests, shall we say. Come now. I'm sure we'll both find it interesting."

Gueryn did the only thing left to him. He struggled with the guards and bellowed his protestations as loudly as his lungs could manage, in the faint hope that someone might hear and bear testimony to his disappearance at the hands of the barshi.

25

FYNCH LAY STILL ENOUGH TO BE DEAD, CURLED ON THE FLOOR of the small cave he and Knave had come to call home these past few days. Knave had worried about the boy's weakness, but Fynch had grown stronger through long healing sleeps and the dog had to assume that this was the way of the magic. No doubt Elysius had done the same. He regretted they had not asked the manwitch more questions about the sickness.

Kestrel had communicated that Elspyth was also healing through long rest periods after her surgery with Master Rilk. Knowing that Elspyth lived and would recover from her injuries had helped Fynch to let go of Wyl's friend and become more focused on the trial ahead and his own health.

Knave understood that the boy had no idea of what they

were up against. Not even he could imagine it, to tell the truth, but he had heard the gravity in Elysius's voice when speaking of his brother and had seen how the manwitch had fretted at the thought of passing the magic, and the responsibility that came with it, to such a youngster. But all of that had paled in comparison to the arrival of the Dragon King. His presence alone had impressed upon Knave the dire task they faced. For the King of the Creatures to come to them from his abode high in the mountains of the Wild, where no man or possibly no other animal had ventured, made it clear that Fynch's trial was more important than any of them could know.

The youngster stirred, his eyelids fluttering as consciousness arrived. Then his eyes opened and he regarded the dog. "You make me feel so safe, Knave," Fynch murmured sleepily.

Knave only wished he could protect the boy from all that was coming toward them. But this was no time to scare him. They needed to be strong together. *I'm never far, remember?* the dog replied.

Fynch sat up and stretched. "I feel better than I have in days."

You must eat, Knave said, unable to hide the elation in his voice.

"You sound like my sister."

Your sister must be a wise woman.

Fynch reached to hug the dog. "I'll eat for both of you." He was able to start a fire with the smallest trickle of magic and Knave quietly marveled at how quickly his friend had accepted his new powers. Fynch did not talk about the wondrous nature of his new skills, but Knave understood that the lad treated this gift as he treated everything in his life—with serious care. The dog knew Fynch would never be playful with the magic or test its boundaries; he would no more send messages unnecessarily than he would try out his own ability to fly.

The boy refused the rabbit Knave had killed for him. "I can't; it repulses me for some reason."

You don't like rabbit?

The boy frowned. "I don't think I like meat anymore. I'll find some berries."

There were some cirron berries growing nearby and Fynch made a meal of them with a knuckle of bread, "I feel well enough to travel now," he said in between tiny mouthfuls.

It's time we made a move, the dog agreed. He was about to say that they should travel as far as they could during the morning, and that Fynch should sleep in the afternoon before sending them about ten leagues east, when Fynch cut across his thoughts.

"I'm going to risk Rashlyn today."

He caught Knave off guard. *What do you mean?*

"I'm tired of all this patience. I'm tired of feeling sick and wearied by the magic. If it's going to be this harmful to me, let's not waste more time. Let's really use it."

What are you talking about, Fynch?

"I'm talking about sending us all the way. I sent you to Werryl, and I know I can do it now for the two of us. I can get us right to the door of the fortress if we feel that bold." Then he grinned shyly. "Perhaps I should send us somewhere a little safer."

No! Knave replied. *Too risky, too dangerous for your health, too—*

"Hush, Knave. I know my limitations."

I'm not sure you do, Knave said testily.

Fynch knew the dog's bad humor was a manifestation of his fear. "Trust me. I think I can blur the magic."

I do not understand. Exasperation gave way to weariness in the dog's tone.

Fynch shrugged. "Hard to explain, but while I was sleeping I think perhaps . . ." He hesitated.

Perhaps what?

"Perhaps the Dragon King spoke with me," the boy finished, embarrassed.

Knave was surprised but he pressed on. *And?*

"I believe I can try to muddy the magic going out, so to speak. Whether Rashlyn senses it or not, I might be able to confuse him sufficiently that he can't lock on to us or what we are."

That's a big gamble.

"Yes, but time is not on our side. I'm getting bad feelings about things."

Things?

The boy pulled a face. "Just a sense; again, hard to explain. I thought it was my fear for Elspyth, but it's more than that. It's Wyl, it's Valentyna. There's something very bad happening in the Razors, something not right."

Unnatural, you mean?

"That's it. That's exactly what I mean. There's a taint of evil on the wind, and it's talking to me in my dreams."

What do you see?

"Two men. Both in pain. I can't really see them, only sense them. One I believe I might know, but I can't be sure . . . I mean, how could I?"

And Rashlyn's behind it?

Fynch nodded glumly. "I think he's the source of what's bad. I could send a creature to find out more . . . perhaps Kestrel even. But that would just be more time wasting. We should go ourselves."

Perhaps that's why the Dragon King spoke to you.

"Yes, that's what I believe. Are you ready?" Fynch said, picking up his small sack and pulling it around his body.

Now?

The boy grinned again, less hesitantly this time. "I've already opened the bridge to the Thicket. It awaits us."

Knave suddenly felt the thrum of magic from the Thicket. He took a deep breath. *I'm ready.*

Fynch put his arms around the dog and Knave sensed the pressure of the air thickening around them. As the Razors began to shimmer around them, Knave braced himself for the landing, unnecessarily. Fynch had mastered his sending skills and had summoned a pillow of air to cushion them as they arrived. Knave was on all fours in a blink and hovered protectively over the little boy, who was vomiting violently into the undergrowth.

Take your time, he whispered helplessly, wondering what kind of toll the magic would take this time, so soon after Fynch's last use of it.

Fynch grasped for his sack and the sharvan leaves. He forced a handful into his mouth, which tasted sour from the recent meal he had just lost.

Knave rebuked himself for agreeing to this madness when he had just managed to get his charge to eat something. *Sip lots of water,* he advised. *I'm going to scout around.*

Fynch said nothing, chewing intently to start the painkilling juices flowing down his aching throat. Using the magic might have been a good idea, but it had taken a huge toll on him. He felt as though he might die.

Knave saw that the boy's eyes were bloodshot, and for the first time, a thin rivulet of blood ran from his nose. The dog felt uncharacteristically angry with everyone: himself, for not insisting that Fynch spare himself, Elysius for passing on the magic, his king for entrusting this lovely child with such a huge task, even Fynch for insisting on sending them so far. He stalked away, his mood as dark as the fur that covered his body, and blended into the cover of the foliage. When he returned, his companion lay on the ground, still and pale. Alarmed, the dog nuzzled the boy, his fear almost making him whine.

"Knave?" Fynch croaked, his complexion ghostly as he raised his head.

I'm here, the dog replied, his relief evident. *There are people coming, and horses, quite a reasonable number of them. We're well hidden, so we just need to remain still.*

"It's Wyl," Fynch said groggily.

The dog was confused. Wyl was in Briavel, with Valentyna. *How do you know?*

"When I sent us, I tried something new." Fynch coughed and blood splattered from his mouth. "I'm sorry," he said, his tone flat.

No! I am, Knave said, his anger at last finding its way into his tone. *This is not right, Fynch. You're going to die if you don't stop overextending yourself.*

Fynch looked at his friend with a sad expression. "I'm going to die soon anyway, Knave," he said gravely.

The dog was lost for words, so Fynch continued, wiping his bloodied mouth on his sleeve. "I cast out as we traveled, trying to lock on to Rashlyn and using the magic of the Thicket to shield us. I found Wyl instead. I think the Thicket did that deliberately."

Why?

"Probably because Wyl is not meant to be in the Razors. He should be in Briavel with Valentyna. The Thicket is warning me."

Did it tell you what to do?

"No, unfortunately. That's up to us, Knave. I think we should just follow at a distance and take stock of the situation. He's surely not here by choice."

Are you up to following them?

"I'll manage," Fynch said.

Knave had to look away, unable to bear the pain in the boy's face. *They'll be a few minutes yet,* he said. *Just lie down until then.*

For once Fynch obeyed.

Crys made a sound of exasperation. "It's too soon."

"I don't want to spend another second in this blood-soaked place," Elspyth said, grimacing as she pulled on her cloak.

"Please, Elspyth. At least let me take you to Sharptyn."

"No, Crys. I want to leave the region. I nearly died here and I'm not talking solely about my physical wounds. Before you arrived . . ." Her voice quavered but she steadied it. "Speaking of which, I still haven't thanked you for bringing the Briavellian Guard."

He waved her embarrassment aside. "Master Rilk said—"

"Master Rilk is a tailor!" Elspyth cut across his words. "I'm grateful to him, grateful to you all, but I'm ready to leave."

"Where will you go? Surely not into the Razors?" Crys beseeched. His expression added new injury to her aching heart.

"No. I'm not fit enough for that. I shall go home first." She looked around her. "This place almost looks"—she searched for the right word—"clean again."

Crys risked reaching forward and buttoning her cloak for her. "Liryk and his men have done a good job."

Elspyth smiled at his gesture but wished he would not show his affection for her quite so openly. "They have. When does the Guard move out?"

"Today, I believe."

"Then my timing is perfect. And you? Where will you go?"

Pain flickered briefly across Crys's open face, but he wrestled his expression back under his control. "Not Briavel. I'm a hindrance there and Valentyna will be making preparations for her journey to Morgravia now."

"Poor soul. She intends to go through with it, then?"

"She has no choice. I don't believe it can be avoided, Elspyth. And with Wyl taking himself off to die again at the hands of Celimus . . ." He trailed off.

"She could just say no," Elspyth blazed, then grimaced at the sour look her words won from her friend. "No, I know. She can't. That would mean war. Do you think the next time we meet Wyl, he'll be the King of Morgravia?"

Crys gave an involuntary bark of a laugh. "Oh, I don't know," he said, a helpless tone in his voice. "Wyl's so stoic. Where did he find the courage to march into Celimus's den, knowing he goes toward a horrible death?"

Elspyth sighed. "I think we're all capable of being heroic when it comes to those we love, Crys," she said sadly, and knew he understood by his equally sorrowful nod.

"Well, a happy ending for Wyl and Valentyna perhaps?" he tried brightly.

"But not for us, eh?" she responded in kind.

"It could be if only you'd let it," he said, then wished he had not. "I'm sorry, Elspyth."

She accepted his apology readily. "Come with me," she said, knowing how badly the Duke of Felrawthy needed the anchor of friendship, and truthfully she herself did not feel like traveling alone.

"Really?" Crys asked, hardly believing Elspyth's words.

A smile lit the petite woman's face. "Why not?" She held up a restraining hand. "But there are terms."

"Of course. No kissing, or any attempt at seduction," he listed, grinning. "No suggestion that Lothryn is a wasted cause or that you're too small, too fragile, too feminine to save him."

She laughed openly now. "I like that you use your wit to hide your emotions, Crys," she said, meaning it with affection.

"It's all I have now. I feel so bruised and battered, I need to hide. Thank you for allowing me to accompany you. I won't let you down, Elspyth." They both understood the unspoken words.

"I appreciate that," she said. "Did Wyl have any ideas for us before he left?"

"Well, he did suggest I stir up some trouble within the Legion."

"In what way?"

"Reinforce the name of Thirsk, remind the men that the Donals were true, insist that Celimus is a destroyer of realms." He ran his hands through his hair. "And a slayer of souls."

She touched his arm. It was all the solace she could offer. "Shall we detour past Pearlis on our way north?"

"Could you stand to? I mean, it's not as direct as you probably want."

Elspyth paused to consider his question. "No, but I'm not really well enough to be any good to anyone, and a couple of extra days will not make a difference to my journey."

"Perfect. Can you ride?"

"Let's take Ericson's cart. He's not going to be needing it," she said, feeling ghoulish at her pragmatism. "You have a horse, don't you?" He nodded. "Then we're set. Let's go do some damage to our king."

Rashlyn stepped back to admire the fruits of his toil. He was drenched in sweat; it beaded into his tangled beard and soaked the already soiled shirt he had worn for days. He chuckled. "Better, definitely better," he muttered, and swallowed a cup of the rejuvenating brew he had made before he began his ugly work.

He knew from past experience that crafting this sort of magic was exhausting, but now he believed it actually drained the life from him. A measure of his essence had been used to create the spell. That was his sacrifice, the price he had to pay to manipulate this magic. But he was becoming stronger, more proficient in his crafting. The dog stood on all fours before him, trembling so badly Rashlyn was sure it would collapse. It snarled, despite its obvious suffering.

"I suspect that was none too pleasant for you," he said to the creature. "In fact, I imagine it was nothing short of excruciating. I'm surprised you lived through it . . . and rather pleased you did."

Again the dog growled weakly, baring its teeth, pulling helplessly at the restraining chain that held it to a ring in the wall.

"How does it feel to be a dirty dog, le Gant? A filthy Morgravian dog?"

The dog leapt forward and managed to make the sorcerer flinch. But the chain dragged it back viciously and it fell over. It lay on the ground, panting hard, eyes glazed, its energy spent.

"Oh, don't die on me so soon, le Gant. I do so want to show the King my handiwork. I'm going to give you to him so he can feed you the crumbs from his table, or perhaps break your ribs with his boot if that takes his fancy. I suggest you change your attitude. You are nothing now, you Morgravian dog. You never were."

The dog snapped once, but so weakly that Rashlyn did not even hear its jaws come together. He was lost in admiration at his skill. The dog could hear and react. The horse Galapek seemed nothing more than a void, but le Gant the dog showed spirit. Very good.

He was so close to full control now. He could hardly wait to present his latest creation to Cailech. Together they would rule not only the men of the land but its creatures and birds as well. Cailech could go to war with the south with bears, wolves, wildcats, even a troop of zerkons under his command—it was more exciting than Rashlyn had ever dared to dream.

And while Cailech might be the most powerful man in the

realm, Rashlyn believed he himself would be even stronger. Without knowing it, Rashlyn had come to the same conclusion as Elysius. He believed that Nature was the reflection of Shar, and if he, Rashlyn, could exert control over Nature's beasts, then surely he would achieve godlike stature himself.

The barshi left the semiconscious dog to lie in its own mess, slamming the door shut on yet another tomb. The dog, hurting deeply and wondering how it could bring about its own death, whined softly as it passed into unconsciousness.

26

WYL SANK INTO A GLUM SILENCE AS THEIR PARTY NEARED THE higher ground and the inevitability of the fortress. The terrain was familiar and once again he felt the weak but nevertheless sickening pull of Romen's fears as what little was left of him recognized where they were.

Cailech had been generous enough to leave Ylena to herself during the journey. At night she was permitted to sleep alone in a tent made from animal skins that the warriors rigged up for her rest. Fresh water was always found for her ablutions and Cailech had even promised a dip in a hot spring where he insisted she would have privacy. He had been formal and courteous in all conversation and their only physical contact had been during the hours on horseback. Wyl realized that Cailech must be enjoying the feel of Ylena's slim body pressed against his chest, and although he made a huge effort to sit as far forward as he could, ultimately by day's end the journey would wear him down sufficiently that, without meaning to, he would find himself leaning against the King's broad, hard body. There were occasions when Cailech, wanting to show Ylena something, would win her attention by gently touching her arm or speaking quietly into her ear as he pointed out a soaring eagle or a particularly jagged series of peaks, so distinctive to the Razors. And each time Wyl would withdraw just a bit further within, to what was purely him.

This was the third morning and they had broken camp a couple of hours ago. Aremys dropped back to ride alongside Cailech. Wyl had been surprised to find that the mercenary had essentially ignored him these past two days, preferring to keep company with Myrt and a fellow called Byl. He guessed that his friend was anxious and embarrassed by the situation in which Wyl found himself.

"I imagine they're restless to be home now," Cailech commented, nodding toward the men Aremys had just been talking with.

"They are. I don't think any of you Mountain People feel comfortable outside the fortress and its compounds."

Cailech grinned. "That's a good thing." He inhaled the sharp mountain air. "Can you smell that, Ylena? Those are tiny white flowers called thawdrops that burst through at the first hint of spring and flourish toward midspring. The fragrance is being blown here from the valley just outside the fortress, which we'll be passing soon. It's quite a sight. I shall pick you some."

Wyl remembered the valley—it had been bare the last time he had passed this way. His stomach clenched at the thought of reentering the Mountain Fortress.

"Your friend is very quiet, Aremys," the King said, amused, as if Ylena were not encircled by his arms, the prisoner of his desire.

Aremys shrugged, not daring to look Wyl's way. "I hardly know her, my lord, to pass judgment on her silences," he said carefully.

"You have us baffled, Ylena, you see?" Cailech said. Wyl could feel the King's face touching the back of Ylena's head as he leaned forward. "Are you not happy to have escaped Celimus again? Can you not share your pleasure with us?"

"I wanted to die, sire. You denied me my revenge."

"How so?"

"I wanted the blood of both Thirsk heirs on his hands,

your majesty. I wanted it mingling with that of the blood of the holy men of Rittylworth and the loyal souls of Felrawthy he had slaughtered."

"And Koreldy's," Cailech said quietly.

"Yes, Romen's too. And that of King Valor."

"Do you think he will kill his bride?" Cailech suddenly asked.

Wyl flinched. "He is capable of it."

The King nodded. "Is that his plan, though, do you think?"

"No," Wyl admitted. "He wants heirs. Perhaps three, to sit each realm," he added craftily.

It did not rattle Cailech as intended. "I have an heir, Ylena," he replied. "His name is Aydrech, and I am hopeful you will give me more sons."

Wyl felt a fresh wave of nausea, all his own. He fought back, unwisely. "I hear that Aydrech is not truly of your blood, sire."

Cailech's right hand left the reins and raised itself in the air. The men behind obediently slowed and stopped their horses, as did Cailech. Aremys looked uncertain, glancing between King and guest.

"What did you say?" Cailech said, his voice hard.

It was too late to retract it; besides, Wyl had nothing to lose. The threat of being touched by this man was coming closer by the minute.

"You heard what I said, your highness, and your very re-action proves its truth."

Myrt had dropped back to Cailech's side. "My king, is everything all right?"

"Move the men forward, Myrt. I have a private discussion to finish."

The big warrior nodded and shot a surreptitious glance to-ward Aremys, who also felt the dangerous tingle in the air but hadn't understood Wyl's words. The other horsemen moved by, averting their eyes, and Aremys made to follow.

"Wait, Aremys," the King commanded, leaping down from his horse with agile grace. He walked around to where he could look his bride-to-be directly in the eye. Wyl knew that stare well. "Now, Ylena. Finish what you have to say or I shall slit your throat here and now."

Wyl remained silent. Aremys shifted uncomfortably on his horse.

"What do you know about my son?" Cailech said, and his tone was now edged with a fire that had not been directed at Ylena previously.

"Only what I said, sire."

"And how do you come by such information?"

Wyl considered his options. Romen could be the scapegoat; no one could hurt him anymore.

"It was Koreldy."

The King looked shocked. "How could he know?"

Aremys wanted to know as well, although he feared Wyl's answer and feared even more this nest of vipers Wyl had seemed to deliberately uncover.

"Did anyone mention to you the love between Romen Koreldy and Queen Valentyna, my lord?" Wyl asked, enjoying watching the surprise flit across Cailech's face, to be immediately masked.

"You jest, of course."

"I have no reason to, your majesty. You heard Celimus tell you that Romen was at Werryl Palace, acting as champion to Queen Valentyna."

Cailech nodded. "She fell for his charms," he said, smiling at an old memory of Romen's flirtatious manner.

"She fell in love, your highness," Wyl corrected. "He was not charming her—he was wooing her."

"It sounds like Koreldy," Cailech said disparagingly. "So what?"

"So he told her things—things he would normally have kept to himself. A man truly enraptured can have no secrets from the woman he loves."

"He told her about my son," the King finished.

"He told her about a man called Lothryn whose wife bore a new son, sire."

"Aydrech is of my flesh, Ylena."

"She knew that, my lord, and mentioned as much. Lothryn explained to Koreldy about the boy. I gather it shocked Romen, as it does me, to learn that you would take another man's wife purely to produce an heir."

At this the King found his lazy grin again, infuriating Wyl. "As I am doing with you. Now I understand, Ylena. You were married to Alyd Donal. I'm sure he won't mind if I bed you, although I am sorry that you see me in such a harsh light. I am genuinely intrigued by you. You have kindled a fire in me I have never before felt burn so bright."

"And I'm supposed to be flattered by that?" Wyl asked incredulously. "What about how I feel? You are treating me with the same contempt that Celimus treats Valentyna."

Cailech did not react to Ylena's stinging words but changed the topic adroitly, frustrating Wyl. Cailech was too wise to fall for his baiting. "You sound as if you admire the Queen, Ylena."

Wyl shook Ylena's head in annoyance. He glanced at Aremys, who looked as anxious as he had looked in the hall at Felrawthy. "I do, more than any other woman I've ever met, sire."

Cailech made a sound of disgust. "This is the same woman who sold you out to Celimus, knowing full well he was determined to kill you."

Wyl's anger flared. "And if you believe that, your highness, you are even more ignorant than the southerners believe you to be."

It happened fast. Wyl felt Ylena's body being wrenched from the saddle. Cailech's strength was immense and her body hung from his hand like a rag doll, the tips of her boots only just touching the unforgiving rock they stood on. Aremys was off his horse in a blink, unsure of what to do.

Cailech dragged Ylena even closer. "Don't you dare use that high-handed Morgravian tone with me, Lady Ylena. Remember, you breathe only because I allow it."

"Then disallow it, sire," Wyl taunted. "Kill me now as you threaten. I don't wish to marry you. I would sooner die. Why can't you understand that I went to Celimus to lose my life?"

The light green gaze narrowed and studied her hard. "You went to Celimus? Willingly?"

Wyl nodded as best he could.

The King let go of Ylena and Wyl explained. "Valentyna

was as determined not to release me from her protection as I was to leave it. She could not help me, sire. But I could help her. Presenting myself to Celimus as if I had been sent by his bride-to-be meant I could probably get the Legion called away from Briavel's borders. Celimus is unpredictable and Valentyna is headstrong; their engagement has been threatened by Morgravia's aggression. So I made the sacrifice."

"Why? Why do you owe her anything?"

Wyl had no ready answer to that question. "Because Wyl died trying to save her, to save her father. My brother must have had good reason to swap his allegiance to Briavel, sire. Can you imagine a Thirsk doing that without cause?"

Cailech said nothing, only continued to stare at Ylena. Wyl looked toward Aremys, whose expression begged him to win back Cailech's trust. "I decided to give what little I had to my brother's cause, my lord. I have no reason to live. Queen Valentyna has every reason to. Don't be misled, my king, Valentyna alone is what stands between Celimus and the Razor Kingdom."

"How so?"

"I think she can influence him. If she handles this right, Valentyna might just guide him from the path of war."

"I don't know her but I agree," Cailech admitted. "Although something happened back there at Felrawthy. I can't be sure but my instincts usually serve me true. I believe Celimus might hold to the promise we made to each other."

"And you, my lord?"

"I have no reason to start a war, my lady, or I would not have wasted my own time or breath in meeting with Celimus."

"I would be lying if I said I was not impressed."

"Perhaps we can build on that, then?"

Wyl looked sharply up at Cailech. "What do you mean?"

"I mean, Ylena, that I understand your reluctance to be here and your fear of the Mountain Kingdom, its people, and its sovereign. But perhaps my determination to forge a lasting peace with the south is a place from which we can build this new relationship. Your life is forfeit anywhere outside of the Razors—you do understand that, don't you?"

Wyl nodded.

"Good. Then take my protection. It is mine to bestow on whom I please. I will not rush you, my lady, but I will make you my wife. I have given my word to our neighbor. It is on that understanding that he released you."

Cailech watched Ylena take a breath to interrupt, and hurried on: "I know you wished for death. I could see it in your eyes. But I will not permit such beauty to be wasted, nor such a feisty spirit. You are the last of the great Thirsk family, Ylena. Surely you wish to see its name flourish again?"

Wyl was ill-prepared for Cailech to touch on the very topic that was closest to his heart, one that provoked a storm of emotion and pain in him. He felt Ylena's eyes water and turned away. It was in that moment of despair that he caught sight of a dark shadow that disappeared almost the instant he saw it. Knave! That meant Fynch was here too. Why?

New fears and confusion erupted. He was cold and he was tired. Ylena's fragile body needed rest and it was obvious he could not provoke Cailech into a swift killing. Despite his private anxieties, he could not help but feel his spirits lift at the thought that his friends were close. He would have to go along with Cailech's plan for now and rethink his options once he was inside the fortress.

And so he gave Cailech a response he knew would please the King. "I wish that more than anything in the world, sire. I just cannot see how the Thirsk name can survive."

"Through me, Ylena," Cailech said gently, greatly relieved by her answer and beguiled by her sorrowful beauty. "I give you this pledge: Any child of ours will bear the name of Thirsk. That would also infuriate Celimus, of course, which is really rather satisfying. Does that please you, my lady? I would allow you to call him Fergys or even Wyl to honor your dead."

"It pleases me, sire," Wyl replied, taken aback by Cailech's generosity.

"Then come, my lady. Let me take you to your new home and allow me to show you off to your new people. I will make you a queen, Ylena."

Wyl sighed and dredged up a wan smile for Ylena's face. "You honor me, sire," he said, his mind racing for a way to escape the Razors again, and quickly.

*   *   *

Fynch could barely raise his head when Knave returned.
It is Wyl, as you warned. I think he is with King Cailech, the dog said.

The news roused Fynch, although he was too weak to sit up. He squinted his eyes. "How do you know it's the Mountain King?"

I heard them talking and I saw the men defer to him. Ylena shares his horse and his cloak is far grander than any of the other men who travel with him.

"How in Shar's name could this have occurred?"

From what I could gather, Wyl was at Briavel but somehow convinced Valentyna to hand him over to Celimus.

"Celimus! Where is he?"

I couldn't tell from their conversation. But I do know Wyl tried to get himself killed.

"He cannot invite death!" Fynch exclaimed, coughing. Knave saw blood on the boy's hand when he took it away from his mouth. "Elysius mentioned it to us, remember—after Wyl stormed out of the cottage in the Wild?"

I do. He risks much—the King got angry but fortunately took no action.

"We've got to see him, Knave," Fynch bleated, feeling helpless.

You don't seem so well. Knave deliberately kept his voice toneless.

"I'll be all right," Fynch replied, lying. He did not fool Knave.

Stand up, then. Let's be on our way. The dog loped off.

Fynch tried and failed. Tried again. Knave reappeared, looming over him. "I'm so sorry," the boy whispered.

The dog hardly heard the apology. *You can't stay here, Fynch. It's too open. The warrior scouts could pick you up.*

"I can drag myself somewhere perhaps?" the boy offered, feeling ashamed.

Use what strength you have to climb onto me.

It was obvious that Fynch understood the depth of his sickness or Knave knew he would have objected. Instead the boy used his reserves of will to drape himself across the large animal's back.

I'm sorry, Knave.

Don't send! Save yourself. Now let me get you somewhere safe and dry.

Knave moved silently and slowly, picking his way over the rocky ground, careful not to dislodge the child lying across him. He hardly felt the weight. The boy fell asleep and the dog was relieved. With sleep there would be no pain.

Where could he take Fynch? Perhaps the Thicket could send them to a safe spot. It had done so before when they were traveling. He called to the magical place; disappointment knifed through him when it replied and he learned that he was no longer connected to it as he had been before. He could feel its magic but only through Fynch's link. Knave no longer had its powers at his call.

He pressed on toward a ridge and sent a plea to whoever might be listening that there would be some protection here from the elements. He hoped that it would not be the final resting place of Fynch the gong boy.

K estrel had tried to reach Fynch but could not raise a response. He had followed the pretty woman and her companion as far as the outskirts of the big southern city known as Pearlis. It was obvious they were headed into its center and he would lose them among the crowds. He sighed as he watched the two blend into the constant flow of people either making for or leaving the main city gates; time for him to leave. Kestrel dipped his wing to the right and made a new course. It was warmer here and he would not have minded a few days of hunting with the sun warming his outstretched wings. Here in the south spring was already turning its face to welcome summer, but the north was where Kestrel was headed—to cooler climes and an intriguing young lad who dared to call himself King of the Creatures.

E lspyth had no idea that the bird of prey had just bade her farewell. She was not feeling at all well and, for all her bravado, thanked Shar's blessing that he had seen fit to send her an angel in the guise of Crys Donal. Her injuries reminded her constantly of her ordeal and the pain sapped her energy. She would never have made it into Morgravia without Crys's strong arms and guiding presence. Reaching Yentro seemed wishful thinking, and the Razors and Lothryn a plain impossibility now.

Self-pity was corrosive and pointless. She pushed away the melancholy that threatened to overwhelm her and permitted Crys to use his body to shield her against the sudden crush of people. They had traveled in the cart until they neared the city and then left it at the roadside for some fortunate finder. Crys's horse carried them both from there, but progress was slow because of the stream of people flocking into and out of Pearlis. Still, it was not nearly as crowded as it had been on Elspyth's last journey into the city, when she had arrived with her aged aunt for the tournament. That felt like a lifetime ago, and yet she would have fingers to spare if she counted back in moons. Had it really been such a short period since she had first clapped eyes on Romen Koreldy in Yentro, before she had learned that he was no longer the dashing mercenary but General Wyl Thirsk of Morgravia?

She thought about Wyl as Ylena—felt a pang of sorrow for his suffering and wondered where he was now. Was Ylena already dead and Wyl walking as someone new?

"A regal for your thoughts?" Crys murmured from behind.

"That you're clutching me too close," Elspyth replied.

He squeezed her harder. "My only legitimate chance," he said.

She ignored his jest. "Is the gate into Pearlis always this busy?"

"Yes, so I gather. Still, it was a good idea of yours to abandon the cart and expensive clothes."

"How does it feel to be an ordinary citizen?"

"Better. For the time being the Donal name is cursed."

"We'd better think of a name for you."

"I can be your brother, how's that?"

"I approve. I've always wanted a brother."

"And if you had one, what would you call him?"

"Jonothon."

"Then that's who I am for the time being. I'll hop down and lead you in on the horse. Hopefully we'll slip by unnoticed."

"There's no register at Pearlis," Elspyth offered.

"Nevertheless, some bright spark might recognize me. Alyd and I are . . . *were* incredibly alike in appearance."

"Good idea to tie your hair back like that, then."

"Thank you, sister. Here we go. Don't look anyone in the eye, but don't avert your gaze too obviously."

"Can't we just talk? You're making me nervous with your instructions."

"So how old would Cousin Jemma be now?" Crys replied smoothly.

They were passing through the main gate and Elspyth risked a laugh toward Crys. "Oh, I think she'd be marriage-able age. I hear she's very pretty."

"I don't like flaxen-haired women. I like dark haired beauties, as you well know," Crys continued conversation-ally. He nodded at a guard, who ignored him, and then he laughed. "I am not marrying her even if it does mean you can come and live in the city."

"We're through," Elspyth said, touching his shoulder with relief.

"Well done."

"Now where to?"

"Lord and Lady Bench are old friends of our family, and they will be able to get some medicines for your pain. You look pale."

"Are you sure we'll be welcome?"

Crys grinned his reassurance. "Trust me."

"Famous last words." She groaned, but felt safe for his confidence. She could tell that the wound on her shoulder had reopened and was glad her cloak was dark enough not to give away their secret. "Let's hurry."

It took longer than Crys had anticipated to wend their way into the quieter, more affluent neighborhood where Lord and Lady Bench kept their family home. In the end, he stabled their horse and hailed a carriage to take them the final half mile.

"This is better, Elspyth. If for any reason their house is being watched . . ."

"Why would it be?" she asked, collapsing into the seat.

Crys gave the driver instructions. "I don't know," he said patiently. "But I highly doubt that Celimus would allow one of the most powerful men left in this kingdom to go about his business without some form of observation."

Elspyth nodded. She did not want to talk anymore. It was all she could do just to hold herself together. The pain had stepped up to a most determined throb, she could feel heat at the shoulder wound, and her head was pounding.

"Infection," Crys muttered when she told him. "You need a physic. The Benches will see to it."

"Let's hope they're home."

Fortunately the Bench mansion was encircled by a huge privet hedge and the driver was able to take them into the sweeping driveway and unload them unseen. Crys paid him some extra coin; it might buy silence should it prove necessary. Then he all but carried Elspyth to the door, which was swiftly opened by a dour-faced servant.

"Is the family at home?" Crys inquired.

"That depends, sir," the man said, looking the shabby couple up and down. "Who is calling?"

"If Lord Bench is in residence please inform him that . . ." Crys hesitated; perhaps this fellow could not be trusted. It paid to be cautious. "Tell him it is an old family friend from Brightstone." Crys remembered that the Bench family had a seaside property in the far northwest.

"I will need a name, sir," the servant said with irritating condescension, closing his eyes as he contrived a fake smile.

Crys took a breath. "Just say it's Booty. Now hurry, man, this woman needs medical attention." Elspyth felt like deadweight in his arms, although she was conscious and gave him a brave grin as the manservant disappeared.

"Booty?" she asked.

"My father's old nickname for Lord Bench. Apparently there's no item he can't appropriate if he sets his mind to it."

They stood in awkward silence for a minute, then suddenly a plump, powdered woman came bustling through some double doors, closely followed by a tall, silver-haired gentleman.

"Shar's wrath!" the woman exclaimed. "Is that woman sick?"

"She is, my lady, and urgently requires attention."

Before Crys had finished speaking, the older woman had turned to the manservant. "Arnyld, why are you still standing there? Send a runner for my physician at once! Tell Physic Dredge to waste no time." She turned back to Crys. "Put her over here, son," she said gently, pointing to a long low bench seat.

"I'm bleeding, my lady," Elspyth began, "I'll ruin—"

"Hush, child," the woman admonished. "Do as you are told."

Elspyth obeyed immediately, sinking to the bench.

Crys took his chance while there were no servants visible, turning and bowing to Lord Bench. He was met by a grim-faced stare.

"I wondered who had the audacity to use old Jeryb's nickname for me to gain entry," Eryd Bench said in his melodious voice. "Introduce yourself truly now, before I call a Legionnaire."

"Lord and Lady Bench, my apologies for arriving in this manner, but circumstances demand it. I am Crys Donal, Duke of Felrawthy."

The couple standing before him blanched. Lady Bench reached for her husband, who helped her sit down next to Elspyth. Crys, looking at their pale expressions, was relieved to know the physic was on his way.

27

KNAVE WHINED SOFTLY, HIS GREAT HEAD ON HIS PAWS, HIS body encircling the sleeping boy, whose breathing sounded dangerously shallow. Something was happening to Fynch, but his close companion could not reach him. All he could do was watch, wait, and pray to the Dragon King that this was not Fynch's time.

Fynch was dreaming. He felt himself flying; the wind

whipped through his hair and whistled past his ears. For a dream, the view around him looked awfully real, and the wind was shockingly brisk.

A voice suddenly spoke into Fynch's mind, and he knew it could not be a dream. *Not long now.*

It was the Dragon King and Fynch realized he was riding him, feeling each powerful beat of his wings as they worked in tandem to drive the creature faster through the air.

My king, Fynch sent, his voice unashamedly filled with awe. *Where do we go?*

To a private place, my son. Somewhere safe. Where you will be free from your pain and where no one can hear us.

Am I truly with you?

Your body is with Knave, Fynch. Your spirit is here.

How can I do this?

It's my way of honoring you.

Honoring me?

We ask so much of you.

Whatever you ask, sire, I give it gladly.

Brave boy. You are more than worthy.

Of what, my lord?

Of Kingship, Fynch.

I don't understand, my king.

You will, my son. That is why I have brought you here.

Wyl felt a sense of despair as they entered the gates of the fortress. Cailech was immediately surrounded by well-wishers welcoming him back, and stealing interested glances toward the golden-haired beauty he had left on the horse. It was Myrt who arrived at Ylena's side to help her dismount.

"May I show you to your rooms, my lady?" he asked, taking her hand to help her from the horse, much to Wyl's discomfort. "The King has requested you dine with him later."

Wyl reached for a gracious smile, though the invitation reminded him of the meeting with Celimus he had been forced to attend while trapped in Leyen. "Thank you, er . . .?"

"Myrt." Aremys appeared at Wyl's side and now offered the formal introduction. "He is a friend, Ylena. You can trust him."

Wyl nodded toward Myrt, who gave one of his rare smiles. Aremys had already explained that Myrt knew about Aremys's suspicions about Lothryn's fate, but as the mercenary obviously could not come clean about Ylena, he would have to remain polite but distant to Wyl's sister.

"I will see you later perhaps?" Aremys said to Wyl, and then to Myrt: "Shall we meet at the stables?"

The big warrior nodded. "Come, my lady," he said, and Wyl had no option but to be guided away, deeper into the fortress of the Mountain King.

F ynch remained curled on the Dragon King's vast back, though the creature had landed. Its darkly vibrant colors seemed to pulse bright one moment and soft the next, illuminating its scales. Fynch felt warm and safe for the first time since leaving the Wild, even though he knew he was not really here. Physically, he remained on a freezing ledge near the home of the Mountain King and he was dying, with Knave's body curled around him.

He twisted to lie on his back, loving the deep connection between himself and the Dragon King. The magnificent beast remained silent while his guest acclimatized himself to the breathtaking scene below. They were on the highest peak of the Razors, but not in the northeast, where Fynch's body lay.

Are we in the Wild, my lord?

Yes, Fynch.

The boy sighed. *If I died now amid this beauty, my king, I would die happy.*

The King did not reply.

I am dying, aren't I, sire?

You have pushed yourself too hard. The magic you have called upon is so potent it is poisoning you.

Elysius managed to live with it, Fynch said.

True, my son. But Elysius did not draw upon the magic of the Thicket, nor was he required to use magic for years on end. He preserved himself by using it sparingly.

I am sorry I have been so careless with it.

The Dragon King twisted his sinuous neck and the massive head came close. A monstrously large eye regarded the tiny figure that lay on its back. *You need make no apology to me, Faith Fynch.*

It moved Fynch to hear these solemn words and tears ran down his face. *I am not afraid to give my life, my lord—I hope you know this. But I am so afraid of failing you that I am impatient to reach Rashlyn.*

The Dragon King gave a murmured growl of agreement. *I know, child. You will not fail us.*

But I am not sure I can recover in time, my king. I will likely end my life where Knave and I lie.

That is why I have brought you here, Fynch, the King said, his voice so deep the boy could feel it rumbling the length of his own body, despite the gentleness of its tone. *I shall restore you. But, as always with magic, there is a price.*

I will pay it, Fynch said bravely. *I wish only for my strength to return so I may to do your bidding.*

I accept your sacrifice, and in return you deserve an explanation. I have seen something in you, Fynch, that you must know.

I felt it too, my lord, the boy admitted. *I sensed you recognizing a part of me I barely know myself.*

Can you not guess, child?

Fynch considered the King's question and closed his eyes. Yes, he could guess, but was this something he truly wanted to know? He assumed the price he must pay for the temporary restoration of his health was death, had already accepted as much. If it had to be sooner rather than later, he would not fuss. He made his decision.

It is connected with my mother, I feel.

Go on.

Fynch felt a breeze break through the protective wings of the huge beast and brush against his cheeks. More tears were falling, but he ignored them. He was not crying because he was sad or frightened; he was weeping because this was the most emotional moment of his life. The Dragon King was about to confirm something he had always known but had held buried within, a secret with far-reaching repercussions. If revealed, it could affect the course of a realm.

I believe I am not of my named father's flesh.

A tremble passed through the Dragon King. *You are correct, my son. So who fathered you?*

Fynch did not want to speak the name. He didn't know why he was so sure it was the truth; all he knew was that he had glimpsed it within himself the moment the Dragon King saw it. While it had surprised the King of the Creatures, for some reason it had not surprised Fynch.

The boy looked out again over the majesty of the Razors, hidden valleys emerging from beneath the snows as spring staked its claim.

I didn't know it would thaw this high up.

We are in the Wild, my son. Everything is possible.

Fynch nodded. The Dragon King was not rushing him to answer, but now it was time. *My mother was fey. At each new moon she would experience a sort of madness. The madness took the form of lust.* He hesitated.

Go on, Fynch.

She would tempt other men. She had no control over it.

And?

I was conceived during one of those moon times.

Yes, you were. Who is your father, Fynch?

My father is . . . He almost dared not speak the name but knew he must. *My father was Magnus, King of Morgravia.*

Indeed. You are part of the dragon throne line and thus a part of me.

Was Magnus aware of who I was during our conversations at Stoneheart?

He felt a strong connection to you, Fynch, as you did with him. But no, he never knew you were of his flesh.

At the great creature's final word, Fynch felt a rush of sadness. It washed over him like a crashing wave but settled finally into peace—the peace that comes with the finality of suspicions confirmed and a puzzle solved. A new sensation took over; a feeling of warmth. He did not know whether it was the dragon himself—but he was aware of some sort of new link between that creature and himself.

Suddenly he felt a sense of intense belonging . . . to both Kings, Magnus and the Dragon.

28

ORD AND LADY BENCH SAT WITH ELSPYTH AND CRYS IN THE Benches' drawing room, which was hung with family portraits and softened with lush furnishings and drapings. Elspyth, determined not to miss out on the conversation, was propped in a comfortable chair. Helyn Bench's physic had examined her and declared that the wounds were neatly sutured; infection had set in only at the shoulder. Fortunately it had been caught in time and the physic promised to send over a special brew that would clear up the problem within days. Rest and quiet were also integral to the healing. Helyn had not hesitated in confirming that Elspyth would remain with them until she was fit and well.

"I cannot impose on you for so long, my lady," Elspyth had protested.

"Child, you'll be going nowhere until the fever is gone and the infection has cleared," Helyn had cautioned, and Elspyth understood there would be no arguing with the powerful woman.

Now the Benches and their guests reclined comfortably. Crys and Elspyth had related the worst part of their tale. A small porcelain brazier burned gently in the corner of the room. Elspyth thought it similar to those the Mountain People favored and said so.

"As a matter of fact, it is from Grenadyn," Eryd replied, "but I'm impressed that you have seen one in the Razor Kingdom and intrigued as to how you lived to tell the tale."

Elspyth blushed. "It is a long story, sir, and after the one we've just told you, I can't imagine you would want more of the same," she said, hoping to deflect his attention from the story of how she came to be so far north.

"Indeed," he said, eyeing her gravely but not pursuing it. After the story of the murder of the Donals, the Benches were already in a state of shock. "Crys, I regret having to tax you further on this subject, but are you quite sure that the Crown was behind the slaughter at Tenterdyn?"

Crys nodded. "My mother died in my arms and her last wish was for revenge. Her haunted eyes spoke of the horrors she had witnessed—the killing of my father and brothers and then the burning of their bodies. The massacre at Rittylworth was also definitely the work of Celimus—Ylena Thirsk confirmed it and Elspyth happened along quite soon after the raiders had left. She took the message from Brother Jakub to my father."

Helyn handed Crys a goblet of wine. "None for you, I'm afraid, Elspyth. Sorry, please go on," she added, smiling softly at the young Duke.

Crys hoped the tremble in his voice would disappear with the help of the liquor. "As I explained, we have been at Queen Valentyna's court. She offered her protection without question. I hadn't expected the diversion of tracking down Elspyth," he said, "or I would have been here much earlier."

"What can we do?" Lord Bench asked. "I feel so helpless."

"Wy—" Crys stopped himself in time. "Ylena suggested that I come to Pearlis and try to stir up some trouble for the King."

"Ylena Thirsk did? Where is that girl now?" Lord Bench demanded. "To tell the truth, I thought she must have gone home to Argorn after Wyl's death. Now that we know about her husband's murder, all the more reason for her to flee Stoneheart."

"No, sir. Ylena was thrown into Stoneheart's dungeons. A mercenary called Romen Koreldy rescued her." Crys quickly outlined how Koreldy fit into the tale, manipulating the truth by telling them that he had made a promise to the dying Wyl to find his sister. "Then, after escaping Rittylworth, Ylena fled to Felrawthy. She carried proof of my brother's murder there with her—which is why Celimus sent

his assassin to find her. Leyen, of course, never—" He
stopped abruptly as both his hosts flinched with obvious
alarm. "Is something wrong?"

"Leyen?" Lady Bench said, her expression aghast. "Is that
the name you used?"

Crys nodded, glancing toward Elspyth.

"Can you describe her?"

Discomfited by Lady Bench's interest, Crys gave a quick
summary of Leyen's appearance.

"But that's her!" Helyn exclaimed. "I know this woman.
She came to our house, for Shar's sake. I have been protecting her from Celimus since I first met her and he began asking questions about her. She told me she was a
messenger—a go-between for the King and Queen Valentyna!" Exasperation rang in her tone.

"She is an assassin, you say?" Eryd said gravely, looking
toward his wife to be calm.

"Well . . ." Crys hesitated. He had made a mistake, should
have used the name Aremys Farrow. But how was he to
know that the Bench family would know Faryl?

"Out with it, young man," Eryd urged. Duke or not, Crys
was still a young pup in Lord Bench's eyes. It was incon-
ceivable to him, even after days of trying to accept it, that
Jeryb Donal was dead. The old rogue had been stronger than
several oxen; he had been destined to outlive them all.
Friendship aside, it upset Eryd deeply to think that Morgravia had lost not just such a fine man but also its finest remaining strategist and soldier. Celimus would pay for that
loss.

Crys looked helplessly toward Elspyth. She knew he was
trapped by duty whichever way he turned: to his parents, to
the realm, to these fine people, to a friend. She hesitated, and
then impulsively leaned forward.

"My lord, my lady," she interrupted. "I have a story to tell
that you will not want to believe—no doubt won't be able to
believe once you have heard it. But I am telling you the
truth, for I have borne witness to it with my own eyes."

"As have I," Crys joined in, a mixture of terror and relief
flooding his body as he saw that Elspyth had made the deci-

sion for him. He hated breaking oath with Wyl, but he hated lying to Lord Eryd Bench even more, particularly as the old man reminded him so much of his own father. And the truth was, they needed allies. Someone had to help share the burden of Wyl's woes. It had sounded fair enough at Tenterdyn to keep this terrible secret, but someone in power had to know of Myrren's Gift. Others must be convinced to rally to Wyl's cause.

Eryd glanced between them. "This sounds dire," he said. He had thought he had heard their worst, but it seemed far more terrible information was yet to be revealed.

"Why do I suddenly feel I don't want to hear what you're about to tell us?" Helyn Bench added, surprised herself that she could resist a tantalizing tale.

"You might regret our sharing this with you, Lord and Lady Bench. But once told, you must promise us you will aid us and act upon it."

"My dear," Helyn said, now truly wishing she had joined her daughter, Georgyana, for a day of shopping, "you make it all sound so sinister. What is this about?"

"It is the story of Wyl Thirsk, my lady, and I shall tell you everything I know, even though he will never forgive me for sharing it."

Elspyth began.

As Elspyth was sharing Wyl's story with a stunned couple in Pearlis, Wyl, in the Razors, was explaining to the women attending Ylena that he preferred not to wear either of the two dresses that had been brought to his chamber.

Cailech had commandeered a suite of rooms as accommodations for Ylena. Once again, Wyl was arrested by the simple beauty of the Mountain People's creativity. A fresco of vines and their fruit trailed the perimeter of each room's ceiling and the whitewashed walls were hung with paintings of the stark Razor landscape. A thick rug on the floor and an equally colorful bedspread added yet more brightness to the natural light flooding in through the huge windows favored by the King throughout the fortress; he liked to bring the mountainscape he loved inside.

The last time Wyl had been in this stonghold, as Koreldy, braziers had warmed each room. Only the endless hallways and cavernous spaces connecting the chambers had been left unheated, and those had been freezing, he recalled. But it was well into spring now and the hardy Mountain People had done away with the heating.

Ylena's body trembled from the cold as Wyl tried again to politely decline the garments. "Thank you, but I prefer my trews," he said.

"Both gowns are woven from the coat of polders, my lady," one of the women assured. Her tone suggested that this was equivalent to being spun from gold.

Wyl was none the wiser for the explanation but was courteous enough to touch the dress and smile. "It is very beautiful," he agreed.

"Please, my lady, we will get into trouble if you do not wear one of these dresses."

"Oh, surely not."

They nodded. "Our king told us to dress your hair as well. He has had fresh thawdrops brought up from the valley."

Wyl looked toward where the women glanced. He had not noticed the vase holding the tiny white flowers Cailech had promised to pick for Ylena. He felt more trapped than ever, and wished he could reach Aremys. Perhaps he should just make a run for it. He could hope someone would bring him down—if he were lucky, kill him. It would likely be a Razor warrior and then at least he could inhabit the body of a man again . . . but if he was felled by an arrow, he might not live to avenge those who had been murdered, or see Valentyna again.

Valentyna. His heart ached as he remembered the disturbed and disgusted expression she had worn the last time they were together. If only he could be a man again, he would somehow make it up to her . . . even if only to apologize on Ylena's behalf for his stupidity.

He realized suddenly that the women were staring at him and the silence had stretched embarrassingly long.

For you, then, Valentyna, he decided, and nodded to the waiting women. "Which one suits me best, do you think?"

The women beamed. One reached out and touched Ylena's hair. "You are so beautiful, you would do either of them justice." Then she took Ylena's hand. "We have longed for the day when our king would take a woman for his own," she said shyly.

Wyl was touched in spite of the horror he felt. "Do you not mind that I am Morgravian?"

She shrugged and looked toward her companion, who made a similar gesture. "That you have captured his heart is enough. We do not question his choice, and in truth there is no one suitable within our own kingdom. Whoever he chose to marry, it would have caused jealousy among the factions. You have no allegiance to any Mountain family. This way he offends no one. And, my lady, rumors abound that our two kingdoms have signed a peace treaty. This makes your marriage to our king even more special. How could we not accept the woman our king loves?"

"Loves?" Wyl repeated, aghast. "He doesn't even know me."

"The King is a great judge of character," the woman said stubbornly.

"He's told you we are to be married?" Wyl asked, further alarmed.

They nodded. "Oh yes," the other woman said. "The news is spreading like fire around the fortress."

"And has he said when?" Wyl held his breath.

They hesitated, sensing his trepidation. "The day after tomorrow, my lady," the older one said finally. "A gown is being stitched from pure white polder—our most rare color. Animals are being slaughtered today for the feast and people are already gathering to catch a glimpse of you."

They saw the noblewoman's hands fly to her face and press against each cheek in horror. Her look of desperation frightened them.

"He will be gentle with you, my lady," the older one assured, imagining the angelic beauty was fearing for her wedding night.

"Oh, stop, please," Wyl said, determined now to find a way to flee or bring about his own death. He remembered the warning from Elysius with despair. It was not possible for him to invite his own death. But randomness was still possible, as young Fynch had assured him. That was what he needed now to save him. A random act—be it madness, violence, or anger. Whatever occurred, he had to be rid of Ylena's guise within the next few hours.

"You're sure of this?" Myrt hissed in a whisper.

Aremys nodded, trying to look nonchalant as he lifted the latch on the side door leading into the stable. He forced himself not to glance over his shoulder. "Where's Maegryn?"

"He's always around somewhere. You'd better have a story at the ready if we're caught."

"Perhaps you should wait outside," Aremys suggested. "I can't risk you getting into trouble with Cailech. Once you're committed, there's no going back."

Myrt shook his head. "I have to see the horse for myself."

The set of his friend's mouth assured Aremys there would be no further discussion. He nodded and stepped into the darkness. His eyes took a few moments to adjust to the minimal light that filtered through the stable's timber boards. A snort told him Galapek was in the shadows to his right. He immediately began whispering a stream of soft words to the creature.

Myrt closed the door and remained silent behind Aremys. He realized he was holding his breath. He watched Aremys raise his hand and place it on the animal's majestic face, and as man and beast touched, he felt a surge of emotion. Was this really Lothryn?

"Lothryn," Aremys murmured. "If you're there, give us a sign. I've brought Myrt." He nodded at Myrt to step forward. "Say something," he whispered.

Myrt moved from behind the Grenadyne and cleared his throat. "If that's you, my friend, prove it."

"I can feel the magic shivering through his body," Aremys said. "He's fighting it; that's why his flesh is trembling." He turned back to Galapek. "Come on, Lothryn, do it for Elspyth. She's alive. She's coming for you. And Wyl's here too!"

The horse reared up onto its hind legs and squealed. Aremys fell to the floor, pain filling his head as a voice, equally pain-filled, growled into his mind, *Turn me loose!*

"It's him!" Myrt whispered as he tried to calm the horse, which was kicking and pounding at the wall. "Quick! He could hurt you."

"He won't hurt me," the Grenadyne said, disgusted with himself for falling. His head throbbed but his satisfaction was intense, as was the awe this sickening magic inspired in him. "It is him, Myrt. He spoke to me. He wants to be turned loose."

The warrior turned an anxious gaze toward him. "What do we do?"

Aremys frowned, as much with frustration as with helplessness. "Well, we can't just let him go. We have to think this through. There's Gueryn to consider, too."

"Forgive me if I don't lose any sleep over a Morgravian soldier," Myrt said. "I care only about Lothryn."

"Understood. Listen—" He got no further. A sudden shaft of sunlight made them both swing around toward the side door where Maegryn had just entered the stable.

"Myrt? What are you doing here? And that's the Grenadyne with you, isn't it?"

Myrt was not as adept at lying as Aremys and his hesitation, as well as the guilty glance toward his companion, was telling. "I . . . that is, we . . ."

"We got back today," Aremys continued smoothly for his faltering friend. "I was hoping we could go for a ride."

Maegryn looked quizzically at them. "But you've been riding for days."

"That's true," Aremys agreed, mentally kicking himself and giving an embarrassed grin. "A lot has happened these past few days, Maegryn. I felt like being as alone as I am permitted to be. Can't think of a better place than in Galapek's saddle."

"Surely you weren't thinking of taking the King's horse without his or my permission?"

"Of course not," Myrt said, regaining his composure. "We were just passing and thought we'd look in on the animal.

Aremys is fond of him—brought him a red apple because he knows he hates green ones."

The stablemaster was not to be put off so easily. "I heard Galapek. What was all the noise about?"

Both men shrugged and Aremys knew they looked more guilty for that single gesture than for any of their stammered responses or awkward pauses. He could tell from the guarded look in the stablemaster's eyes that Maegryn was suspicious of their intentions.

"Where are you going?" Aremys said when the man turned away. He knew very well where Maegryn was headed, but he was desperately stalling for time.

"The King, if he'll see me. I'm sorry but I have my orders."

"Who from?" Myrt demanded.

"Rashlyn."

"Since when do you take orders from him?" Myrt spat.

"Since le Gant went missing," the stablemaster replied. "The barshi insisted that anyone acting suspiciously around the King's horse would meet the same fate."

Aremys felt a chill move through him. "What do you mean, 'fate'?"

Maegryn shrugged, fortunately not realizing that Aremys had no way of knowing of the Morgravian prisoner. "According to the barshi, le Gant has been dealt with."

"Dealt with!" Myrt repeated. "I thought only the King made decisions about our prisoners?"

"Listen, Myrt," Maegryn began, his anger stoking fast now. "I hate Rashlyn. You of all people should know that. But I won't interfere in the King's business—you should know that, too. Lothryn, Haldor rest his soul, learned the hard way about crossing the King. I don't intend to be given into Rashlyn's keeping because I've invoked the ire of King Cailech. I can't help you."

"Is that what's happened?" Aremys pressed. "Rashlyn took le Gant?"

Maegryn looked down. "I don't know what's happened. I suspect Rashlyn took him from the dungeon, yes."

"What are we coming to, Maegryn, when we are too

scared to speak out?" Myrt asked. He did not mean it as an accusation; it was more a sad-sounding reflection on his own shortcomings.

"Lothryn stood up to the King and Lothryn paid the price!" Maegryn yelled. "I don't have his courage."

"True. And where is Lothryn, do you think?" Myrt asked, advancing on the stablemaster.

"Be careful, Myrt," Aremys murmured. His senses had become highly attuned over the years to the feelings of men in a blood rage, and Myrt seemed close to losing control of his emotions.

"I . . . I don't know. Dead, I suppose," Maegryn answered, stepping back. "Don't threaten me, Myrt."

"An honorable death, do you think?"

Maegryn nodded slowly, uncertainly.

"He's not dead. He's alive!" Myrt boomed, close to Maegryn's face. "Rashlyn told us as much. It's just taken me a while to work it out."

Maegryn's expression was shocked now. "Alive? Where?"

"Here, Maegryn. Right beneath your nose," Myrt said, a cruel tone to his voice that Aremys had never heard before. Myrt was too upset. This was dangerous.

The stablemaster frowned, stepped back again, closer to the door. "What are you talking about?"

"I'm talking about magic, Maegryn. I'm talking about Rashlyn and his sinister ways."

"I don't understand," the man muttered, licking his lips nervously. He looked deeply scared now, as if he too sensed that the situation had turned nasty.

"You'd be right to feel petrified," Myrt went on, noting the man's fear. "Lothryn is in your care."

Maegryn's eyes widened, the nonsense of Myrt's words giving him courage. "You're talking in riddles, man. What's he saying, Grenadyne?"

Aremys hesitated. Myrt's emotions had gotten the better of him. Sharing what they knew with Maegryn, who was as loyal to Cailech as any of his warriors and did not share Myrt's single-minded dedication to Lothryn, was a dangerous idea. "Maegryn," he started, his mind racing, "it's going to be hard for you to believe us—"

"Galapek *is* Lothryn, you fool!" Myrt interrupted, spitting his fury and advancing on the cringing stablemaster. "Rashlyn, with the King's permission, used his dark magic to change him into Galapek. That's why you don't know where the horse came from, and why the King is so careful about who rides him or asks questions about him. And that's also why you've been sworn to secrecy. You've always known there was something odd about the whole situation surrounding the horse. Admit it, damn you!"

"Lothryn?" Maegryn repeated, shaking his head in confusion. He looked at the huge horse and saw the anger in its eyes then returned his anxious gaze to Myrt. "No," he said, his head moving slowly from side to side in denial.

"You know it's true, Maegryn. You've had doubts of your own from the start. Right from the beginning when Cailech said he would break this horse's spirit and earn its loyalty with trust. What do you think that whole charade was about, eh? The King was humiliating Loth, destroying his closest friend, his truest follower, and then rebuilding him in the form of a beast. A mute beast that would have to carry the King on his back for the rest of his life and thus pay homage like any slave or lowlife. An honorable death was too good for our best warrior, Maegryn. The King wanted to make him pay; he wanted revenge and humiliation for Loth's betrayal."

Maegryn retaliated, reacting to the pain of the truth he knew he was hearing. "Lothryn chose the Morgravian woman over his own king, his own people!" he cried.

"And he deserved to become this, did he?" Myrt boomed. "An animal! He still lives, Maegryn. That's the worst of it. He knows. He's trapped inside that body, in agonizing pain."

The stablemaster shook his head again, as though he himself were in pain. "No. This isn't true. Can you prove it?" he demanded, looking between the two men. "Show me how this is Lothryn. How can you know?"

Aremys answered in a tone of such resignation, Myrt knew they had lost the opportunity of convincing Maegryn. "I can feel the taint of the filthy magic."

"That's it, Grenadyne—your word? And what . . . you are gifted with sentient power?" He looked at his fellow Mountain Man. "Have you gone mad, Myrt? You would trust this foreigner over your own king?"

"It's the truth, Maegryn."

The stablemaster gave a harsh laugh, feeling a small measure of control return. "The truth?" he scorned. "Says who? Another prisoner? For that's what he is. I have no gripe with you, Farrow, but don't ask me to take your word over that of my king."

Aremys said nothing, knew nothing he could say would change the stablemaster's mind.

"You don't know anything of substance, Myrt," Maegryn continued. "You're just believing the Grenadyne. Have you heard Lothryn speak? Has the horse communicated anything to you?"

Myrt shook his head, anger trembling through his body. "He spoke only to Aremys."

"To Aremys!" Maegryn repeated, still more scorn in his tone. "No proof, nothing but this man's say-so, and you're prepared to believe that Lothryn has been turned into a horse. Does that not sound ridiculous to you?"

Myrt nodded. "It does, but not when you say that same sentence with Rashlyn's name attached to it. The barshi is evil and you know it. His influence on the king is dangerous. Lothryn felt it and said as much to me. I don't think our king ordered this. I think Rashlyn did. I believe, as Lothryn did, that the barshi is able to sway the King against his own wishes."

"Rashlyn uses magic against the King?" Maegryn clarified, aghast.

"Yes. That's what I now believe. I think he can persuade Cailech to agree to things he would not choose himself."

Maegryn put his hands up in a warding gesture. "That's enough, Myrt. I don't want to hear any more. You speak treachery against our sovereign and it is my sworn duty as one of his men to make this betrayal public. I'm sorry."

The stablemaster had just opened the door when he felt the breath cut off from his lungs as huge, powerful hands closed around his throat. He let go of the door's iron ring, gasping. Fear pounded through his ears and the blood pumped desperately through squeezed veins and arteries. As if from far away, he heard the Grenadyne shouting at Myrt. He found enough strength to twist around to see through his bulging eyes the rage in the bigger man's face, but he could not loosen the warrior's grip to beg for life. "I'm sorry too," were the last words he heard before Myrt intensified the pressure and crushed his victim's neck. Maegryn slumped in his killer's arms, dead.

Aremys, shocked, stood frozen in place. He was angry with himself for not foreseeing Myrt's rage and preventing the killing. But the deed was done. Instead of accusations he offered help. "Where can we hide the body?" he said matter-of-factly. Myrt was in a state of shock, his rage gone the moment Maegryn had died beneath his fingers. He did not reply, crouching instead by the corpse. "Come on, man! It's done with. You can't bring him back. We have to hide him."

"I'm a dead man. We Mountain folk are strict about killing our own kind."

"We're probably both dead men anyway. Come on, help me. We have to hide him and buy some hours."

"For what?" Myrt said hopelessly.

"Everything's going to unravel, my friend. The King is marrying a woman who does not want him and whom he does not know well enough," Aremys responded. "Strange stuff is going to happen—believe me. Time is our enemy now. I know you don't want to, but you have to choose between Lothryn or your king and you have to do it now! This is what I wanted to avoid, why I asked you to remain outside."

Myrt nodded sorrowfully. "I made my choice, Grenadyne. I chose Lothryn."

Aremys continued, more gently this time. "All right, then. We now know we are in the presence of your friend, and we must find a way to release him."

"Can we?" Myrt asked, his spirits lifting.

"By death if necessary," Aremys answered gravely. "We need to find out more from Rashlyn."

"He has Cailech's protection," Myrt warned.

"Not while the King is enamored of Ylena Thirsk, he doesn't. We must get to Rashlyn now . . . and perhaps he will lead us to Gueryn."

"I told you, I don't care about the Morgravian soldier."

"But I do. And so will Ylena Thirsk when she finds out her guardian is a prisoner here."

Myrt looked at him, startled. "Her guardian? Does the King know that?"

Aremys shook his head. "I shouldn't think so but I'm going to tell him. I'll seek an audience with the King. You establish where the barshi is and keep him from Cailech at all costs."

"And Galapek?"

"Will have to be patient a little longer," Aremys said softly, turning to stare at the stallion in the shadows. "Myrt, this choice you've made—you do understand you'll have to leave the Razors?"

"Escape, you mean?"

Aremys nodded. "I won't let you go alone."

The warrior sighed. "This is how Lothryn must have felt. Damned if he did and damned if he didn't. I betray those I love whichever choice I make. I'm sorry, Aremys. I can't promise I'll leave."

It was best not to force the issue, Aremys realized. The circumstances would no doubt make all the decisions for them. "Come on, we've got to hide this body," he said.

Myrt nodded. "I know where."

29

ADY HELYN BENCH RELUCTANTLY HELD HER HUSBAND'S
jacket as the man she loved slipped his arms into the
sleeves. "I wish you wouldn't," she began again.

He turned in her arms and hugged her. "My mind is made
up, my dear. I don't like this cloak-and-dagger stuff. I think
we must air the grievances tactfully."

"Eryd," she said, fear combining with exasperation, "how
tactful can you be when you're about to accuse someone of
murder?"

"Indeed," he said, and pointed to a silk scarf. "Would you
help me with that, please?"

She flounced to the chair and picked up the length of silk
draped across it. "And not just anyone," she continued. "The
King!"

"Helyn, in case you haven't noticed over the years, I am
not a dimwit."

"Taking witnesses won't stop him!" she cried. "He'll just
have you all killed."

"Don't be ridiculous, woman. Kill me and then Lord
Hartley? Then I suppose he'd have to kill Lord Jownes and
Lord Peaforth because they would follow in our footsteps.
And then who else would be left to advise, to cajole, to ad-
minister this city? He needs us."

"Please don't go. Don't do this."

"I shall know from the way he reacts whether or not he is
lying."

"Eryd!" Helyn pleaded, just short of a screech, hating the
way her husband closed his eyes in despair. "Do you believe
that the Donals are not dead? Not hacked to bits, raped,

burned? Or that the massacre at Rittylworth was a misunderstanding and that the monks are in fact live and well?"

"No, Helyn," he said, and the tone in his voice chilled her. She wished she had not resorted to sarcasm. He was deeply angered now; she had overstepped the mark. "Please do not speak ill of the dead. I am painfully aware of the deaths of my friends the Donal family and the innocent men of Rittylworth."

"I'm sorry, Eryd, I—"

He cut her off, too angry to hear more. "Enough, wife. The three remaining lords of Morgravia cannot disappear! Now hush your ramblings and get this scarf tied, or I shall be late."

"What did you tell the others?" she asked, resigned, understanding there was nothing more she could do to stop her husband from walking into the dragon's den.

"All that we know."

"Not about Wyl Thirsk, surely?"

"No. That revelation I am keeping to myself until I can see this phenomenon with my own eyes."

"Do you believe our guests, though?"

He nodded, slowly, reluctantly. "How could I not? Their tale is so shocking and mysterious, no one could make it up. Jeryb Donal's son would not lie to us, Helyn. You can see it in his face that he is as petrified of this . . . this Myrren's Gift, as they call it, as he is intrigued by it. We have known Crys Donal since he was a babe in arms. He is as open a man as any, I am sure. No, there is no lie there, but I can't accept it fully yet."

"That Wyl Thirsk walks in the body of his sister, you mean?"

"That he was the Koreldy assassin, that he was Leyen, whom you delighted in so much, that, yes, he has become his sister."

"But it does make sense, doesn't it, my love?" she said. "It is odd that a Grenadyne mercenary would bother to rescue his enemy's sister from the dungeon of his benefactor." Eryd nodded. "Then take her to safety before going to look for that Widow Ilyk person."

"Is that the seer's name?"

"Yes. I'm embarrassed to admit that she has done readings for me in the past."

"It's all nonsense, Helyn. You know that," Eryd grumbled.

"I thought so until now," she replied, hurrying on. "Then the Grenadyne is trapped, taken into the Razors, and instead of bargaining his way out—as presumably he could have done with that Mountain King—he risks everything to get Gueryn le Gant and Elspyth away. Does that sound like a hardened mercenary, or like Wyl Thirsk trapped inside the body of one?"

"I agree, Helyn. It's not that I need convincing. I just—"

"So then he makes his way to Briavel to offer his protection to Queen Valentyna. Why? Well, of course, he'd saved her life once before from a potential assassination attempt and had fought to save her father's too, losing his own life in the effort. But then King Celimus comes along and it all goes wrong. Wyl gets killed by the King's own assassin, Leyen—"

"They called her Faryl."

"Whatever her name was. That girl, as much as I liked her—and I guess now it was simply Wyl I was liking all over again—was not used to womanly things."

"What do you mean?"

"Well, the baths. Remember I told you?"

"You must have."

"And you weren't listening as usual," she admonished. "She was so hesitant about going into the pavilion—that's where we first met. She was terribly embarrassed about showing her body, and let me tell you, Eryd, no woman who looks like that is ever coy about her body. She had no idea about the soap leaves, and when I mentioned the razing of Rittylworth, her whole demeanor changed. That's because it was Wyl, fearing for his sister."

Eryd nodded. "I understand, Helyn. I want to believe it, but I believe what I see with my own eyes, not hearsay."

"I know. As you say, though, it's too chilling not to be real. I need no further convincing."

"About what, Mother?" came a light voice, and the Benchs' daughter, Georgyana, slipped into the room.

"Were you listening?" her father asked, anxious that his young, fanciful daughter had heard more than he wished.

"No. But I wouldn't tell you if I had," she answered, and pulled a face at him, at the same time taking his hand and squeezing it. That father and daughter worshiped each other was obvious. Helyn sometimes wondered how they ever found room for her in their lives. "Did you meet our guests, darling?" she said.

"No," Georgyana said, shaking her long golden curls.

"We have visitors downstairs," her father said. "I suppose you came in through the back like a servant?"

"I'm hungry." His daughter pouted. "I wanted to see what was cooking."

"Well, come and meet them," Helyn said, glad of Georgyana's noise and distraction.

"Do I have to?"

"You'll like them," she assured.

"Who are they?"

"The Duke of Felrawthy and a lovely girl called Elspyth, from the north."

"Oh, another stuffy old man like father?" Georgyana said, winking toward Eryd.

"Far from it, my love," Helyn replied. "Crys Donal is one of the best-looking men in Morgravia, and soon to be the most eligible when word gets around of his new status."

"Ooh! What are we waiting for, Mother?" her daughter squealed. "Off you go, Father. Bring me back something small and sparkly."

Eryd rolled his eyes with exasperation. "I am hoping for an audience with the King, Georgyana."

"Well, steal me something from the palace, then." His daughter giggled as she left the chamber.

Helyn gave her husband a searching glance. "My love, please—"

"Don't say it," he warned gently. "You know I will be."

She said nothing and left, fearful of letting herself down with tears.

Knave was amazed at Fynch's recovery. His surprise drew a grin from the boy. "Truly, I am well," he said, stretching. "I'm even hungry."

No headache?

"All gone . . . for now."

How can this be?

"The King came."

The Dragon King? Again! He was here?

The boy nodded. "He came to me in my dreams. I flew with him, Knave. He carried me to the Wild."

You were here all the time, Knave said quietly. *I noticed you were restless in your sleep, though. I feared it was pain . . . death.*

Again the boy smiled, gently and without smugness, but Knave noticed something new in his expression. Some knowledge, perhaps.

I don't mean to pry, Fynch, but you appear miraculously well.

"I am," Fynch said, laughing. He stood. "And I don't need sharvan either. He healed me."

The King did?

"Yes. He said he would restore me so I can fulfill my task."

Suddenly Knave could not look at him; he understood the way of things. *But nothing comes without a price, am I right?* he asked, sadness in his voice.

"Don't dwell on it," Fynch replied softly. "I am at peace, my friend. The King shared something with me that has made me happy. Happier than I have ever felt before."

And this sharing was a secret?

The boy nodded.

I understand, Fynch. I'm glad you feel so well. I hated to watch you suffer.

"I know. You are a better friend than any I could wish for," Fynch said, hugging the large dog. "Now," he continued brightly, "I must eat something and then we must go. I am strong now, Knave, and ready to face our enemy."

Knave said nothing. When he first clapped eyes on the small gong boy in Stoneheart, he had not anticipated that he would lose his heart to him in friendship. He had never guessed he would come to resent the burden placed upon his shoulders by the Thicket.

It was as though Fynch read his thoughts. "If we don't destroy him, Knave, he will destroy the world we love and the Thicket. The magical creatures will die and the Dragon King will be exposed. We have no choice."

Knave did not respond but Fynch sensed the resolve in the dog and knew that his words had reminded his companion of their duty.

Eat, Knave finally said. *We have a journey to finish.*

The Duke of Felrawthy was getting on famously with the unashamedly flirtatious Georgyana Bench. From the moment they had touched hands, the young woman curtsying to the Duke, Elspyth realized Crys might never stare at her in that sad-eyed, wistful way again.

She was surprised how it hurt, tried to shake it off as simply feeling clingy about the person who had rescued her from death, but she knew deep down it was all about her longing for love. She did not want Crys Donal—of this she was sure, for she loved only one person—but she would be lying if she did not admit to enjoying the Duke's attention.

It was embarrassing when Lady Bench dropped in on her private thoughts. "Forgive my daughter, my dear."

Elspyth reddened and smiled awkwardly. "Not at all, Lady Bench."

"Oh, do call me Helyn," the woman insisted, touching Elspyth's arm as they sat together, withdrawn from the animatedly chatting pair.

"Thank you, Helyn," Elspyth said. "Crys and I are great friends. I think terror and fear bring people painfully close, and we have shared much, not the least of which was learning of his family's deaths. But our relationship is platonic, I assure you."

"You have been very strong for him, Elspyth. Don't underestimate how he might feel."

Again Elspyth smiled, sadly this time. "He's made that perfectly clear, actually," she said. "But I love another, Helyn, and I really must make tracks soon to return to him. I'm glad, truly, that Crys and Georgyana are getting on so well. He needs a reason to smile and a woman who will enjoy him."

Lady Bench lifted her eyebrows. "I know I shouldn't speculate so soon, but it's true that they would make a marvelous match. Eryd would be delighted to join our family with the Donals."

"Where is Lord Bench?" Elspyth frowned, not really wanting to discuss a potential love match between Crys and Georgyana.

Helyn Bench grew serious and looked away from her laughing daughter and into Elspyth's soft eyes. "He's gone to the King."

"What?" Elspyth started to rise, alarmed.

"No, wait," Lady Bench soothed. "You need to understand."

"Lady Bench, he is sworn to secrecy about Wyl Thirsk!"

"And that secret will be kept, my dear. Have no fear, we are not about to start broadcasting news of magic in this city. We only stopped burning suspected witches less than a decade ago, as you would know."

"So what will Lord Bench say to Celimus?"

Helyn Bench's face darkened. "I believe he intends to confront the King—in his wonderfully articulate and polite way—about the Donal family and no doubt Rittylworth." She put a hand in the air to stop Elspyth's oncoming tirade, then noted the fear in Elspyth's face. It reflected her own anguish, although she hoped she was disguising it well enough.

Elspyth glanced toward Crys, who was clearly entranced by the vivaciously pretty girl who had engaged him in such lively conversation. She returned her gaze to Lady Bench. "I think his action is unwise, Helyn."

Her carefully chosen words sent a chill through her companion; they echoed her own anxiety. She began to weep, no longer able to hide her worries.

"Oh, Helyn, please don't. Can we reach him?"

The older woman shook her head. "And he is adamant anyway. He would not listen to me earlier when I begged him not to do this."

"What is his reasoning?"

"He believes in sovereignty, Elspyth. He desperately

wants our king to act like the true Crown of Morgravia, to behave with care and compassion and to listen to wise counsel from his own lords."

"Eryd has listened to our horrific story and still believes he can change this cruel King into a compassionate ruler?" Elspyth asked, shocked.

"He believes we must follow the rules of our kingdom. Talk before action. No accusations before all information is sought and gathered. He does not intend to ruffle feathers, Elspyth. Eryd will be careful."

"Listen to me," Elspyth said, enunciating carefully as if talking to a dimwit. She did not mean to act condescending; she was frightened. Petrified, in fact. She knew Crys had noticed her distraught body language when he excused himself from Georgyana and crossed the room. "Helyn, Eryd is in grave peril. His life is at stake. So is yours and that of your daughter. The moment he raises this topic with the King, he will broadcast how much we know and the King will instantly see him for the danger he has unintentionally become."

Helyn was weeping again. "I feared as much."

"Elspyth? What has happened?" Crys asked. She told him briefly and watched him pale. "The King killed my father on a simple suspicion and then had the rest of the family executed just for good measure," he said. "Lady Helyn, forgive me, but Lord Bench has signed his own death warrant. We have to get you out of here. Immediately. I'll ready transport. Pack only essentials, and warm clothes. We're going north."

Helyn Bench, trembling, reached toward her daughter. Georgyana, however, began to protest. "This is preposterous. I have engagements and—"

"Be quiet, Georgyana, and do as you're told!" Elspyth admonished. "We're trying to save your life." Suddenly she could no longer feel the pain of her recent injuries. Fear had taken it away.

Crys tried a different tack. "Georgyana," he said, amazed at how his stomach flipped when she turned those huge eyes on him, "I could not live with myself if anything should hap-

pen to you." His expression pleaded with her to follow them
without further protest.

Clearly she saw something else in that expression, something Crys thought he had disguised. "Oh? Could you not,
Lord Donal?" she replied, and her smile said it all.

E ryd Bench and his colleague sat in a small waiting chamber at the foot of Stoneheart's war tower. Eryd had no
idea why they had been escorted here, but Chancellor Jessom emerged just as he began to privately question the logic
behind this curious venue.

"Lord Bench, Lord Hartley, it's good to see you on this
mild eve. Are you both well?" The visitors made all the right
noises and Jessom continued: "My apologies to have kept
you waiting. The King, as you can see, is working from his
war room tonight—I hope you don't mind meeting with him
here?"

Eryd was slightly less anxious for Jessom's warm greeting. "Not at all. I am grateful he could see us at such short
notice." He looked toward Hartley, who simply nodded in
agreement. Lord Hartley had offered to come along as support when Eryd had confided his reservations about the truth
of the slaughters at Felrawthy and Rittylworth.

Jessom smiled benignly. It was not an expression that
came easily to him, particularly in the light of the situation.
Two lords asking for an audience at sudden notice, and Lord
Bench at that—it all smacked of trouble. "Thank you, Lord
Bench. As you know, his majesty has only just returned from
the north. I'm sure he will be pleased to tell you more when
you see him."

"I look forward to it, Jessom," Eryd replied. "I heard he
was at Tenterdyn?"

"That's right," Jessom said carefully.

"And rumor has it a meeting of Kings took place there."

The Chancellor attempted another smile. "No smoke
without fire, Lord Bench. Perhaps you might inquire of the
King for more information. I am a simple chancellor."

"Nothing simple about you, Jessom," Eryd said, deliberately softening his voice to avoid giving offense.

Jessom did not respond; he simply bowed to the two lords. "Not long now, gentlemen." He exited the room, to return several minutes later. "Lord Bench, King Celimus will see you now, alone."

Eryd looked toward Hartley, who stared stonily back. "Go ahead, Eryd. You speak for all of us," he encouraged.

"This is unusual. We are both here for an audience with his majesty," Eryd tried to explain, but the thin Chancellor shrugged.

"My apologies, Lord Bench. The King requests your presence only."

Eryd nodded. Too late now for anything but compliance. He would just have to be especially careful with the slippery sovereign.

"Will you wait?" he asked Hartley, who nodded. "Thank you, Chancellor," he said, gesturing for Jessom to lead the way. At least with Lord Hartley in attendance, he had someone to vouch for his arrival and presence, even if the other man could not bear actual witness to his meeting with the King.

He followed Jessom, filled with intensifying trepidation as his wife's cautions rang in his ears. Perhaps this had not been such a good idea after all. Perhaps Hartley had not been the right person to accompany him. He was an unmarried man, his only son dead of the fever some years back.

Which had been precisely the King's thinking when he heard of the arrival of the two lords. "Separate them and take Hartley down to the dungeon," he had ordered.

"But, sire," Jessom had said, startled. "Could we not wait and see what it is they wish to discuss with you?"

"We know what they're here about, Chancellor!" the King had said, voice rising. "They're here because they don't believe that the noble family of Felrawthy was slaughtered by Razor warriors. They suspect this because word has gotten around that I was meeting with the Barbarian King. It's not hard to follow their thought patterns, Jessom."

"No, sire. But the dungeon is a fairly radical step for someone of Lord Hartley's status."

"So is death, Chancellor. Be careful I don't ask you to kill him for me."

At which point Jessom had kept his thoughts to himself. Experience told him it was the same old argument, one he would never win. Expecting the King of Morgravia to show restraint was a waste of energy. He was a power unto himself, not caring for any advice. In fact, if Jessom was truthful with himself, he was well past the point of believing there was a prosperous future to be shaped under Celimus. His personal dreams of becoming a kingmaker had been cracked by Rittylworth's shame, shattered by Felrawthy's calamity, and, he suspected, were now well on the way to dust, for he did not expect to see Lord Eryd Bench live out the night. Not if Bench was here to question the King's actions and motives, no matter how elegantly couched those accusations might be.

The fragile treaty with Cailech would also be broken soon enough, Jessom suspected, and was saddened by it. The Mountain King had shown tremendous courage and foresight in his actions and the Chancellor rather admired his man Farrow for brokering the meeting. The mercenary had been under intense pressure—especially with that business about Ylena Thirsk—but still he had shown himself to possess a cool head even within the eye of a storm. These men could be valuable to Morgravia and yet Celimus was systematically destroying any chances of retaining their loyalty. How much longer would the nobility put up with his ways? Not long, Jessom suspected, and he was not about to be the King's scapegoat.

Their only chance, in truth, was Queen Valentyna. The marriage presented opportunities, and not just in deflecting attention from Celimus's ugly deeds. Valentyna was bringing something positive and shiny bright into the lives of Morgravians. The people were looking forward to a dazzling queen and the pomp and ceremony of a formal wedding. Valentyna's beauty and composure, not to mention her personal power and wealth, were the sparkle that had long been missing in Pearlis—not forgetting the promise of heirs. She was the ideal diversion from all the death and destruction. These would not go away, of course, but they would be put aside for a while—perhaps long enough to lose some of their potency, by which time Valentyna of Briavel would have worked her own magic simply through her presence. With the people's hearts won, no one—not even the lords—would want to upset the balance between the two realms with difficult questions. Sleeping dogs would be left to lie, as they say, Jessom thought as he guided Lord Bench up the tower stairs. He could hear the old man puffing behind him.

His mind turned again to Valentyna and he had a sudden sharp thought. Perhaps his own loyalties should be aligned with the Queen. She was intelligent and wanted peace and prosperity for her nation; that meant she was open to advice and still young enough to be malleable. Perhaps it was to Valentyna he should dedicate himself; he could be not a kingmaker but an empire maker.

Jessom arrived at the King's chamber feeling far more lighthearted than he'd felt when he began the climb. He looked behind him.

"All right, Lord Bench?"

"Yes," the man wheezed. "I had forgotten the tower was so tall."

"It is deceptive," Jessom answered, tapping on the heavy timber door.

"Come!" the King called.

Jessom swung the door open and announced the visitor.

"Eryd," Celimus said, beaming from behind the desk. "I imagine you are familiar with this chamber, eh?"

The voice was so friendly that Lord Bench felt himself relax momentarily. "Yes, my lord. Your father spent much time here briefing us in years gone."

The smile remained fixed on the King's face, bright, dazzling, and, Eryd suddenly realized, predatory. It was the first time he had seen right through to the heart of the young man. He had always considered him supremely clever and quick-witted and felt these were qualities that would serve him well as King. He had heard troubling stories from years ago, when Celimus was something of a hell-raiser, but had put them down to youth and riches. Like most of the nobility, he had hoped that despite the cool relationship between Magnus and his son, Celimus would shine as King if the right people were around him. He himself had always intended to be a pillar of support and wise counsel for this new King.

But too many of the lords were muttering that, for all their advice, the King was making his own decisions without reference to the council. He did not even show the courtesy of informing some of the most senior people of his plans. The proposed war with Briavel had come out of nowhere and had escalated so fast it had ignited a private war of its own, with many of the senior officials—such as Lord Hartley—quietly declaring that permitting the King to continue in this way was too dangerous. Such treacherous talk, even in private, was seriously disturbing. Civil unrest was the last thing the realm needed.

"Are you all right?" the King inquired, and Eryd snapped to attention.

"Yes, your majesty. My apologies. I think I was taken aback there momentarily by memories."

"But we have a new sovereign on the throne now, Lord Bench," Celimus admonished, and although his manner was genial, there was bite in the sparkling tone. "I know I can count on your loyalty."

Eryd coughed. "Of course, your majesty."

"Which is why," Celimus continued, "I am glad you came this evening. Where is your lovely family, by the way?"

Eryd glanced at the Chancellor, who was handing him a glass of wine. Jessom's expression was blank, giving no clue as to why the King would ask such a curious question.

"Er . . . at home, sire. Why?" Eryd sipped, recognizing a superb southern red, fruity and earthy, with hints of juniper and blackberries. Normally he would relish the opportunity to share such a fine drop, but the King's carefully couched question turned the wine instantly sour on his tongue.

"Oh, no reason. I just thought it would be lovely to see your charming Georgyana again. It would have been a pleasure to have you all here," Celimus replied evenly.

The answer arrived as smooth as silk, but as sugary sweet as it sounded, Eryd was not fooled. He felt suddenly dry-mouthed and the ball of fear in his stomach, which just moments ago had been almost negligible, suddenly grew exponentially. Unless Eryd was mistaken, the King had just made a supremely well-disguised threat. Eryd sipped again from the glass, a bigger, more nervous gulp, but could hardly bring himself to swallow. His throat suddenly felt as though it were closing up.

"To your good health," Celimus said, and raised his cup. Lord Bench was paying scant attention. His thoughts had fled to Helyn and Georgyana.

"Tell me why you came," Celimus said, suddenly turning to business.

Eryd was feeling light-headed. He thought it was anxiety, but he noticed how warm the room had become even though there was no fire burning. He tugged at his collar to loosen it. "I wished to talk to you about Felrawthy, your majesty."

He saw the King glance toward his chancellor and the subsequent twitch of a smug smile was not lost on Eryd. So the King had expected him. Had anticipated this meeting. They were lost.

"Oh yes? What can I tell you, Lord Bench?"

Eryd was feeling worse by the moment. His vision was blurred and his thoughts were swimming. He forced himself to stay focused. "I heard a rumor, your majesty, that you have signed a treaty with the Mountain King." He was sure he was slurring his words.

"That's right, Eryd, I did. We are now peaceful neighbors. I had hoped to make this announcement at my wedding, as the icing on the cake, you could say." Celimus laughed softly at his own jest. "But it seems my learned lords are well ahead of my news."

Eryd drew a shaking hand across his forehead. "Forgive me, your majesty, I suddenly feel very unwell."

He heard the King tsk-tsk comfortingly. "Oh, dear. Some more wine perhaps?"

"No, no, thank you," Eryd said, pulling his goblet away from Jessom, who was suddenly at his side. "I think I should go, your highness. Perhaps we could continue this talk when I am feeling better. Tomorrow?"

"Sit back, Eryd, and listen," the King said. It was said in

a friendly manner but was clearly an order. Lord Bench obeyed, hearing a soft ringing in his ears.

"I think you came here this evening to see if you could shed some light on the slaughter at Tenterdyn. Would I be right?"

As if no longer in control of his body, Eryd nodded his head. The movement felt painfully slow. He could hear the King's voice, but it came to him as though he were deep inside a well, echoing around his mind.

"Good. And I believe you might have heard something along the lines that I ordered the killing of the Donal family? I think I'm right in presuming it might be Crys Donal who told you?" Celimus said, still friendly and speaking softly.

Again against his wishes, Eryd nodded, as if compelled to give the King what he wanted.

Celimus smiled. "Thank you, Eryd, for your honesty. I'm afraid I can confirm that I did give that order, and I regret that my men missed the Donal heir, who, I assume, is now running around Briavel causing trouble and sending people like you these treacherous messages." Eryd frowned. Had he heard right? "Is this not making sense, Lord Bench?" the King asked gently. "I suspect you are wondering now about Lord Hartley, or perhaps about those closer to your heart . . . your wife and your beautiful child? I would forgive you for not paying any further attention to me, for you have good reason to be worried about your family."

Eryd tried to stand, but found himself paralyzed.

"My apologies, sir," Celimus continued, as nonchalantly as if he were discussing the weather. "I took the precaution of poisoning your wine. Won't be long now. I think I'm right, aren't I, Jessom, in that Lord Bench would be experiencing some sort of paralysis now?"

Eryd could not turn to watch the Chancellor's nod. If he had, he would have seen the disgusted expression on Jessom's face, and known that the man had murdered one of the most powerful men in the realm tonight only under threat of his own death. He heard Jessom's whisper, though, as the Chancellor removed the goblet from his catatonic grip.

"Forgive me, Lord Bench," he said, and then was gone, stepping aside to reveal the heinously grinning face of the King of Morgravia

"You are dying, Eryd, in case you hadn't quite grasped it. We shall say it was your heart. I will ensure a proper ceremony for your funeral, you can count on it, and all your noble friends will come and pay their respects. I'm afraid I can't promise the same for your women, although I will make you an oath that they won't suffer, how's that? Pretty Georgyana, such a shame."

Eryd began to growl unintelligibly, the only voice left to him now. His vision had turned dark, and although he could hear, he no longer listened. The cruel words were too painful. He felt his chest constricting and his heart seemed fit to burst from the little space it had left. He tried again to move, but it was useless.

His last coherent thought was that the King had gotten it wrong; for all his smug satisfaction, he had no idea that Crys Donal had returned to Morgravia and was in fact already in Pearlis. Perhaps, Eryd thought as his breathing came in shallow gasps, the young Duke had already taken the Bench women and escaped, for he would surely not have liked the news of this visit to the King. *Please don't let Georgyana die,* he prayed as the paralysis took him and he gurgled a final heaving gasp. He died, eyes wide open, saliva dribbling down the dark robes he favored.

"Check him," Celimus ordered.

Jessom obliged in silence, seeking a pulse at the neck. He shook his head. "Dead."

"Good. That is a most effective weapon, Jessom. I might ask you to use it again sometime. I gather you didn't enjoy that death." Jessom did not reply and the King did not care. "You've already sent the men?"

"They left for the Bench household not long after the two lords' arrival, sire."

"Hartley knows too much."

Jessom knew it was wasted breath to try to convince the King not to kill again tonight. "I shall see to it, your majesty."

"Arrange for him to be dealt with by men you trust, Chancellor. I want no wagging tongues."

"May I ask, your majesty, how we are going to explain the disappearances of Lord Bench and Lord Hartley?" Jessom risked.

"That is what I pay *you* for, Chancellor. Don't trouble me with details. Be gone."

Jessom turned, and as he did, so did something inside him.

30

YL ENTERED THE SAME IMPRESSIVE CHAMBER HE HAD BEEN ESCORTED to as Romen Koreldy. Once again he was greeted by the Mountain King, who immediately dismissed the two warriors he was speaking with.

"Ylena," Cailech said, moving swiftly from the huge windows where he had been gazing out across the valley. "You look enchanting." He kissed her hand and moved back to the panoramic view, this time with her in tow.

Wyl closed his eyes with revulsion but permitted the courtesy. "Thank you for the fresh clothes."

"Can't have you looking like a man all the time," Cailech replied, his light green eyes sparkling in the dying light. "Are you hungry?"

"Not especially."

"Mountain People are always ravenous," the King admitted. "I'm afraid you'll have to be polite and pretend you're eating plenty. Just push the food around if you must, but let the kitchen know you've appreciated their efforts tonight."

Wyl nodded. "Of course."

"Your hair is so beautiful and soft," the King said, reaching a hand to touch Ylena's carefully dressed hair.

Wyl stepped closer to the window, trying to avoid the

King's caress. "You certainly live in a magnificent place," he said, keeping his voice steady, mind racing. He had to escape. No ideas had presented themselves, save death, and he was not permitted to force that. The Quickening was sinister enough without antagonizing its magics. He thought about those who were still left to him—Fynch, Elspyth, Aremys, Gueryn, hopefully, and, of course, always Valentyna. He was terrified that Myrren's Gift might strike at them if he broke its laws, and he could not risk those precious lives.

"This is your home now, Ylena. I hope you'll come to love it in the same way that my people do."

Cailech watched the Morgravian noblewoman smile wanly at him. "May I ask you a question, sire?"

"By all means. Come, sit, let me pour us something to enjoy while we talk."

Sitting was good, Wyl decided, for there were no chairs in the room that could take the two of them. "Thank you," he said, walking deeper into the chamber toward the hearth.

"I had a fire lit. I presumed you might be feeling the cold."

"Just a bit," Wyl said, and shivered for effect, making the King grin.

Seated, Wyl broached the subject that had burned on his lips ever since meeting Cailech again. "My lord, I have learned that someone very precious to me was sent into the Razors a little while ago with a scouting party."

The King did not reply, simply arched an eyebrow in query as he handed Ylena a small, exquisite glass of a honey-colored wine that looked syrupy and delicious. "This is my personal favorite. Please enjoy."

Wyl nodded his thanks and sipped. It was Romen's distant memory that recalled the wine—a burst of sharp fruit that somehow was also achingly sweet—but it was Ylena's mouth that smiled with pleasure. Again the King grinned.

"He is Morgravian," Wyl continued. "An older man. His name is Gueryn le Gant."

Cailech's expression remained unchanged. "Yes, I know of him."

"Is he alive, sire?"

"I don't know."

Wyl's heart twisted in his chest. He had to be especially cautious here. He could not let on that he knew anything more than Ylena herself could know. "I see. But you had him as a prisoner?"

"That is correct."

"Can we find out if he has survived, my lord?"

"That depends."

"On what, your majesty?" Wyl drew on all his sister's sweet manners.

The King put a finger to his lips at the sound of a knock on the door. "Come," he called.

A servant appeared. "Forgive me, your majesty. Warrior Borc wondered if you could spare a moment. He said it's extremely important."

Borc! Wyl remembered the name all too well—the man had nearly prevented their escape from the fortress the last time.

The King showed his irritation at being interrupted. "Very well. I can spare only a moment, and tell him it had better be vital news." The servant disappeared. "Forgive me, Ylena," Cailech said. "This won't take long."

Wyl nodded, a polite smile on his sister's face.

Borc entered nervously. Wyl stiffened as he saw that the man still carried himself with a limp—the legacy Romen's sword, wielded by Wyl's hands, had left.

"This had better be good, Borc," the King warned. "I have company."

The young warrior nodded toward the noblewoman, embarrassed, and made a low bow to his sovereign. "Please forgive me, sire, but I bring dire news."

"Dire?" the King repeated, not taking the younger man seriously. "Get on with it, then, man."

"Should I speak freely?" the warrior asked, glancing again toward Wyl.

"I would have said so otherwise," Cailech replied, his tone brusque.

"Yes, your majesty," Borc bobbed another bow. "I . . . er, well, I was passing the stable earlier this evening, sire, and there was a terrible commotion from within. It was your stallion, my lord."

"And where was Maegryn?" the King asked.

"That's what I'm here to tell you, sire. Maegryn is dead."

The King paused deliberately in an attempt to steady his erupting emotions. "Killed by the horse?" he asked, mind racing as to whether Lothryn could or would do such a thing.

"No, your majesty. Killed by our own and the Grenadyne."

"What?" Cailech roared, no longer caring for control.

Wyl stood and backed away, his own mind in a swirl of confusion. What could have happened between Aremys and Galapek to provoke such a thing?

"Farrow was there?" the King demanded.

Borc nodded. "It was not Farrow who did the deed, though, sire."

"Tell me." Cailech's face had darkened, his eyes narrow. Wyl knew the look, had seen it through Romen's eyes. A storm was raging beneath the seemingly calm expression. The men had forgotten Ylena in the shock of the news and he frantically scanned the room for a way out. But there was no side door, no entry other than the one presently blocked by Borc. He was trapped.

"It was Myrt, sire."

The room became deathly silent. Even the air seemed to thicken in that moment of dread.

Cailech's voice, when it came, was strung taut. The impact of a second betrayal from a trusted warrior hit hard, and he half whispered, half groaned, "You are sure of this?"

The man nodded, eyes darting toward Wyl and anxiously back to his king. "I was taking a tumble with a girl, sire. Forgive me. We were in the hayloft above your stallion's stable when two men came in. I recognized Myrt immediately, and of course the Grenadyne was easy to distinguish even in the low light of the stable."

"Go on," the King urged, his body tensed like an animal ready to pounce on prey.

Borc looked as though he regretted the whole idea of bringing this alarming news to his sovereign. *Gone is the smugness now, eh, Borc?* Wyl thought, deriving momentary pleasure from the uncertain expression on the warrior's face as he tried to explain something the King did not want to hear yet insisted on being told.

"Myrt and Farrow, they . . ." Borc looked embarrassed.

"What? What did they do?" the King demanded.

Borc took a breath. "They talked to Galapek, sire."

Wyl had not thought the atmosphere in the room could get more potent with foreboding or that the King could hold himself more still or more tense, but he saw he had been wrong.

Borc tried to fill the silence. "The Grenadyne spoke to the horse as if it could hear him, sire, and so did Myrt. They . . . well, I feel awkward about this, sire," he said, looking to his king for help.

"Say it!"

"They called your stallion Lothryn."

Cailech swung around, a sound of anger combined with anguish escaping his throat. He swatted at the clay flagon nearby and it shattered on the granite floor, the smell of honey and syrupy-sweet wine wafting through the chamber.

"Finish it, Haldor damn you, Borc!" the King said, rounding on his warrior. It was the first time Wyl had ever seen Cailech lose his control.

Borc swallowed. "The horse reared when they called to him, sire, then it began to scream and kick at the walls. Farrow told Myrt that the stallion wanted to be let loose."

"Did they do that?" Cailech demanded.

Borc shook his head. "Maegryn interrupted their planning. He questioned what they were doing around Galapek. Myrt seemed unsure at first, sire. The Grenadyne did all the talking, said he wanted to go out for a ride or some such excuse. Maegryn said he had to report them because the barshi had given orders since the disappearance of the Morgavian prisoner that anyone acting strangely around Galapek was to be singled out."

Wyl kept Ylena's gaze on the floor but sensed the King steal a glance toward her at the mention of Gueryn. He worked hard to give the impression that she was embarrassed to be sharing this information and did not react to the mention of the prisoner.

Borc was racing to the end of his sordid tale, clearly uncomfortable and eager to leave. "Maegryn said he was coming to see you, sire, and that's when Myrt grabbed him. Farrow told him not to, but there was blood rage there, sire, Myrt couldn't stop. He strangled Maegryn but I didn't stop to see what they did with the body, your majesty. I jumped from the small window upstairs and came straight here, although I gather the Grenadyne is also on his way to see you." He looked behind him as if Aremys might already be standing there.

"And Myrt?"

"Has gone to find Rashlyn, your majesty. Farrow wants to know what has happened to the Morgravian prisoner. Maegryn mentioned that he thought the barshi had taken him for his own uses."

Cailech twisted away in angry thought, staring out of the window. He could only barely see the great shadows of the mountains in the distance now as darkness fell quickly upon the Razors.

"Borc."

"Sire?"

Cailech's voice was as cold as the ice that covered the Razors' peaks in midwinter. "Assemble the senior warriors. Tell the gatekeeper no one leaves, not even our own. Send reinforcements to the portcullis. Have several guards posted on every gate—even those into the town. Neither Myrt nor the Grenadyne is to be permitted access in either direction. Release the dogs. Understand?" Borc nodded. "Send Rollo to me immediately with one other of his choice—have runners sent for him if necessary. Tell Rollo everything and then find Myrt." Borc bowed and departed.

The King turned slowly to face Ylena. Wyl set her face impassively and took the lead. "I'm sorry, your majesty, that I witnessed that. I'm sure it was a private concern."

"It was not your fault, Ylena. I should have taken more precaution."

"That man of yours was speaking about Gueryn le Gant, wasn't he?"

The King nodded, staring so intently at Ylena that Wyl felt himself falter slightly. Perhaps it was not a good idea to question Cailech right now. But there might never be a better opportunity, and time was their enemy. "Gueryn le Gant is my guardian," he said. "When our mother died, Gueryn was all we had, for my father was away at Pearlis with the King. When I was sent to Stoneheart to be raised as the ward of King Magnus, Gueryn was there too. He is family. He is all I have left." Wyl made Ylena's soft tones beseeching.

The news took the King by surprise, but he had no time to respond, for there was another knock. Once again he hushed Ylena with a gesture. Both knew who it was going to be. The same servant appeared with an expression of apology, but Cailech hardly noticed.

"Is it Aremys Farrow?" he asked before the man said anything.

"Yes, sire."

"Send him in."

Aremys was shown in and Wyl immediately sent him a look of warning.

"Sire, you were expecting me?" Aremys said smoothly, trying hard not to show his surprise.

"I guessed you would come around soon enough," Cailech said, his tone casual and his body language relaxed. Behind him Wyl shook his head toward Aremys, desperately cautioning him against saying anything incriminating.

Aremys faltered. The smile he would normally give to the man he now considered a friend did not arrive.

"Care for a cup of wine, Farrow?"

"No, sire, I came here only briefly to pass on a message. Forgive my interruption, I thought it was important."

"Apparently there are a number of important messages to be communicated tonight," Cailech replied.

The cryptic reponse was not lost on Aremys. "I can come back later, sire." He saw relief move across Ylena's face and then froze as Cailech also glanced toward her.

"No, please, come and join us," Cailech said affably. "I'd like to share some wine with you."

Wyl looked at the shattered flagon and Aremys followed

his glance. Something dangerous had occurred here tonight; tempers had frayed. "Are you well, Ylena?" he asked, suddenly wondering whether Cailech had hurt Wyl.

"I am, thank you, Aremys. I was just about to tell the King about Queen Valentyna and all she told me of Romen's tales of the Razors." Aremys nodded, frowning slightly, and Wyl took the risk of saying more. "You know, about how Romen's escape was aided by Lothryn, and how he later worried about what might have happened to the brave warrior who betrayed his king."

Wyl himself had fast reflexes but Ylena's body moved more slowly than he was used to. He saw the King's sudden action but as Ylena could not avoid the hard, stinging slap. Ylena's small body flew across the room, gashing a leg on a small table and sprawling across a chair before tumbling to the granite floor. Wyl lay still. From the terrible pain, he suspected Ylena's slim shoulder had dislocated during the awkward fall.

Wyl heard Cailech ranting above his sister's body. "Do you think I'm stupid, Ylena?"

Wyl had no choice; he spoke quickly to his friend. "He knows about Maegryn," was all he managed before he felt himself lifted easily from the floor and flung again across the chamber. He glimpsed Cailech's enraged face and heard his roar of anger. Ylena's body crunched awkwardly against the stone fireplace and this time her leg snapped, the bone poking through the skin. Fresh pain klaxoned through her frail body. Wyl released a scream, partly out of helplessness, partly designed to keep Cailech's attention away from Aremys. It was too late, though— Cailech's men had arrived, among them someone Aremys clearly recognized.

"Hold him, Rollo!" the King commanded, pointing at a startled Aremys, who had remained frozen, unsure whether to run toward Ylena or out the door. Either way he left his decision until it was too late and Wyl closed Ylena's eyes with despair. He moved her bleeding, broken body into a sitting position and prayed the King would not hurt her further. He could handle the physical pain, but the battering of Ylena both at Tenterdyn and now here was more than Wyl could bear emotionally.

"Be still, Farrow!" Cailech commanded. "There is no escape."

Aremys obeyed. "What is this about, your highness? I thought I was a free man."

"You were," Cailech said, advancing on his new victim, Ylena forgotten. "Until Borc brought me some dark news."

Aremys wore a confused expression. "What news, sire?"

"You snake!" Cailech spat. "Am I that gullible, Farrow? Perhaps I am," he said, answering his own questions with a weariness in his voice. He smiled suddenly, ruefully. "I trusted you. I thought you were on our side."

"King Cailech—" Aremys began.

"Don't, Grenadyne," the King warned. "Don't begin to spin any lies. Rollo, is everything secured?"

The man nodded. "Borc and some others are seeing to it, sire."

"Myrt?"

Rollo looked uncomfortable at the mention of the senior warrior's name. "He is being followed to the barshi's quarters, sire, as you ordered."

As soon as Aremys heard Myrt's name, he lowered his chin and his body slumped slightly in the grip of the men. They were all as good as dead now. He looked over at Wyl, equally helpless at the other end of the room, and felt something inside him break.

Rashlyn had been experiencing an inexplicable sense of doom for the past few hours. The Stones, which he had cast for himself, kept showing him the coming of a dragon. It made no sense. Dragons were creatures of myth, as were winged lions, unicorns, and other strange beasts worshiped through the ages—and still revered in Morgravia. The Stones had never given him such a picture before and yet they insisted, time and again. Considering that he had cast the Stones only a few times in his life on his own behalf—and had always found them accurate—this was wildly unsettling.

He had been pondering this curiosity for many hours,

wondering at what it could mean for Cailech and, more to the
point, himself. Now he felt a light was dawning: Perhaps the
vision pointed toward the changing of a sovereign in Morgravia. It had come to him that the King of Morgravia sat
upon the dragon throne, and that the King's emblem—and
mythical creature of the Crown of Morgravia—had always
been the dragon. So did the coming of the dragon shown by
the Stones mean a new king for the southern realm?

That made little sense, however, for the present King was
young, virile, and seemingly in excellent health, according
to Cailech. Perhaps they were suggesting that the marriage
of Celimus to Valentyna would change the Crown somewhat, bringing a new queen to the throne. Except the Stones
were specific; they spoke only of the dragon and a new coming. Valentyna was not in any way connected to the dragon
throne; nor, to Rashlyn's knowledge, did the Briavellians
have any link to the mythical creatures in the manner of
Morgravia.

No, he pondered, pulling at his tangled beard, this was
specifically about the Dragon King. There it was again:
change. Before Cailech had left for Morgravia, the Stones
had spoken change and Rashlyn had thought they referred to
something sinister. As it turned out, Cailech had returned triumphant, not only with a new truce and a peaceful neighbor
but with a bride as well. Rashlyn nodded to himself, con-
gratulating the Stones on their accuracy. Change had indeed
occurred for the King of the Razors. Everything had
changed for the better.

But now this . . . this time it felt sinister, threatening. The
Stones pointed toward the coming of the dragon, but he had
done this casting purely for himself, not on behalf of
Cailech. This foretelling was about him. Was the dragon
coming for him?

Deep in his thoughts, he jumped in alarm as the door of
his chamber crashed open and Myrt's huge body filled the
doorway.

"Good evening, barshi," Myrt said. The words were polite, but the tone and the expression on the big man's face
belied them.

"What are you doing here?" the small man stammered, immediately summoning a spell of protection.

"I've come for the truth about Lothryn—or should I say Galapek?"

Rashlyn was intrigued by the big man's discovery; he held back the magic he had prepared to hurl. "What do you know?" he asked, his voice light and taunting.

"Where is the Morgravian prisoner?" Myrt responded.

The barshi gave a mad cackle. "I'll be happy to show you," he said, and pointed to the corner, where a large gray dog was sitting, chained and quivering.

Myrt, aghast, was unsure whether to take the deranged barshi seriously, yet somehow knew he was being shown the truth. "Gueryn?" he asked the dog tentatively.

The dog whined. It was in obvious pain, but it pawed the ground in frustration and strained against its chain.

"Like my work, Myrt? It's so much better than Lothryn, whom I'm afraid I must have killed in the process. As you can see, le Gant is alive within the beast and fully aware of his new status."

"You fucking—"

Myrt got no further. Pain exploded in his head and his nose and ears began to leak blood.

"Shut up!" the barshi screamed. "Or I won't even give you a choice of what I turn you into, you stupid fool." Myrt was moaning unintelligibly and clutching his head. "I guess that hurts, eh?" Rashlyn continued. "Well, listen to me now, big man. I'm going to take away the pain and then you are going to tell me who else knows my secret."

Myrt shook his head vigorously and blood spattered the barshi. Rashlyn seemed not to notice; instead he stepped up the punishment and the warrior's eyes bulged as a fresh wave of pain hit.

"Do just as I say, Myrt," Rashlyn warned. His fingers moved slightly and the warrior was pushed back and held against the wall. "Better?" he asked, dispelling the pain.

Myrt shook his head, refusing to cooperate even as his body was released from its agony.

"Who else knows?" Rashlyn asked, moving toward the warrior.

"Just me and, I presume, the King," Myrt spluttered. Although the pain had lifted, the toll on his body was significant enough to make him gasp still.

"Oh yes, the King knows. It was his choice to punish Lothryn that way, you see. I think it's beautifully subtle. And Galapek is so magnificent—"

Rashlyn suddenly stopped and cocked his head, as if listening to something. He turned slowly, fear coursing through every fiber of his being.

"What?" Myrt asked.

"Shh!" Rashlyn cautioned, swiveling his body from the window to the door, then back again. "It's coming," he murmured.

Myrt, connected to the barshi through the madman's magic, also sensed the approach of something. Stunned by the immensity of power that was being communicated, he whispered, "What is it?"

"The dragon," Rashlyn replied, suddenly releasing his magic hold on Myrt as his own fears got the better of him.

Myrt fell to the floor, hitting his knees hard and yelling in protest. He was forgotten as the barshi began to spin around in the chamber, a look of terror on his face. Myrt took advantage of Rashlyn's confusion to drag himself across the floor to the dog, which cocked its head toward a key on the table. Myrt nodded, reached for the key, and unlocked the chain that secured the dog. It barked once and stretched itself on unsteady, gangly legs.

Blood was running freely from Myrt's nose; he only noticed it now. He tried to wipe it away, but more replaced it. He was thinking he should ignore the weakness imposed by the barshi's magic and somehow make his way to the door, crawling if necessary, when the doorway was filled by a large figure.

"Hello, Borc," he said, disdain lacing his tone. He did not like this young man, whom he blamed for Lothryn's capture and torture.

The warrior looked over at Rashlyn, who seemed to be in

a trance, mumbling to himself. "What have you done?" he demanded of Myrt.

"Nothing. He's off in his own world, muttering about the coming of a dragon or something. Why are you here?"

"Why are you on the floor . . . bleeding?" Borc continued angrily, dismissing the question leveled at him.

"The last time I checked," Myrt began, working hard to ignore the weakening sensations in his body, "I was your superior, Borc. Do I need to remind you of how to speak to a superior?"

"And the last time I checked, Myrt"—Borc sneered— "you were busy murdering someone."

"Ah," Myrt replied, hiding his shock. He would not give this sniveling youngster the satisfaction he surely craved of watching the most senior of the warriors groveling to him.

"I told the King," Borc added triumphantly.

"Yes, I'm sure you have, you arse-licking fuck!"

Borc's reply was cut off as a boy appeared to step through the granite blocks of the high tower's wall. He was surrounded by a shimmering light that momentarily blinded the three men in the chamber before it dissipated. The boy looked around at them and Myrt realized this was no vision; the boy was flesh and blood—scrawny and small but terrifyingly real.

Rashlyn's wildness intensified. "Who are you?" he screeched.

"I am your destroyer, Rashlyn," the boy said.

Then everything happened very fast. Rashlyn leapt through an open window. The drop meant certain death, yet Myrt was certain he glimpsed the barshi hovering in the open air before he disappeared from view. The boy smiled before seeming to dissolve back through the wall. Borc watched him too, openmouthed and filled with disbelief. It was his slowness to recover that gave the gray dog a chance to leap, bringing the man down.

Myrt watched in horror as the dog, its limbs still trembling, struck for Borc's throat. Myrt reached for his dagger, but so did Borc. The younger man was strong and he struck at the dog with the blade, wounding it many times in its side.

But the creature refused to let go. It had the warrior by the throat at last, seemingly experiencing the blood madness that comes over a beast when defending its life or those it loves just as it comes over a man.

Myrt raised himself painfully, still suffering the effects of the magic, and all but fell onto Borc and the dog. The animal was growling fiercely now, its huge jaws locked around the man's neck, tearing at his throat. Borc made one final valiant effort and managed to sink his blade into the animal's chest. The dog screamed and rolled away, but Myrt moved quickly. He would mete out death on behalf of the dog who had saved his, Myrt's, life. Raising his dagger, he struck deep into Borc's lacerated throat and hit the artery he was looking for. The younger man stared with dismay at the plume of blood that erupted, and grabbed his neck in a sad attempt to retain the precious liquid. He even managed to drag himself to his knees before Haldor claimed him and Borc of the Mountain People fell heavily across the prone dog, dead.

31

RYS DONAL RODE ERYD BENCH'S CHESTNUT MARE THROUGH the Pearlis town gates, nodding to the watchmen as he passed.

"Shar guide you," they called to the lone rider, who raised his hand in friendly salute but said nothing in return.

Not long afterward a black carriage, like any other public carriage that plied its trade on the streets of Pearlis, also left the gates.

"How long, Gordy?" one of the watchmen cried as the driver paid his toll, recognizing him from the pool of men who entered and exited the city many times a day with paying passengers. The man shrugged and the gatekeepers caught sight of two women in the carriage whom they recognized as Lady Bench and her daughter. "Evening, Lady Bench," one said, showing the right courtesies.

Helyn Bench smiled back, the men never knowing how much courage that gesture took. The younger woman did not look at them at all. "Onward, driver," Lady Bench called.

It was at least another fifteen minutes before a petite figure, cloaked in blue, walked a horse out of the city gates to whistles of approval from the men. It was not dark yet, so they could see her pretty features set in a pale face. Fortunately for Elspyth, they could not see the dark bloodstain on her cloak or the fierce effort it required for her to urge the horse to carry her gently beyond the reach of King Celimus. She forced a smile and said, "See you soon, lads," as if she were only going to be away for a few hours, then she too disappeared down the road. She knew she had two bends to get past before the third one would remove her fully from the watchtower's view. It felt like a lifetime and she wondered if the guards were wondering why she was riding so slowly down the road.

Finally she caught sight of Crys Donal. He rushed toward her, and as much as she wanted to be composed and not show how sick she was, Elspyth all but fell from the horse as she leaned toward him. As they had done before, the strong arms of the Duke of Felrawthy cushioned her and carried her gently to a patch of soft grass. "I'm sorry you had to do that, but—" he began.

"Hush, Crys," she replied. "There was no other way. It would have looked too odd for Georgyana to ride out after her mother's carriage, especially alone."

"We can only hope those guards make no connections. Two of us were strangers and easily forgotten," Crys reassured. Elspyth noticed how his gaze softened when it fell upon the Benchs' golden-haired daughter. She felt another pang and reminded herself that Crys did not belong to her. She had pushed his gentle advances away too often. She was spoken for . . . if, perhaps, only by a dead man, she thought sadly.

Crys glanced toward Lady Bench, who sat on a mile-
stone staring straight out before her, clearly dwelling on
thoughts of her beloved Eryd. He walked over and put his
arms around her. She was a friend of his mother's, who was
about the same age. He tried to imagine how Aleda must
have felt watching Jeryb Donal die. Crys was sure Eryd
was dead by now too, and knew the effect of his death on
Lady Bench would be no less painful than if she had witnessed it.

"I'm so sorry, Helyn," he said softly.

"Are you sure it's useless, Crys? I mean—"

He cut off her teary words; they were too painful to listen
to again. "We cannot risk Georgyana, Lady Bench. You must
see to her safety first. I promise you I will return to Pearlis,
but first I insist on ensuring that you three ladies are out of
danger." He hugged her again, suspecting that her inclination was to send Georgyana on with him and take her
chances back in Pearlis. "Please, Lady Bench. Celimus
showed no mercy to my parents, or my brothers, the
youngest of whom had barely reached your daughter's tender years. He will have no qualms about killing you, Lord
Bench, Georgyana, and anyone else who looks to be getting
in his way."

"In the way of what?" she said.

"Of whatever it is that he wants," Crys replied. "He is
mad, Lady Bench. He dreams of empire. The upcoming
wedding is a sham. He will destroy Valentyna and Briavel
one way or another—it just appears more respectable if he
can do it diplomatically. Listen to me," he said, taking the
liberty of turning her face toward his earnest one. "If he was
prepared to murder my father, who was the most loyal of
Morgravians, then he will respect none of his senior coun-
selors' lives. Please trust me."

"So you think Eryd is already dead," she said, her voice
flat.

There was no point in attempting to placate this woman
with empty words after making her and her daughter flee for
their lives. "I do."

She did not break down into sobs as he had expected; she

did not even shed another tear. Instead she echoed the words of his mother. "Avenge him," she said, "for our sakes."

"Celimus has many deaths to answer for, my lady. I intend to make him accountable for each of them, rest assured."

She squeezed his arm, unable to speak for her tumbling emotions.

"Come, we will ride in pairs now," he continued. Elspyth was breathing hard, and Crys reached for her hand. "Can you go a bit farther?"

"Yes, let's go," she said, enjoying, despite herself, his touch in front of Georgyana.

"You and Lady Bench ride together, Elspyth. Georgyana can come with me," Crys said, instantly putting to rest any delusion that he was not utterly infatuated with the young noblewoman. It was fitting that he should align himself with his own kind; they would make the most handsome of couples, Elspyth thought. She scowled privately but convinced herself that her acid mood was caused by the throb at her shoulder.

"Where are we going?" Georgyana asked, unaware of the sour emotions the pretty woman by her side was feeling.

"They will expect us to go north," Crys said, "as we all have homes and links there."

"So we go south?" Georgyana finished for him. He smiled indulgently.

"Yes, my lady. South to Argorn."

Jessom stared at the sputtering candle. Its erratic flame held his attention in the otherwise darkened room. His thoughts were distracted, roaming. A light perfume wafted up from the soap leaf he had used to wash his hands after touching Eryd Bench's body. He had killed twice himself, and had had many deaths carried out at his order, but none had ever felt like this one. Lord Bench's death had been as unpleasant as it was unnecessary. Unpleasant because Jessom had been forced to administer the poison personally and very much against his own will, and unnecessary because it had achieved nothing but another dirty secret to keep hidden.

He linked his newly washed fingers as he contemplated the afternoon's pointless proceedings. To the King, the report of another killing, no matter how high ranking the victim, was akin to hearing that a kitten from the kitchen cat's latest litter had died. *He just kills on a whim,* Jessom thought bitterly. Bench and his fellow lord could have been so easily diverted, sent on some special mission even, but left alive, retaining their importance in the fabric of Morgravian life. "Shar knows, that fabric is wearing very thin," the Chancellor muttered.

If even Lord Bench had been questioning the King and his motives, then this was surely the end of the road, for Eryd Bench would never have considered making his concerns public without much soul-searching. How many others had doubts? Jessom wondered. How many others disapproved of the King's actions?

"Civil unrest is next." Jessom finished the thought aloud.

It would only take someone like Crys Donal, now the Duke of Felrawthy, to stir up sufficient emotion and the civil unrest could turn into an uprising. Jessom was not so naive as to believe that the famous Legion would not follow its instincts, which would be screaming in favor of Lord Donal after what had happened in the north. The Legion had suffered several blows recently—enough to provoke the men into turning against the King they hated.

Jessom listed them in his mind: Alyd Donal, Wyl Thirsk, Ylena Thirsk, most of the Donal family, Rittylworth's holy community. Even the death of King Valor of Briavel was beginning to be viewed suspiciously, particularly given that Wyl Thirsk had been in Werryl on the King's business when he had lost his life alongside Valor. Jessom had heard mutterings that the circumstances of the two deaths were not as cut-and-dried as they were said to be. Then there was Jorn, a popular lad around Stoneheart—his torture and death had hit hard, and for what result? The Legion had not recovered from the deaths of its own men either—all in the pursuit of missing taxes. Too many had been impaled and left to die long, horrible deaths. Celimus was too cruel, too quick to punish without consideration of the repercussions. As for all the mercenaries who had lost their lives—well, few cared, but Jessom was tired of killing for no good reason. Almost all could have been spared; they had been on the Crown's side anyway.

He slammed his hand down on the table in frustration. And now Lord Bench was dead and Hartley was languishing in the dungeon. Jessom had finally rebelled against Celimus. He would find a way to spare Hartley yet; he refused to kill pointlessly again.

Jessom lit a fresh candle and extinguished the sputtering one with a pinch, hardly feeling its warmth on his fingertips. He was too deep in thought about his own future. He assessed his options. They were few and mostly unpalatable. He could remain with Celimus and stay loyal to his belief that the King of Morgravia was too strong to be challenged. He could raise the Legion himself by telling its officers the truth, but then what? They could unseat Celimus but there was no heir, which potentially meant some distant relative from Parrgamyn perhaps laying claim to the throne. Jessom's experience of the Parrgamyse told him that this was not a wise path. Alternately, he could argue that a new dynasty be created from within—with someone like the new Duke of Felrawthy, perhaps—but such a transfer of power would be messy, full of internal strife, and not guaranteed to be successful or bloodless. Third, he could leave. Disappear tonight and begin a new life elsewhere. But where? And if Celimus survived as King, he would have Jessom hunted down. The Chancellor could not bear to dwell on what the King would do with him when he was caught . . . and he was sure he would be caught, even if it took Celimus years.

That left one last option. And as he reflected on its merits, he realized it was, without question, not only the best of the alternatives but was perhaps his most inspired idea ever. If it worked, he would never have to worry again. If he failed, it meant an horrific death. He must take precautions.

He would need the help of an expert in fashioning a failsafe capsule of the juice of the Deathbloom, a plant so rare most people had never heard of it. If he was caught in this last and desperate measure, then he would not hesitate to bite down on the capsule, which would deliver death so swiftly that no one would even realize what had occurred. By then, his body would be stiff in the rigor the plant's poison so effectively provoked.

He smiled thinly. "Not that I intend ever to take that capsule," he whispered.

Wyl stared at Aremys through Ylena's glazed vision. He must have passed out momentarily, he realized; he had slumped to one side and must appear dead. It looked as though the fight had gone out of the Grenadyne. The King was pacing before him, poking his finger into his chest, sneering at him with cutting words. The two guards on either side of Aremys looked uncomfortable. Wyl fought the pain back as Gueryn had taught him and righted Ylena's frame against the hearth. No one saw his movement; everyone was intent on Cailech.

Wyl had to move, broken leg and dislocated shoulder aside. Go down fighting—was that not the Legion's way? He rallied his spirit and called upon everything left within him to find the strength to move toward Aremys.

"So you don't deny Maegryn's murder?" Cailech demanded of the mercenary, his anger back under icy control.

"No, sire. It was a mistake."

"Mistake!"

Aremys blinked. There was no way out of this, no possible explanation—except the truth, of course—for the death of the stablemaster. Aremys no longer cared about Cailech and the peace treaty or about the Mountain People. In truth, if he boiled it down, he cared about the man trapped in the broken woman's body in the corner, he cared about a man driven mad with pain and anguish by being transformed into a horse, and he cared about bringing about the death of a southern king.

Nothing much else mattered—not even his own life, it seemed, because it had not occurred to him to include it in his list. He stole a glance at Wyl and realized he had moved. Not dead, then; brave Wyl was forcing his broken body toward him. What could the two of them achieve against two huge warriors and an enraged king who was now reaching for his blade?

"Lost for words, Farrow? Perhaps this will loosen your tongue," Cailech said, swiping his knife across the Grenadyne's face.

Aremys saw the red splashes spatter Rollo's face. The man blinked but said nothing. To his own credit, Aremys hardly flinched. Perhaps it had been too fast. How he found the strength he would never know, but he enjoyed it. "Haldor be praised that your blade is kept so keen, Cailech. I didn't feel a thing."

The King's gaze narrowed as he watched the bright blood drench the face of the man he had called friend, the man he had thought might fill the yearning gap that had been caused by the loss of Lothryn. But this man was now facing death *because* of Lothryn.

"Why, Aremys? You could have had it all with me," Cailech said, a touch of sadness creeping into his tone.

"Because you are a puppet king," Aremys replied, defiance rising in him as he accepted death. He could see the pulse at Cailech's temple beginning to throb.

"Explain yourself, Farrow."

The mercenary shrugged, reveling in his nonchalance. It was amazing to let go of fear; he suddenly felt empowered. This was how Wyl must have felt when he was baiting Celimus into killing Ylena at Tenterdyn—except Wyl had not expected to die, he thought, a rueful grin creeping across his bloodied face.

"Answer me!" the King roared, raising the blade.

"I'm not afraid to die, Cailech, so threatening me will not help you learn what you need to. But I shall tell you anyway. You are a puppet to Rashlyn. Ask your men. Ask Rollo here what he thinks of your mad barshi and the way he controls you. Ask poor Myrt, who would have crawled over the very ice caps for you but hates you now for what you have done to Lothryn at the barshi's whim. You are controlled by the mad sorcerer. He uses magic on you, my king, and makes decisions for you."

Aremys felt the change of atmosphere in the room immediately. The grip of his captors lessened and he saw Cailech's face move through a series of expressions from disbelief to rage.

"You lie!"

"No, Cailech. Look at your men. Ask them. You turned Lothryn into a beast. Galapek is an abomination—abomination—but it was not your idea, was it, sire? It was Rashlyn's. And now the Morgravian prisoner has disappeared. Where is Gueryn le Gant, your majesty? Magically twisted into another abomination, that's where. Can your people trust you with this sort of misery and sorcery hanging over them?"

Before Cailech could respond, Rollo broke in. "My king, is this true? Have you used magic on Lothryn?"

Cailech's hesitation in replying was damaging.

"And now he's going to have Myrt killed, Rollo, because he knows the truth too."

Rollo dropped his hands from Aremys and his second followed suit. "I cannot permit this, sire," he said, shaking his head, disbelief raging in his eyes. "I hate the barshi. But I loved Lothryn like a brother, and Myrt is our leader even though you are our king. You would kill the two men I trust most? Rashlyn is evil, sire."

Cailech's eyes darkened in the granite face. "Do you challenge me, Rollo?"

The warrior backed away. "I don't know the truth, sire. I don't understand any of it. If Myrt killed Maegryn then I wish to hear why. I want his side of the story, not the words of Borc, who would sell his own grandmother to get into your good books."

"I order you to take this man to the dungeons," Cailech said. His words were slowly spoken and chillingly intense.

Rollo shook his head with equal slowness, hardly believing he was defying his own sovereign. "Not until you bring Rashlyn here . . . and Myrt."

The room had become still with tension. Cailech stared at Rollo and then back at Aremys. His silence was telling as he considered his options. Finally he nodded wearily. "Go. Bring them both here."

Relief flooded the warrior at the King's capitulation. He

wasted no time, nodding first to his second to follow and then to Aremys, who would have liked to thank Rollo for his courage. It was pointless, though. As he stared at Cailech and the King returned the glare, both knew the Grenadyne would not live a few moments beyond the warriors' departure.

As the door closed behind the two Mountain Men, Cailech rounded on Aremys.

"I know you don't intend to let me live long enough to clap eyes on Myrt again, sire," Aremys said, playing for time.

"How instinctive of you, Farrow. I'm glad we understand each other."

"Lothryn got to be a horse. Nothing so exotic planned for me, Cailech?"

"Nothing leaps to mind," Cailech growled, stepping closer.

"Or do you have to wait for the puppeteer to arrive to make the decision for you? So he can cast his magic and make you dance precisely as he wishes?"

Cailech shook his head in mock disgust but Aremys could see him grinding his jaw. And then his hopes were destroyed. Cailech turned nonchalantly to gaze down at the figure of Ylena Thirsk, who had painfully and silently crawled the length of the room, a trail of blood behind her.

"Ah, Ylena, good. You've arrived painfully, I see, and just in time to watch your rescuer die. I think Aremys was counting on you to divert me while he took care of me, although I have to wonder what he had in mind, as neither you nor he carries a weapon. Perhaps he was going to bite me to death." The King laughed. "Here, my dear, let me help you," and he reached down almost tenderly to pick her up.

Aremys felt his gut twist. It was over, then. Cailech was right; he had been counting on Wyl to achieve some diversion. Between them they might have been able to get the blade from Cailech and hold him off until the others returned.

"There we are," Cailech said, placing a grimacing Ylena into a chair just in front of Aremys. "Now you have a good view." He lifted her skirt to look at her leg and made a tutting sound. "Nasty. That must really hurt. I'm constantly impressed by your courage, Ylena." He returned a savage gaze to Aremys. "How would you like this done, my friend? Throat? Gut? Heart?"

"May Haldor rot your soul, Cailech!" Aremys said, helplessness washing over him. He looked once more upon Ylena. "I'm sorry I failed you."

"You haven't yet," Wyl answered. "Remember who I am. Use me!" he urged.

Cailech smiled. "Such a brave pair. What is it between you two? I could almost feel jealous. You seem to have each other in some sort of thrall. It's not ardor or lust, for I would have sensed that. It's more than that—"

Aremys was not going to listen anymore. "Get on with it, then, and look to your back, Cailech. Celimus will never allow you or the son you foisted on Lothryn's wife to live." He rolled the die once more. Perhaps in Wyl's fighting words there was a chance yet. "I've already told Celimus about Aydrech. Security in case you did not keep faith with me. He'll come looking for you both. The boy will not live to see a year, I predict."

That was it. That was Cailech's weak spot, he realized. His love for the child and his desire for an heir were more important than anything else in the world to him. Aydrech was his softness.

Cailech's subsequent howl at the biting threat was filled with a venom that Aremys had only previously experienced in battle. It was beyond anger or fear. It was a rage people reach when there is nothing else to care about but the kill. Many hardened fighters spoke of the moment when nothing but blood—the enemy's blood—could cleanse them of that hatred and wrath. Aremys watched the blade rise and closed his eyes, expecting to die. It was up to the gods now.

It was no god that came to his rescue that day but a damaged man trapped in a woman's body; broken and bleeding, he somehow found the strength to push the enraged King still further.

"And Celimus will not spare the child any pain," Wyl said,

watching the blade also. "He'll probably drag Aydrech behind his horse, or simply impale your weeks-old son . . . he might even roast him and feed him to the royal hounds," he goaded the King.

This time Cailech roared as the blade descended and it was Ylena who took the mighty blow that nearly cleaved her in two, cutting flesh and sinew, cartilage and bone, finally coming to rest buried between her breasts.

Her sad, lovely eyes met Aremys's as she fell to her death at last. Her gaze was triumphant.

Cailech groaned. The sound was deep and guttural, and filled with rage. He was bent double, his body shaking and his large hands clutching his head as it swung angrily from side to side, as if in denial. The Mountain King suddenly arched his back and clenched his fists, his expression a contortion of such pain that Aremys took a step back. Cailech let out a final low and desperate growl, slumping forward before he straightened, staring at the bright blood on the hand and arm that had dealt the murderous blow. The King took a deep, shuddering breath and lifted his formerly light eyes to meet Aremys's.

Aremys, hating to have put Wyl through more pain, noted their curious ill-matched color and did not know whether to cry with relief or share the despair of loss. He laid his hand onto the hard, muscled arm of King Cailech and whispered, "Welcome back, Wyl."

Wyl Thirsk, now King Cailech of the Razors, flexed his broad shoulders and sighed. "Let's go find our friends," he growled in Cailech's deep voice.

32

FYNCH SAT CROSS-LEGGED, STARING AT THE MAN WHO HAD brought so much hatred and destruction into the world. Now he must die.

Rashlyn did not know Fynch could see him, but he could feel the boy, sensed his powerful presence here among the Razors. He looked so small and helpless; how could a child possess such potent magic?

Rashlyn had fled without thinking, but leading the boy into the small wood behind the fortress now seemed like madness. Perhaps the child would die of cold. Perhaps he himself might. He summoned a spell to warm himself and pondered his next move.

It was not in Fynch's nature to be violent, but he was a destroyer whether or not he cared for the role. The blood of the dragon line pounded in his veins and the Dragon King himself demanded this of him. He would not fail. He might die but he would not let his king down.

Not far away from him sat Knave, silent, filled with dread and powerless. His part in this adventure was over. He had guided Fynch to Rashlyn and now all he could do was bear witness.

It seemed to Knave that the barshi had disappeared, but still Fynch sat and waited.

How do you feel? Knave could not let go of his concern.

Well enough to face what I must.

Does your head still pain you?

Yes. There is no more sharvan, before you ask.

Where is he?

Hiding, he thinks. He is confused and frightened, but he will face me soon enough.

Are you frightened?

No.

I am.

Don't be. This is what you and I were meant to do.

Who are you, Fynch? Please share it with me before . . .

Knave hesitated.

Before I die? Knave did not reply and Fynch did not force it. *I am the son of King Magnus of Morgravia, half brother of Celimus. I am of the dragon's blood.*

Is that what the Dragon King saw in you?

Fynch nodded.

What does it mean?

Nothing really, Fynch said, shaking his head gently. *Hardly anyone knows. My mother, and she's dead. The Dragon King, you, and me. Magnus perhaps, but he is cold in his tomb.*

Shouldn't you tell someone?

Fynch smiled and shrugged. *Best kept between us. I know who I am now and where I belong. It is enough. That's why the Dragon King took me away as I slept—he wanted me to know the truth before I faced Rashlyn. He restored me temporarily so I could fight a king's fight.*

Where is the barshi?

Over there, Fynch said, pointing into the wooded area. *He thinks he is hidden.*

Invisible?

Apparently. But I see him.

Fynch, what are you planning to do?

Nothing.

What does that mean? You won't fight him.

He must attack me.

But you'll then respond?

Wait and see. Be brave now, Knave; you've told me that often enough.

I don't want to see you die.

Hush, here he comes.

When Jos arrived at the antechamber outside King Cailech's meeting room, he was greeted by a look of disdain from the servant who was manning the desk. "Are they sending half-wits to the King now?"

"Shut up," Jos growled, towering over the man and glad to note that the words sounded perfectly enunciated. "Do your job and let me do mine."

The man sneered but backed away and knocked at the door. Curiously, the King opened it himself. This dismayed the servant. He was not used to talking to his majesty in person. "Er, sire, there is a messenger for you."

Wyl looked over the servant's head to the bear of a lad behind him. No memory of his face registered within Cailech. "Who are you?"

"Jos, sire. I've been sent by Rollo."

The King looked back into the room, spoke briefly, then nodded. "Come in."

Jos entered to find the Grenadyne wiping blood from his face with a dampened linen and a woman, clearly dead, laid out on the floor with the King's cloak covering her face.

The King looked at him with a stony expression. "I believe you know Aremys," he said. Jos nodded, his eyes riveted on the dead girl. "This is Ylena Thirsk. She turned out not to be a good choice as a bride."

"What did you have to tell us, Jos?" Aremys prompted, the blood finally cleaned away, although the wound still seeped slightly.

The warrior turned his confused gaze on his king and bowed. "Apologies, your majesty," he said, remembering his manners and the message he had been sent to deliver. "Rollo sent me. They've found Myrt; he's badly injured. Borc is dead. Rashlyn is nowhere to be seen."

Wyl sighed. "Where is Myrt?"

"In the barshi's tower."

"All right. Jos, I would consider it a personal favor if you would have Ylena Thirsk's body shrouded and readied for travel on horseback. I'm returning her to Morgravia, where she belongs. Please use people we trust; no one with a loose mouth—you understand?"

"Of course, your majesty."

"Good. Then please ready horses for myself and Farrow."

Jos's eyes sparked with pleasure. He was rarely involved in any tasks other than lifting, carrying, and general menial tasks around the fortress. "Certainly, your majesty."

"And Jos, after we depart, I am leaving Myrt in charge. Rollo will be his second and I am appointing you Rollo's deputy."

The hulking lad looked toward Aremys and could not subdue a beaming grin. It did terrible things to his already twisted mouth—which is why he rarely smiled—but that did not matter anymore. "Thank you, your majesty," he repeated, bowing again. "You carry on, I'll fix everything here," he added, hoping the King understood him.

He did. "Good lad."

The King and Aremys left hurriedly, with strict orders that only those whom Jos permitted were allowed to enter the King's meeting room. Jos gave a twisted smirk toward the servant, who was not quick enough with his bow to miss the young man's sarcastic gesture.

"How do you feel—or is that a stupid question?" Aremys asked as they strode through the corridors.

"Shaky, but I'm getting used to Cailech's body. Relieved to be a man again."

"A king, don't forget." Aremys watched Cailech's face break into a reluctant grin. "You wear him well."

Wyl took no pride in knowing he had just destroyed another life. "Cailech fought me. I wasn't sure I could win."

"Inside, you mean?"

Wyl nodded. "Such anger. I don't know what he saw— presumably me, the real Wyl Thirsk, but perhaps he glimpsed Romen as well. Who knows? But whereas the others capitulated in shock, he was savage in his intensity to hang on to life."

"It's a pity he had to die. Cailech had admirable qualities. He was a good king most of the time."

"Without Rashlyn he would have been the greatest sovereign of his time," Wyl agreed.

"We have another king to worry about now," Aremys reminded.

"Poor Ylena. I so wanted to keep her whole."

"You did her proud, Wyl. Don't dwell on it. She's at peace now—and we aren't. I presume we're headed to Pearlis?"

Wyl shook Cailech's proud head. "Werryl. I have to see Valentyna, if I can make it before she leaves for Stoneheart and Celimus."

"You can't prevent the marriage," Aremys warned, knowing it was a waste of breath.

"I know. I just have to see her. Do you know where we're going?"

"Yes. Up these stairs and then out across the courtyard toward that tower over there. And what makes you think the Queen of Briavel will take kindly to a visit from the King of the Razors?"

"Valid question. I'll think of something. Knave is here, by the way; I saw him before we arrived at the fortress."

"Does that mean the boy is here as well?" Before Wyl could answer, Aremys added beneath his breath, "Remember to acknowledge your people, King Cailech." He nodded toward a group of warriors approaching.

Wyl received their salutations appropriately, Cailech's essence guiding his gestures and facial expressions. He answered Aremys: "Yes, Fynch is most likely here too, though I can't for the life of me think why."

More people, more polite salutations, and then Firl, the lad Aremys had allowed to beat him during swordplay when he had first arrived in the Razors, greeted them. "Your highness; Farrow," he said breathlessly, bowing.

Wyl nodded. "How bad is he?"

"I'm not sure, sire. We can't find Rashlyn to help."

"Have any other healers been called?" Aremys asked.

"Arrived a minute ago."

Wyl pushed Cailech's tall body past the young man and ran up the stairs with Aremys directly behind. Rollo's men were guarding the door but automatically stepped aside at the sight of the King. Wyl entered the chamber. He had anticipated the worst but was surprised to see Myrt sitting up.

It was Aremys who spoke first. "I hope you haven't made us run up those fucking stairs for nothing, Myrt."

His jest broke the tension and Rollo and Myrt grinned

while Cailech's face twitched in that way it did when he was amused but thoughtful. Wyl had realized he still had to win Rollo's trust and clear up the business of the barshi and his effect on the King.

He immediately addressed Rollo. "We need to speak."

Rollo raised his hands. "The fact that Farrow is still alive, sire, says plenty. Forgive my insubordination of earlier."

"Already forgotten, though we will speak more about your concerns shortly," Wyl replied. He moved toward Myrt and glanced at the dog lying on the floor, Borc's body next to it. The dog was deathly still and had puncture wounds on its body. For some reason Wyl felt dizzy and nauseous. It was not the sight of the animal's blood, but the feeling that it was tainted with magic.

"Are you all right, sire?" Aremys asked, noting the King's sudden change in demeanor.

"Is that Rashlyn's dog?" Wyl said, fighting an urge to throw up.

Myrt did not understand what had happened, but he had watched Cailech's interaction with Rollo and desperately wanted to trust his sovereign. He glanced toward Aremys now, who nodded reassuringly, then motioned at Rollo, who moved to shut the door. "Best to keep this between ourselves for now, sire."

Wyl frowned. "Speak," he said, moving away from the animal and positioning himself where he could suck in some fresh air from the open window.

"According to the barshi, the dog is . . ." Myrt hesitated, looking embarrassed, and glanced again at Aremys. The mercenary had only just become aware of the smell of magic. He no longer had to touch the beast to know it was there; he could sense it. The reek was not as bad as it had been with Galapek, but it was there all right. He despaired for Wyl at what he knew was surely coming.

Wyl followed Myrt's gaze, sensed the awkwardness. "Say it, Myrt."

"Yes, sire. Um . . . Rashlyn was boasting that the animal is the Morgravian prisoner. He used sorcery to turn him into a dog."

The King's face was suddenly a mask of anguish. "He what?"

Aremys moved to Wyl's side. "Careful now," he muttered. "You mean like Lothryn?" he asked, already knowing the truth as he looked back to Myrt. The big man nodded, his eyes fearful.

Aremys decided to impress some reassurance on these men, now so apprehensive around Cailech—and with good reason. If only they knew who Cailech's puppeteer was now. "We can speak freely," he said to the Mountain warriors. "The King has accepted that he's been entranced by Rashlyn on occasion and magically urged to agree to things he would normally never entertain. We've deduced that the spells only work if the barshi is close to the King, or his majesty would never be free of his hold—as he is now. He will execute the barshi when and if we find him."

He looked directly at Rollo. "It is because of this sorcery that our king was convinced to allow Lothryn to be . . . changed," he said carefully. "It was not his idea. He would never have agreed to something so horrific, so against our law of honorable death."

Wyl spoke up as if in a trance, stunned by the horrifying news about Gueryn. "He will never have that effect on me again. I am free of him. Do you men believe me?"

Something in the ferocious timbre of his voice and his cold, hard gaze had the right effect. Both Myrt and Rollo nodded.

"I will find Rashlyn and kill him," he added, and they believed him. He moved to crouch by the dog and stroked it tenderly, battling the revulsion caused by the magic. "Gueryn still breathes."

"He saved my life, sire," Myrt said. "Borc would have killed me if not for the animal's courage."

Wyl stopped himself from saying all that he wanted to about Gueryn's bravery; he was fighting back tears and took a moment to compose himself. "I will personally deliver Rashlyn to whichever god will accept him," he said.

"No need, sire," Myrt said. "You haven't heard the rest of my story." And he described the mysterious arrival of the boy through the tower walls, bathed in light and claiming to be Rashlyn's destroyer.

Wyl closed Cailech's eyes. "His name is Fynch," he said into the heavy silence that followed Myrt's startling revelation. "He is known to me."

No one dared ask how or why, which was fortunate, Aremys thought, because he could not imagine how Wyl would explain it. Cailech looked haggard, he noted. It had been one shock after another for Wyl: his sister, then Gueryn, now Fynch . . . not to mention another death, another body, another person to learn about.

"And you are recovered?" Aremys asked Myrt, taking the attention off the King so Wyl could gather his thoughts and emotions.

"Rashlyn used his filthy magic on me to weaken me, but the effects are wearing off. I'm ready to do your bidding, sire."

"Good!" Wyl growled. "Because you and Rollo are being left in charge here."

"Where are you going, sire?"

"To Briavel," came the reply. It provoked surprise and confusion on the men's faces, but Cailech's tone suggested it would be imprudent to argue. "Who is Maegryn's second? Call for him," Wyl commanded.

Rollo nodded and opened the door to the guards. "Get Obin. Hurry!"

"Gueryn's life is to be saved, so help you all," the King muttered. Rollo and Myrt exchanged another confused look. "Where did Rashlyn and Fynch go?" Wyl continued.

"Sire, as I said, one floated out of the window, the other through the walls," Myrt said, shaking his head. "I think I may have been seeing things."

"No, you weren't," the King replied, deadly cold. "You were witnessing two sorcerers throwing down the gauntlet at each other in a fight that has nothing to do with us."

It had come to Wyl now what this was about. He sensed that it was related to the sense of doom he had felt for Fynch when he had left him in the Wild. He pieced it together as he paced the room, waiting for Obin, who he hoped could save

Gueryn. Elysius must have died, Wyl guessed, and he remembered now the strange sensation of loss he had felt upon arriving in Briavel, courtesy of the Thicket. He had dismissed it as worry at leaving Fynch and his fretting over Ylena, not to mention being magically tossed hundreds of miles across the land. But perhaps Myrren's Gift had kept him linked with Elysius and he had felt the strange little man's death. *But you didn't die without luring Fynch into your web of despair, did you?* he thought savagely, suddenly hating Elysius.

He addressed the men again, his anger at Fynch's awesome responsibility and what had been perpetrated on Gueryn spilling into his tone. "Everything that has occurred tonight stays between us and a young warrior called Jos, whom I've appointed as your deputy, Rollo. In my absence, Myrt makes the decisions for our people. Agreed?" The Mountain Men exchanged worried glances. "Is that clear?" Wyl shouted.

"Yes, sire," the warriors said in unison, neither Myrt nor Rollo wanting to point out that nothing was clear about tonight. Not the King's strange behavior, nor the incredible sight of a ghostly boy appearing through granite walls; not Rashlyn jumping through an open window and hovering outside, not the talk of sorcery or men being changed into beasts. Nor why Myrt, who really did not want the task, was now leading the Mountain People.

"What about Lothryn, my lord?" Myrt risked.

"I'm going to find Rashlyn. Before I kill him, he will restore Lothryn and Gueryn le Gant." No one wanted to ask what would happen if the magic could not be reversed.

"Aremys," Wyl said.

"Sire?"

"Stay with the dog for me. If he dies . . ." Wyl could not finish. "Just see him cared for. I'll meet you all at the stables in one hour."

Fynch bowed, much to Knave's surprise. "Rashlyn," he said. "I have been sent."

The barshi had appeared as if out of nowhere. He looked rattled.

"By whom?"

"Can you not guess?" Fynch asked, echoing a king, a dragon, who had promised him so much not long ago.

"Elysius?" Rashlyn whispered in wonderment.

Fynch nodded.

"Why could he not face me himself?" the barshi demanded. He sounded deranged, his voice controlled and soft one moment, high and angry the next.

"He is dead."

"Then I do not fear you," Rashlyn cackled.

"You should," Fynch said, unfazed by the madman's baiting. "Elysius was not the only one who wishes you destroyed."

Rashlyn sounded arrogant now. "I know dozens just among the Mountain People who would slit my throat happily, if not for the King. I have his protection."

"Not anymore, I'm afraid."

That won the barshi's attention. "What do you mean?"

"Cailech is dead."

Rashlyn could not speak as he tried to absorb the terrifying news. Then: "I don't believe you. You're just a child."

"My age makes no difference. You have no protection now; Cailech will not save you. In fact, I would imagine the King of the Mountains is stalking you this very minute for the abomination you have imposed upon two men."

Rashlyn stared at the boy through wild eyes. "You just said he's dead. How can a dead man stalk me?"

Fynch simply grinned.

"Why are you here?" the barshi screeched. "If Cailech is dead then I am lost anyway, as good as dead."

"Not good enough. We wish to destroy you."

"We?"

Fynch nodded. "The Dragon King and I."

The sorcerer looked at the boy, puzzled by the riddles he was giving for answers. He regarded the self-possessed child from beneath hooded lids and asked the obvious. "Who is the Dragon King?"

"He is the King of the Creatures."

"And who are you?"

"I am the Dragon King," Fynch replied, and opened a bridge to the Thicket.

Wyl ran on long, muscled legs that covered the hard ground easily. Before leaving the tower, he had taken a deep breath and laid his hand once more on the barely breathing dog. Its eyes were glazed and blood seeped from its nostrils; its tongue lolled on the floor from between its jaws and it was all Wyl could do not to weep as he whispered to Gueryn to hold on. The dog did not move and Wyl left, not risking another word for fear his voice would break.

"Let him live," he prayed to Shar as he ran now. He felt the wood calling to him—sensed the hum of a powerful magic and recognized it as the Thicket. The Thicket and something else, something bright and powerful and good, overlaying an ugliness that he presumed was Rashlyn.

He burst into the clearing, drawing his sword, and pulled to a sharp stop when he saw Fynch standing there, bathed in a fierce glow of golden light. Knave was nearby and instantly covered the gap between himself and the new arrival, nearly knocking the King over with his welcome.

"Hello, Wyl," Fynch said, not turning his gaze from Rashlyn. "I'm sure you know who this is," he added.

"Fynch," Wyl replied, feeling a new sense of awe as he looked at the small gong boy who had so suddenly been infused with power, who was so composed . . . so brave.

"King Cailech, I—" Rashlyn began. He looked still more confused, his gaze darting between boy and man.

"I am not Cailech," the familiar voice said, turning a hard gaze on Rashlyn. "I am Wyl Thirsk."

The man groaned. "The General? You can't be. I . . . I would know it."

"Your eyes deceive you, Rashlyn," Wyl replied. "You didn't know me when I came here as Romen Koreldy either. Your brother's magic has given me the power to possess others. Clever, eh?"

"No! I won't believe this," the man said, shaking his head to deny what he knew to be true. The man looked like Cailech but did not behave like Cailech; worse, Rashlyn could almost taste the magic emanating from his former protector.

"You know I speak the truth," Wyl said.

"Tell me how," the barshi begged. "I must understand it!"

"Not until you lift the spell on Gueryn le Gant," Wyl demanded.

The wild man's mouth split into a thin, cruel smile beneath the tangle of his beard. "I cannot. It is irreversible."

Wyl took an involuntary step toward Rashlyn, his hand going to Cailech's sword.

"Don't," Fynch warned. "It is what he wants."

"And Lothryn?" Wyl demanded, already knowing the answer.

"Even more of a problem. At least with your friend le Gant, I knew what I was doing. Didn't hurt him as much. But Lothryn—that was horrible, even for me. He could not have survived it. You're wasting your time. The barbarian scum is dead."

It was Cailech, not Wyl, whose anger and grief rose now, who raised the sword and ran at the barshi. Wyl could not help but join with Cailech's lust to hack the magic man from skull to feet.

"No!" shouted Fynch, and Wyl felt Cailech's body slammed to a halt, high in the air. "Do not attempt to kill him. That is my job," the little boy commanded. His tone demanded respect.

Rashlyn screeched with laughter. "Now even your own people work against you, Thirsk. Perhaps I should kill you."

"You cannot. My protection will repel anything you cast against him."

Rashlyn sneered at Fynch. He moved his hands and a huge flaming ball roared toward Cailech's suspended body. Wyl held his breath, but the ball of flame bounced against something he could not see and fell away helplessly to extinguish itself in a nearby pool of thawing snow.

"Wyl, I want you to go now," Fynch said.

"I can't leave you."

"You did before and you will again. We walk different paths now."

"Will I see you again?"

"I think not."

"Fynch—"

"Don't, please. There is nothing to say except that I have loved you as a brother. Go now and do what you must."

"I need Knave."

"I know. He will come with you."

I am not leaving you, Fynch, the deep voice growled in the boy's head.

You must. It's the only way we can save Wyl. You are his guide now.

I don't understand.

You will. Now go.

Fynch . . .

Knave, go!

"Rashlyn is running," Wyl warned.

"He cannot escape me."

"Why do you have to do this?" Wyl's tone was pleading.

"Because no one else can."

"Let me go, then," Wyl said wearily, and felt Cailech's body lowered gently to the frosty ground. "What about Gueryn and Lothryn?"

"I do not know," Fynch said, knowing he was breaking Wyl's heart. "I must deal with Rashlyn."

And you will die, Knave crashed into Fynch's mind.

So be it.

"Do you and Knave talk?" Wyl asked, noting the odd silences and the expression on Fynch's face.

"Yes, ever since Elysius passed his magic to me."

"I thought he must have done so," Wyl said, feeling helplessly sorrowful.

"Wyl, Valentyna is to marry Celimus in a matter of days. You cannot save her that trial; you know that, don't you?" Wyl nodded. "But I know you wish to see her and you have something to tell her."

"I do?"

"Tell her everything. Let there be no secrets between you. She must understand who you really are."

"I cannot!" Cailech's expression became dismayed.

"You must. Please, trust me," Fynch urged. "And in turn she will trust you."

Wyl had no answer to Fynch's request. The boy had never been wrong before.

"Now please go. It is time I faced the barshi."

"Who are you, Fynch?" Wyl asked fearfully.

Fynch's face broke into a beatific smile. His golden hair seemed to radiate a bright glow, which spread to outline his tiny frame. "I am the Dragon King, Wyl," he said, and vanished.

Knave threw back his huge black head and gave a chilling howl, silencing the twittering birds that had come home to roost among the trees and echoing throughout the Razors. It was the heralding of death. Wyl knew he would never see the brave boy again. Somewhere deep inside he felt a part of his heart break. No tears and no amount of time would ever heal the loss.

33

OBIN HAD TAKEN ONE LOOK AT THE GRAY DOG AND SHAKEN HIS head. Aremys nodded, sad for Wyl. Another death he had not been able to prevent, and knowing his friend as he did, Aremys was sure Wyl would blame himself for this one too. One man; so much sorrow. Myrren and her father had plenty to answer for in Shar's plane. Aremys thanked Obin and then, wrapping the dog in a sheet he found in Rashlyn's rooms, hefted the animal into his arms.

"I'll take you to Lothryn," he murmured to the dog, who was still breathing in short, desperate pants. The dog whined but its eyes did not open.

When Aremys finally made it to the stable, staggering under the weight of the large animal, he heard Galapek whinny. The horse knew; Lothryn knew. Another man had been broken by Rashlyn's twisted magic.

Aremys laid Gueryn down in some fresh straw and lit a lamp. He explained to the horse who this was, all self-consciousness about talking to a horse gone. The animal reared, angry, and Aremys tried to calm him with soft words and soothing hands. As he touched the stallion he sensed the enormous and agonizing effort Lothryn was making to communicate with him. The horse was begging to be set free. Aremys was torn with indecision. Footsteps approached and the new King of the Razors stepped inside the stable, immediately flattening himself against the wall.

"Fight it, man," Aremys said, realizing Wyl had been overcome by the tainted aura of magic. "You'll get used to it, as I have."

Wyl lost the battle momentarily, gagging and then retching into a corner. "Oh, Shar." He groaned. "What has he done to them?"

Galapek whinnied again, a sound that nearly broke Wyl's heart. He forced himself to find composure, wiping his mouth on Cailech's sleeve, and in so doing, seeing Gueryn lying in the straw.

"Could Obin save him?" he asked.

Aremys shook his head. No point in lying.

Wyl leaned against the wall again, closed his eyes and groaned. The sight of him, so filled with anguish, made Aremys look away. How much more could Wyl take, he wondered, before he gave up on his fight? Or, more likely, found a way to take his own life.

A huge black dog entered the stable, startling Aremys out of his bleak thoughts. "Shar's wrath! I've never seen a dog so big."

"Meet Knave," Wyl said, flat-toned.

"Ah, the famous beast," Aremys replied. "May I?" he asked Wyl, his hand reaching to stroke the animal.

"Knave alone decides," Wyl said, and Aremys detected just a hint of humor in the tone. Perhaps Wyl would get through this, after all.

"Hello, Knave," the Grenadyne said, risking touching the

great head. Knave growled with pleasure as Aremys scratched his dark brow.

"Welcome to the chosen few," Wyl said, coming back from the dark place where he had been moments ago. "Knave is particular about who he lets touch him."

The black dog gave a deep-throated, suspicious bark and walked over to the horse first. Galapek did not flinch. Knave sniffed the creature and whined gently. Then he padded over to where Gueryn lay dying. This time he growled softly and began licking at the wounds of the gray dog.

"Speak to Lothryn," Aremys suggested, wanting to divert Wyl's gaze from the touching but painful scene in the straw. "Breathe through your mouth; it makes it easier."

"That's how Fynch overcame the major hurdle of being a gong boy," Wyl said, his mind going back to a time when he had lived the simple life of a Legionnaire.

"Where is Fynch?" Aremys asked.

The fragile shell Wyl had built around his emotions fractured again. "Gone to his death, fighting Rashlyn."

Aremys regretted his question. "I don't understand."

"You don't have to. None of us do, except perhaps Knave. It is not our battle."

The big man had no idea how to respond, so he left it, turning instead to the problem in front of them. "Come, Lothryn can talk to us."

Wyl stepped up to the horse. "He's beautiful despite that repulsive magic."

"So true. Touch him."

Wyl did so and his eyes widened. Startled, he fought the reek of the evil magic and laid his head against the sleek forehead of his rescuer and friend. "Lothryn," he wept, "it's me, Wyl."

The magnificent horse nuzzled him, as if in thanks, and Aremys too felt the telltale sting of tears.

Wyl, the horse whispered weakly into his mind, *I knew you would come. Didn't expect you to look as you do now.*

"I'm sorry I took his life."

Don't be. He lived it fully. Paid the price for his decisions.

"We will find a way to restore you."

Turn me loose, I beg you. Tie the dog onto my back and let us go.

"Aremys," Wyl gasped, "touch him. Hear what he's asking."

The Grenadyne laid a hand on Galapek and shared the conversation.

I must save my strength, Lothryn said, *what little is left. Please, put Gueryn on my back and turn us loose.*

"Why?" Wyl beseeched.

I don't know, in truth. It seems right. Don't leave us here like this.

"Do you know how to rid yourself of this guise?" Aremys asked, heart lurching with hope.

No. But something is compelling me to leave.

Wyl frowned. "Why take Gueryn?"

Do you want him to die here . . . in a stable?

Aremys grimaced at the harsh words. "Where will you go?"

I don't know. Give him to me. You must leave. Let us do the same.

"We could lose you forever," Wyl pleaded.

You've lost us already. Let me try—let me see what or who this is calling to me.

Wyl nodded, resigned. "Let's do it," he said to Aremys.

They fashioned a sling from the linen in which Aremys had brought Gueryn to the stable and found a sack to hold the dog. Knave finished tending to the gray's wounds.

"Odd that he would do that," Wyl commented absently.

"An instinctive attempt to heal the wounds perhaps?" Aremys offered.

"Or simply Knave's way of showing his sorrow."

"He can breathe easily through the sackcloth," Aremys said.

"He won't be breathing much longer," Wyl said, stroking the dog's face.

"Come on, Wyl. You have to be strong," Aremys warned. "Like Fynch."

The fighting words rallied Wyl's flagging spirits. "Yes, you're right. Fynch is off fighting a lost cause; I should at least try to hold myself together." He hefted the injured dog into the sack and together he and Aremys tied the sack to the sling, then to the saddle on Galapek's back.

Aremys watched the King reach again toward the majestic face of Galapek.

"Haldor protect you, Lothryn," Wyl said.

Shar go with you, Wyl. We shall see each other again.

"Elspyth will kill me in an ugly fashion if we do not," Wyl joked, trying to lighten the heavy moment.

Lothryn did not reply, simply waited for Wyl to make his farewell to Gueryn.

Wyl cupped the gray dog's face in his huge hands and kissed it, hoping that love and honor would somehow pour through his touch and reach the brave, dying man trapped inside.

"As One," he whispered to the dog, and then the horse was off, moving through the great doors Aremys had pushed open and cantering off into the blackness of the night.

R ashlyn felt compelled to return to the clearing, even though every fiber of his being told him he should run. But he was too curious about the boy, Fynch, and his self-proclaimed title of King of the Creatures.

"Come, Rashlyn," a voice called, startling him, for he could see no one. Then Fynch shimmered before him. "It is time."

"For what?" the barshi screamed at the child.

"For you to die," Fynch replied, a new gravity in his voice. He had left behind everyone he loved, deliberately cutting himself away from Wyl and Knave. He knew he could not carry out his task, could not offer himself as sacrifice, if they were near.

Sacrifice. He understood now. It had taken some time to ponder its meaning and recognize how he must apply it to this battle with Rashlyn. It meant more than death. It meant yielding.

Faith Fynch. Sacrifice.

The first wave came as Rashlyn hurled a magical avalanche of blows at Fynch, screaming with madness and anger as he loosed his powers.

Around them the creatures of the mountains quietly gathered in awe. They had instinctively known for many hours that something momentous was about to occur, although they had not been exactly sure what. Now they knew. Zerkons, ice bears, deer, snow hares, even the birds who had been spreading the news since dusk, gathered side by side, predator and prey, forgetting their fear or hunger as they witnessed a wild man doing battle with a creature they had never seen before, a creature they knew of only from stories handed down through the ages. A dragon.

Rollo, Myrt, and Byl saw Cailech glance at the muslin bundle that had been carefully tied to one of the Mountain King's most trustworthy horses. They could see past the stern expression to the emotional battle going on inside. Wyl steeled himself not to look at Ylena's corpse again. It was over. Her life was spent and had been given bravely, as all the Thirsks before her had given theirs.

Beside Cailech's horse stood a huge dog. He explained its presence to the Mountain Men. "This is Knave. He is going to help us with what we must do, and is one of the reasons why Rashlyn no longer has any hold on me."

"Where is Rashlyn, sire?" Myrt asked. He seemed fully recovered from the barshi's attack.

"He is dead," Wyl risked, hoping he was telling the truth.

"And Lothryn, your majesty?" Rollo added.

They deserved to know the truth. "I have released him. Aremys here can talk to him and that was what Lothryn wanted."

Rollo gasped. All the talk of magic had been confusing enough, but was the King saying that the Grenadyne could communicate with the magically created animals? "What! How?"

"Myrt knows," Wyl replied. He was not in the mood for further discussion. "He will explain. Right now we ride for Briavel."

"May I ask why, sire?" Myrt said. His tone was hesitant but his manner firm.

"To make a new peace treaty, this time with a queen who needs the support of the Mountain People."

"Against the Morgravian Crown?" Myrt asked, quickly grasping his king's intent.

It was Aremys who replied. "Celimus has no intention of keeping his promise to the Razor Kingdom. Our only hope of peace is with Briavel."

"But, sire," Rollo pleaded. "She is marrying Celimus. Her loyalties stand with him!"

"Not necessarily," the King replied in a tone that discouraged further argument. "I need you to trust me. I have not yet led our people astray. I will not do so now."

"Shouldn't we come with you, sire?" Myrt asked, far preferring to ride headlong into danger with his king than to take over royal duties.

"No. I need you here, Myrt. You and Rollo will keep everyone steady. And in case the horse returns—he will need friends, allies who know the truth." He said no more. It would not serve any purpose to get their hopes up that Lothryn might be restored.

Myrt asked anyway. "Can the spells be reversed?"

"It's my keen hope they can be. According to Aremys, it is why Lothryn asked to be released."

"Where has he gone?"

"We don't know," Aremys replied. "But he took the gray dog with him. We just have to hope he knows more than we do, now that Rashlyn is finished."

Myrt nodded unhappily, a glum Rollo by his side. "Haldor keep you safe, sire."

Cailech nodded back, appreciating the warrior's suffering and his wish to protect his king. "It is better this way, Myrt. We two can slip into and out of Briavel far more subtly than a pile of Mountain barbarians storming Werryl Palace."

"Get word to us the usual way," Myrt said, cocking his head toward a small box fastened to the side of the horse that carried Ylena.

Wyl frowned, taking a moment to delve into Cailech's memories. He understood. "I hope those pigeons are strong fliers," he said.

"The best," Myrt answered. "Rollo's top birds," and he grinned toward his companion.

"All right. Keep faith. Look after Aydrech. If anything

happens, if Celimus sets a raid, the boy must be protected at all costs."

The big man nodded. "I will take care of him personally."

"Good," Wyl said, adding: "Rotate the watches regularly. I have no idea whether Celimus will attempt anything or not."

"Possibly not with a wedding so close," Aremys commented drily.

"Nevertheless," Wyl replied, "the child's safety is paramount." He leaned down and clasped each man's hand in farewell, suspecting that neither of these loyal Mountain warriors would see their king again.

T he horse arrived at the edge of the wood. Lothryn was drawn toward the trees, and as he entered their cover he felt the pulse of magic emanating from somewhere deep inside the forest. He also noted that he was feeling stronger, more himself, than he had felt since the change had been inflicted on him. Pain continued to be his companion, but he believed it had lessened ever so slightly.

Lothryn was reassured by the connection between him and the dog. He could feel its heartbeat, weak but still there. *Hang on, Gueryn,* he passed through the link, even though he had no idea whether the trapped man heard him or could even register something as subtle as another's thoughts.

Still following the compulsion, Lothryn pushed deeper into the wood until he came to a clearing. He stood at its fringe and looked in wonderment at the sight that confronted him—a huge dragon coated in a shimmering armor of scales. Its serpentlike neck was twisted and the great head was thrown back, but there was no sound. The great beast was silent as wave after wave of sickening magical power pounded its body. The deathly magic was a sickly brown color, impenetrable by light. And Rashlyn was dealing the blows, his face a twisted mask of hate.

Lothryn was tempted to rush forward and pummel the barshi with every last ounce of strength he could muster from Galapek's powerful body, and yet something stopped him. He stared at Rashlyn and knew that if hate, madness, and despair could be embodied, they would look exactly like the sorcerer before him. Although Rashlyn looked exhausted, he was standing and seemed to be in control of his powers. He muttered a stream of unintelligible words; the dragon faltered.

Looking around, Lothryn became aware of other creatures—dozens, no scores of them—clustered among the trees and dotted around the nearby foothills. He even saw zerkons, and flinched in fear, before he realized they were paralyzed by the same awe that he was experiencing.

A dragon! Who would have thought they truly existed? Lothryn had always considered them creatures of myth.

Fight back! Lothryn begged.

He won't, replied a voice, startling him.

He twisted to see who it was. A bird on a nearby branch stretched its wings. *Who are you?* the horse asked.

I am Kestrel.

And who is that? Lothryn tossed his head toward the dragon.

That is the King. The King of us all. And he is sacrificing himself to save us. He was once Fynch.

I gathered Fynch was a child.

He is so much more.

But I see him as a dragon, Lothryn persisted. *There's no boy there.*

He is still a child physically, but the dragon reflects who he truly is.

Kestrel's explanation served only to confuse Lothryn. He looked back at the dragon, which staggered slightly. *Why doesn't he use his powers? Surely he can topple a man!*

Oh yes, he could overcome the sorcerer with ease, but he refuses to kill. That is the child in our king. He made a pact with himself, I think. I sensed it when he first spoke to me. There is no violence in Fynch. He agreed to destroy Rashlyn but in his own way.

Lothryn felt his spirit lurch with grief. Wyl's friend, now—like all of them—somehow changed by enchantment. *So how can he beat the barshi?*

Kestrel's sorrow was immediate and apparent. *By taking everything that is Rashlyn. He will absorb the storm of magic, consume the pain, devour the evil. Already his glow lessens. When they began, the King of the Creatures burned golden bright. See how the murky evil has dimmed him.*

But then he will die himself, Lothryn said, aghast.

I suspect so, Kestrel agreed, bitterness in his voice. *But not before Rashlyn burns through his power until there is none left.*

Lothryn needed to ask no more. Both creatures fell silent, keeping vigil with the other animals of the mountains, still gathering to pay homage to their king.

34

WYLAND AREMYS SET OFF FROM THE FORTRESS IN THE DEAD OF night, Knave trotting at their side. The Grenadyne chanced airing his concern to the grim-faced King at his side. "We cannot travel the Razors successfully at night, Wyl. Surely you know that the way down is treacherous?"

"I do. We won't be going far," came the reply.

"If you're intent on this mad journey into Briavel, why not leave at first light? We would easily make up the poor advantage of departing now."

"I'm sorry, I haven't explained myself," Wyl said, turning to look directly at his anxious friend. "Leaving by horse was purely for appearances."

"What?"

"I have another method, much faster—though horribly unpleasant."

"Has becoming a king gone to your head?" Aremys began to sound truculent. The night's proceedings had worn down his emotional reserves. He was tired, angry at losing Cailech, furious at failing Lothryn and Gueryn, sad for Wyl, and altogether sick to the back teeth of magic. He must have murmured the last thought aloud because Wyl answered him.

"Well, just a little more magic to go. It was you who gave me the idea."

"Me! Whatever are you talking about?"

"I'm talking about the Thicket, Aremys. We will use the Thicket to travel."

That won the Grenadyne's attention. He felt his belly clench and could not speak for a few moments. Finally he said, "How?"

"Knave. It's why I insisted he come."

"He looks none too happy about it."

"He isn't, believe me. I've never known him to be this aloof."

"Because he had to leave behind Fynch?"

"Correct. The two of them are inextricably linked."

"But you told me he was your dog."

Wyl sighed. "It's complicated," he said, smiling sadly. "Knave loves us all and has protected all of us. Now he is having to suffer each of us dying, and me so many times over."

Aremys was eager to get away from the painful subject. "So how can the dog help us?"

"He is of the Thicket. He is our connection to it."

"And?" Aremys was still baffled.

"Remember how you suddenly found yourself between the fringe of Timpkenny and the Razors . . . ?"

Aremys frowned, then understanding dawned. "Oh, no. You jest, surely?"

He saw Cailech's eyes—now settled back to their pale green—sparkle in the light of the flaming torch he carried. "Not this time, my friend."

Aremys began to stutter, words falling out on top of one another. "But how do you summon it, command it, control it?"

Cailech's shoulders shrugged and a twitch of a grin at his mouth disappeared as rapidly as it arrived. "We just have to trust the Thicket."

"That place is no friend of mine, Wyl. It cast me out, remember? What if it hurts me this time?"

"It won't."

"You sound so confident," Aremys blustered.

"I am. The Thicket will not hurt either of us—first, because we travel with Knave, and second, because of our connection to Fynch. The boy means everything to the Thicket, I believe."

"How do we know it can do this?"

"It threw me all the way to Briavel in seconds," Wyl said.

Aremys gasped. "I didn't know that."

"There is so much you don't know," Wyl said, his voice laced with regret. "Such as the fact that Fynch will die this night, doing what he has done since I first met him."

"Which is?"

"Acting out of sacrifice, loyalty, love. He has always put others before himself." Wyl sighed, then added, "You also don't know that Valentyna will marry Celimus, come what may."

Aremys felt utterly baffled. "What? But I thought we were going to Briavel to try to prevent it."

He saw Cailech shrug. "I can't read the future," Wyl said. "Elysius told me that she will marry the King of Morgravia."

"Why do we go, then?"

"Because Fynch told me that Myrren's Gift is still subject to randomness."

Aremys looked quizzically at the King of the Mountains. They were moving slowly, often raising an arm to acknowledge scouts and guides on higher ridges who were recognizable only by the flicker of their small fires. A special flame burning on top of the fortress told these guards that their king was passing through the mountains, so the two men had no fear of being attacked or stopped. "I don't understand any of this, Wyl."

"I hardly understand it myself," Wyl admitted. "Fynch believes that random acts can still affect the outcome of Myrren's Gift."

"And so you will try to do something to prevent the Queen marrying Celimus, is that right?"

"In truth I don't see how I can. I think I am going simply so that I may see her before I die again."

Aremys reined in his horse and Wyl followed suit, knowing his statement was too provocative to be ignored. "Why?" his friend demanded. "Stay as Cailech. Just think of all you can achieve. Let's turn back. You say yourself that you cannot affect the outcome of the marriage. We have friends here, loyal people. You are a king. You can live. Stop the gift now!"

"Only one thing will stop it, Aremys," Wyl said, weariness in his tone.

"What?" the Grenadyne asked.

Wyl raised Cailech's head and looked his friend directly in the eye. "When I become the sovereign of Morgravia."

"Celimus?" It came out as a choked exclamation.

Wyl nodded, deadly serious. Aremys was shocked to the core. "Is that what this is all about? Myrren's Gift is to make sure that you become him?"

Cailech's face twisted into a snarl. "It's about revenge. Myrren suffered at Celimus's hands, so she and her father worked out a way to make him suffer in return."

"But why involve you? You did nothing but offer her pity."

"I am nothing but a pawn in this complex game," Wyl said softly. "She has used me to avenge her torture, which Celimus so enjoyed."

The big man's horror was written on his face. Wyl recalled his own despair at the discovery of the truth of Myrren's Gift. Perhaps it was even worse for the mercenary, Wyl thought. Often watching those you love suffer was more intolerable than living through the suffering yourself.

"Wyl," Aremys began, recovering himself. "This is worse than I could ever have imagined, I'll agree, but can you not think of it in the more positive light that you will be King of Morgravia and your queen will be Valentyna? Can the knowledge that you will be together soften the damage that has been done? You cannot bring back those you have lost, but perhaps you can make their lives count by making Morgravia great again. Sire heirs with Valentyna and establish a new dynasty. Imagine it—Morgravia ruled by you, not Ce-

limus. One more death, my friend, that's all it will take."
There was a new brightness in the Grenadyne's voice, as if
suddenly he felt everything could be righted.

Wyl looked down at his new large hands with their promi-
nent knuckles and long, blunt fingers. He had thought of the
same scenario many times since learning of his destiny. And
every time he tried to convince himself that this terrible
episode of his life could end happily, he hit a wall. The wall
was called Celimus. "Aremys," he said softly into the chill
spring night. "I don't want to be him."

Aremys had not considered that. "You have no choice."

"I will not live as Celimus," Wyl said slowly, defiantly. "I
would sooner die."

"But you will have everything—"

Wyl cut him off. "I will have nothing but hate and despair.
You don't understand. When I become someone new, much
of who they are remains with me. I have their memories,
their dreams. I have their ways and mannerisms. I have their
darkness, Aremys. I will not live as the person I hate most in
this world, who in turn has hated the Thirsks for two
decades."

"So what are you going to do—die again?" Aremys's tone
was heavy with sarcasm. Wyl remained silent and continued
staring at Cailech's hands.

The Grenadyne shook his head slowly with disbelief.
"Tell me you're not planning to die once you're him, Wyl?"
he urged, a fresh wave of fear washing across him. He realized that once Wyl became Celimus, he would no longer
have Myrren's protection. He would be as vulnerable to
death as anyone.

Wyl spoke in a grave tone. "When it happens—and it will,
for my destiny is to become the sovereign of Morgravia—
you will end my life once and for all."

Aremys was rocked by Wyl's words. "I won't," he
shouted. "I won't do it."

"You will! You will do it because I demand it. I will be
King of Morgravia, don't forget, and I will command you."

"Command me?! Upon the threat of what—pain of
death?" Aremys yelled.

Wyl ignored him, kept speaking. "We shall set it up as an accident. It doesn't have to be by your hand as such, if that revolts you too much. We can manipulate it through others. But you will help me to achieve my death. I think I would like an arrow, clean and swift, to the heart. I would prefer it to be you, Aremys, as I know you shoot accurately. This is about friendship, love, loyalty."

"No, Wyl. What about Valentyna?"

"I can't think about what might happen after my death. That will be beyond my control. But Valentyna will be released from her sentence of being married to Celimus, free to return to Briavel and begin her life afresh."

"But it's not *him*. It's you."

"Valentyna will not know that. She will look at me with disgust; she will detest my touch and speak my name with loathing. No, Aremys," Wyl said sadly, "I would rather be dead, truly. Elysius said I cannot contrive for others to kill me, but I am counting on the fact that once I have become Celimus, as Elysius and Myrren intended, the gift will have run its course and will no longer be able to hurt me or those I care about."

Aremys shook his head; it was too painful. They had battled against so much, but for what? "Don't make this decision yet," he beseeched. "Fynch warned of the randomness—let's wait and see how it all turns out."

Wyl recalled Fynch begging him to tell Valentyna the truth, and was reminded once again that the boy had never led him astray. Fynch had always been true. "Fair enough," he said. "We will not discuss it again until I become Celimus, after which I will give you one night's grace, which I shall spend with Valentyna, and the next day I will expect you to take my life. Agreed?"

Aremys was cornered. "Agreed," he said, deeply unhappy.

"Good," Wyl replied, feeling suddenly brighter for airing the decision he had been brooding on for so long. Now it was time to ask for the Thicket's help.

"Come, we'll try from here," he said, pointing to a small outcrop of rocks.

"Do you know what you're doing?" Aremys asked, leading his horse in the direction of the rocks.

"Not really, but the journey will take too long by conventional means. I have to try."

Aremys sighed audibly. "So what do we do? Turn the horses loose or remain on them?"

Cailech shrugged his broad shoulders. "I haven't even brought anything for her," he said, his mind elsewhere.

Aremys lifted his eyes to the heavens and asked Shar to help them. "Come on, Wyl, what do we do?"

Wyl collected his thoughts. "Knave," he said, "please, would you call on the Thicket? I need it to send us to Werryl Palace, like it did for me before."

Knave could not explain to his friend that he no longer enjoyed the same contact with the Thicket as he had in the past. There was nothing for it now, he realized; he would have to contact Fynch . . . if the boy was still alive.

Letting his mind flood with the trace that was Fynch, Knave cast out to him, begging him to be alive, to answer him . . . not because he needed his help but because he wanted to hear his sweet voice again.

Knave. It sounded more of a groan.

Always here, the dog answered, keeping his voice steady even though he was frightened by the pain communicated in the single syllable of Fynch's response.

Is Wyl safe?

Yes. Knave knew not to waste time on small talk. Fynch was fighting for his life. *We need to use the Thicket to travel quickly to Briavel. I'm sorry to—*

Wait. There was a silence and then Fynch was back; his voice sounded even more fractured and filled with pain than just moments earlier. *I've set up a bridge. Use it, but hurry— I can't hold it together for long.*

Fynch, what's happening?

Hurry, Knave. Please.

Knave closed his eyes in grief. It sounded as though Fynch were near to death. He reached toward the Thicket, feeling guilty at drawing on Fynch's waning reserves. He could not understand it. Fynch was strong in his power. Surely he could easily overcome Rashlyn?

It was Rasmus who answered the unspoken question. *Fynch is following his destiny, Knave. You must do what he has commanded. The Thicket will allow this request.*

There are horses too, Knave replied, disguising his rising fear for Fynch.

The owl made a sound of disgust. *Wyl Thirsk never makes it easy,* the bird said testily. *We'll have to be careful how they land. Tell the two men to sit on horseback. Then we only have to control three "parcels."*

Just two. I plan to return to Fynch.

No. You have been commanded. You must do as he wishes. Now make ready.

Knave cut the link angrily, unused to feeling such emotion. He felt a keen loyalty to Wyl and would give his life for him if asked, but with Fynch it ran much deeper. It was love. Not something you turned your back on.

Thank you, Fynch, he sent, filled with sorrow.

He could barely hear the reply, but he felt it. *I love you, Knave. Farewell.*

And then the boy cut their link. Knave whined softly, feeling a deep and irreplaceable loss, then turned to Wyl and gave a low growl.

Aremys shook his head. "Do you understand him?"

Wyl nodded. "Sort of. I've been around him long enough to grasp what kind of message is being communicated."

"And that one meant . . . ?"

"We wait." He turned to Knave. "I know you're hurting, boy, but I need you to come with us."

Wyl's comment was timely. Knave realized, as much as he hated to admit it, that he was not of much use to Fynch right now. But Wyl needed him for to this trip to Briavel. That settled it. He would go.

The men began to dismount, but Knave barked.

Aremys frowned. "What now?"

"Wants us to remain on horseback, I think," Wyl said. "Is that right, Knave?"

The dog gave a familiar growl and Wyl nodded to his friend. "Yes. I guess we're taking the horses."

"This will take some explaining at the other end," Aremys said as the air around them began to thicken.

"Here we go," Wyl cautioned. "It's not pleasant, I warn you."

"I think I remember that much," was all Aremys had time to say before he felt a huge pressure on his body and all went dark.

The blinding golden light that had initially shimmered around the dragon had gradually dimmed to a soft glow, taking on a dirty bronze color. The dragon's wings hung limply and each breath was labored, but still it stood upright, absorbing the magic slamming into its body.

"Die, beast," the barshi screamed, clearly confused as to why the creature would not retaliate. "You came here to destroy me," he yelled. "Yet you can't even shield yourself against my magic."

He blasted the dragon again with a powerful spell and saw the beautiful beast stagger for the first time, its head drooping.

Fynch! Lothryn screamed.

He can't hear you, Kestrel warned. *He won't listen anyway. He is dying, wants to die . . . has to die, I think.*

We must do something, Lothryn cried. He was feeling much stronger, and was restless, frantic to help Fynch.

We are. We bear witness to his sacrifice.

We stand by and let him die? But we could save him! We could all rush at Rashlyn together and destroy him, Lothryn tried.

Kestrel tutted. *He is already being destroyed.*

What do you mean?

With every spell the sorcerer weakens. He cannot feel it yet, but we can see it. His magic is a filthy brown, tainted and ugly, not bright and golden like that of the Dragon King. The man has been careless—he has used most of it up.

And?

Fynch will absorb the evil magic until there is no more left in the sorcerer. And in doing so, he sacrifices himself.

A collective groan echoed around the forest and up to the mountain ridges as the animals saw the dragon slump to one side, its golden light no more than a slight wash of color.

Rashlyn was laughing maniacally. "It is you who dies, you fool. Am I so strong? Can you not fight me? I am the King of the Creatures, not you. I will rule them. I can change them and bend them to my will." He shook his bony fist toward the animals who watched. "You will all hail me as your king. Look at the dragon now. He dies. I have vanquished him and I shall take all of his power and wield it as I will."

It was true. The King of the Creatures had rolled onto his side and was breathing so shallowly that death was surely imminent.

If Lothryn had not been mesmerized and moved by the boy's courage, he would have closed Galapek's eyes. But he could not do that. Instead he focused on Rashlyn, and because he was helplessly linked to him through the evil man's filthy magic, he could feel the barshi summoning everything he had within. Curiously, Lothryn felt himself grow even stronger. The pain had diminished; his flesh no longer twitched and trembled. He sensed Rashlyn gathering all his power to hurl at the dying dragon.

"Finish it!" the animals heard their king whisper. Fynch's words were met by a hysterical cackle from Rashlyn.

The barshi unleashed a primeval howl and launched every ounce of magic he possessed toward the dragon. The animals who had gathered to pay homage bore witness as Fynch, King of the Creatures, rolled back onto his clawed feet again in a last defiant show of strength and will. He too loosed a roar—a death roar—which every creature felt rattle through its chest, and he accepted the powerful killing spell, absorbing the twisted magic. And then, with a mighty effort, he went on sucking hard at the barshi, whose twisted face of triumph turned to surprise. He was no longer giving his magic; it was being stolen from him, pulled in a great and dirty arc into his opponent.

I will take it all from you, Rashlyn, the dragon vowed.

Lothryn and Kestrel watched in awed silence as Fynch, howling with anger, dragged the very essence of the barshi's being into himself and consumed it in golden fire. The brilliant light pulsed brightly around the dragon before extinguishing itself.

The King of the Creatures fell, reducing in size and stature until, where the mighty dragon had stood so proudly just hours earlier, the tiny shape of a boy lay curled tightly into himself on the forest floor.

Each creature present cried out in sympathy and then, as if on a given signal, all but the zerkons began to move toward the child, who looked as though he were sleeping. One by one they nuzzled or sniffed the tiny body, each softly giving thanks for the sacrifice that had been given to preserve their lives and their ways.

In Briavel, Knave threw back his head and howled a sound to chill the souls who stood nearby. He did it again and again and Wyl knew the black dog was grieving for Fynch.

He lowered King Cailech's head in grief. "Fynch is dead," he said to Aremys, and the mercenary knew better than to offer hollow words of comfort.

A man staggered between the trees, his body burned and shriveled, his hair flaming. His tangled beard was a blackened mass and patches of charred flesh ate at his face. His eyes were unseeing, scorched black, and he moaned, arms outstretched as he blindly felt his way. He began to scream and his empty cries echoed off the mountain peaks and returned to taunt him.

"Yes, scream, you evil bastard," a voice said.

"Who speaks?" shrieked Rashlyn, swinging around in the direction of the voice.

"It is Gueryn le Gant."

"The dog?" Rashlyn whispered.

"The man," Gueryn said, and it sounded like a threat. "You have no more magic, Rashlyn. You cannot bind me and so I have been freed." He looked at the horse next to him, sorrow knifing through him. "I see his magic was not used with such sophistication on you, my friend. You remain entrapped."

Having felt his spirit soar with untold joy at seeing Gueryn whole, Lothryn experienced the sickening fall of disappointment at realizing that he, of course, remained as Galapek. He turned his great head toward the man but could no longer communicate with him by sending thoughts.

Gueryn lifted his finger to his lips to calm Lothryn. "We will find a way," he whispered to the horse, knowing the man inside could hear.

"How did this happen?" yelled Rashlyn, his voice trembling. "You were stabbed, dead."

"The other dog, Knave, healed me. He licked each of my wounds, sealing them with his own magic. He sensed I would be returned if you lost your power."

"Lost my power?" the barshi echoed.

Gueryn advanced on the wild man. He could smell the charred flesh and took great pleasure in noticing injuries that would normally turn his gut. "Try your magic now," he taunted. "If you can."

Rashlyn reached inside himself and, discovering his loss, screamed in despair.

Gueryn laughed. "Fynch may not have had the desire to kill, but I do, Rashlyn," Gueryn said. "I do." He moved toward the staggering man, who was now walking in circles, arms outstretched. But then, looking up, Gueryn had a far better idea. Most of the animals had scattered at the demise of their king, but one type of creature remained. They were gradually closing in on the three that remained in the clearing, but Gueryn could see that their attention was focused on the charred man.

"Ah, a better idea," he said gleefully. "A fitting one, Rashlyn."

Spinning toward his voice, Rashlyn began to weep. "What?"

"Do you know what zerkons look like?"

The barshi fell to his knees, pleading for mercy. Gueryn laughed, amazed at the man's audacity. "Go to your god, Rashlyn, and I hope he burns you in eternal fire."

Gueryn bent down to the boy, not wasting time to check for

a pulse. He lifted the tiny mass of limbs and cradled the child in his arms. Fynch's head rolled against the soldier's chest. Gueryn called to Galapek and rapidly hefted himself onto the stallion's broad back, Fynch all but weightless in his arms. "Lothryn, if you wouldn't mind taking us out of here . . . ?" he asked.

Galapek's powerful frame carried them swiftly from the clearing as two massive zerkons descended on the screaming man, who understood all too well, blind or not, that death had finally arrived. Only one creature remained to witness the barshi's bloody end—a kestrel, perched high in a tree's branches.

35

AREMYS THOUGHT THAT COMING TO WERRYL WAS A STUPID idea. It was clear from what Wyl had said that Knave would prefer to be back in the Razors, and even Wyl's good sense must have warned him against reentering Briavel. And yet here they were, taking deep breaths to recover from the magical travel and preparing to waltz up to the Queen of Briavel and present King Cailech, sworn enemy of the southern realms and newly agreed partner-in-crime with the treacherous Morgravian monarch.

"Do you think the Queen will start screaming like a banshee or do you imagine she'll keep her composure and offer the Mountain King high tea?" Aremys said sarcastically. "That is, if we make it past the hail of arrows."

"We'll send Knave," Wyl said, smoothing back Cailech's long golden hair. "How do I look?"

Aremys laughed, harsh and brief. "Like the fucking King of the Razors."

"I meant," Wyl replied calmly, "am I untidy?"

Aremys shook his head. "What does it matter? Let's go, Wyl, and get this done with."

"Trust me, my friend. She will see us."

"And kill us," the mercenary growled.

"Not with Knave leading us, she won't. She trusts the dog more than she trusts me."

"Who is 'me,' Wyl?" Aremys asked angrily.

"Romen," Wyl corrected. "You're welcome to remain here," he offered, tiring of the Grenadyne's bitterness even though he understood.

"No, it's always fun watching you die," Aremys cut back swiftly. He regretted the words instantly as he saw pain sweep across Cailech's face, the eyes darkening with barely contained sorrow. "Forgive me, Wyl." He groaned. "I didn't mean that."

"I know you didn't," his friend said softly. "I just have to see her once more, Aremys, before I become Celimus and am forced to see her through his cruel eyes."

"How will it happen, do you think? The Queen will turn you over to him . . . again?"

"Probably," Wyl said, resigned to his fate. "Come, I hope she has not already left for Pearlis."

Valentyna was taking a late supper with Liryk. Conversation was hard won with her this night, just a day before their departure to Pearlis. She was trying, of that the commander was certain, but gradually her gaze had clouded and now she had withdrawn into her private, no doubt grim, imaginings of life as Celimus's queen.

Liryk wished he could spare her the sorrow she was feeling, but he thought of her father and imagined how proud Valor would be of his only child. She was giving Briavel a brilliant gift—the gift of peace.

He watched her pushing food around her plate, her fork never once lifting any of it toward her mouth. The only sound in the room was the clink of cutlery against porcelain. She lifted her beautiful face, aware of his gaze.

"Forgive me, Liryk."

"Nothing to forgive, your highness."

Valentyna smiled wanly. "My thoughts are elsewhere this eve—a bride's prerogative, I think." She tried to widen the smile but failed. Tears welled instead.

They both started at the sound of a knock at the door.

"Let me, your majesty," Liryk offered, rising to answer the messenger. He returned tight-lipped and frowning.

"Important?" she asked, presuming it was for him. "Don't fret, you're excused from my dazzling repartee this evening." He gazed at her, wishing he did not have to tell her anything, wishing they could leave for Pearlis tonight. "What is it? Not bad news, please . . . unless"—she laughed harshly—"it's to tell me that Celimus has unexpectedly and tragically died."

"Far more intriguing, your highness. Knave is on the bridge."

She stood. "Knave's back! Is Fynch with him?"

"No, your majesty." Liryk's hesitant tone snapped her to attention.

"He's not alone, though, is he?"

"He brings with him two men. One is Aremys Farrow."

Valentyna's mouth dropped open. "The man Ylena Thirsk and the Duke of Felrawthy spoke of—the one brokering the peace treaty with the Mountain King?"

Liryk nodded.

"And who accompanies him?" Valentyna asked, then frowned at Liryk's silence. "Come on, Commander, the suspense is irritating."

Liryk wiped away the perspiration coating his forehead. "King Cailech of the Mountains, your majesty."

The silence that met his words felt as heavy as the dread in his own heart. He watched the Queen's hand fly to her throat; to her credit, she gave away nothing more than the initial shock. Visibly gathering her composure, she turned toward the double windows, unlatched and threw them open, then stepped out onto the balcony.

He joined her in looking down upon the famous Werryl Bridge to where three figures stood, surrounded by soldiers. One was familiar; as if on cue, the dog raised his great dark head and looked directly at Valentyna. Valentyna felt that penetrating gaze cross the substantial distance between them and pierce her heart. She had to stop herself from clutching her breast, where an old ache, barely buried, resurfaced to taunt and frighten her.

"He has brought him back to me," she whispered to herself.

"Beg your pardon, your majesty?" Liryk said.

Valentyna closed her eyes momentarily then calmly replied, "Bring them to my study."

"Your majesty, I don't—"

"Now, Liryk, please. Search them and remove their weapons."

"Yes, your highness."

She disappeared from the balcony, leaving Liryk to look down upon the strange trio once more.

"Now what have you sent us, Shar, to disrupt her peace?" he muttered.

Valentyna splashed icy water on her face and took several deep, steadying breaths as she held the drying linen to her cheeks. She groaned. What was happening to her?

She raced through the questions that were alarming her. How could Knave know the Mountain King? Why bring him here? How could they have come so far without encountering the Briavellian Guard? It was impossible, she realized. Unless they materialized out of thin air, two riders and a huge dog would not escape notice.

Knave's return inevitably reminded her of Fynch and she recalled his last conversation with her, when he had implied that the man she loved was not decaying in a tomb within the palace crypt. *If I suggested this was simply a dead body and not really the Romen Koreldy you loved, what would you say?* he had asked, shocking her. And she had replied that it was cruel to ask such a thing. Still, he had tried, dear Fynch, to make her understand something which she could not believe, and yet now felt so deep in her heart. *Although Romen's corpse lies here before us, that the man you knew—the man you loved, your highness—is not dead.*

Looking down at the trio on Werryl Bridge, she had felt as

much, even though neither of the two men looked remotely like Romen. She hesitated even to say the word, but it hovered nevertheless on the tip of her tongue. Magic.

"Magic," she said aloud, recalling Elspyth's warning about being open to different ways of understanding. She had spoken of reincarnation and told her that love might return in the shape of another. Elspyth had been trying to convey a message; Valentyna had heard it in the urgency of her tone, her desperation to imply something important while not actually saying it. Elspyth had said that love might even present itself as a woman and Valentyna had laughed. Yet Ylena Thirsk had tried to give her love. Valentyna had rejected it, disgusted and upset that a woman would make such an approach to her. *But that was no ordinary woman, was it?* she thought to herself now, throwing down the linen and staring at her reflection in the mirror. *If you were truthful to yourself, you would admit there was an attraction there. You could not explain it if you were asked to, but if your life depended on it, you might whisper that Ylena behaved with you as a man would . . . as a particular man would.*

Helpless tears rolled down her face as she permitted the truth of her thoughts to be unleashed for the first time. Ylena Thirsk had walked and talked like a woman but acted like a man. She had even had that curious habit of pulling at her ear and pacing when deep in thought.

Say it! she urged herself.

"Like Romen," she whispered to the mirror. "She kissed me like Romen did."

Thoughts clamored and clashed in her head until she could no longer bear it. She heard a gentle tap at the door and gave herself one last look in the mirror. She looked tousled and unsure of herself.

Fynch had connected Romen with Wyl Thirsk too. The boy had told her a long time ago that he believed Romen embodied General Wyl Thirsk, the redheaded, shy, and courageous emissary from Morgravia who had saved her life and given his own in an attempt to save her father. Both her father and Wyl had died, but somehow Romen had survived.

Romen, a mercenary in the pay of King Celimus . . . a mercenary who, upon his return to Pearlis, had searched out and rescued Ylena Thirsk.

Valentyna thought about the men on the bridge. Fynch had told her that Knave responded to no one but those Wyl Thirsk loved. Wyl hardly cared for Romen Koreldy or King Cailech or indeed Aremys Farrow, another stranger. And yet the dog had brought all three of these men to her. Why . . . if they weren't connected to Wyl?

The tap at the door came again. Valentyna dug deep and found enough strength to call out, "Enter." Even so, she was not ready emotionally for the two strapping men who stepped into the room behind Commander Liryk, both towering over him. Knave pushed around their legs and bounded toward her.

Tears came to her eyes at the sight of King Cailech, along with the unshakable, inexplicable feeling that she was once again in the presence of Romen Koreldy. She pretended her tears were for the dog and bent to pat his head and then hugged him fiercely, whispering "Thank you," although she was not sure why.

The rattle of guards' weapons as the door closed behind her visitors reminded her who and where she was. Valentyna straightened, ignoring her wet cheeks, and raised her eyes to meet the warm, dark eyes of Aremys Farrow and the cool yet burning gaze of the Mountain King, who was staring at her hungrily.

"Gentlemen, forgive me. As you can see, I am overwhelmed to see my friend Knave again," she said, amazed that her voice sounded so steady.

"Your majesty," King Cailech said, bowing low, "the apology is all ours for disturbing you at this hour."

Valentyna felt a thrill tingle through her body at the warmth in his tone. His voice was as deep as she had expected, yet also layered with humor and something else . . . affection, she thought fancifully. She curtsied, paying due respect to a king. "You must be Aremys Farrow," she continued, turning to the bear of a man who stood awkwardly beside the king. She stepped forward and extended her hand. "I have heard about you from Lady Ylena Thirsk and the Duke of Felrawthy."

Aremys took her hand and kissed it. "Your highness," he said.

"Come," she said, "are you hungry?" Both men shook their heads. "A drink, then, of my father's finest wine. I cannot imagine the tale I am about to hear about how two men of the Razors—one a king, no less—covered hundreds of leagues of my realm without a single guard spotting them."

"Indeed," Farrow muttered.

"Valentyna."

Something in the way Cailech said her name made her heart leap in her breast.

"Yes, Cailech?" she responded, and they both smiled at the sudden lack of formality.

"May we speak as sovereigns . . . in private?"

She noted how Aremys Farrow glared at the King. It was an odd reaction, unless theirs was a friendship that extended beyond that of monarch and bodyguard.

"Of course," she offered, glancing toward Liryk, who looked astounded at the suggestion.

"Your highness," he began.

Valentyna held a hand in the air to stop her commander, knowing precisely his concerns but somehow not at all daunted by them. "Can we trust you, King Cailech?" she said.

"Far more than you can your husband-to-be, Queen Valentyna," he responded, and Valentyna saw Liryk close his eyes with despair at the King's inflammatory words.

Aremys was fuming as Commander Liryk escorted him from the room. Nevertheless, he could not blame his friend. Ever since a treacherous king had sent him on a mission of death, Wyl had known nothing but violence and despair, frustration and sorrow—save a few days in Briavel, as Romen, when he had wooed a queen.

And here he is doing it again, Aremys thought, not realizing he had voiced that thought.

"I beg your pardon," Liryk said. He looked as angry as Aremys felt.

"I'm sorry, Commander. It's been a long journey," the mercenary said. He noticed the man's eyes widen in further wrath.

"Yes, I'd like to talk to you about that, Master Farrow."

Aremys sighed. He had no idea how to explain their mysterious arrival. "Actually, first I need to relieve my bowels," he said, knowing this remark would throw off even the most persistent pursuer. "Also, I am famished and I need to bathe and rest. Then I shall attempt to answer all of your questions, I promise. But please remember, I am only a bodyguard to my king. A foot soldier, if you will. It would be best if you saved your wrath for him."

And with that, Aremys Farrow took himself off in the direction Commander Liryk, filled with surprise at the rebuttal, pointed. Aremys just hoped Wyl had some plan to get them out of Werryl as easily.

Valentyna, self-conscious and uncharacteristically blushing, showed the tall Mountain King toward the comfortable sofas in her study. "Are you cold, sire?" she asked, then her face fell as he smirked. "Ah yes, how silly of me, I hear your people don't feel the cold."

He shook his head gently. "I'm sorry. By all means, let us sit by your fire."

She smiled. "I'm afraid I do hate to be cold," she admitted, "although I must give the fire away soon. Each eve is milder than the next these days."

"Which means summer is beckoning," he reminded. She did not miss what he left unspoken.

"Is that why you are here?"

"Yes," but he seemed to hesitate, as if unwilling to broach the subject. "This is a most pleasant room."

"Thank you. Is Farrow your friend?"

He grinned at the odd question. "As a matter of fact he is."

"Which would explain his fury at being asked to leave?"

He nodded. "No doubt, although he has no right to feel that way."

"Indeed, sire. I hear that you don't treat your friends all that well," she baited, handing him a cup of wine.

"I can't imagine what you refer to, Valentyna," the Mountain King responded calmly.

"I refer to Lothryn, your second in command, your closest friend. The man you murdered."

"He is not dead," Wyl answered simply. His mind raced. Why in Shar's name had he come here? How would he explain any of this to her? What could he possibly say—other than that he worshiped her—that would make her listen to him, prevent a courier being sent to Morgravia that night?

"Not dead?" she spluttered. "But Elspyth told me—"

"Elspyth is wrong, your highness. I have left Lothryn alive in the Razors."

Valentyna knew that there was no love lost between Cailech and Elspyth. But every fiber of her being screamed at her that this man was an impostor, in the same curious way Ylena Thirsk had seemed to embody someone else, and she decided to test him. "Elspyth may never live to hear that good news, my lord."

"What?" Cailech said, spilling wine on his hand as he leaned forward in his chair.

Intrigued by his reaction, she continued: "The last I heard, she was near death and being carried to Pearlis—or so Liryk tells me."

The King's face drained of color. "What happened to her?"

"Why do you care? She is a Morgravian slut to you, surely?"

She watched the King hesitate, his gaze darkening as he collected his thoughts.

"I care," was all he said. "Is she alive?"

"Yes," she said. "But that's all I know."

Wyl put the cup down and, without realizing it, began to pull at an earlobe as he thought on this news. He did not see the sudden sick expression that crossed the Queen's face. Presumably Crys Donal was with Elspyth, he decided. He asked as much and the Queen nodded. He could not know that she did not trust her voice to speak, her eyes riveted by the habit she had seen four people demonstrate now, starting with Wyl Thirsk.

"Valentyna," Cailech began, but the Queen was no longer interested in the strange game that was being played out between them. She stood suddenly and demanded, "Why is it that Knave sits at your side? He belonged to Wyl Thirsk and looks kindly only on those Wyl loved. So why does he choose to accompany you?"

Wyl could no longer stand the tension between them. He put down his wine and stood also, facing the woman he so loved. He was very close and a head taller than she. To her credit, he thought, she did not flinch. The defiance in her eyes only fired his desire more and he took her hand and pulled her toward him. This time he would kiss her as a man, and to hell with the consequences.

Valentyna did not fight him. She did not think she could have resisted even if she had wanted to. Cailech, King of the Mountains, had a raw and blistering charisma that burned around him like a halo. If her heartbeat had increased for Romen, it was hammering for Cailech, and if her body had yearned for Romen's touch, it cried for Cailech's so strongly that she was tempted to throw herself down before the hearth and have him take her like the barbarian he was purported to be. The ardor she had felt for Romen was nothing compared with the carnal desire she felt for this golden man who was standing too close, his huge hands gripping her upper arms, their faces a hairbreadth apart, the fire of passion burning between them.

Wyl found his courage. He touched his lips to hers, instantly becoming lost in a sizzling rush of desire and need he had hungered after for too long.

The fire had burned so low it was only glowing embers, but neither noticed the cool of the air. Their naked bodies were still entwined and to Valentyna it was as though they were one. She could not feel where her lean limbs ended and his muscled limbs began. They lay facing each other and she stroked his golden hair while he held her in an embrace she never wanted to leave and stared at her in a way that made her heart leap all over again.

"Perhaps I should have asked first?" he said.

She laughed, full-throated and tinged with a devil-may-care happiness she had never thought she would feel again. "Particularly as it was my first time," she said, pulling a face.

"I'll kill myself if I hurt you," he said fiercely.

"That's not the sort of comment I would expect from a barbarian king."

"We are not barbarians," he said, dropping his hand away.

Her expression betrayed her anguish. "Oh, Cailech, no, I didn't mean it that way. It was a jest. It's just that . . ."

"Just what?" he asked softly, returning his hand to the crook of her back, resting it in the soft dip before the rise of her buttocks.

She felt his fresh arousal and smiled to herself as she realized what power women had over men. Even Kings were vulnerable. No weapon, no threat, no blood; a woman's body was all it took to make an enemy king compliant. Cailech should have come and seen her before to discuss the problem in the north—she and her kind could have solved it in an instant, she thought, delighting in the fact that she had just lost her virginity to him, and did not have to gift it to Celimus.

"It's just that I feel as though I know you," she risked, daring to venture toward her wild thoughts of earlier.

"You do," he said gently, watching her carefully.

She sat up, her breasts high yet irresistibly heavy and rounded. Wyl could not believe he was really here with her, and more, she was not merely returning his affections but was inviting them, loving them. He too sat up and reached toward her, but she took his hands and put them into her lap.

"We've known each other less than two hours, Cailech, and we've spent more than half of that time making love. No preamble, no honeyed words, no romantic gestures. It's impossible that I would act this way—impossible! But I felt a burning for you from the moment we met. Before, in fact. I watched you from my window as you stood on Werryl Bridge, surrounded by guards, and my heart was pounding for you then."

"Valentyna, I—"

"No, wait. I have to say this." She smiled, suddenly embarrassed, and pulled around her the dress she remembered him unbuttoning not so long ago. "There are a lot of voices crowding in my mind—a boy called Fynch, for one, whom I adore." She noticed something dark flicker across his face at the mention of Fynch, but she pressed on, determined to say what had been niggling at her for so long. "He once said something profound to me, which I dismissed as a child's fancy. I think now I was wrong. Then a friend of mine from Yentro, Elspyth, encouraged me to open up my heart to someone else after I was betrayed by the man I loved, Romen Koreldy."

Again Wyl tried to speak and again she hushed him, this time with a hand to his lips. Tears welled in her eyes at the mention of Romen. "A noblewoman called Ylena Thirsk came to me to offer her help and then gave herself up like a sacrifice to King Celimus so that the Legion would be withdrawn from our borders. You were there at Felrawthy, Cailech; you would have met her. It was a lie that I sent her to him. It was all her own selfless idea to walk into the dragon's den."

He nodded and she saw grief in him. "Where is she now?" she asked, almost too frightened to hear the truth.

"She is dead, Valentyna. She showed the courage to match her name. The Thirsks have always been true to Morgravia and yet both Wyl and Ylena pledged themselves to you. They both loved you in their own way."

His words made her weep openly. "Who killed her?"

"I did," he whispered.

She looked at him, not understanding. "You?"

He nodded so sadly she had to believe him. "It was an accident. I rescued her from Celimus—he had planned a horrible death for her, which I won't sully your presence by describing. Suffice to say it was up to his usual cruel and humiliating standard. Aremys and I took her away from Felrawthy and into the Razors."

"What happened there?"

"She did something very brave—may I leave it at that? I find it painful to think on."

Valentyna heard the tremor in his voice. The description Romen had given of Cailech was of a man who was anything but tender as this man was. In fact, nothing she had seen of the Mountain King matched the description she had heard of the arrogant sovereign. But then, all that was hearsay—always secondhand. She needed to find out the truth for herself.

"I will grieve for Ylena. She was my friend."

It was Wyl's turn to take a chance. "She told me you parted on bad terms."

Valentyna pushed her hair back from her face. "We parted amicably, although there was something between us . . . Ylena tried to make love to me," she stammered, surprisingly herself with her candor.

Cailech looked down at their linked hands. "Yes, she told me her error. Wished she could take it back."

"I wish I could have reacted differently. I was flustered and tactless with her." Valentyna paused. "But, Cailech—how is it that Knave favors you in the same way he favored Wyl Thirsk, Fynch, Ylena, and Romen?"

I could tell her, he thought frantically, *and see what happens.* Or he could preserve the lie and not trouble her life with talk of magic. Already a plan was forming in his mind. Now that he had possessed her so completely, he knew he could never let her go, never allow her to be with Celimus. The most daring yet logical scenario seemed to be to call the Mountain warriors into Briavel and take their chances on war with the Legion. If Crys Donal had taken his advice, he would be stirring up trouble within the Legion anyway, and with powerful people such as the Benches behind that push, perhaps Celimus would not have so many of his Legionnaires to count on.

Wyl made his decision. "I have a plan, Valentyna, which may prevent your marrying Celimus. It is dangerous, and spells death for some Briavellians, but I believe it is the right path for your realm. You know that Celimus has killed so many, not the least of whom was your father," he said, hating to see how his words brought tears, "and so perhaps it is the way you want to go anyway. Until now I haven't been able to help you. I thought you were as trapped as I am."

She looked at him and frowned. "You're not making sense. Why are you trapped?"

It was time. This had not been his intention when he set out from the Razors, but then he had not expected that he would be holding a naked Valentyna in his arms. Sharing her body had changed everything. He swallowed hard, wondering at how she would react. "I have to tell you something," he said.

"I hear fear in your voice," she replied. "Why does what you are about to say scare you?"

"Because it requires an honesty I have been unable to find before with you. I was scared it would push you away."

She shook her head. "But you have never met me before," she said, feeling the soft hairs lift on her arms and behind her neck. This was it. This was what she had searched her soul for.

"I have met you before, Valentyna. I first met you and fell in love with you in this very chamber. Your father was present and we took supper together and you laughed at me because was I too short in your opinion to be an emissary from the King of Morgravia."

If time could stand still, if a heart could stop beating, if all breath could cease and one could still live, Valentyna believed these things are happening to her now. She kept silent, her eyes riveted on Cailech's.

"And when I met you again, my beloved"—the King reached for his trousers, pulling from them a handkerchief—"you gave me this."

Valentyna started sobbing now, deep, heartfelt sobs. She shook her head in denial. What she had wanted to hear suddenly sounded too frightening to contemplate. "I gave that to Romen Koreldy," she pleaded, squeezing Cailech's hands so tight her own felt numb. "He was a Grenadyne nobleman, a mercenary."

"He was me," Wyl said gently, tears welling in his own eyes. "It was me you loved, Valentyna. Romen was dead—you never knew the real man. I am Wyl Thirsk and I was trapped in Romen's body."

Words failed her. It was as if she were listening to a language she did not understand. He continued, driving the painful understanding deeper into her heart.

"I returned to your life as Ylena, my own sister. My brave girl tried to stand up to Romen's killer."

"Hildyth, the whore," Valentyna whispered.

"Her real name was Faryl. She was an assassin sent by Celimus to kill Romen, which she successfully achieved, except that it was me inside Romen's body and the magic, known as the Quickening, forced me to take her life. She died instead." He pulled Valentyna close, and to his surprise, she permitted it. He went on, determined to tell her everything. "Ylena heard about Faryl. She took her chance at Tenterdyn as I raced to catch up with her and Elspyth, and a lucky blow killed me once again, this time compelling me to take my sister's life."

Valentyna sobbed audibly.

"I had to see you, to try to help you," Wyl went on. "I came back to Werryl and tried so hard not to make a fool of myself, but still I succeeded in doing so. I have loved you, Valentyna, since that very first night. I'm sorry for humiliating you and making you feel so bad about Ylena."

Valentyna took the linen handkerchief from his lap and dried her eyes. She told herself to find some strength. Her father would be ashamed to see her so undone, although it was unlikely he had ever faced anything this daunting in his long life. She sniffed and tried for a watery smile, but failed. She raised her hand to wipe away Wyl's tears, too.

"I think I knew it then. Your sister showed too many masculine traits—habits I recognized as belonging to Romen. But I just couldn't make myself believe something so incredible. And so," she continued for him, "Ylena lost her fight again and became King Cailech; is that right, Wyl?"

To hear her speak his true name was more than he had ever dreamed. He kissed her, stroking her hair. "That's right," he said. "I'm Wyl. I'm so sorry for lying to you, but I was just trying to protect you."

"From myself," she said harshly, "because I wouldn't accept the existence of magic." She thought of all the occasions Fynch had tried so hard to convince her.

"Don't blame yourself," Wyl urged. "I would not have believed it either had it not happened to me."

"But you see, Wyl, others believed you—I presume Aremys knows?" He nodded. "You see. You have people who trust you. I hate that I did not."

"You didn't know!" he said, desperate not to upset her any further.

"I saw the clues. It was all there for me. Knave did everything but speak to me," she cried. "But . . . if you were Romen, does that mean that Romen wasn't real?"

"Oh no, Valentynta, no! Don't cry. Romen was real, as real as I am here. I was Romen; he was me. It's me, Wyl, who loves you, who said all of those things to you as Romen."

"You," the Queen said, dazed. "Wyl Thirsk. Poor red-headed Wyl."

"That's right," he whispered, sad to feel her draw away from him. "It's always been me. I stopped you giving yourself to Romen that night; I planned the feast celebrations; I gave you the dove mask and told you I loved you. I wore the black mask and fought Celimus. I would have killed him too, if not for you. It broke my heart to see my betrayal reflected in your eyes."

She stared back at him, wanting to believe but struggling to absorb such shattering news. He understood.

"Know this, Valentyna. Whatever happens now, I have loved you with all my heart. I love you now and I will love you forever, whoever I am. There is nothing you could ever do to make me feel another way, and I shall never give my heart to another. It is yours."

Valentyna sighed. She was too overwhelmed. She had no more words.

He rescued her. "May I tell you my plan?"

She hesitated, then seemed to relax. "I don't really know how to reply to your sweet words. I . . . I loved Romen, and I cannot give you—whoever you are—up."

Wyl nodded, afraid, yet daring to hope she might be able to love him back.

"Wyl," she began again, but was interrupted by a frantic

knocking. Her soft expression turned to one of terror. "Quick, we must dress!"

Wyl was into his few garments in moments, and was impressed at how quickly and deftly the Queen slipped into her gown despite the intimidating banging on the door. "Stall for time," he hissed, helping her button the back.

Valentyna was about to call some excuse for the delay when the door burst open and Aremys rushed into the room. He took in the scene in a second and a look of deep apology swept across his face, but the palpable sense of fear that entered the room with him caused all three to forget their embarrassment.

Valentyna was at his side rapidly, praying to Shar that none of her men would notice her dishevelment or guess that her gown was still undone at the back. "We'll be fine, thank you," she said, closing the door on the anxious guards.

"What is it?" Wyl asked, stepping to Valentyna's side and finishing off the buttons on her dress.

"Celimus," Aremys answered. He could not hide the distress in his voice.

"What? Here?" Valentyna rushed to the windows.

"I'm afraid so. Come on, Wyl, we leave now!"

"You called him Wyl," Valentyna said, turning from the window and the riders flying Legion colors below. It was true, then. Out of Wyl's affectionate embrace, the intimate moment lost, the reality felt harsh and suddenly ridiculous.

Aremys shrugged, sheepish. "Well, your highness, I assume he has told you the truth. Is that right, Wyl?"

Wyl nodded, glancing toward the Queen with a heavy heart. It was over so soon . . . before he had even had a chance to put his plan into action.

"Wyl!" Aremys repeated. "We must go, now! My apologies, your highness."

Wyl did not move.

"Go!" Valentyna urged, catching Farrow's infectious anxiety. "Please. The Legion is entering the palace."

"Is Celimus here?"

"I don't know. I can't—"

Aremys interrupted, angry now. "He's here in person, Wyl. I beg you, let's go."

King Cailech took some time to right his clothes, then a calm smile broke across the rugged face that truly reflected the mountain region that had raised him. "This is meant to be, Aremys," he said, voice soft and sad. "This is it, the culmination of Myrren's Gift."

"No!" the Grenadyne yelled, striding toward his friend. "We can escape. If you won't think about yourself, think about Valentyna and how your presence here will reflect on her."

Wyl had not considered how Celimus might react to finding him here. Aremys was right: He had to leave, if just to protect Valentyna from any suggestion that she was consorting with the enemy behind the Morgravian King's back.

"What are you talking about?" Valentyna said. "Why is this meant to be?"

Aremys caught the stern glance from Wyl and knew this was one secret he had not shared. The mercenary shrugged; he knew when to keep his own counsel.

Liryk saved them further argument by barging in, all protocol disregarded. He was startled to see Aremys. "Who let you in, Farrow?"

"I let myself in, Commander. I lied to your guards; they let me through."

"This is preposterous, your majesty," Liryk blustered. "I am supposed to be taking care of your security and it seems anyone can come and go as they please."

Valentyna took charge, concerned now that Celimus might catch her in Cailech's company. "Liryk? What did you come here to tell me?" Her tone brooked no further delay.

The Commander adopted a formal tone old Chancellor Krell would have been proud of. "My queen, I am here to tell you that King Celimus has just arrived in the bailey."

Valentyna took a steadying breath. "Thank you. King Cailech cannot be seen here and I need to . . . tidy up."

Liryk frowned, still flustered at finding Farrow in the room with them. *If only he knew what had happened,* Wyl thought. It would have been safer for Valentyna had Farrow been there all along.

"King Cailech," Liryk said, "I will organize an escape

route and divert the Morgravian party, but you must leave now. You have made your peace with Celimus—now let us make ours!" The vehemence in his voice surprised them all. "Your majesty, please go ahead to your chambers. I will let your husband-to-be know that you are not far away." He emphasized the word "husband," taking in her disheveled clothes and the heightened color in her cheeks. Looking around the room, he saw that the rug was crumpled and the lavender stalks strewn on the floor were crushed in one spot. Their fragrance overlay another one he knew well from places like the Forbidden Fruit . . . no, he certainly did not want to take his thoughts down that path. One more day and Valentyna would be on her way to Pearlis, where she would marry King Celimus and finally unite the two realms. Liryk would permit nothing to get in the way of that vision.

Valentyna felt cornered. She nodded at Liryk. "Thank you, Commander." Then: "King Cailech, it has been enlightening," she said, extending a hand. The Mountain King kissed it too long and too tenderly for Liryk's liking.

"Come, gentlemen," the commander urged. "Your highness, I will wait for you in the main salon."

"Use the secret door," she said, and he nodded.

Liryk did not miss the long, meaningful glance exchanged between his queen and the Mountain King, but pretended to ignore it, feeling more relieved with every step he and the two visitors took closer to the door and the passageway that would lead them out of the palace.

Cailech turned just before ducking to enter the secret stairwell. "Valentyna, remember all that I've said. It's the truth." And then he was gone.

Valentyna stared as the door closed behind him, leaving her alone. Leaving her to face Celimus and a desperately unwanted marriage while her heart's light burned fiercely for Wyl Thirsk.

36

REMYS HAD PERSUADED WYL AS FAR AS THE GATES, HURRYING
Cailech's bulky form down into the bowels of the
palace. The guard accompanying them directed them to a lit-
tle-used gate, which brought them out into a courtyard near
the chapel.

When Aremys cursed their lack of weapons, Wyl remembered that Koreldy's blue sword was stored in a secret spot
in the chapel. Against the guard's wishes they hurried in,
startling Father Paryn.

A familiar voice greeted them. "Aremys!" Turning, they
saw young Pil, who had escaped with Ylena from the massacre at Rittylworth.

"You know these men, child?" Father Paryn asked the
novice.

"I know Farrow—we met at Felrawthy, Father. But I don't
know his friend."

"Pil," Aremys said, his voice spilling its relief. "This
is—"

Wyl would not permit it. "I am King Cailech of the Razors," he said, bowing.

Father Paryn's face drained of color. To his credit, young
Pil recovered quickly and bowed. "Why are you here, your
highness?" the novice asked.

"We're running from King Celimus," Aremys growled,
hurling an angry glance Wyl's way.

"King Celimus is here?" Father Paryn asked.

"I'm afraid so," Wyl said calmly. "We must not be found
or it will look bad for the Queen, you understand?" Clearly
neither of them did, judging from their confused expression.

Wyl pushed on; confusion could be helpful now. "Anyway, we need Romen's sword."

"No fighting in the house of Shar, King or not," the priest cautioned.

"There won't be, Father. We just want to take the sword and leave. I promise no blood will be spilled."

It was too late. There were shouts outside and the guard accompanying them shrugged. "I'm sorry, sire," he said, "I shall have to turn you in. I've been briefed by Commander Liryk not to risk the Queen's reputation."

Wyl nodded. "I understand."

"What?" Aremys roared. "Wait!"

"Be quiet, Aremys," Wyl commanded. He turned quickly to Father Paryn and Pil. "Hide him," he said, indicating the Grenadyne, "and help him escape the palace compound. I ask no more than that you give him Koreldy's weapons. Queen Valentyna will thank you for it," he added, then lied: "She has sanctioned it."

Both holy men nodded dumbly, watching as King Cailech of the Razors strode out to meet the Legionnaires and the Briavellian Guard.

"Quick!" Pil said, and with no choice left to him, Aremys Farrow hung his head and followed the novice.

A few minutes later he heard the soldiers enter and receive a predictable roasting from Father Paryn for bearing arms in the chapel. They tried to explain but achieved nothing but the threat of damnation in Shar's eternal fire if they did not leave at once. "Curse you all for disturbing a man at prayer," the priest called after them.

Pil left Aremys in a small room behind the main chapel while he went for news from Father Paryn. "Where did they take the King?" Aremys asked when Pil returned, wondering how he might free Wyl from a company of Legionnaires and the Briavellian Guard.

"I gather he's in the guardhouse. There are soldiers everywhere. Is he really the King of the Razors?"

Aremys looked sorrowfully at Pil and nodded before adding, "He was also Ylena Thirsk, Faryl of Coombe, and Romen Koreldy."

The boy's eyes widened. "Wyl Thirsk!" he exclaimed in a hushed tone of wonder.

"That's right. And now the King finally has him in his clutches."

"What are we going to do?" Pil asked, terrified.

Aremys knew that trying to rescue Wyl right away was pointless. He needed time to think it through, and Celimus would not do anything too risky on Briavellian soil just before his wedding. No, he would save Cailech for some sort of spectacle after the marriage ceremony, no doubt.

"You're going to stay here and keep our secret," he told the novice. "And I'm going to take Koreldy's sword and make my way to Pearlis."

"That's where he'll be taken, I gather. To Stoneheart."

"Good work, Pil," Aremys said, knowing the praise would help the frightened young monk.

"Is there anything else I can do?"

"Lead me out safely and then let the Queen know that I've escaped."

"Do you need a horse?"

Aremys shook his head. "Too risky and Celimus is too smart. No, I'll go on foot and hitch a ride somehow."

"There are plenty of nobles and merchants headed for Pearlis, Master Farrow," Pil said excitedly. "I'm sure you can get a lift with one of them."

The Grenadyne tried to smile but failed. "That's what I'll do, then."

Most of the nobles making the journey to Pearlis for the royal wedding had their own men for protection, but Aremys was counting on the strata of society below the nobles not having reliable security. A number of middle-class families had decided the opportunity to witness the marriage ceremony combined with the sight of the great city of Pearlis was irresistible, and were also preparing for the trip.

After lying low in the northern part of Werryl for a couple of hours and carefully watching the procession of travelers, Aremys offered his services to three couples who were obviously traveling together. Aremys knew he possessed one of those inherently honest faces, which in this instance won favor with the ladies—along with his suggestion that although Briavel was relatively safe, Morgravia was riddled with bandits who preyed on wealthy merchants.

And so Aremys found himself sitting alongside Mat, a purveyor of fine foods to the nobility, who was driving the carriage that carried the rest of the party, while another man, Bren, brought up the rear, riding one of the two fresh horses they had brought along.

"I've never seen a sword tinged with blue like that," Mat commented.

"Aye," Aremys answered, more sadly than he meant to. "It belonged to a friend who gave it to me as a gift."

Mat whistled. "Some gift. Must have set him back a penny or two. My brother's a craftsman in weapons, but I've never seen him work on anything like that."

"I believe it was made by Master Craftsman Wevyr."

"At Orkyld," the man said in awe.

Aremys nodded. "He was a good friend."

"I guess so," Mat agreed, some irony in the grin he cast the Grenadyne's way. The two men settled into a comfortable silence as the carriage cleared the city and headed onto the main road that led to Morgravia.

37

ALENTYNA DESCENDED THE STAIRCASES TO THE MAIN SALON, feeling as though she were now two people: the one who was presently contriving a welcoming smile for her betrothed, whom she despised; and the one who—in mind, certainly—was fleeing with King Cailech and Aremys Farrow.

The truth of the Mountain King's identity had still to sink in fully. It was all she could think about, her mind moving back through the time she'd spent with Wyl as himself, as Romen, as Ylena. As much as she wanted to find holes in the story—just one would do—comparing Romen with Cailech yielded frightening similarities, and when she threw Ylena into the mix, it left her numb. Why had he never tried to tell her?

She answered her own question: She never would have believed it. Not when he was Romen; not even with the miraculous arrival of the chaffinch that had seemed to herald Ylena's visit. She had considered the finch's song a timely coincidence, not magical, but she now realized it must have been magic of some kind. She thought of Fynch; Wyl had not had time to tell her how he was, nor enough of his idea of how she could avoid marrying Celimus. What would she not give to hear it now! She had considered every possible scenario and had not been able to find a way out. Only a few more steps now, she realized, emerging from her disquieted thoughts, and Celimus would be kissing her hand and offering sugary platitudes. What could he be doing here? Well, he could just turn around and go home. She still had one more day before she had to leave for Pearlis.

She took a deep breath and nodded at the guards outside the salon as they pushed open the doors for her entry. Valentyna had already pictured King Celimus bowing elegantly, then striding majestically forward, smiling widely with those perfect teeth. She had already planned her own contrived expression—a delicate balance of surprise and feigned pleasure that he was in Briavel. But she did not have to contrive any surprise. It slapped her hard in the face when she swept into the room only to be confronted by a snarling, struggling Cailech and a smugly grinning King of Morgravia.

"Valentyna, my love," Celimus said expansively, "look what I found sneaking out of your palace like a rat."

Valentyna stopped, unable to breathe. She saw Cailech shake his head, knew what he wanted her to do. Her heart broke. Again; it was happening again. Once more he was offering himself up to save her.

Everyone was waiting for her to speak.

"I've already explained," Wyl yelled, shaking off his captors' hands, "that I never got to speak with the Queen." Valentyna noticed the manacles around his arms and ankles.

"I heard you the first time, Cailech," Celimus spat, turning back toward his bride. "My dear, is this true?"

Don't hesitate, Valentyna, just agree, Wyl prayed.

For Briavel then, she decided, rapidly assessing her helplessness in the situation. She summoned her most regal tone and hurled it back at Celimus. "Of course it's true," she answered tersely. "Who is this man?" She pointed toward Wyl—presumably Aremys had escaped. "And how dare you hold anyone against his will in my court, King Celimus."

That startled him. He was not prepared for her wrath, having already decided she was as guilty as the Mountain King in conspiring against him.

"Your majesties." Liryk stepped in. "Allow me to escort the prisoner to a secure place and perhaps then you might discuss—"

"Yes, why don't you do that, Commander," Valentyna agreed, cutting across his words and seizing control. "This is unforgivable, King Celimus. You called him Cailech. I still don't know who he is."

Celimus had also regained some equanimity. "Don't you? Let me introduce you to the treacherous King of the Razors, who just days ago was signing a peace treaty with Morgravia at Felrawthy."

Valentyna feigned shock, hiding her despair as the man she had loved through so many lives was led away.

Cailech turned his head, spoke over his shoulder. "I'm glad you have finally met me, your majesty." The word "me" was loaded with meaning. "We'll meet again," Wyl said.

"Oh, I'm sure you will," Celimus said. "I'll insist my wife is present for your execution."

She saw Cailech's sad smile and did not understand it. Dismissing everyone, she swung around on Celimus the minute the door had closed. "How dare you, sir!"

"Valentyna, please," he cajoled. "I came with only romantic intentions. My chancellor suggested that it would be wonderful for both our peoples if we could be seen together.

His idea was that I bring an escort to accompany you on this symbolic journey across our two realms. I know I should have sent word, but it sounded like such a worthy plan, I was excited and in a hurry to catch you before you left Werryl Palace. I've had a special carriage made, my love, emblazoned with our new heraldic device, which my craftsmen have been designing for months now. It flies the colors of Briavel and Morgravia, sweet Valentyna. We have woven the crimson with the emerald and violet so beautifully, it seems we were always meant to be one."

Valentyna was taken aback by his enthusiasm. She could see that the idea of this marriage had great merit for the people of their realms, but she hated surprises being sprung on her at the best of times, let alone by the hated King of Morgravia.

She had promised herself one day. One final day to mourn the loss of her status. One night to remember with love the touch of Romen, of Cailech . . . of Wyl Thirsk. Now Celimus had taken that from her too.

She wanted to react, to scream her frustration, sob her grief. But the man in front of her was dangerous, and she needed to respond with her head, not her heart. She nodded slowly, affecting calm. "What do you plan to do with Cailech?"

"I'm not sure yet. I shall be taking him with us to Stoneheart."

"Surely you don't mean a trial and execution?" she wondered, a new terror chilling her. He could not die again. She could not lose him as she had lost Romen.

"I said I don't know. Death would be my choice."

"Why must he die?" she demanded.

"That you need to ask such a question baffles me, Valentyna," Celimus replied calmly, but followed it with a condescending smirk.

"But you said yourself that you'd just signed a peace treaty."

The King's famous temper began to stoke. He had done well to get this far without losing his patience. "Which he broke by setting foot into Briavel—and that, I might add, is a whole new mystery. How the King of the Razors can infiltrate your realm and cover almost its entire length without being noticed is a puzzle."

"It certainly is," Valentyna replied abruptly. "Which is why I don't agree to any decision on your part, sire. He is my prisoner, on my land. I will decide his fate."

A new note crept into Celimus's voice, one she had not heard before but one she was very sure was more characteristic of this cruel King of Morgravia. Gone was the affected brightness, the sugary tone. "I'm sorry, Valentyna, you will not. I've noticed how you deal with treachery—you send it off to a brothel for the night."

If only he knew how deep his words cut. "Leave me, Celimus," she commanded, not trusting herself to say more.

He impaled her with a stare, which she returned with defiance, and then he nodded. "Fine. We shall leave tomorrow as you had planned, and Valentyna, you had better wipe that scowl off your face by then. I will marry you, and I will reserve the right to execute my enemies if they are found on my soil."

"You mean my soil, don't you, Celimus?" she spat, trembling from the hate that was threatening to overwhelm her.

He shook his head. "It's mine from now on, Valentyna. Get used to the idea. We can marry and please our realms and I'll provide peace for your people. Or we can do it the hard way and I promise I will slaughter every man, woman, and child of Briavel if it comes to that."

She had not thought he could shock her, but the venom with which he spoke now—in a way she had never been spoken to before—chilled her. She felt the wispy hairs on her arms stand on end. That was no way to speak to a queen, especially in her own palace, but she was powerless to stop him. The only weapons she had left were words. She threw them at him now.

"You are a snake, Celimus. Wyl Thirsk was right."

"Wyl Thirsk is dead, Shar rot him, as you will be if you don't put on a happy face, come serenely to Pearlis, and take those wedding vows as planned."

"I would rather be dead," Valentyna snapped recklessly.

"That's your choice," her fiancé snarled. "No more woo-ing, Valentyna. This is your new life as my queen. You are not my equal. The only good you'll do me is to give me the sons I crave, and believe me, if you won't give them to me willingly, I will take my pleasures as I see fit."

W yl sat glumly in the guardhouse. Much as he wanted to please Celimus, Liryk could not bring himself to have the King of the Razors incarcerated in the palace dungeons. Legionnaires were posted throughout the guardhouse, one for each Briavellian soldier.

"Did Aremys get away?" Wyl asked Liryk.

The man nodded. "You shouldn't have hesitated, sire."

"It was wrong of me to run."

"Your pride aside, this is all very dangerous for our queen."

"She handled it well. I won't make any further problems for her. Thank you for maintaining our secret."

The old soldier sighed. "I'm not sure I understand your coming here, or now your calm acceptance of what is certain death at the King's hands."

"This is how it is meant to be," Wyl said, resigned to his fate. "This is Myrren's Gift playing out precisely to plan."

"Myrren's Gift?"

Wyl smiled. "Take no notice of me."

Liryk was baffled but his relief that Valentyna seemed to be compromising with Celimus overwhelmed his curiosity. "How did the King know? He sent men looking for you immediately upon his arrival."

"It was my horse," Wyl replied, grateful for Cailech's memories.

"What?"

"I gave Celimus my white stallion as a gift at Felrawthy. He fell in love with it, so I insisted he have it because I had its twin back at the fortress. Identical."

Liryk understood. "He saw your horse, the twin."

"He's probably riding its brother. How could he miss it? You won't tell him about Aremys, will you, Liryk?"

The old man shook his head. "No, sire. I want no further

grief for her majesty. No one needs to know about the mercenary, and the Briavellian Guard can be trusted to keep the secret."

"Thank you."

"I shall see to your comforts, sire. We leave for Pearlis tomorrow at dawn."

Wyl nodded, no longer caring.

Valentyna escaped her anger and Celimus by taking her horse out, refusing to have him accompany her. This would be her last ride as a single woman through the woodland of Briavel and onto the moors. Next time—if there was a next time, she thought, remembering the King's threat—she would be married to Celimus. She would have the grand title of Queen of Briavel and Morgravia, but it would be an empty title.

She glanced back at the odd medley of guards following her, comprising her own men and Legionnaires. Celimus was taking no chances with her. There was nowhere to run and hide anyway, and it would be unseemly for a monarch to flee her own realm. No, Valentyna was made of sterner stuff. She would face this trial, would bestow the gift of peace upon her people as she had promised.

But the memory of Cailech's touch still burned in her mind and on her body. It had been such a rushed, frantic episode and yet she could remember each moment of it, relive it in her thoughts in a delicious slow-moving scene. She could still not quite grasp that she was no longer a virgin; it had all happened so fast. She could never have planned for this, and yet nothing gave her greater satisfaction—nothing!—than knowing her greatest possession had been given to the man she loved, not the one who would steal it from her under false pretenses.

Cailech . . . no, Wyl, she reminded herself, was such an enigma. He had claimed she had known him as Romen and yet she knew so little about him really, other than that he loved her, would die for her—had died for her. Poor Wyl, she thought. She could not imagine how he had survived the killing of his sister . . . wished she could ask him, have time with him. That was impossible, she knew, but she would do what she could. She would marry Celimus and give everything of herself toward preserving the life of the King of the Razors. Even if she could never see him again, it would be enough to know that he lived. Celimus would not execute Cailech because she would forbid it.

She had taken the wrong approach with Celimus, she realized. All she had done was anger him, corner him into making rash statements. Her father had always said she must learn to curb her tongue. Being a good royal, he had cautioned, was about diplomacy, careful choice of words, and always giving oneself time to consider. She had ignored his advice in her behavior with Celimus, and it had cost her. He had obviously been shocked to find Cailech in Werryl and, like a wounded animal, had struck back. She should have sensed the danger lurking there; Valentyna admonished herself for such clumsiness. If she was going to survive in the Morgravian court, she would have to play Celimus more intelligently than she had today. She must fuel his vanity, make him feel omnipotent, make herself irresistible. Valentyna slowed Bonny to a walk, in no rush to be back in the palace, and remembered how powerful she had felt just hours before, realizing what a woman could do to a man. For all his strength and stamina, his status and bearing, Cailech had been too vulnerable. Faced with naked desire and a compliant partner, he had become putty. Could she achieve the same with Celimus?

She recalled that Chancellor Krell had intimated that, if she approached the marriage with the right attitude, she could use her feminine wiles to get what she wanted. Her revulsion for Celimus aside, if she could play the role of affectionate Queen, impress his people and thus please him, she might be able to enjoy small wins of importance to her.

Her first priority was Wyl. She understood that there was no changing his status as prisoner; Celimus would want to make an example of him. So be it. But she would put all her efforts into ensuring that this was the extent of the punishment. They had lied once already. No doubt Wyl could dream up some clever reason as to why he had come to Briavel. Surely there must be a feasible explanation. She pondered, found the wisp of an idea. It might work. She would need to get word to Wyl.

38

HE JOURNEY ACROSS BRIAVEL AND INTO MORGRAVIA PASSED uneventfully. In any other situation, Valentyna would have truly enjoyed the trip and the chance to mix with her people, for they came out in the hundreds to wave the royal procession through their towns and villages. And what a procession it made: The Briavellian Guard was in full formal dress in emerald and violet, while the Legionnaires looked dashing in their crimson and black. Trailing the rear came a cavalcade of nobles, dignitaries, servants, and attendants, not to mention Madam Eltor's personal retinue in charge of the Queen's wardrobe, as well as cooks, pastry makers, and bakers—all the people required to provide a joint wedding feast that blended Morgravia's culinary specialties with Briavel's fine foods.

And in the midst of the brightly colored entourage rode a smiling king and queen, graciously accepting the crowd's blessings for their happiness.

"You can almost believe it," Valentyna commented, aiming a shy smile toward the King.

He did not look at her, but she heard the softer tone in his voice. Perhaps it was hard work being vicious all of the time, she thought. "Why not? They love you. They love me for marrying you and for bringing peace to the realm."

"It is a good thing, Celimus."

"Do you mean that?"

She caught a posy thrown by a young lad and blew him a kiss, which won a roar of approval from the happy mob. "I regret my behavior of yesterday, and indeed throughout our courtship."

He finally looked away from the mass of happy faces and turned to her. "And?"

"I wish us to start again, here and now. Neither of us has parents to guide our choices, no family to lean upon." She sighed. "We are trying to achieve something extraordinary: two young monarchs, new to their thrones, forging peace and prosperity. I did a lot of soul-searching last night, Celimus, and realized that what you have worked so hard to bring about will become a landmark era in the history books."

Celimus's expression was skeptical. "But last—"

"Yesterday was different. You frightened me and I was rattled to think that King Cailech had infiltrated Briavel without my knowledge. Did he tell you why?"

"No. I thought I'd find out courtesy of Stoneheart's clever men of the dungeons," the King offered unkindly.

Valentyna did not react. Celimus, like any bully, was always looking for ways to hurt others. Instead she planted the first seed of her lie. "Cailech told Liryk that he wanted to meet with me to talk about a surprise festival he was thinking about throwing in your honor."

It was clear that Celimus had not expected this. "My honor!"

"Yes. He wanted to hail you as the region's peacemaker, bringing long life and prosperity to the three realms." She held her breath through the pause that followed, forcing herself to look back and wave to the crowd, smiling calmly despite her fear.

"That might change things," Celimus said softly.

Instead of leaping on his words and giving away her excitement, Valentyna shrugged. "Yes, well, it is of no matter to me, but perhaps you can find out more in due course. It would be a pity to lose a friend in the Razors when you have worked so hard to establish the truce."

"Indeed," he said drily, but it was obvious that the notion

that Cailech had not been in Briavel for sinister reasons had been successfully planted. She would need to water it subtly throughout the journey, Valentyna realized.

"To get back to what I was saying earlier, my lord, you can rely on me to be faithful and dutiful. Let us make this marriage the success everyone wants so badly."

He laughed derisively. "I know you don't love me, Valentyna."

"As you don't me, sire," she countered with care. "But that doesn't mean we cannot be a successful royal couple. Respect, affection, cooperation—surely these are all qualities we can work to achieve?"

"Surely. But I don't understand."

"What puzzles you, sire?"

"The change of heart. One minute you are a spitting cat, the next a kitten."

"I dreamed last night of my parents, Celimus," she lied, trying not to recall her true dream of Cailech's passionate embrace, his ardent yet gentle touch, his kisses so tender and deep, his declarations of love . . . she felt herself going hot in all the wrong places.

"Yes?" the King prompted.

"And . . . they urged me that this was a match made by Shar for the good of the realms. They told me that Shar's angels, if we let them, will guide us to hold our marriage fast and be good to each other. That we will have sons—strong boys—four of them," she said, feeling nauseated by her own creative invention. "Are you superstitious, Celimus?"

"Not really. Why?"

"This morning I found a white rose on the bush my father planted for my mother at her death."

Celimus looked at her quizzically, although she could tell he was intrigued. "What is the significance?"

"Ah, perhaps it is only in Briavel we believe this. Legend has it that if a white rosebush produces a single bloom, which opens before any other buds show themselves, any dream of the previous night is destined to come true."

"No matter whether it is good or bad?" he asked.

"That's correct. That is why I went looking for the rose,

because my dream was so profound, so vivid. I could see our sons, Celimus—dark, strapping boys, like their father."

He grinned. "That's very interesting, Valentyna. I'm pleased that you feel so positive suddenly."

"I intend to be a good wife to you, sire. I will make you proud and happy."

Celimus looked into her clear blue gaze and saw no guile. He reached across the distance between their two horses, his white, hers black, and took her hand. The crowd gasped, then cheered uproariously when King Celimus bent to place his lips against the back of the hand of his queen.

Valentyna felt nothing but revulsion. She was relieved she had chosen to wear gloves.

Wyl was traveling among a different cavalcade but toward the same destination. Tied, gagged, and thrown in a covered wagon, he was driven hard. There were no stops for food or rest. Fresh horses took over at various points until, just by the smell of the air, he knew he was approaching Pearlis. Wyl had lost track of time and thought. His mind felt like a skein of tangled wool.

"Stoneheart ahead!" he heard a soldier cry, and smiled to himself. Death was upon him. Myrren's Gift was reaching its climax and the Quickening would come to an end.

He hoped Aremys had made his own way to Pearlis, and that his friend would keep his solemn promise to end Celimus's life the moment the change occurred. He thought briefly of Fynch's caution about randomness, and took solace from it. It was randomness that had given him Valentyna by the fireside not so long ago. Nothing could ever take away that time of exhilaration, that delicious loss of thought and control, that intense passion that had sealed his love for her.

Valentyna was his. They were one, coupled in love and desire; it had been an exquisite pain when they reached that final dizzying, breathtaking pleasure in each other. He had known her in a way no other had. Her maidenhood had been given gladly, lovingly, and he had taken it with a trembling, feverish joy. Celimus might marry Valentyna but the Queen

of Briavel belonged to the King of the Razors . . . to Wyl
Thirsk.

He would not swap his lying with Valentyna for anything—not even in exchange for his life. He could die happily now, for he was loved—and loved as Wyl Thirsk. She
had uttered his name.

His thoughts were interrupted by soldiers unfastening the
hood of the cart. He cast a final thought toward Knave,
wished he had had a chance to say goodbye to the faithful
dog. He did not struggle as rough hands dragged him from
the cart and led him to a place in the depths of Stoneheart
from which few people returned.

For the first time in his life Knave had neither mission nor
magic to call upon. He was still driven, though, urged by
a force more complex than anything he had known before. It
went by the name of sorrow.

He had hidden himself in the palace compound, close
enough to watch the guardhouse for any movement on Wyl's
part. He had made sure that the Grenadyne had gotten safely
out of Werryl and had seen him organize transport with
some Briavellian folk on their way to the wedding festival in
Morgravia. Then he had returned to the palace and kept Valentyna company during her ride, watching her fall so deeply
into thought that her horse could have probably stopped and
grazed without her realizing it.

He had watched Celimus prowl around the guardhouse,
giving orders to his Legionnaires, making sure they remained alert and that nobody visited the prisoner without
his express permission—not even the Queen. The palace
had finally settled down for the night, although a constant
quiet movement of servants prepared for the departure the
next day.

Knave had wandered away to the woodland, where he had
spent favorite times with Fynch. He found the spot where
they had slept the night, where he had heralded the death of
Romen Koreldy with a piercing howl into the dark. He lay
there, his head on his huge paws, as the hours crawled by,
and he mourned the loss of the boy he had come to love, the

boy who had given his life to destroy the enemy of all that was good and natural in the world.

Knave threw back his huge head and howled in grief. It seemed the Thicket heard him, for once again he felt himself connected to its magic.

Knave? came a voice.

Rasmus. He groaned, his throat swelling from the pain of his emotion.

We promised Faith Fynch we would aid Wyl Thirsk, the bird said.

Knave waited, his head hung low. He did not want any more instructions.

Go to Argorn, Rasmus finally said. *Find Felrawthy's duke and return him to Pearlis, where he will meet Farrow.*

And then?

They will know what to do. Go now. The Thicket will send you.

Knave closed the connection, too numb to care what happened now that Fynch was gone. Very soon he was hurtling through the dark toward the region of Morgravia that had produced Wyl Thirsk.

39

WYL SAT ON THE COLD FLOOR OF ONE OF STONEHEART'S DUN-geons, his head resting on his knees. Moments earlier he had turned to prayer, beseeching Shar to watch over and protect Valentyna, to heal Elspyth, to restore Lothryn, and to welcome Ylena and Alyd, Fynch and Gueryn into everlasting life. As the list of souls lengthened he had stopped, overcome by distress. How many lives had been lost or destroyed because of Celimus? Wyl's anguish deepened as he accepted that he was helpless now. There was nothing he could do from the dungeon except wait for Myrren's Gift to mete out its final crushing blow and hope that Aremys would keep his promise.

And so he sat in silence, wishing the guards would come for him and speed his death. A strange tingling sensation coursed through his body and then a blue shimmering light forced him to look up. He recognized the feeling—it was connected to the magic of the Thicket.

"Fynch," he whispered as the shimmering coalesced to reveal a vision of his young friend.

Hello, Wyl, the boy said into his mind.

"Are you alive?"

Not in the way you mean.

"Then you died during the battle with Rashlyn?"

Wyl, Fynch interrupted gently, *my time with you is short.*

"What is it that I must do?"

Just trust me.

"To do what?"

To forge a Bridge of Souls.

Wyl remained baffled by Fynch's visit. It had been inspiring, calming even, to see the ghostly vision of his friend and hear Fynch speak so surely. He had insisted that Wyl trust him, and Wyl did—but that was all Fynch would tell him, other than to promise that the Bridge of Souls would save his life. His instructions to Wyl were simple. When Wyl needed to be saved, all he had to do was call out Fynch's name. But, in truth, Wyl did not believe there was any escape from this dungeon or from his fate. He appreciated Fynch's attempt to soothe him, but he was thinking only of death now—real death. There would be no returning from the end of Aremys's sword.

Wyl looked around the cell, touched the cold black stone that encased him. Not so long ago Stoneheart had been his home, a place that embraced him with the love of Magnus and the security of his title as General. Now it was the lair of his foe and its cold walls would witness his death twice over in the coming hours.

Wyl's gaze roamed absently in the dim light, which filtered through from an outside cresset. It fell upon an inscription scratched into one of the bottom stones. AVENGE ME, WYL, it said. His heart pained. He had come full circle. This was surely the work of Myrren. She must have suffered in this very cell all those years ago. Her touching plea still had the ability to move him.

He hated Celimus for being the cause of so much suffering. As if on some silent signal, he heard the click of boots on flagstones. There was only one person who walked with that arrogant stride. He turned away, did not want to see the King gloating over his rival's downfall.

Liryk had gotten a message through to Wyl from Valentyna, saying that she had found a way to explain Cailech's presence in Briavel. Liryk had watched Cailech shake his head at the idea, but had not had the heart to relay the Mountain King's attitude to the Queen. Wyl had no intention of making excuses.

He soon discovered this was also the reason for the King's visit late into the night.

"Tell me, Mountain King, was there a good reason for your visiting Briavel without an invitation?" Celimus gave a soft, deprecating laugh as he flicked an invisible mote of dust from his jacket. "You see, the Queen seems to think you had very fine intentions of joining forces with her to plan some special festivities on my account." He shook his head with mock embarrassment. "How very jolly."

"I would not plan any festival around you, Celimus, other than your funeral," Wyl enjoyed saying.

The King laughed in obvious delight. He clapped his hands, loving Cailech's bitterness. "You obviously want to die, my friend. Valentyna was surely throwing you a lifeline here."

"Thank her for her generosity," Wyl said. "And I'll wait to see you in Shar's eternal fire. We'll settle our score there, Celimus . . . if not sooner."

Celimus had looked at him quizzically, not understanding his final words, but Wyl did not elaborate. Intent on having the last laugh, the King gave his dazzling smile. "Is there anything I can do for you in the meantime?" he asked.

"Yes. Do it yourself."

"Pardon?"

"You heard me. Kill me yourself."

Celimus made a sound of disapproval. "I might miss and merely injure you—oh dear, that could be messy and painful."

"I'll risk it. Let me feel the touch of your blade."

Celimus smiled and nodded. "Perhaps. We shall see what mood I'm in tomorrow. Sleep well, your highness," he said, leaving with a chuckle.

Wyl felt even more hollow than before. Not once but thrice had he betrayed her. First as Romen, later as Ylena, and now as Cailech. She would never forgive him. He sat in the darkness, the bleak atmosphere matching his thoughts, disturbed first by the scuffling of rats and then by the sound of yet another arrival.

Once again there was no need for introductions. "King Cailech, I regret to find you here, sire," Chancellor Jessom said. "Is there anything I can get you?"

"Other than the key, you mean?" Wyl murmured, refusing to turn toward the King's servant. He would make him speak to his back.

"A rug perhaps, sire?"

"You forget that I am of the Razors, Chancellor. We don't feel the cold."

"A candle, then. Let me at least light this grim space for you, my lord."

"Do what you wish. It matters not to me."

"I meant what I said, King Cailech. I regret to see you incarcerated here. When the rider gave the news of who was being brought here, I thought the man must have been duped, charmed by a hedgewitch."

"Be careful talking of witches in here, Jessom. Or you'll find yourself on this side of the bars."

The Chancellor cleared his throat, sounding abashed, and Wyl heard the rasp of a clay plate being pushed through the bars. Shadows leapt across the bars as a soft light eased the darkness.

"There, that's better, surely," Jessom said.

"What are you looking for, Chancellor? Absolution?"

"What do you mean?"

"All the deaths—you must have so much blood on your hands."

"I don't understand you, sire."

"Why not? I am speaking the same language you do."

"But what could you know of me?" Jessom replied. "We are all but strangers."

Wyl admonished himself to be careful. It was true: Cailech would hardly know the Chancellor, other than by name and sight from Tenterdyn. However, the truth was, he was not of a mind to be careful anymore. He wished Celimus would hurry up and bring about the final death in Myrren's ghastly plan. He ignored Jessom's question and posed his own instead. "Where is your king?"

"Asleep, I hope. He has a big day tomorrow."

"So the wedding goes ahead as planned?"

"Yes, sire. Why would you think otherwise? I'm afraid the city will shortly degenerate into mass celebrations and drunkenness. It is but an hour to dawn."

"The Morgravians want the marriage as badly as the Briavellians," Wyl commented, more to himself than for the Chancellor's hearing.

"Of course. It is a brilliant union."

"Not for Valentyna."

"Why do you say that, sire?"

"He will destroy her."

"He wants her very much."

The words fired a new anger in Wyl and he swung around to face the Chancellor. "He wants what she brings him, Jessom. He wants to own the glittering jewel of Briavel, and everything else that Briavel can give him. He doesn't care about Valentyna. He wants her body and the sons she can provide, the peace and prosperity she brings. The people love her, and because of her they will love him, for surely they hate him right now."

Jessom cleared his throat. "You seem to have a very deep understanding of the south, King Cailech."

Wyl grunted. "It is my business to know these things.

Mark my words, Jessom, if he destroys her—and he will—
the people will rise up against him. Already I suspect there
are mutterings within the Legion. The right whisper in the
right ear and the army will move against the Crown. You
know it is powerful enough."

Wyl realized that the Chancellor was actually paying attention to what he was saying. Perhaps the man had not
come here to bait him after all. If he could sway this powerful person, he might be able to help Valentyna from beyond
the grave.

Jessom interrupted his thoughts. "The King has placed his
own people in senior positions in the Legion. They would
not move against him," he said.

As far as Jessom was concerned, Celimus had played out
his last vicious act. Imprisoning and executing the King of
the Razors, with whom only days ago he had signed a peace
treaty, was sheer madness. But Jessom's first attempt at arguing against killing the Mountain King had failed and a second could have dire consequences. Jessom knew Celimus
saw killing Cailech as a way of ridding himself of the final
obstacle to becoming Emperor. But he did not agree. It was
a mistake.

"When someone like Eryd Bench knows the truth of
what's been going on, his voice alone will be enough to turn
the Legionnaires," Wyl assured.

Jessom could not guess how King Cailech could know of
Eryd Bench, but that did not matter now. The death and destruction had to stop. Unification and peace were at hand.
But Jessom feared Celimus was not the monarch to lead the
Morgravians to greatness. Whenever the King took a dislike
to someone or felt in any way threatened, he turned to
killing. Such a sovereign would ultimately destroy the region. "Lord Bench is dead, sire, I'm sorry to say."

Jessom was astonished to see Cailech react as if he'd been
punched. The Mountain warrior's head rocked back, his
eyes closed in agony, and he threw his body toward the bars,
gripping them with white knuckles. "Dead?"

"I'm afraid so, King Cailech."

"How?" Wyl rasped.

"How else?" Jessom replied, revealing more of his private feelings than he had intended. "Let's just say our king took umbrage at Eryd Bench's gentle inquiries about certain events in the north."

Wyl groaned. His hands fell away from the bars and he slumped against the wall, slowly sliding his tall body to the ground. "His women—Lady Bench, Georgyana?"

"Do you know them?"

"Are they safe?" Wyl yelled, no longer caring how he might be confusing the Chancellor.

Stung by the Mountain King's venom, Jessom answered truthfully. "They escaped. A servant told our men that two guests had arrived, a man and woman. The woman was injured; dark-haired, small, attractive. The man was probably Crys Donal of Felrawthy." He surprised himself by offering so much information. There was something compelling about Cailech. He seemed entirely different to the arrogant, sharp-witted man he had met in the north.

"Elspyth," Wyl whispered. "No sign of where they went?"

Jessom shook his head. "May I ask why this interests you, sire?"

"No. But I will tell you this, Chancellor Jessom: Your days as a powerful adviser to the Crown are numbered. Mark my words, you will be dead at the hands of your king in a matter of days . . . perhaps hours. You will be lucky to see out the next few days." Wyl enjoyed the sudden insecurity that coursed across the angular planes of the Chancellor's pale face.

"He needs me," Jessom said.

"No, he doesn't, Chancellor. I can sense your disgust at his actions. If I can, he already has." Jessom heard the ring of truth in the Mountain King's warning.

"He doesn't know that Lord Hartley still lives," Jessom muttered to himself, his agile mind racing.

"Lord Hartley?"

The Chancellor looked up, his thoughts clearly elsewhere. "Yes, Celimus ordered his death, but I let Hartley go—he's in hiding now. I can call upon his help to rally the other nobles against our king."

"Not before the King kills you," Wyl said cruelly. "But I have an idea, Jessom. It's too late for me—and for you, I fear, unless . . ."

The man's mortified expression was quickly replaced by wrath. It was not death he feared, Wyl realized. It was loss of power, wealth, and position.

"Unless what, sire?" Jessom asked. He was composed again, his tone curious.

"Unless you put your considerable knowledge and influence behind Queen Valentyna. Protect her, befriend her, put your faith in her. Someone else will deal with Celimus. Trust me on this. He will not live to see old age. He may not even live to see out the spring. But the Queen can live to a ripe age if she is given the right defenses. She can win over the Legion, she can woo the nobles. Through her, Morgravia can achieve peace with Briavel and retain the truce with the Razors."

"The Mountain People will make war on Morgravia and Briavel if you are executed." No more diplomatic language, Jessom decided; King Cailech knew he could not escape his fate. There was a bargain being made here. He was not sure he understood it, or why Cailech cared about peace in the region, but Jessom was a pragmatist. Cailech was right: Valentyna was the future, especially if she were to quickly become pregnant by Celimus. Then nothing but the Queen and the heir—the true Crown of the newly unified realms— would matter.

"You echo my thoughts so closely, King Cailech, it is uncanny."

"Come closer, Jessom. I have something to tell you and I do not wish to be overheard."

"I cannot save your life, King Cailech," Jessom warned candidly.

"I understand," Wyl said, extending Cailech's blunt fingers through the bars.

Jessom smiled thinly. He was curious to hear the bargain this imprisoned, doomed King could offer. The Chancellor stepped closer but drew his blade to show the man of the mountains that he was not naive. He would shake hands cautiously.

"No need for that, Jessom. I have no intention of anything but sealing our bargain."

Palm met palm and Cailech's fingers closed around Jessom's hand. The King was smiling, and Jessom suddenly realized there was something unnerving, something predatory, in that expression. The Chancellor balked, tried to release himself from Cailech's grip, but it was too late. A shimmering blue light flowed around their hands. A seal.

40

ALENTYNA STOOD FORLORNLY IN A GRAND CHAMBER AT Stoneheart, her heart as cold as the dark stone surrounding her. Madam Eltor had permitted only her most senior and trusted assistant to help her dress the Queen. Valentyna sensed rather than saw the surreptitious glances between the two older women as they took in her grief-stricken expression.

"Come now, my queen," her seamstress tried once more. "Please don't stain your face with tears."

"There are no more tears left within me," Valentyna replied.

"This is your wedding day, your highness. The happiest day ever for the people of Briavel and Morgravia," the assistant risked.

"Not for me, though," the Queen replied, not caring that her words provoked a raising of the assistant's eyebrows and a stern gaze from her superior.

The women had worked fast and fluidly. Valentyna was already stitched into her gown, although Madam Eltor had tut-tutted, warning, "You've lost weight, my girl. This was perfect last week."

Valentyna just shook her head. "Let's get this over with."

"That will be all, Maud," Madam Eltor said, dismissing her assistant. "I hope I don't need to remind you that what is discussed in our presence always remains private."

Maud curtsied and left hurriedly, the news no doubt already spilling out of her that the Queen was going to her wedding as full of grief as when she had attended her father's funeral. "Valentyna!" the seamstress snapped. "Stop this!"

"I don't love him," she said, balling her fists and closing her eyes, trying to get a grip on her spiraling emotions.

"We don't care!" Madam Eltor replied, deciding that harshness was the only solution now. "He brings us peace. I regret that you are the currency with which we buy it, your highness, but it is too late for you to turn back."

Valentyna was stung. "Yes. Of course, you're right. Forgive me."

The seamstress's voice softened. "Be stout of heart, Valentyna. You are Briavel's jewel. The brightest jewel now in Morgravia's crown. Imagine how proud you would make your father today."

"Yes, by marrying the man who murdered him," Valentyna muttered.

Her companion gave a gasp of shock and Valentyna realized too late that hurting Madam Eltor achieved nothing. The truth of Valor's demise did not change the fact of his death or her decision to marry Celimus. She hated the way she veered between courage and weakness: One moment she felt she could make the marriage work, would bear his children, would make Briavel safe and prosperous. The next, she plunged into gloom, remembering that passionate hour in Wyl's arms. How could she wipe that from her thoughts? How could she lie with Celimus this evening and not feel anything but revulsion?

Because you must, she told herself in a small, urgent voice. *Because Briavel's future rests upon it.*

"I'm all right," she reassured her seamstress. "My nerves are jangling. I'll be fine once we leave for the cathedral, I promise. Put the veil on."

Madam Eltor did not believe her, but she obediently

draped the exquisite veil over Valentyna's head and face, then stepped back to admire her work. "You are breathtaking, your majesty. The Morgravians will fall in love with you instantly."

Valentyna found a small smile for her lifelong friend. "I'm ready," she said.

Celimus had ordered a glistening white carriage to convey his bride to the cathedral. It sported the new device linking Morgravia and Briavel: the intertwined initials of the King and Queen painted in their national colors. Four stunning white horses, imported from Grenadyne, pulled the carriage. Accompanying the Queen were members of the Briavellian Guard, beautifully outfitted in emerald and violet. A proud Commander Liryk waited, as did all the crowd, for the first glimpse of the Queen.

As if Shar himself had ordained it, the sun appeared from behind a cloud and bathed the main square of Stoneheart in a dazzling golden light. The people screamed their delight as the Queen appeared on the steps of Stoneheart's main entrance in that same moment. Trumpets sounded above the din, and without a male family member to do the honors, it was left to Commander Liryk to walk stiff and proud up those stairs to escort her. He bowed low before her, as did all gathered.

Valentyna was moved. A lump formed in her throat and she recalled the similar tumultuous welcome she had been given on her arrival into Pearlis. She and Celimus had had a deafening, exhausting couple of hours making their way through the cheering city. Everyone had seemed to be waving squares of linen in the colors crimson, black, emerald, and violet, creating a sea of moving color that mingled the two realms more effectively than any device she and Celimus could have arranged.

She curtsied low and long to the people. The gracious acknowledgment drove them into even wilder applause. Liryk smiled at her action. "You are already their queen," he said, his breath catching.

Valentyna thought she might cry again. "I hope my father is watching," she managed to say.

He took her hand and squeezed it. "He will be cheering alongside your beautiful mother, both of them so proud."

"Thank you, Liryk, for all you have done for me. I'm sorry I have been difficult in recent times."

"Your highness," he said with genuine reverence. "I am your servant."

Valentyna was warmed by the sentiment of her commander and the pride his words evoked within her. She vowed once again to somehow exist alongside Celimus without fracturing the peace their two realms considered so very precious.

"Come, Liryk. Lead me to my husband."

Wyl could hear delirious cheering as he was led out of the dungeons into a courtyard he had never seen before.

"Has the Queen left the palace?" he asked one of the senior soldiers, a man he recognized.

"I think so," the man answered, embarrassed by his task. This was a king, after all, and they had been led to believe a peace agreement had been made with the Mountain dwellers.

"And where do you take me now?"

The man hesitated and checked that the manacles were secure on their prisoner. "We have orders to move you, King Cailech."

"That doesn't answer my question, soldier," Wyl insisted. "I asked where."

To his credit, the soldier looked directly into the hard gaze of the Mountain King. "To the block, sire."

Wyl sighed. "I see." Celimus was wasting no time in executing his northern rival. He wondered if the cruel sovereign would force Valentyna to witness the death. He knew that Celimus would revel in the grisly notion. And she would have no choice. Executions were something royalty had to face whether or not they had a stomach for it. And

Valentyna would not be watching a stranger die, as Celimus assumed; she would be watching the head of the man she loved be severed and lifted in triumph above his slumped corpse. He hated to think about how this would hurt her very soul, and did not want to ponder how she would respond to his transference into Celimus.

Wyl heard the crowd cheer again and imagined the Queen of Briavel's procession to the cathedral. She would be serene, he decided; she would rise above her sorrow and do her realm justice. Her gown would be simple, with little if any adornment, as was her way. He imagined she would wear her raven hair loose, and smiled sadly to think how the bridal veil would be a welcome sheath between herself and the reality of her situation, a barrier between herself and Celimus. But not for long. Once their vows were exchanged, the King would claim a kiss to seal the holy pact made before Shar, raising the veil and tearing away Valentyna's last protection.

Wyl could not help but recall how he had fallen in love with Valentyna at first sight. Dusty and dressed in riding breeches, she had had smudges on her cheeks and her hair had been falling about her face. She had reeked of horse and leather. Yet it had been his pleasure to kiss her hand and his heart's desire to ask for it in marriage, even on behalf of another. A smile had broken across her face like new sunlight; he had bathed in its warmth and his heart had become instantly hers.

But that was over now. It had all gone so terribly wrong. Above the roar of the crowd he could hear the cathedral bells pealing, heralding the impending marriage. Soon she would be the Morgravian Queen, married to his enemy, and he himself would be past caring about.

Wyl felt sick. He stumbled slightly and the soldier walking by his side instinctively threw out a steadying hand. "I'm not used to being in chains," Wyl lamented. The man nodded, clearly awkward.

And so I move between Kings today, Wyl thought, *and then I die.* He had not lived out the great Thirsk tradition of death on a battlefield; instead he would succumb to death enmeshed in a battle of magic he could not win. He was nothing more than an unwilling puppet.

"Wait." Wyl stopped, suddenly anxious. "The King will be present, I take it?"

"Yes, sire."

Relief flooded him. "Good. I want him to share my death," he said, surprising the Legionnaires around him by smiling fiercely.

Aremys had arrived only hours before the wedding procession, exhausted and dirty but relieved that he had made it to Pearlis in time. He used his strength to bully his way to the front of the crowd, earning disgruntled grumbles. One man risked hurling his displeasure at the bear, who simply turned and scowled at him through dark, hooded eyes. "Shut up!" was his reply, and all within earshot did just that.

Valentyna caught her breath at the first sight of the famed cathedral of Pearlis. Bells were pealing and heralds trumpeted her arrival into its grounds. She tried to imagine what Celimus was feeling inside the cathedral. Satisfaction, she decided. He had won. It seemed he always did where she was concerned.

Meanwhile, inside the hushed cathedral, King Celimus took the nod from Jessom that the Queen's carriage was pulling into the compound. The man looked thinner and more vulturelike than ever. Celimus had heard the whispered jokes about his chancellor's likeness to a carrion bird. It was actually a very good description, particularly today, he thought, wondering what was passing through Jessom's sharp and slippery mind. He did not trust him as he once had. There was defiance lurking behind that well-guarded facade. The King was not fooled: Jessom would switch allegiance in a blink if he thought the cards were going to fall the wrong way. And Celimus had begun to believe that the Chancellor might be considering his future quite carefully.

Jessom's fierce disagreement with the King's latest idea regarding King Cailech's execution had further fueled Celimus's mistrust. Where did the Chancellor's interest lie that he would advise so strongly against taking the Razor King's life?

"Is everything ready?" he whispered.

"Her majesty arrives, sire, yes," Jessom confirmed.

"Not her, you fool. Cailech?"

Jessom nodded in that slow, reptilian manner of his. "As you ordered, sire."

"Good. Now get out of my way. You're blocking the view of my latest conquest. This is a good day, Jessom. A very good day. Two monarchs will be brought to their knees before me." He laughed quietly, straightening the front of his black jacket. He knew he was resplendent in dashing crimson and noir with flashes of gold and a cape of the blackest yarn lined with the fiery red of Morgravia. He was looking forward to claiming Valentyna's maidenhood tonight and did not plan on being gentle about it. A husband must impress on his wife that he was in charge.

A remys watched with a heavy heart as Valentyna alighted from the carriage, aided by Commander Liryk. He had mixed feelings about the Briavellian who had helped him escape while at the same time aiding in the capture and imprisonment of King Cailech.

The Grenadyne assumed that Wyl was already cooling his heels in Stoneheart's dungeons. During the frenzied dash from Werryl to Pearlis, he had focused only on getting to the capital and finding a way to help Wyl. The promise he had made to Wyl burned brightly in his mind now. Would he be able to do it? Could he murder his closest friend? He had watched Wyl's strange journey through three lives and had come to love him in the way that King Cailech had once described his feelings for Lothryn: brotherhood, friendship, loyalty. Aremys felt an intense sorrow for Wyl's suffering, but he was not sure he could find the courage to kill the man he loved as a brother, even out of kindness.

Aremys pulled himself out of his dark thoughts as Valentyna approached. She looked more beautiful than he could ever have imagined, gliding alongside Commander Liryk, smiling softly to the crowd and carrying herself proud and erect. As she passed, and the cheering around him increased to its highest volume, he roared her name, not really expecting her to hear. Amazingly, she did, swinging around toward his voice.

When she saw him she faltered. "Aremys," she mouthed as she passed, and he lifted a hand in greeting. They were both thinking the same thing: *Wyl.* When she cast a last glance over her shoulder, looking at him through her veil, he nodded his encouragement to her.

And then she was gone in a fanfare of trumpets, through the massive double doors of the cathedral, swallowed into its dark depths and an uncertain future.

Crys Donal had seen the bride too, but had not been able to make eye contact with her—not that she would have recognized him if he had. His yellow hair was now a deep brown and he sported a beard and mustache, also darkened. Gone were the fine clothes, replaced with the uniform of a Legionnaire. He blended into the crowd perfectly, and as neither King Celimus nor those he kept close knew Crys Donal by sight, he felt relatively secure.

He used his height and newly assumed status to shoulder his way through the crowd toward the cathedral. It was acceptable for him, as a Legionnaire, to be seen crossing the unmarked line that separated onlookers from the participants, particularly when an officer hailed him.

"Soldier, are you on duty?"

"No, sir," Crys answered crisply. "Just part of the cheering crowd."

"Well, you're back on as of now. Get down to the cathedral's entrance and move that mob back. The happy couple won't be able to get out of the church if we don't create space for the carriage to come through."

"Understood, sir. Right away."

"Good lad," the officer said, and moved on.

Crys was jogged down the street in front of yet another sparkling new carriage designed for this special day. Black with crimson flourishes, it bore the King's personal device and its gold dragons glinted in the sunlight while bunting in emerald and violet flickered in the spring breeze. Other soldiers had been sent in as well and Crys joined them in pushing back the happy mob.

"If you tread on my foot again, I'll rip that beard off your chin, sonny," one big fellow said.

"Hello, Aremys," Crys murmured, and won the shocked gasp he expected. "It's Crys."

Aremys grinned in spite of his bleak mood. "Good to see you, Donal."

Crys looked around to see that no one was watching them. Not only could no one hear, but no one cared. The mood was festive and fun-filled. All the people wanted was their new queen and they chanted her name ceaselessly.

"The King won't care for that much," Aremys commented.

"He'll have to get used to it. It's her they've turned out in the thousands to see."

"Crys, I heard about your family. Shar, I'm so sorry, lad. I wish—"

"I know," Crys said softly. "Everyone does."

Aremys nodded. "Where's Elspyth?" he asked, then wished he had not when he saw how the youngster's face darkened.

"Come with me," Crys said. "They'll be an age yet and we need to talk."

He dragged Aremys out of the crowd and away from the main entry of the cathedral, finding a slightly more quiet spot around back. Crys told him everything but saved the worst until last. "A new infection has her in its grip. She seemed all right for a while and I assumed she would recover after the physic in Pearlis pronounced her wounds in good shape, but the trip to Argorn was too hard for her. By the time we got there, she was feverish again and high-colored."

"Why did you leave her?"

"Knave arrived—you know, that strange dog of Wyl's?" Aremys nodded. "Out of the blue, just walked into Argorn Manor."

"And . . .?"

"Elspyth rallied slightly at seeing him; she obviously understood better than I that he had come for us. Don't ask me how he knew where we were."

"You don't want to know," Aremys said. "It goes hand in hand with the Quickening and magic." He grimaced at the news of pretty Elspyth's sickness. "Is she under good care?"

"Yes. She had to stay in Argorn, of course, no chance of more travel. Another physic has seen her, but you know, Aremys, it's a bit like she's given up on herself, as though she doesn't want to fight anymore. It was so nasty what she went through." He shrugged awkwardly. "I just think she's accepting death."

"Go back there, then. Make her fight!"

Crys shook his head. "No, I'm no good for her. It's tricky—there are two other women there. Lady Bench and her daughter, Georgyana. The daughter is . . . well, she's lovely, and . . ."

"And what?" Aremys quizzed.

"Shar, but you can be dense sometimes, Farrow. I like her and she likes me. I think being around us makes it worse for Elspyth. She's so in love with Lothryn, as you know, and it hurts her to see us falling for each other."

"But that can't kill her, surely?" the big man growled.

"No, but that infection might, especially when she denies herself food, fights the medication, can't sleep—won't even try. She talks about leaving to find Lothryn, weeps that he's in pain, that he's been changed somehow." Crys ran his hands through his newly dark hair. "But she was lucid when Knave arrived. She seemed to know that he wanted us to go with him. I'm ashamed to say we had to tie her to the bed to stop her trying to accompany us."

"She's no good to anyone here," Aremys said gravely.

"I'm not sure any of us are any good here. She wept when I left, said we'd never see each other again. It's left me hollow, I can tell you."

"You're sure the women are safe there?"

"No one knows they're there, and Argorn has sealed its

collective mouth. What about your story—what's happened since we parted? Where is Wyl? More to the point, *who* is Wyl?"

"Would you believe me if I told you he is currently King Cailech?"

It was Crys's turn for disbelief. Aremys told him the whole story.

"So he's here right now? That's why Knave came for us."

"In the dungeon. I have no idea what's planned for him, though."

The Duke of Felrawthy turned ashen. "I think I do," he said. "Hurry, we must get to the dungeon. But first we need to disguise you as a Legionnnaire."

41

HE NEWLYWEDS EMERGED ONTO STONEHEART'S LARGEST balcony, known as the wedding balcony because it was the place where so many Morgravian Kings had presented their new queens to the people.

Valentyna's heart was pounding yet she felt somehow numb. It was done. The ceremony within the cathedral had dragged on, but she had spoken clearly when asked to take her vows, had even found a smile for the despised man beside her as she uttered the words that bound her to him for life. Their exit from the cathedral had provoked a rapturous noise she had not imagined possible. As the royal couple had walked to their new carriage, its dominant colors not lost on Valentyna, she had been showered with rose petals from blooms especially cultivated beneath glass. Their pastel colors joined the fresh whites of spring flowers. Underfoot, just before her, she had noticed a spray of lavender; it was so out of keeping with the roses and so dear to her heart that Valentyna had turned toward the man who'd thrown it. The Legionnaire had grinned, and she had suddenly recognized the Duke of Felrawthy despite his disguise.

"Thank you," she mouthed, but much as she wanted to bend and pick up the purple heads of her favorite flower, she had not wished to draw the King's attention to it. He was far too sharp not to wonder who had thought to throw lavender to the new Queen. She had stepped on it instead, crushing the heads and releasing the fragrance briefly before Celimus had helped her into the open-air carriage.

The noise had been deafening as they had made their slow way back toward the castle. Valentyna had searched for Aremys or Crys but had not seen either again. Inside the carriage the time had seemed right, so she had reached inside the small cream velvet pouch she carried.

"This, my lord, is for you," she had said in the sweetest voice she could muster, knowing she had to preserve the fragile bond they had formed.

Celimus had looked puzzled as he took the small, exquisitely lacquered box. She knew he was captivated by the way his mouth opened when he saw the gift inside.

"It is a lovely ring, Valentyna," he had whispered, and kissed her, much to the people's joy. "Will you put it on me?"

She did so. "I'm glad you like it."

"I will wear it always. I have something for you too," he replied. "It's being readied for you now."

"Oh?"

"A special surprise," he had promised, turning away to wave to the crowd.

And now she found herself waving from the wedding balcony to the sea of people below who had crowded into the main square before the castle.

"They are so proud of you, my lord," she said above the din, leaning close to be heard. She hated her obsequiousness.

"And they love you. I knew they would. You are very good for me," he replied. She knew he did not mean it as a romantic compliment. Celimus meant it literally: Valentyna made him look better; she was good for his image.

There was truly no hope for them, she thought. She would

struggle her entire life to be a sugary-sweet doormat just to
keep the peace between them. She could not do it. Just maintaining the delicate truce forged by her careful words on
their journey into Morgravia was destroying her soul. She
hated him. And tonight she was expected to respond passionately between the sheets with him. As she gazed out
across the ocean of smiling faces, Valentyna felt she would
rather die than have Celimus touch her intimately.

It seemed he had the same scene on his mind. "Tonight,"
he began, "when all the formalities are done with and we are
finally in bed, I mean to teach you something."

Valentyna tried but failed to sound seductive or indeed
even interested. "That sounds rather intriguing, my lord.
What can you mean?"

"I mean to teach you that I am not someone to be trifled
with."

Valentyna felt her body chill. He meant to hurt her. "I
don't understand, my lord." She tried for levity in her voice.

"I will teach you how the King of Morgravia expects his
Queen to behave."

"Have I disappointed you during the marriage proceedings?" she asked, all other sounds now fading to the background as she focused on his voice alone.

"You lied to me, barefaced and at a particularly poignant
moment. I am hurt by this."

She could not imagine Celimus emotionally hurt by anything, least of all words. "I don't understand, Celimus," Valentyna said, more firmly now, her mind racing. Which
particular lie might he be referring to?

"Cailech denied your story to me in person last night. Of
course I had hoped it was true, hoped I was the one who had
jumped to the wrong conclusion."

Something in Valentyna died. Wyl had refused her gift of
life. "I . . ." She struggled to form a response.

"Now," Celimus began brightly, waving to the people and
encouraging her to do the same, "I can forgive you this mis-
demeanor. You have behaved perfectly since our arrival at
Pearlis; I believe that you did not invite Cailech to Werryl,
nor did you know of his arrival there or his intention to stir

up war using Briavel as an ally. My belief is that you lied to save further bloodshed; you hoped to preserve the peace between the three realms. And I am delighted by the wedding gift you have given me. So I forgive you. But you will learn an important lesson tonight."

Valentyna began to say something, but he hushed her with his hateful hand against her mouth, replacing it quickly with his lips, much to the crowd's delight and her disgust.

"Hush, my love. Take your medicine and be pleased it's not more harsh. I appreciate that you are a virgin, though I cannot promise to be as gentle as I might have been a few days ago. Wave farewell to your people now and let me cheer you with my own special wedding gift as promised."

"I—"

"Hush. I shall wait while you change. I want you to wear crimson, the color of Morgravia."

A remys followed Crys blindly as they made their way to the Legionnaires' barracks. Stoneheart was like a town in itself—a maze of streets and openings, corridors and courtyards. When they finally reached their destination, the barracks were virtually deserted. Everyone was either on duty at the wedding or joining in the celebrations. Crys was able to sneak into the provisions office and take the biggest uniform he could find.

"I have no idea if this will fit," he said, returning to the small outbuilding where he had left Aremys, "but it's genuine Legionnaire, so it should do the trick and get you past security. Everyone's so preoccupied anyway—they'll see the crimson and black and no questions will be asked. Let's face it, it's likely none of the guards on duty around Cailech are going to be proper Legionnaires anyway—they're probably all mercenary impostors."

"I hope you're right," Aremys grumbled. "I'm sensing we have to get into the dungeon, right?" Crys nodded grimly. "Don't you think it will be heavily guarded, no strangers permitted?"

"We're not strangers. We're guards."

Aremys did not have the heart to argue. "Lead on," he said.

At the dungeon Crys discovered that the royal prisoner had been moved.

"We've been sent along to make up extra numbers. King's orders," Crys said to the officer there, trying his best to sound as uninterested as possible. "Who is the prisoner, anyway?"

The man ignored him. "Who sent you?"

Fortunately Crys knew the senior officers and captains of the Legion. "Captain Berryn," he said, giving the name of one of the more aggressive captains.

The man's tone changed instantly. "All right, how many of you?"

"There's two of us but I don't know how many others he is sending. We were told to report to you here," Crys lied.

"Why can't they send a runner and inform us of what they want? I'll tell you, it was different in the days when the Thirsks ran this outfit."

Crys shrugged, feigning indifference.

"Get your companion and follow me. I'm on my way there now. And listen, sonny, this is no sideshow, all right? Today we execute a king and you will behave with due respect. Is that clear?"

"Yes, sir," Crys said, straightening, glad that Wyl was at least being accorded due respect.

Crys and Aremys remained silent as they walked a few steps behind the officer. The man was so preoccupied with what was ahead that he ignored them totally anyway.

They arrived at the courtyard at almost the same time as the King and new Queen, but both had eyes only for the prisoner.

"Cover up, you know the drill," the officer said, handing them black hoods from a small sack he carried. He left immediately to confer with one of the captains on the other side of the courtyard.

Crys explained the hood to Aremys in a low whisper. "It's an old custom dating back to the first persecution of witches and sorcerers. It was held that empowered people had to see a person to cast a spell against them. The mask was introduced to ensure that anyone present at an execution would be impervious to their magic. The belief died out over the centuries, but soldiers are still required by tradition to cover their faces at executions."

"Suits me," said Aremys. "At least we won't risk being recognized by the King or Jessom."

Valentyna stood in the crimson gown Celimus had ordered made for her and then demanded she wear. She did not notice the trio of Legionnaires arrive in the courtyard. Anger, fear, and the hideous injustice of the position she found herself in quickly gave way to a feeling of desolation when her gaze followed the King's pointing finger. Chained to a post like an animal, but still looking proud, was Wyl: tall and golden, fury burning in his eyes and a defiant set to his jaw. Now she felt weak, overcome by a combination of terror and an overwhelming rush of love.

Wyl's light green gaze left her and fell on Celimus. A smirk crossed Cailech's face and he raised a fist and turned the clenched fingers toward his Morgravian counterpart. A northerner would know that this was the sign that the tribes of the Razors gave to indicate a declaration of war.

Crys looked helplessly at his companion, not understanding.

"He's baiting the King," Aremys muttered.

"Why? Surely there's enough bad feeling?" Crys whispered.

"Wyl is trying to ensure that the King will personally kill him, although I'm not sure the Quickening obeys such laws."

Dawning had spread on the Duke's face beneath his hood. "He will be our king, then?"

Aremys nodded as they watched Wyl being unchained from the post. But not for long, he thought in private anguish.

Valentyna felt as though she could no longer breathe. Tears were streaming down her face.

"I didn't know you cared for him that much, my love," Celimus cooed.

"Why must he die?"

"Because he can't be trusted. He will always be a danger to us."

"But killing him will merely enrage the Mountain People

and encourage them to wage their own war against both our realms."

"You have no realm now, beloved."

"What?"

"Briavel is now part of Morgravia. I now rule both our realms—that's my job. Your job is to swiftly become pregnant with my sons and be a smiling, loving wife. You will no longer worry about realms, politics, war, strategy—I shall take care of all that. And I am not in the slightest bit intimidated by the Razor Kingdom."

Valentyna could not stand to be beside him for another moment. With a final glance toward Cailech's granite expression, she feigned weariness and asked to be excused.

"Soon enough," Celimus said. "But first let me deliver my gift to you."

"What do you mean?" she asked, fresh anxiety washing over her.

"You must bear witness, my love. I am executing King Cailech in your honor. He will never trouble you again."

"I refuse—"

"You refuse me *nothing,* wife! Remember, you belong to Morgravia now . . . and to its king."

42

YL WAS LED UP ONTO A HASTILY BUILT WOODEN STAGE. Despite that touch of theater, it was a lonely scene for a king's end. The only witnesses were the two royals, a few guards, the Chancellor, and, of course, the masked executioner, who had just arrived.

Wyl was not afraid. The truth was, he could not wait to die again, and feel the Quickening release him from Myrren's Gift and the curse she had brought over his life. He would not have to live long as Celimus. Just long enough to be with Valentyna again, to hold her once more.

And if it all went sadly awry, he would still live—this time as a burly man of enormous strength and stature. Wyl had taken the precaution of discovering the executioner's name: Art Featherstone. He wondered briefly how, in the guise of the executioner, he would ever contrive to get close enough to Celimus for Myrren's Gift to come into play again, but gave up the line of thought. Whoever could have thought that Wyl would become Romen, or that Faryl would claim Romen's life, or that Ylena—he faltered on hearing her name in his thoughts—would kill Faryl and become her brother's host. And now here he was, the King of the Razors, about to become the King of Morgravia . . . or the burly executioner.

He had done his best to plant the seed, without actually inviting death—surely Celimus would find the temptation to personally separate King Cailech's head from his body irresistible? It would be another triumph for the Crown.

A huge Legionnaire came up with a cup of water. "Orders," the man said toward the executioner, who nodded, uncaring.

Wyl's spirits lifted at the sound of the man's voice. "Aremys," he whispered as the Grenadyne gave him the cup.

"I beg you, don't make me keep the promise," Aremys muttered beneath his breath.

"You will keep it if you care anything for me," Wyl growled.

Aremys stared into the green eyes, then nodded sadly. "As One," he said, walking away.

A single trumpet sounded and Wyl noticed for the first time that Valentyna was dressed in a crimson gown. The color of Morgravia. The color of blood. She was solemn-faced and looked intensely frightened. He wished he could spare her this—had hoped against hope that Celimus would come without her.

Valentyna would not look at anyone—not even at Wyl. He could not blame her. It must have felt like a shocking betrayal to hear that he had denied her fabricated story. He understood, but it did not make it any easier to see her ignoring him. Was it just two days ago they had been making love at Werryl? As the killing blow fell he would cling to that, remember what it felt like to lie naked with Valentyna and love her as she loved him.

Celimus guided his wife to a pair of thronelike seats hurriedly erected in the courtyard. He kissed her hand, winning a sickly grimace from the Queen. Her expression did not seem to matter to Celimus, who was now announcing why the King of the Mountains was to die.

Wyl looked toward Jessom as the King spoke and remembered the strange blue light entwining their hands in the dungeon, binding them to each other. He wondered if Fynch was right, if the Chancellor might somehow provide that random element that could outwit Myrren's Gift. Turning his attention back to Celimus's speech, Wyl heard that he was to be sacrificed as a wedding gift to Valentyna. At this, he withdrew into himself, praying to Shar that the King of Morgravia would see fit to gift Valentyna by making the killing blow himself.

Valentyna had withdrawn too. There was nothing to live for anymore. Soon she would have to witness the death of the man she loved, his head savagely removed from his neck with, hopefully, one swing of a cruel sword. It was too much for her heart to bear.

And after all of that, all that was left for her was Celimus, who had made his despicable intentions very clear. Her notion that she might be able to dupe him into believing she was true had been naive. Celimus was too sharp to fall for that ruse, although he would still expect her to treat him as she had promised, even if she was pretending every minute of every day.

He would continue to hurt her, she knew—first taking Wyl from her, then Briavel, no doubt ultimately taking away every son she bore. Her life would be utterly controlled by him. Bile rose to her throat as she imagined what he was going to do her tonight. Rape, she was sure, would be the very least of it.

Celimus had finished explaining his reasons for executing the treacherous Mountain King and the sudden silence dragged her out of her thoughts. She looked at Cailech, whose shirt was being cut away to reveal his broad torso, sculpted with muscles. She remembered that body well, riding above her in an urgent rhythm, each thrust taking her to a higher level of pleasure.

Chancellor Jessom, looking appropriately somber in black robes, gravely pronounced the Crown's sentence on the accused. "Have you anything to say, Cailech, King of the Mountains?" he asked finally.

Wyl spoke clearly. "Legionnaires, remember who you are. Remember your oath to protect and serve Morgravians above all others. Above all others," he stressed, "even above your king—"

"Enough!" roared Celimus, enraged.

At the King's signal, the beefy executioner backhanded the prisoner, who stumbled but did not fall, despite his manacled ankles.

Wyl knew the guards were probably not Legionnaires— Celimus would not risk them witnessing such an unlawful execution. Nevertheless, he hoped the insult had been sufficient to provoke Celimus into swinging the death sword himself.

"Get on with it!" the King ordered the executioner. "My wife and I wish to continue our wedding festivities."

"You accuse me of treachery, King Celimus. I'm surprised you aren't carrying out that threat you made in the dungeon! Or are you too squeamish to risk my blood on your fine garments?" Wyl roared, hoping his lie would get lost in the alarm his words would prompt. He knew he must not try to force death, but perhaps he could needle Celimus into picking up a weapon and killing him in wrath, as Cailech had killed Ylena. "My hunch is that you have never killed anyone yourself but always get others to do it for you, you sniveling coward. A poor shadow of your father," he added, sneering.

His challenge was greeted with stunned silence as all gathered turned to watch the young King of Morgravia.

Celimus's voice sounded as cold as the ice from Cailech's own mountains when it finally came. "I made no threat but you should be assured that I have never been scared to spill your blood, Cailech."

"Is that so? I'm sure you'll never prove such a claim," Wyl taunted, laughing.

Valentyna could not bear it. Wyl had already severed the lifeline she had thrown him and now he wanted to make sure that Celimus chopped his head off? Why? Surely he would prefer the accurate swing of an executioner over the perhaps deliberately clumsy hacking by a man whom he'd just publicly scorned? Wyl had gone mad. He would die painfully and then Celimus would—

Valentyna caught her breath audibly as the realization hit hard. And then Celimus would become Wyl!

Oh Shar! He was doing it deliberately so that Celimus would die and Wyl would take over his body, becoming the King, and her husband. Wyl would live on because of Myrren's Gift! Now her breath came hard and fast and her pulse began to race. She stood. "Do it for me, Celimus!" she cried, her cheeks flushed, her heart pounding.

The King swung around in surprise. "You want me to kill him?"

"Yes," she demanded. "He has driven a wedge between us with his underhanded dealings. I hate him. I hate his treachery. Kill him, Celimus. Do it with your own hand so that we are free of his curse on our lives. That would be my ultimate wedding gift, sire." She curtsied low, ensuring that her husband saw the swell of her breasts.

Celimus grinned ferociously. He looked like a wolf closing in on its prey as he peeled off his cloak, the crimson lining reminding everyone of the blood he would shortly spill.

Valentyna could hardly believe it. Her spirits were soaring with the hammering of her heart. She would have Wyl. She would have Romen. She would have Cailech. He would be Celimus, but the real Celimus would be dead. *Thank you, Myrren,* she whispered. *Thank you, Shar.*

"Come, stand closer, my love," Celimus called to her. "You must share in this, my wedding gift to you."

Cailech was forced to his knees. Valentyna, no longer afraid, glided confidently toward the husband she despised, her eyes locked on the man who would soon be her one love. She leaned forward and kissed Celimus, making it as tender as she could. She wanted him to know how much this meant to her.

Wyl felt sickened by the kiss and closed his eyes. He knew Valentyna had guessed what was going to happen; he had seen it reflected in the blaze of her eyes and the hungry expression she suddenly wore. But he did not believe she could live alongside him once he was in the body of the Morgravian King. Celimus had damaged them both too much. *Hurry, Shar damn you,* he thought, opening his eyes and silently urging the King on. He lowered his head to the block and bared his thick neck.

But Celimus hesitated. He too had noted the change in his wife's demeanor. The kiss was a surprise, especially after his threat on the balcony barely an hour ago. He thought about her behavior since: one moment despairing, the next filled with a fervor he did not know she possessed. She looked rejuvenated, excited . . . she looked hungry. What could possibly have had that effect on her? Surely not the mention of blood. Even the little he knew of her confirmed that she was far from bloodthirsty—she was marrying him simply to prevent bloodshed. No, it was not that. Yet her whole manner had changed at the suggestion that he kill Cailech himself, galvanizing her into this lustful creature. Her eyes blazed with a passion he had not seen since that night in Briavel when they had danced together. And even then he had felt sure the fervor had not been for him.

Celimus's sharp mind worked across every possible scenario but came up wanting. He could find no logical explanation for this odd change of heart. Valentyna had lied to save this man's life, had wept at the thought of him dying just moments earlier, yet now she was begging for his execution at the King's own hand. His instincts screamed that there was duplicity here, but he could not get to the truth. He would test her.

"No!" he roared. "The King of Morgravia will not tarnish his wedding day by dirtying his hands with blood."

"But, my lord," Valentyna cried, "this is for me. I want his head."

"And you shall have it, I promise." Celimus turned back to the executioner. "Do your job: Behead the treacherous sovereign on behalf of Morgravia and Briavel," he ordered.

Celimus took Valentyna's hand and led her back to their thrones. She felt breathless with panic. The King had thwarted them. If Myrren's Gift continued, Wyl would become the bald-headed executioner. What a terrible irony, she thought. Only weeks ago she had scorned Fynch for believing in magic, and now here she was pinning everything on the hope of an enchantment. If that hope failed, Valentyna knew in her heart that she would not lie with Celimus tonight . . . or any night. She would take her own life if need be.

She shook her mind clear as the executioner lined up for his single killing blow. The least she could do for Wyl was bear witness to his brave death. She watched the big man raise his sword slowly, carefully, smoothly. It reached the apex of his swing and was about to fall with its severing blow when she heard herself shriek, "Wait!" The man teetered and then stopped, looking angrily toward King Celimus for guidance.

"What is it, Valentyna?" Celimus asked smoothly. Perhaps now the truth of her strange behavior would reveal itself.

"Let me do it, sire," she begged, for his hearing only. It was the only way out for her.

For the first time since she'd known him, Valentyna saw hesitancy and alarm on his face. "You would kill this man?"

"For you, Celimus. It is the only way I can resolve the difficulties between us."

"Through his death?" he queried, wondering if she had gone mad.

"Yes," she whispered. "He will release us. You will know I am true to you if I do this."

Celimus shook his head, baffled. Nevertheless, the shock of her suggestion titillated his sadistic streak. He rather liked the idea of her executing Cailech. Such an act would haunt her forever, offering further opportunity for exploitation. She would be even more easily controlled when her demons rose to remind her of this ugly spectacle. It would also, of course, show her to be a strong person, either terrifying or inspiring the onlookers—either way suited him.

He studied her and she stared back at him hungrily. There was no doubting she meant her words.

"It is not a pleasant thing you request, Valentyna. You will have to live with this memory all of your life."

"You have no idea how important that notion is to me, sire."

He shook his head, as if washing his hands of her. "As you wish."

He turned to the executioner. "Bind the prisoner's mouth," he ordered, knowing Cailech was likely to make a fuss when he learned of this new and exciting turn of events. The idea of his queen killing a man made Celimus feel like rutting. His mind slithered toward the bedchamber. An heir would be made tonight, he was sure of it. He would have his first son before next spring.

Wyl looked around, confused. He watched Celimus stand once again, hoping against hope that the King had had a change of heart and would deliver the killing blow. But it was Valentyna who walked toward him.

"No!" he shouted from beneath the bindings, but it came out as a strangled cry. His eyes were wide with horror at her decision.

Valentyna glided toward him in her bloodred gown and Wyl was suddenly reminded of his dream at Tenterdyn. This was it. No dream, but a premonition. She bent toward him, tears streaming down her face. "Forgive me," she whispered, and he roared his anguish, not caring that it appeared he was about to die cringing like a coward.

The executioner pushed Cailech's head down onto the block again. "Don't make it harder for her," he growled. "She'll never survive it if she misses."

Wyl knew the man spoke the truth and he stopped struggling. He did not want to become Valentyna. He did not want her to sacrifice herself for him. He could hear her shallow, terrified breathing. The courtyard was so silent he was sure he could hear her heartbeat too. It was too much for his own bleeding heart. Wyl closed his eyes and begged for a miracle that might thwart Myrren and her cursed gift.

Fynch! he called silently

Valentyna lifted the sword. She took a moment to pray for her own soul before she screamed her despair, pouring her sorrow, pain, and anguish into the downward sweep that severed King Cailech's head from his neck.

She sank slowly to her knees in his blood, her heart aching, tears streaming, and waited for the change to come over her body. She had no idea what to expect or how the magic worked. All she knew was that she would accept him gladly. This would be her ultimate sacrifice, the final demonstration of her love.

Behind her, Celimus's dark olive eyes sparked with the fire of lust for this woman and the joy of knowing his final enemy was slain. He was Emperor now—and perhaps Valentyna had just shown herself worthy of the title of Empress.

Nearby, Chancellor Jessom's body sagged and he hung his head as he struggled slightly to breathe. He would need to gather his composure quickly.

The King of the Razors' body was slumped forward over the block. The executioner bent to pick up the head, which had rolled to his feet. For the umpteenth time he wondered whether the brain remained alive just long enough to know its head had been removed from its body. At the King's nod, Art Featherstone placed the head of the Mountain sovereign in a leather sack. He would take care of the body once the royal party had departed.

Valentyna felt nothing. Not even a single tear. Was she now Wyl? Had her soul left her body? She was confused. Her hands were slick with his blood, and through her wet eyes she could focus on nothing else.

"Come, Valentyna," said the voice she hated more than any in the world, and then she felt the King of Morgravia's touch. She turned away from the headless body to look at Celimus and knew in that instant that something had gone terribly wrong. It had all been a lie. The Quickening was not real. Cailech was dead and the story about Wyl Thirsk must have been some sort of cruel ruse. She was alive and her husband awaited her.

"Jessom," the King said.

The Chancellor looked up and cleared his throat. "Sire?"

"Help Queen Valentyna to her chambers. I will see you both there shortly."

"Yes, your majesty," the Chancellor said, offering his arm to the Queen. Her pale skin was spattered with blood. "You, guard," he called to Aremys, and beckoned. Aremys moved silently toward the Chancellor; he could not risk being recognized. "You look a burly enough fellow. Help the executioner remove the body immediately and lock it away. Bring the key to me. No one is to be permitted entry. Is that clear?" Aremys nodded.

Jessom looked directly at Crys. "And you, take an inventory of all present, including guards and the herald. I want the names brought immediately to me in the Queen's chambers. Is that understood?"

Crys, puzzled, nodded beneath his hood, avoiding speech for the same reason Aremys had.

Jessom looked as stunned as the Queen by the afternoon's events. Moving with uncharacteristic awkwardness but quickly, he hurried Valentyna from the scene of death, and using back corridors that only he seemed to know about, he got the silent, shivering bride to her suite of rooms.

43

HANCELLOR JESSOM WAS SURPRISINGLY TENDER WITH HER, but Valentyna was too lost in her own darkness to notice. He wet a square of linen and wiped her face and hands clean of the blood, and tried gently to get her to talk. There were important things she must understand before the King arrived.

"What can I do to help you, my queen?" he whispered,

wondering how to revive her from this stricken state before he began to explain his new situation.

Valentyna was in utter turmoil. What had gone wrong? She was still herself . . . and Cailech was dead. She had killed him, and Wyl had not possessed her. Everyone had lied to her. Fynch, Elspyth, Cailech . . . but why? She groaned involuntarily. It was a sound of such anguish that she saw fear pass across the hook-nosed Chancellor's face. Why was he showing her such concern?

"Your majesty?" Jessom whispered, trying to bring her back to the present.

"Kill me," she whispered. "Before I have to spend a night with him."

"I cannot do that, your highness."

"Then I shall kill myself," she said, color flushing her ghastly, almost yellow complexion.

She saw him flinch. "Please don't, your majesty. Listen to me: I made a promise to King Cailech yesterday that I would offer you my protection. Rest assured, my word is true. I am now your servant, your highness." He broke protocol by taking her hand and placing it on his heart. She tried to pull it back, repulsed, but he held it firmly in place. "You must trust me," he begged her. "King Cailech—"

She cut across his words. "Why do you offer your allegiance to me? You are the King's man."

"You must trust me, please," he repeated. He took her dull silence as agreement. "The King is on his way here, your majesty. I have important information to share with you, but let me organize some refreshment so it arrives before Celimus does. I will be only moments." He swiftly exited the chamber.

Valentyna did not move, knowing he would not leave her alone long enough to end her life. It briefly occurred to her that the Chancellor was treating her far more kindly than she had expected. Perhaps the Mountain King had indeed managed to persuade him to watch over her. Jessom could not protect her, however, from Celimus's attentions tonight. She felt bile rise again, thought she might be sick. It mattered not—by tonight she planned to be dead herself. Jessom returned. He was breathing hard, as if he had been running. "Ah, here we are now, your highness. Please drink this."

"What is it?"

"The King's favorite wine. It has a rich and full flavor. It suits only the heaviest of foods because it tends to overpower other tastes, but then the King does not take a midday meal and thus favors the heaviness."

Valentyna wondered why the Chancellor was giving her such an in-depth description of the wine. Perhaps he thought she needed educating on Celimus's preferences.

The door suddenly opened and the King of Morgravia himself stood before her. His cheeks were flushed and he looked triumphant. "You were magnificent, Valentyna," he said, laughing. "Do you still have his blood on you, you savage Briavellian?"

"I washed it away, your highness," Jessom said softly. He was ignored by both King and Queen.

Valentyna stood and curtsied. "I don't know what came over me, sire."

"I do," Celimus said, taking the proffered goblet of wine from Jessom without even looking at his chancellor. "It was a wonderful demonstration of patriotism. I am proud of you. To us," he said, raising his glass.

"To us," Valentyna echoed. She thought of her father's small dagger, which she had packed and brought with her to Morgravia. It had been for the sake of sentimentality that she had wrapped it so carefully in muslin and laid it among her things. Shortly it would serve a different purpose, bringing welcome death when it opened the arteries at her wrists.

Celimus drained his glass. It was swiftly taken away and refilled by Jessom, then returned as surreptitiously.

"Are you feeling up to the feast, my love?" the King asked.

"I will change, I think," Valentyna replied drily, looking at her stained gown.

The King sniggered at the jest. "Of course, go ahead. The nobles can wait. I'll hang on to the gown for posterity, though; Cailech's dried blood will make an amusing keepsake."

"More wine, sire?" Jessom said, stepping forward.

Valentyna watched Celimus drain his second glass of wine and knew that by tonight he would be intoxicated and even more determined to keep his promise. Jessom filled the glass for a third time and Valentyna grimaced, wishing the Chancellor would stop plying the King with so much liquor.

"I won't be long," she said. She was backing into her dressing chamber when she saw the King stagger slightly.

"Are you all right, sire?" Jessom asked.

"Shar, but I feel a little odd," Celimus said.

"Well, I imagine that's the poison I put in your glass, sire," Jessom offered matter-of-factly.

Valentyna's mouth fell open. "Poison?" she echoed. Her gaze moved from the King's suddenly haggard expression to the victorious face of his chancellor.

"Yes, your majesties," Jessom replied. "Valentyna, you don't love the King, I most certainly don't love the King, the nobles despise him, and Morgravia will hardly miss him—I decided we were all better off without him."

Celimus tried to move toward the Chancellor, but succeeded only in twitching awkwardly.

"Ah yes, I think the paralysis must be setting in by now, and because you drank two . . ."—Jessom gave a soft chortle as he checked the glass decanter in his hand—"almost three glasses, each with a hefty dose of the poison, it will work fast. So let's talk swiftly."

Celimus made to speak, but nothing of sense came from his lips. He spilled the tiny amount of liquid left in his glass down his front, the glass itself rolling off his lap and hitting the edge of the chair before falling to the floor and shattering.

"No matter, sire, we can clean that up along with your corpse. This is a wonderfully lethal potion Jessom discovered just recently. It kills cleanly, without a giveaway smell and no telltale signs left behind on the body. I'm afraid it's not a very pleasant death for the victim—no doubt quite similar to the one Eryd Bench would have experienced," Jessom went on. "A hideously agonizing end, which is less than you deserve, sire, if I might say so."

Valentyna was slowly shaking her head in disbelief; Celimus bared his teeth ferociously.

"Not long now, sire, I promise. Your highness"—Jessom turned to a stunned Valentyna—"if you have anything to say to him, say it now. We have about ten minutes at most before his heart stops."

She had never been more unnerved. "You have really poisoned him?"

The Chancellor nodded. "I had to run back to Jessom's rooms to get the vial, which is why I was so out of breath, your majesty."

She frowned. "Why do you speak of Jessom as though you were elsewhere?"

"Oops. How forgetful of me," the Chancellor replied, clearly enjoying himself. He gave a sly grin that Valentyna did not understand. "Look at me, Celimus," he demanded, his voice no longer playful as he moved to stand in front of the King. "Watch carefully."

Chancellor Jessom closed his eyes; Valentyna could swear she heard him softly call the name Fynch. A blue shimmering light appeared around his body, burning him, dissolving him. Then her hand moved to her mouth to stifle the scream of disbelief, for beneath the shimmering, another man was emerging. As Jessom disappeared into the blue furnace, it was Cailech who lifted his proud head, Cailech's eyes that opened to look into hers, Cailech's beloved face that looked at her with such love.

Valentyna felt herself tremble and she began to weep, unable to understand what was happening. Could this be true?

Thank you, Fynch, Wyl whispered across the miles. And deep in the heart of the Thicket, a boy smiled.

"It is I, Valentyna," Wyl said gently.

She shook her head, hardly daring to trust him. "I killed you."

"You killed Jessom."

"How?" Her voice was a groan.

"Fynch made it possible for me to swap places with Jessom temporarily, and for the Chancellor to impersonate Cailech. He called it the Bridge of Souls."

"Magic?" she whispered.

"That's right, my love, a clever glamour and a transference between bodies. Fynch came to me in the dungeon and asked me to trust him. I was not of a mind to grasp what he was offering; I only believed it myself when I realized Cailech was screaming and yet it was not me making that sound. Fynch gave his last reserves for us, Valentyna. He worked out that if Myrren and her father could weave such a curse, though he could not undo it, he could reweave it to truly make it a gift."

"A gift of life?"

Wyl nodded. "In the truest sense. I don't plan on changing again. I hope you like me enough as Cailech." Valentyna put her head in her hands, overwhelmed by emotion. Wyl took her in his arms and kissed her bent head. Then he looked across to Celimus; the King's eyes were disbelieving and glassy, and spittle dribbled through lips pulled back in a rictus of anger.

"I think we just have enough time for me to tell you a story, Celimus," Wyl said coldly. He settled Valentyna in a chair and held her hand, but stared directly at the dying King as he spoke briefly and succinctly, starting in the dungeon of Stoneheart, where a young woman named Myrren was being tortured and a boy named Wyl Thirsk offered her pity.

Valentyna felt awed at hearing the story in its entirety. Somehow it was fitting that its full telling should take place before the man who had been the source of it all. Myrren was truly avenged now.

"And Jessom?" Valentyna asked when Wyl was finished. She needed to understand how the Chancellor's fate had become so closely linked with her future happiness.

"Jessom was a parasite, Valentyna. He might not have made the cruel decisions himself, but he saw that they were carried out. The blood of too many people was on his hands. It was fitting that he should suffer for his sins. I suspect he was ready to swap allegiances, but instead the Bridge of Souls saw to it that he swapped bodies."

"So you knelt there and let me pretend to kill you," she said, aghast.

"It wasn't easy. You must know I was happy to die, and I had hoped to die by Celimus's hand," he said, glancing at the

King. "Fynch warned me once of the power random acts had to affect the Quickening, but I could never have foreseen that you might make such a sacrifice. Fynch could, and he took appropriate precautions."

"He knew I would do such a thing?"

Wyl shook his head. "None of us did. Not even you, I imagine. Fynch just seems to see the larger picture. I think he understood that an unpremeditated action might change the pattern of life, and he put his Bridge of Souls in place so that I might be saved, come what may."

"That child is too clever by half."

Wyl fixed her with his green gaze, knowing he could not hide the truth from her. "I believe Fynch is dead, Valentyna."

Her throat swelled with fresh grief. "No!"

"He used what was left of his spirit to help us. It is a long story, my love—one I shall share with you later. First I must finish my task here."

Celimus groaned. His fingers had shaped themselves into claws and Wyl had no doubt that the King was in pain.

"It's over, Celimus," he said, feeling very little satisfaction at seeing the once-proud sovereign arch in death's paralysis. "Let Shar's Gatherers take you now, and may our god alone have the generosity to show you mercy."

Celimus found one last spurt of energy to gurgle his fury and suddenly Wyl felt a sharp pain, like a blade of ice, cutting through Cailech's body and forcing a cry from him.

"What is it?" Valentyna said, grabbing his arm. Wyl barely felt her touch or heard her; his vision dimmed and he could no longer see the chamber around him. But he knew where he was. He was with Celimus.

You! Celimus whispered.

And Wyl understood: This was Myrren's parting gift, her final vengeance. She was showing Celimus the truth.

I'm glad you can see me at last, Celimus. It was no longer Cailech before the King, but a short, redheaded man. Wyl Thirsk, General of the Morgravian Legion.

The Legion and the nobles will not permit it, Celimus screamed into the mind of his nemesis.

You forget, they do not see me; they see only a crowned

*monarch you yourself have forged a truce with. Very few
know I was captured and incarcerated, and even fewer know
of my death.*

*You will not take my throne. Morgravia will never accept
a Mountain King.*

*I don't have to. You gave your throne to Valentyna the mo-
ment you married her, Celimus. She is the ruler of both
realms now. But I will become sovereign of Morgravia when
I marry her. I have to, you see, to fulfill Myrren's Gift and
rid myself fully of the Quickening. It demands that I be sovereign.*

The King of Morgravia screamed his despair into his
rival's mind as he sighted Shar's Gatherers approaching.

44

HERE WAS A KNOCK AT THE DOOR. "CHANCELLOR JESSOM?" A
voice called.

"It's Aremys and Crys," Wyl said, closing the eyes of the
dead King. He had hoped to have a few minutes alone with
the Queen, but the Grenadyne had obviously done his duty
quickly. He strode to the door and pulled it open. Instantly
the color in the two familiar faces before him drained as they
gazed upon the ghost of a man they had watched die just
moments before.

"What in Shar's name—" Aremys began.

"Hush, come in quickly," Wyl said. He felt sorry for their
shock, but there was no time to spare for niceties. "Shut the
door behind you. Hello, Crys. Oh, I think I should say 'carving knife.' " He grinned.

The newcomers entered the chamber tentatively. At the
same moment, they spotted the familiar figure slumped in a
chair.

"Celimus is dead?" Crys whispered, his gaze moving to Valentyna and then returning with fresh fear to Wyl.

Wyl nodded.

"Wait!" Aremys demanded. "What's going on? Cailech is dead! I watched it happen. I waited for the Quickening but saw no evidence of it. I feared you had died for good."

"As you see, I'm very much alive," Wyl replied, taking a grim pleasure in his friend's shock. "It was Fynch. He worked out a way to channel his own magic to save me without disturbing Myrren's Gift."

"How?" the two men asked at once, awe in their voices. Then Crys nudged Aremys and both bowed to their queen. "Your majesty," they said, embarrassed at their lack of courtesy.

Valentyna smiled and shook her head. "I'm too unsettled to even notice any lapses in protocol."

"Tell us," Aremys said, turning back to Wyl. "What did Fynch contrive?"

"He swapped me with Jessom."

"So Jessom was executed?" Aremys said, his wonder obvious.

"Fynch called it a Bridge of Souls," Wyl answered. "He came to me in the dungeon. He begged me to trust him and mentioned the Bridge of Souls, but he did not explain it and I didn't ask him to elaborate. My mood was grim, and much as I treasured seeing him once more, I didn't think anything could change the course I was on."

"I thought you'd become the Queen," Crys finally said, his relief evident. "No disrespect, your majesty," he said to Valentyna.

And then suddenly Aremys had Wyl in a bearlike hug. Wyl reached out a long arm to encompass Crys in the embrace. Valentyna had to look away, the rush of emotion she felt at witnessing their relief echoing her own. She wished she could join them, but sensed this was a special moment between the three men. There would be time ahead for her and Wyl to share their feelings.

Finally the men pulled apart. The newcomers examined for themselves the cooling corpse of King Celimus.

"What happened?" Aremys asked, delight obvious in his voice.

"Jessom poisoned him—I mean, I did. As soon as the King was as good as dead, I was released from the glamour and could reveal the truth to him."

Aremys scratched his head, unsure of what to say or do. He followed his gut instinct and knelt before the two royals. "Your majesties, my sword is yours to command. Although do not ask me to use it on you now, Wyl."

The King laid a hand on the warrior's bowed head. "I won't, Aremys, my great friend. Only we four know of what has truly occurred today. No one else need ever find out."

"So you will remain as Cailech, is that it?" Aremys asked carefully as he stood. "But Myrren's Gift demands that you become sovereign of Morgravia!"

Valentyna spoke up. "We shall marry as soon as it is feasible. It must be with the nobles' permission, but most blessed my strategic marriage to Celimus. Why not a second union in the name of peace?"

Crys Donal nodded. "That's true. And there are rumblings among the true Legionnaires about a civil uprising backed by key nobles. It doesn't seem to be idle gossip any longer. I just have one question: How will you explain the King's death?"

Wyl began to pace the room. Shocked and overwrought as she was, Valentyna could not help but smile to see Cailech's large hand tug at his earlobe in a gesture unique to Wyl Thirsk.

"Jessom poisoned the King and then fled," Wyl said. "The only other person in the chamber was Valentyna, but she had retired to her dressing room to change into her gown for the wedding banquet. She saw the Chancellor pour the wine for the King before she left the room—and we still have the wine in the decanter to prove that it was poisoned. When Valentyna returned, ready to attend her wedding feast, she found the King in his death throes and raised the alarm. You and I, Aremys, had come to pay our respects to the newly married couple, and so were on hand to hear the Queen's cries. We hunted down the Chancellor and dispatched him quickly and without honor, as befitting a traitor. That will also explain his corpse's headless state, should news of it get out."

Wyl paused and looked at his friend. "Is this all right with you?"

"My pleasure to be responsible for his death," the big man replied. "I'll ensure the body is disposed of carefully too."

"What about the executioner?" Valentyna asked. "He will know that it was Cailech I executed, not Jessom. And there were a few guards in the courtyard too."

"Apparently they were all mercenaries, your majesty," Crys offered, "not true Legionnaires, and I have a list here of their names, as Jessom—I mean, Wyl—ordered. We can easily track them down and either pay them to keep their silence, or use other means. Same for the executioner."

"The executioner need not die. He is a good man," Wyl said, remembering how Featherstone had asked him not to make Valentyna's task any harder. "When you find him, bring him to me. I shall explain." He offered no further explanation and no one pushed him for one.

"What reason do we hazard for Jessom's betrayal of the King?" Crys asked.

Wyl tugged at his ear again. "I can say I had a discussion with Jessom the night before the wedding and shared with him my understanding that Celimus intended to lay the blame for so many deaths at the Chancellor's feet. The King would have needed to explain to the nobles somehow, and that would be an ideal solution. And so they will assume that Jessom killed Celimus out of revenge. Let's be honest, few of the nobles are going to grieve at the news of the King's death."

"They'll probably have to grit their teeth to prevent themselves from cheering, if truth be known," Aremys commented.

"Then we have the perfect opportunity at the wedding feast to explain our position," Wyl continued. "We should be as honest as we can. Celimus is dead—we cannot escape this."

"I shall throw Felrawthy's support behind Valentyna as

the new sovereign of Morgravia," Crys Donal offered. "Hopefully others will follow the Donal lead."

"That's generous of you, Crys," Valentyna said, "but I worry about Morgravia accepting me. Surely there is another family they would argue is more suitable?"

"They might," Crys said, "but that family is my own; we are distantly related to the Crown. And I would not accept— believe me, it's the last thing I wish for. I belong in the north and you, Valentyna, already have one crown on your head. In marrying Celimus, you accepted the second."

"He's right," Wyl said. "And I think they will accept you if the right voices are behind you. We must speak with Lord Hartley too—he is a powerful voice and will probably be the most pleased among the lords to hear of Celimus's death, as he only just escaped being killed himself. We can thank Jessom for that mercy." Wyl turned to Crys. "You can't be seen here. The nobles have been told that Cailech slaughtered your family, so it's unthinkable you would even be in the same room as him. In fact, you should change into your formal wear, get your hair color back to normal, and join the nobles to hear what is said at the wedding feast."

Crys nodded. "So I know nothing of this, right?"

"Correct," Wyl said. "But we shall be revealing the fact of Celimus's death at the banquet, so you can have your say then."

Valentyna said aloud what they were all thinking. "I know this is all a lie, but Celimus and Jessom deserve no better."

Aremys had one last question. "What about the Quickening?"

Wyl smiled and turned to Valentyna. "I believe the magic will be satisfied if I become sovereign of Morgravia through marriage, instead of through Celimus," he said. "That is, if Queen Valentyna will have me?"

Crys and Aremys had left them, and Wyl and Valentyna were finally alone. Wyl took Valentyna's hand, ready to pour out all that was in his heart, when there came a knock at the door. He smiled sadly and nodded at her to answer it. "We have a lifetime ahead of us, my love," he said, kissing her fingers.

The Queen took a moment to compose herself, then called out, "Who is it?"

"It's Renton, your majesty."

My page, Valentyna mouthed to Wyl. She went to the door and opened it a crack, to hide the interior of the chamber from curious eyes. "Yes?" she said.

"The nobles are gathered in the banquet hall, your highness. They await their king and queen."

45

TALL MAN CLUTCHING A CHILD WALKED INTO A SUNLIT CLEARing, emerging from the tangled mass of the curiosity known as the Thicket. He was followed by a magnificent black horse.

Gueryn looked at the boy in his arms, pale and lifeless, and wanted to cry. To him, the death of young Fynch was the embodiment of all of his sorrows. The passing of the courageous child echoed the bravery of so many who had died since that terrible day the witch Myrren had died, bequeathing Wyl Thirsk a strange and painful gift. Gueryn had no idea what he was doing in this strange place that reeked of magic, but he had been drawn here, with Fynch and Galapek, as if he no longer controlled the direction in which he moved. What must he do next?

His wonderings were answered, somewhat disturbingly, by an oversized owl, who pierced him with a grave yellow gaze and said into his mind, *Put him on the ground, please. The Thicket wishes to feel him.*

Gueryn obeyed. He had seen so much—felt so much—that was strange, not even a huge talking bird could shock him now.

We of the Thicket are pleased to see you are restored, Gueryn le Gant.

Gueryn bowed to the bird. "It was Knave, I believe, who saved my life."

He is here. You can thank him yourself, Rasmus said, turning his head toward a massive black dog who was bounding out from the shadow of the yews.

"Knave!" Gueryn called, kneeling to greet the dog. "I owe you my life," he whispered to his savior, hugging him close.

The dog barked and then, as he looked at the child on the ground, whined sadly, sniffing every inch of the boy's body.

"Can you help Lothryn?" Gueryn asked, the plea evident in his voice.

A great evil has been wrought upon this beast, Rasmus replied. *I cannot undo it.*

Gueryn laid his hand on Galapek's strong neck. Had this journey been for nothing, then? As he mourned the tragic fate of the Mountain Man, the sun-drenched patch where they stood was suddenly darkened by a great shadow. Gueryn looked up and was astounded to see a huge figure descending upon them.

The King comes, Rasmus said reverently.

Now Gueryn could make out the shape looming above them. "A dragon?" he whispered, overcome by awe.

The massive creature landed, shaking the ground. Its scales shimmered with dark, seemingly ever-changing colors.

Gueryn was on his knees in veneration in a second. He lifted his head a fraction and dared to stare, goggle-eyed, at the fantastic creature before him.

Welcome, Gueryn le Gant, it said. *We owe you our thanks for returning Faith Fynch to us.*

"Can you help him, sire?" Gueryn pleaded.

Not in the way you would like, the dragon's deep voice answered gently. *But although Fynch's life among your kind is over, he will live on in a new form.*

The dragon turned its attention to the trembling horse. *Come to me, poor Galapek.*

The stallion moved to stand before the King of the Creatures and effected a gracious bow of sorts. Gueryn instinctively stepped back from the horse and the dragon as he sensed the thrum of a powerful magic gathering. The clearing exploded into a dazzling golden light, which burned for several moments. It blazed like a huge fire; he could feel its warmth and hear its crackle as it flamed around them, then suddenly disappeared. The rays of sunlight seemed dull by comparison.

Standing where Galapek had been was a huge man. His body was shaking and his head was thrown back, mouth open in silent prayer.

"Lothryn!" Gueryn called, tears flowing freely down his face and into his straggly beard. He ran toward the Mountain Man and grabbed him just as he toppled, taking them both heavily to the ground.

Let him recover for a few moments, the dragon advised. *He is weak now and will remain so for some time.*

Gueryn nodded. "When I was bringing Fynch here, I thought I heard the boy call Wyl's name. It was the only word he uttered. Did I imagine it?"

Fynch did not die at Rashlyn's hands, as you suspected. He died because he chose to relinquish his spirit and his power.

"What do you mean, your majesty?" Gueryn asked.

Fynch was a sacrifice, the Dragon King said, and Gueryn heard genuine sorrow in the creature's tone. *We demanded so much and he accepted all that we asked of him, giving his life freely. His one request was that he use his power to aid your Wyl Thirsk. Rashlyn did not kill the boy. Fynch was far stronger than even we had anticipated.*

"But I thought—"

You heard true; Fynch did call Thirsk's name. He needed to send himself a long way to reach Wyl, and he was so weakened by the fight with Rashlyn that he had to make a decision. He could not maintain life in his body and also send himself to Wyl.

"He chose Wyl?" Gueryn was shocked. He had assumed that Wyl was dead, but perhaps not all hope was lost.

Fynch made the ultimate sacrifice for his friend. He gave his life.

Gueryn bowed his head. He grieved for the child but badly wanted to know that Wyl lived. "And Wyl Thirsk?" he asked, frightened to hear the reply.

Wyl Thirsk lives, le Gant, as the Mountain King. And Celimus is dead.

Gueryn's mouth dropped open in shock, but no words came. Finally: "I don't know what to say," he admitted. He could tell that the dragon, along with the strange creatures he now noticed gathering around the fringe of the clearing, was hurting at the loss of Fynch. Even the Thicket itself seemed to be pulsating with a sense of sorrow.

We shall provide horses to take you and Lothryn from here, was all the dragon replied.

Lothryn spoke as a man for the first time in a long time. It hurt, just as it hurt to breathe, even to think. "Elspyth?" was all he could manage. The dragon turned to regard him with huge black eyes. *She clings to life, Mountain Man. Go to Argorn in Morgravia, and hurry.*

Both men paid homage once again to the King of the Creatures. But there was still one thing left to ask.

Gueryn cleared his throat and looked at the tiny bundle on the ground beside him. "The boy? Should I take him back to his family or . . ."

We are Fynch's family now, the dragon replied gently. *He is one with me and my flesh.*

"I don't understand, sire," Gueryn said, helping Lothryn to his feet.

Fynch was no ordinary gong boy. He was sired by Magnus, King of Morgravia.

Gueryn paled. "Did Magnus know?" he asked, astonished he could sound so composed.

No.

"What are you telling us, your majesty?"

That Fynch is the true Dragon King. As you know, the Kings of Morgravia have always been bonded exclusively to the dragon. No one else but they are permitted to claim union with me.

Gueryn shook his head with wonder. "Do you mean, your majesty, that Fynch was a prince of Morgravia?"

Now Celimus is dead, he becomes a king.

"There must be something you can do, great one," Gueryn said, looking around wildly. "Surely Fynch can be saved?"

There is something I can do, Gueryn, the dragon said patiently. *Watch.* The two men looked on incredulously as the creature of legend tenderly lifted the tiny boy in its huge claws. A blaze of golden light surrounded Fynch the instant the dragon touched him, and the gold in turn was fringed by a riot of dark iridescent colors that echoed the creature's ever-changing hues.

We are one—dragon and King united. The dragon's voice boomed deep in their minds as he wrapped his vast wings about the tiny body, cocooning it. Then he threw back his head and roared in triumph. As he did so, his scales turned to gold, dazzling and sparkling in the drench of sunlight. He opened his wings to their full breadth and both men inhaled sharply. Fynch's body was gone.

And then a new voice spoke to them. *Thank you, Gueryn, Lothryn. Courageous Knave. I shall never forget you.* It was Fynch.

Knave leapt up and let loose with a howl that even the men could tell was one of victory. They clung to each other, tears and laughter mingling as they shared in the creatures' triumph that Fynch lived on.

Farewell, Fynch called. *This will be our secret. I trust you will honor it.*

The dragon beat its powerful wings and the resulting wind drove the two men backward. They held on to each other as the great beast lifted effortlessly into the sky, disappearing toward the east, into the Wild.

Rasmus broke the awed silence. *It is time for you to leave us,* he said, looking to where two horses emerged from the yews. *They are yours now.*

Gueryn nodded, still tongue-tied from all the emotions surging through him: sorrow and joy, elation and awe.

Elspyth is in Argorn, as you have been told, Lothryn, Rasmus continued matter-of-factly. *Wyl is in Stoneheart, Gueryn. We shall not meet again, although Knave has agreed to accompany you. Brace yourselves, the Thicket is sending you . . .*

They arrived moments later beneath the cover of a small stand of trees. The air was sweet-smelling and Gueryn instantly recognized their surroundings as the region of Argorn. He knew precisely where they were: in a small copse barely an eighth of a mile from the Thirsk family estate.

He looked at his companion. "How do you feel?"

"I'm not sure. Weak enough to lie down here and never get up again, yet so energized by the thought that Elspyth is close that I could run all the way to her."

"Then do that, my friend. And when you reach her, hold her tight and never let go. Bring her to Stoneheart as soon as she is well. She may be in a position to bear witness to some events, and I'm sure you will have things to work out for your people in the Razors."

Lothryn smiled. It felt strange to be happy, to know pleasure again. "Thank you, Gueryn. May our realms never be enemies again."

"Between you and Wyl, I'm sure you'll see to it."

"I shall raise Aydrech as a proud ally."

"Hurry to the capital," Gueryn reminded him. "I'll let Wyl know you are coming."

The two men embraced and then parted to follow separate paths. The Mountain Man rode toward the grand manor, where an ailing woman waited for him. The Morgravian, with a huge black dog coursing beside him, galloped off toward Pearlis.

EPILOGUE

Cailech's long arms reached around Valentyna and hugged her close. They were standing on the small balcony of Magnus's old war tower. It was the only place Wyl could think of where they might truly be alone.

"Do you have to go to north so soon?" she asked.

There was amusement in his voice. "You'll handle yourself brilliantly and I'll be back before you know it, Valentyna. The meeting with the nobles went better than we could have dreamed. You already have them twirled around your little finger."

She shook her head with wonder. "Thanks to Lord Hartley coming out of hiding and revealing just how treacherous Celimus was, even to his own nobility."

"We shall be married by summer's end, how's that?"

Valentyna nodded glumly, knowing it would not be appropriate any sooner.

Wyl continued. "I know you understand that I want to be with Crys when he returns to Felrawthy. We shall grieve together at Tenterdyn and our prayers will cleanse it."

The Queen sounded uncharacteristically sulky when she replied, "Crys is so smitten with Georgyana Bench, I'm sure he'll hardly notice your presence." She saw his expression turn serious and was instantly contrite. "I'm sorry. I'm just so scared of losing you again."

"I know," he said gently, kissing her head. "You won't lose me again, I promise you."

"How long will you be gone? It was Aremys who told me you'd be going to the Razors. Were you too scared to share that news with me yourself?"

Wyl laughed. "Yes, as a matter of fact. I may be Wyl to you, but I have to make an effort to be Cailech to everyone else. I must return to the Razors and do the right thing by his people."

"You're going to appoint Lothryn to rule in your stead?"

He nodded. "It's fitting. The people will understand that now that I am planning to marry the southern Queen, I will spend a lot of my time here. But an absent king is not good for their needs, so Lothryn will administer the realm—and far better than I can, I'm sure."

"There's a child, though, is that right?"

"Yes. Cailech fathered the boy, but on Lothryn's wife. Loth has always thought of Aydrech as his own and now he can rightfully raise him as his son."

"Will he be King?"

"Yes. Bastard children are recognized as heirs in the Razors."

Valentyna nodded. "It must feel good to put everything back into balance again," she said. "I'm so happy for Elspyth, too. She's glowing. Did you ever think things could work out so right after everything felt so hideously wrong?"

Wyl turned her to him and kissed her softly, his lips lingering on hers so she could feel the tenderness and passion behind his affection. "I never thought I would win you. I told myself that the time at Briavel would be enough, if that was all I could have. Shar has blessed me."

Valentyna pulled him closer still and whispered into his ear, his golden hair tickling her face, "Shar has blessed you with more than you think."

He pulled away and looked at her quizzically.

"Shar, but for a king, you can be thick, Wyl Thirsk!"

"What am I missing?" he begged, laughing at her insult.

"Marry me fast, my lord, for I am pregnant. It seems we shall have the first royal heir to the joint throne of Briavel and Morgravia by the close of next winter."

She watched the light green eyes of the northern King—soon to be a southern king too—fill with tears. She continued talking, knowing he was at a loss for words. "If he's a boy we shall call him Wyl Magnus—then your name shall live on and our son will take a favorite name from both Morgravia and Briavel. And I'd better start remembering to call you Cailech all the time—do you mind?"

Finally Wyl found his voice. "And if we have a princess?"

"Ylena, of course. What else but a name that signifies such courage and represents so much love in both our lives?"

"Valentyna . . ." Whatever else Wyl was going to say was choked by a soft sob of joy. He hugged her tight, showering her hair and face with kisses. "If I died right here and now I couldn't be happ—"

"Don't! We're both going to live until we're so old we will need servants to help us on and off the privy."

They laughed among their shared tears. "That's right," he said. "We shall grow old and creaky together."

"Make Aremys bring you home to me quickly. I can only believe you are safe while I can see you, hold you," she said fervently. Wyl understood. He would have to be very careful with Cailech's body until they were married and he was rightfully King of Morgravia.

Valentyna sighed, looking out across the landscape. "It's beautiful here. I miss my woodlands but this is certainly a wonderful view. I feel like I can see all the way to Briavel."

"That was the point. This war tower was built so it offered a view in all directions, but especially toward Briavel."

"Well, we shall give this tower a new purpose. I shall dream something up by your return, King Cailech."

He grinned, and as he did so a shadow fell across them. "What's that?" he said, shading his eyes against the sharp sunlight as he looked up.

"I can't imagine," Valentyna said, squinting into the sky. "An eagle?"

"Not in these parts, and it's too big anyway."

Knave, who had been slumped drowsily close by, leapt to his feet and began to bark.

"What is it, Knave?" Wyl asked. He was rewarded with an answer from a voice he had never thought to hear again. *Hello, Wyl.*

Fynch! he sent back. *Oh Shar—is it really you?*

Tell Valentyna. She can't hear us—she's not linked

through the Thicket. And fret not, I've made myself invisible to all but you three.

"What is it?" Valentyna asked, baffled.

"My love, you won't believe it." Wyl grinned, feeling a shaft of happiness spear his heart. "It's Fynch! He's alive."

"Where?" Valentyna asked, amazed.

"Up there," he said, pointing. *What are you?* he sent.

A dragon! He heard the boy laugh in his head and the sound was one of pure joy.

Read on for a preview of the
new trilogy from Fiona McIntosh

ODALISQUE
Book One of the Percheron Saga

A sweeping new epic fantasy trilogy
set in the famed harem of an exotic palace
and rife with forbidden love, treachery,
betrayal and possession

The prisoners, chained together, shuffled awkwardly into the main square of the slave market of Percheron; six men, all strangers and all captives of a trader called Varanz, who had a reputation for securing the more intriguing product for sale. And this group on offer was no exception, although most onlookers' attention was helplessly drawn to the tall man whose searing, pale-eyed stare, at odds with his long dark hair, seemed to challenge anyone brave enough to lock gazes with him.

Varanz knew it too; knew this one was special, and he sensed a good price coming for the handsome foreigner well worth the effort it had cost six of his henchmen to firstly bring the man down and then rope him securely. It puzzled him why the man had been traveling across the desert, of all places—that in itself a perilous journey—but but and also moving alone, which meant almost certain trouble, particularly from slavers renowned in the region.

But Varanz had a policy of not inquiring into the background of his captives; perhaps to ease his conscience he didn't want to know anything about them, save what was obvious to his own eye. And this one, who refused to name himself, or indeed mutter much more than curses, was clearly in good health. That was enough for the merchant.

Trading for this cluster of slaves opened at the sound of the gong. The Master of the Market called the milling crowd of buyers to order: "Brothers, we have here Varanz Set Number Eight." His voice droned on, extolling the virtues of each on offer, but already the majority of potential buyers were in the thrall of the angry-eyed man, clearly the pick of the bunch and the only one of the six who held his head defiantly high. Sensing a lively auction, the Master of the Market decided to state more than the obvious of healthy appearance, strong structure and good teeth. "He was found emerging from the golden sands of our desert alone, not even a camel for company. Brothers, I'd hazard this one will make a fine bodyguard. If he's canny enough to travel our wasteland and remain as well as he looks, then I imagine he has excellent survival skills."

"Can he fight?" one buyer called out.

Varanz arched an eyebrow and looked toward the slave, wondering whether he'd finally get something out of the man. His instincts were right.

"I can fight," the man replied. "In fact," he challenged, "I demand to fight for my freedom."

A fresh murmuring rippled through the crowd. An oddity in Percheron's slave market was its ancient and somewhat quaint rule that a slave who was captured as a free person had one chance to buy his freedom—with a fight to the death. The Crown covered the cost of his loss, either way, to the trader. It was one of the Market's oldest customs, set up by a Zar many centuries earlier who understood that such a contest from time to time would provide entertainment for the otherwise tedious business of trading in human cargo.

Such fights were rare, of course, as most prisoners took their chances with a new life as a slave. But now and then one would risk death in the bid to win back his independence.

Varanz strolled over to the man now that he knew his tongue was loosened. "You understand what you ask for?"

"I do. It was explained to us on the journey here by one of your aides. I wish to fight for my freedom. I also wish to speak with your Zar."

At this Varanz smirked. "I can't imagine he will want to speak with you."

"He might after he watches me best twelve of his strongest warriors."

Varanz was speechless at the man's arrogance. He shook his head and walked to the Master, briefly explaining in a quiet mutter what the slave was proposing. Now both of them returned to stand before the man.

"Don't try and talk me out of it. I want my freedom back. I will pay the price if I fail to win it," the slave warned them.

The Master had no intention of attempting to thwart the proposition of some sport after an already long and wearying day in the market. He could see that Varanz was unfazed, knowing that he would get a good price either way.

"What is your reserve, Varanz?" he asked.

"No less than 200 karels for this one."

The Master nodded. "I will send a message to the palace for authorization," he said; now turning to the man, he insisted, "You must give us your name."

The slave knifed them with a cold gaze. "My name is Lazar."

The palace did more than give authorization. A runner returned swiftly with the news that Zar Joreb, his interest piqued, would be in attendance for the contest. "You understand how unusual it is for The Zar of Percheron to visit the slave traders," Varanz informed Lazar.

The foreigner was unmoved. "I wish to speak with him if I succeed."

Varanz nodded. "That is up to our Zar. We have told him you have offered to fight twelve of his men to the death. This is no doubt why he is coming to witness the contest."

"It is why I suggested so many."

Varanz shook his head, exasperated. "How can you best a dozen fighters, man? There's still time to change your mind and not waste your life. I will ensure a cozy position for you. A fellow like you will find himself in high demand by a rich man to escort his wives, families . . . take care of their security."

Lazar snorted. "I'm no nursery maid."

"All right." Varanz tried again. "I know I can sell you as a high caliber bodyguard to a man who needs protection while he travels. I'll find you a good owner."

"I don't want to be owned," Lazar snarled. "I want my freedom."

The trader shrugged. "Well you'll have it, my friend, but you'll be carried off in a sack."

"So be it. I slave for no-one."

Their conversation was ended by the Master of the Market hissing for silence—a troop of Percheron's guard had arrived, signifying that The Zar's karak was just moments away. Varanz nodded to one of his aides to escort the rest of the prisoners to the holding pen. Trading would resume once this piece of theater was done with.

"I wish you luck, brother," he said to Lazar and moved away to stand with the Master, who was marshaling all the other traders into a formal line of welcome. The Zar finally arrived flanked by several of the Percherese Guard, his karak carried by six of the red-shrouded Elim, the elite guardians of The Zar's harem who also provided bodyguard duties to royalty. The Zar's entry between the slave market's carved pillars of two gryphons was heralded by the trumpeting of several of the curled Percherese horns, and everyone who was not attached to the royal retinue instantly humbled himself. No one dared raise his eyes to The Zar until given formal permission.

No-one but Lazar, that is.

He was on his knees because he had been pushed down but he brazenly watched The Zar being helped out of the karak; their gazes met and held momentarily across the dust of the slave market. Then Lazar dipped his head, just a fraction, but it was enough that The Zar knew the brash young man had acknowledged the person who was the closest thing to the god Zarab that walked the earth.

The Guard quickly set up The Zar's seat and the Elim unfurled a canopy over it. Zar Joreb settled himself. He had a wry smile on his face as the Master of the Market made the official announcement that the prisoner, Lazar, captured by Trader Varanz, had opted to fight for his freedom against a dozen warriors from the Percherese Guard. No-one watched the Master or even The Zar. All eyes were riveted on the dark foreigner, whose wrists and ankles were now unshackled and who was disrobing down to the once white, now gray and dirty loose pants he wore beneath. They watched his measured movements, but mostly they watched him study the twelve men taking practice swipes with their glinting swords, all bearing smirks, none prepared to take the ridiculously outnumbered opposition seriously.

The gong sounded for silence and the Master outlined what was about to happen. It was a superfluous pronouncement but strict protocol was a way of life for Percheron's various markets, especially in the hallowed presence of The Zar.

". . . or to the prisoner's death," he finished somberly. He looked to Zar Joreb who, with an almost imperceptible nod, gave the signal for combat to begin.

Those who were present at the slave market that day would talk about the fight for years to come. Lazar accepted the weapon thrown toward him and without so much as a hurried prayer to his god of choice strode out to meet the first of the warriors. To prolong the sport, the Guard had decided to send out one man at a time—presumably they intended to keep wounding the arrogant prisoner until he begged for mercy and the death blow. However, by the time the first three men were groaning and bleeding on the ground, their most senior man hurriedly sent in four at once.

It didn't make much difference to Lazar, who appeared to the audience to be unintimidated by numbers. His face wore the grim countenance of utter focus; he made no sound, never once backed away, always threatening his enemy rather than the other way around. It was soon obvious that his sword skills could not be matched by any of the Percherese, not even fighting in tandem. His fighting arm became a blur of silver that weaved a path of wreckage through flesh, turning the dozen men, one after another, into writhing, crying heaps as they gripped torn shoulders, slashed legs, or profusely bleeding fighting arms. To their credit, the final two fought superbly, but neither could mark Lazar. He fought without fear, his speed only increasing. Cutting one man down by the ankle, Lazar stomped on his sword wrist, breaking it, to ensure he did not return to the fray, and some moments later, fought the other into exhaustion until the man was on his knees. Lazar flicked the guard's sword away and gave a calculated slash across his chest. The man fell, almost grateful for the reprieve.

The slave market was uncharacteristically quiet, save for the cries of bleeding, paining men. Varanz looked around at the carnage, his nostrils flaring with the raw metallic smell of blood thick in the air, and he raised his eyebrows with surprise. No one was dead. Lazar had mercilessly and precisely disabled each of his rivals but claimed the life of none.

Throwing down his sword, Lazar stood in the circle of hurt warriors, a light sheen of perspiration on his body the only indication that he had exerted himself. His chest rose and sank steadily, calmly. He turned to The Zar and bowed long and deeply.

"Zar Joreb, will you now grant my freedom?" he spoke finally into the hush that had fallen.

"My men would surely seek death than live with the dishonor of losing this fight," was Joreb's response.

Varanz watched Lazar's curiously light eyes cloud with defiance. "They are innocent men. I will not take their lives for a piece of entertainment."

"They are soldiers! This was a fight to the death."

"Zar Joreb, this was a fight to *my* death, not theirs. It was made clear that I either win my freedom through death or through survival. I survived. No one impressed upon me that anyone had to die as part of the rules of this custom."

"Arrogant pup," Joreb murmured into the silence. Then, impossibly, he laughed. "Stand before me, young man."

Lazar took two long strides and then went down on one knee, his head finally bowed.

"What is it you want, stranger?" The Zar demanded.

"I want to live in Percheron as a free man," Lazar replied, not lifting his head.

"Look at me." Lazar did so. "You've humiliated my Guard. You will need to rectify that before I grant you anything."

"How can I do that, Zar Joreb?"

"By teaching them."

Lazar stared at The Zar, a quizzical look taking over his heretofore impassive expression, but he said nothing.

"Become my Spur," Zar Joreb offered. "Our present Spur must retire soon. We need to inject a fresh approach. A young approach. You fight like you're chasing away demons, man. I want you to teach my army how to do that."

Lazar's gaze narrowed. His tone sounded guarded. "You're offering to pay me to live as a free man in Percheron?"

"Be my Spur," Zar Joreb urged. This time there was no humor in his voice, only passion.

The crowd collectively held its breath as Lazar paused. Finally, he nodded once, decisively. "I accept, but first you owe Varanz over 200 karels apparently."

Joreb laughed loudly in genuine amusement. "I like you, Lazar. Follow me back to the palace. We have much to speak of. I must say, I'm impressed by your audacity. You put your life in danger to get what you want."

"It was never in danger," Lazar replied and the semblance of a smile twitched briefly at his mouth.